PRAISE FOR
THE LAST LAIRD OF SAPELO

"*The Last Laird of Sapelo* is a heart-wrenching and beautiful story of a man and his family brought to its knees by the Civil War. Life-changing choices must be made and personal integrity brought to bear during the nineteenth century when the South was swept into a brutal and complicated war. T. M. Brown brings the history of the Spalding family to vivid life with a sure and clear voice, an eye for Southern landscape, and an ear for captivating narrative. Based on a true story, this is historical fiction at its finest."

—Patti Callahan Henry, *New York Times* Best-Selling Author of *The Secret Book of Flora Lea*, patticallahanhenry.com

"As Union forces descend on Georgia's barrier islands during the opening stages of America's Civil War, the South's first casualty is its monetary lifeline — its burgeoning cotton empire, Dixie's "white gold." Distinguished author T.M. Brown's historical novel *The Last Laird of Sapelo* spares no punches in this riveting, gut-wrenching saga of the minuscule line separating independence and freedom."

—Jedwin Smith, Author of *Fatal Treasure* and *Our Brother's Keeper*

"T.M. Brown raises the bar for Civil War-era historical fiction. Using compelling, well-researched details, Brown writes with confidence and lyricism about neglected parts of the conflict and its impact on the coastal islands of Georgia. Civil War fiction fans need to add this novel to their bookshelves today!"

—George Weinstein, Award-winning Author of the *Hardscrabble Road* series, Executive Director, Atlanta Writers Club, Atlanta Writers Conference Director

"As you walk the beaches, dunes, and maritime forests of Georgia's barrier islands and gaze over the vastness of their pristine marshes you will almost certainly sense the history that permeates this unique area. Author T. M. Brown has a taken a small but vital part of that history and brought it to life in *The Last Laird of Sapelo*, a fictional work based on actual people and events as the Civil War comes to coastal Georgia and South Carolina.

"The story centers on Randolph Spalding, a wealthy landowner on Sapelo Island who, as a Confederate officer in the early stages of the conflict, must prepare his beloved island paradise for the ravages of a war he had hoped could be avoided, while finding ways to protect his family and slaves from the growing threat of Union attack.

"Brown paints a portrait of a man who must fill a number of essential roles: commander of inexperienced and sometimes unruly troops, family patriarch who must send his wife and children inland for safety, and paternalistic master feeling responsible for his slaves who are endangered by the troops camped on Sapelo yet resist leaving the only home they've ever known. The weight of duty is almost more than he can bear.

"Spalding and most of the major characters in *The Last Laird of Sapelo* are actual historic figures, and though their thoughts, actions, and experiences have been fictionalized, the narrative rests on a solid historical foundation.

"As I read this novel, I was impressed by the amount of research required to bring authenticity to every page. Brown made me feel as if I were there, feeling the ocean breezes, smelling the tide-washed mud of the marshes, experiencing the chaos of battle, listening in on the dialogue of a wide range of characters caught up in the life-shattering event that was the Civil War.

"*The Last Laird of Sapelo* is an impressive achievement that brings great insight to the impact of war on the normally serene and always beautiful Georgia coast. It's a story that needed to be told, and T. M. Brown has done it in a masterful way."

—John Pruitt, Emmy Award–Winning News Anchor, Author of *Tell It True*

"Regardless of the fiction label, this book is based on real people of the 1860s and reads like the author was there. The story of the Spalding family and Sapelo Island is a well-researched and very personal glimpse of 19th-century Georgia and a family caught up in events they cannot avoid. Mike Brown has brought this family and coastal Georgia to life!"

—Steve Quesinberry, Author of *Better Men: Coweta County and the Vietnam War*

"Much has been written about the historic battles fought between 1861 and 1865, but other aspects of the war were just as pivotal, especially the Union blockade of southern ports that put a stranglehold on supplies desperately needed by the Confederacy.

"Set in the first year of the blockade, *The Last Laird of Sapelo* illuminates lesser known but crucial events in coastal Georgia and South Carolina through the true story of Colonel Randolph Spalding, a noted Sapelo Island cotton planter. Spalding questions the wisdom of Georgia's secession in 1861, but once his native state declares her independence and joins the Confederacy, he ardently supports her cause, determined to do all that he can to defend his new country and preserve a home and legacy for his family.

"Colonel Spalding's struggles and sacrifices are vividly depicted as he faces the reality of powerful Union naval forces threatening the coasts of the Carolinas and Georgia, and he is forced to move his family and many slaves inland to safety, ultimately abandoning his beloved island plantation. Early in the war he is given command of Confederate troops stationed on Sapelo Island, and gets his first taste of real fighting when he and his men are called in as reinforcements at Port Royal, South Carolina—only to find that the battle is as good as lost by the time they arrive. General Robert E. Lee figures in the novel in his early efforts to organize coastal defenses in the deep South.

"This is well-researched, engaging historical fiction that brings to life a dramatic and little-known story of America's bloodiest war."

—Karen Stokes, Archivist and Author at
South Carolina Historical Society

"The sea islands are a series of large barrier islands that lay along the Southern coast from Charleston to Jacksonville. Broad sounds penetrate the region in from the sea, flooding the meandering rivers and creeks that wind through the great tidal salt marshes teem with fish, shrimp, crabs, oysters, alligators, marsh hens, herons, osprey, and eagles.

"In colonial and antebellum times, these islands were homes to plantations of rice and long-staple sea island cotton - great, largely self-sufficient estates supporting a community and an organic way of life as old as Feudal Europe.

"Author T. M. Brown - who is intimately familiar with the region and his subject matter - gives the reader a comprehensive portrait of the region and the way of life of a great estate before it vanished forever with his novel *The Last Laird of Sapelo*. The book centers around Col. Randolph Spalding, the patriarch of a great estate on Sapelo Island, Georgia, and the extended family and interdependent patriarchal society there before it was violently atomized by the War Between the States and the coming of a new world order.

"Mr. Brown's work presents the reader with an informed and sympathetic portrait of a portion of the Old South untainted by the specious presentism or vindictive political virtue posting that corrupts so much of portraiture today. I recommend it highly."

—H. V. Traywick, Jr., Author of *Empire of the Owls: Reflections on the North's War against Southern Secession*

"In *The Last Laird of Sapelo*, Mike Brown does a masterful job of telling the historic story of how the Civil War changed forever the Spalding family, their slaves, and the crucial barrier island of Sapelo on which they lived. He shares in detail the bonds between the Spalding family members and their servants without skirting the inhumanity of slavery. The compelling read was extensively researched and provides an interesting account in story form of how the conflict negatively impacted the owners and other inhabitants of Sapelo Island, including Randolph Spalding, who answered the call to defend the cause of the Confederate States even though he didn't favor Secession. *The Last Laird of Sapelo* provides an important insight into helping us to understand one of the worst times in the history of our country."

—Harry J. Deitz Jr., Author of *Covey: A Stone's Throw from a Coal Mine to the Hall of Fame, Our Father's Journey: A Path Out of Poverty,* and *Journal of a Caregiver: A Story of Love and Devotion*

"I knew nothing of either Randolph Spalding or of Sapelo Island before reading this book. But from the first chapter on, I felt thoroughly immersed in 1860s coastal Georgia as the Spalding family grappled with the challenges of war. Mike Brown's vivid imagery and his mastery of historical detail deliver a powerful story I am already eager to read a second time."

—Lawrence W. Reed, President Emeritus, Humphreys Family Senior Fellow and Ron Manners Global, Ambassador for Liberty

"T. M. Brown's *The Last Laird of Sapelo* takes us on an unforgettable journey, one marked with uncertainty, turmoil and tragedy, and fierce, unyielding loyalty. We travel with hope and caution along the barrier islands of Georgia through a brief, but maybe somewhat forgotten, period of the Civil War. The result is a brilliant fusion of history and fiction. As a gifted researcher and storyteller, Brown delivers an experience. Lifting the curtain on the daily lives of Randolph Spaulding and his family and Sapelo workers, he invites us into their intimate conversations, revealing their doubts and thoughts and dreams. Ultimately, we are moved and inspired by both fear and bravery. *The Last Laird of Sapelo* comes alive through the rich details of true events and a well-developed cast of characters. Even Brown's beloved Sapelo Island is a character, teaching us about her history and the people who love and protect her. There is so much to learn from this journey, and all its lessons are embedded in the pages of this book. As soon as you meet Colonel Randolph Spaulding, you will understand."

—Helen Stine, Author of *The Truthful Story*, helenstine.com

"T. M. Brown's meticulous research and weaving of story within *The Last Laird of Sapelo* delivers coastal Georgia and the saga of Colonel Randolph Spalding vividly and deftly to the page."

—Robert Gwaltney, Award-Winning Author of *The Cicada Tree*, 2023 Georgia Author of the Year, robertlgwaltney.com

"T. M. Brown's new historical novel, inspired by the life of Randolph Spalding of Sapelo Island, Georgia, fame, portrays the difficulties he and his family face after Georgia secedes from the Union. Exploring the complicated dynamics that engulf this storied family in the Civil War, Brown illuminates the unavoidable challenges and realities of a nation at war and, ultimately, the consequences of the hard choices. Fans of Civil War–era fiction won't want to miss this book!"

—Rebecca Bruff, Author of *Trouble the Water*

"*The Last Laird of Sapelo*, by T. M. Brown, is the story of one man's tragic death in pursuit of justice, as his way of life, too, dies in the flames of a war that he had tried his damnedest to avert.

"Sapelo is one of the barrier islands off the coast of Georgia. As this story opens, the War Between the States has just begun, and the Confederacy plans to use those islands as a bulwark against the Union gunboats that assuredly will extend their blockade of Savannah all the way down the coast. If the blockade succeeds, then the South's cotton, the fuel of its economic engine, will languish in Southern warehouses instead of sailing to buyers and allies across the sea.

"Colonel Randolph Spalding, the last laird of the title, committed to the war despite arguing vehemently against it. Now an officer in charge of building a garrison on his own land, he's caught between military duty and personal responsibility.

"As the Llaird of Sapelo, Spalding is duty-bound to protect his family and his property, including more than three hundred enslaved people.

"The Spaldings consider themselves 'enlightened' slaveholders, giving their slaves more time and 'freedom' to work for themselves and have leisure, as well as sturdy houses and decent food. Their neighbors call them fools. The Confederate soldiers see the slaves as their rightful prey.

"His military duty is to keep those soldiers in line. His personal duty is to keep his people safe. When those lines get crossed, he moves heaven and earth to make it right. Even if those lengths will cost him his own life.

"This fictionalized biography illuminates a little-known, but pivotal, part of the US Civil War: the defense of the Confederate coastline as it happened on the ground, in tiny communities.

"Spalding draws readers into his own story, telling it through letters and diary entries over the first year of that terrible war. His first-person perspective on those early months, at a point when hopes were high but organization was lacking, foretells the inevitable cost of this fight. The Civil War will exact a bloody cost no matter who triumphs on the battlefield.

"Despite the deplorable cause for which he fights, Spalding's internal conflicts, filled with intense emotion, make him a riveting character. He faces the scant triumphs and ultimate tragedies of a man who fights to preserve his world, only for it to disintegrate in his grasp.

"*The Last Laird of Sapelo* will fascinate readers interested in the unsung facets of the US Civil War, those looking for a nuanced approach to the origins of the conflict, and anyone interested in the details of military organization—or lack thereof—in nineteenth-century warfare."

—Chanticleer Book Reviews, 5 Stars

The Last Laird of Sapelo

by T. M. Brown

© Copyright 2023 T. M. Brown

ISBN: 979-8-88824-042-7

All rights reserved. No part of this publication may be reproduced, stored in a retrieval system, or transmitted in any form or by any means—electronic, mechanical, photocopy, recording, or any other—except for brief quotations in printed reviews, without the prior written permission of the author.

This is a work of fiction. All the characters in this book are fictitious, and any resemblßance to actual persons, living or dead, is purely coincidental. The names, incidents, dialogue, and opinions expressed are products of the author's imagination and are not to be construed as real.

Published by

3705 Shore Drive
Virginia Beach, VA 23455
800-435-4811
www.koehlerbooks.com

THE LAST LAIRD OF SAPELO

A Novel

T. M. BROWN

VIRGINIA BEACH
CAPE CHARLES

To my mother,

Mary "Pat" Brown
June 10, 1931 to January 26, 2023

Her unwavering love remains.

FOREWORD

By Lawrence W. Reed

When I first saw the title of T. M. Brown's latest novel, I thought, *I know what a laird is, but what is a sapelo?*

I was born and raised in Pennsylvania and lived in Michigan for thirty years. A little less than 20 percent of my seventy years have been spent as a resident of a Southern state—specifically the town of Newnan in north Georgia—so forgive me for knowing so little about an area just a few hundred miles southwest of me. But now, thanks to Mike, I know that Sapelo is a coastal island—and not just *any* coastal island, but one rich in history and fascinating people.

Before this book, I thought *tabby* was one of the more common names for a house cat. Now I know it's a kind of concrete made with oyster shells.

What took me so long to learn this? The best answer to that question is another one: What took Mike Brown so long to write this wonderful novel?

As an accomplished author of historical fiction, Mike knows how to tell a story from the past and bring real but long-dead figures to life. This novel does not read like an aerial view of an island through the clouds from 30,000 feet. As any well-told story should accomplish, you'll feel as you read along that you're on the ground, in the very midst of the challenges, joys and travails of Randolph Spalding, his family and acquaintances. You can't help but empathize with the main characters, warts and all, and find yourself asking, "What would I do in a similar situation?" As a result, the further along I journeyed through *The Last Laird of Sapelo*, the more I became emotionally caught up in it. And when I got to the end, I wished there was even more to read.

Though this is a work of historical fiction, the fiction aspect amplifies the historical part, much more than the other way around. Readers will finish it with a much-improved understanding of what plantation life was like (albeit on one of the more enlightened such places) in mid-19th Century coastal Georgia during one of the most turbulent times in American history. You will appreciate the character of a good man because the author provides indispensable context—the cultural, economic, and political background—that framed Spalding's decisions and behavior. Perhaps if everybody read *The Last Laird of Sapelo*, we would be a more understanding, thoughtful, reflective, and introspective people. Smarter too.

The famed Pulitzer Prize-winning author of Southern tales, Eudora Welty, explained the powerful magnetism of a good book. In *One Writer's Beginnings* (1984), she wrote:

> *It had been startling and disappointing to me to find out that story books had been written by people, that books were not natural wonders, coming up of themselves like grass. Yet regardless of where they came from, I cannot remember a time when I was not in love with them—with the books themselves, cover and binding and the paper they were printed on, with their smell and their weight and with their possession in my arms, captured and carried off to myself.*

I know now what she meant by that, and because of *The Last Laird of Sapelo*, more great works of historical fiction are in my future.

There is resolution to the story that Mike Brown tells here so well. No reader will feel he's been left hanging in mid-air. Perhaps it will elicit reactions that won't entirely match mine. But I can say as a very satisfied reader that it brought forth a wide range in me, from a whiff of nostalgia to a renewed appreciation for how remarkable individuals deal with difficulties most of us can only imagine.

To the pantheon of excellent works of historical fiction, we can thank Mike Brown for bringing us *The Last Laird of Sapelo*.

Lawrence W. Reed
President Emeritus, Foundation for Economic Education
Newnan, Georgia
www.lawrencewreed.com

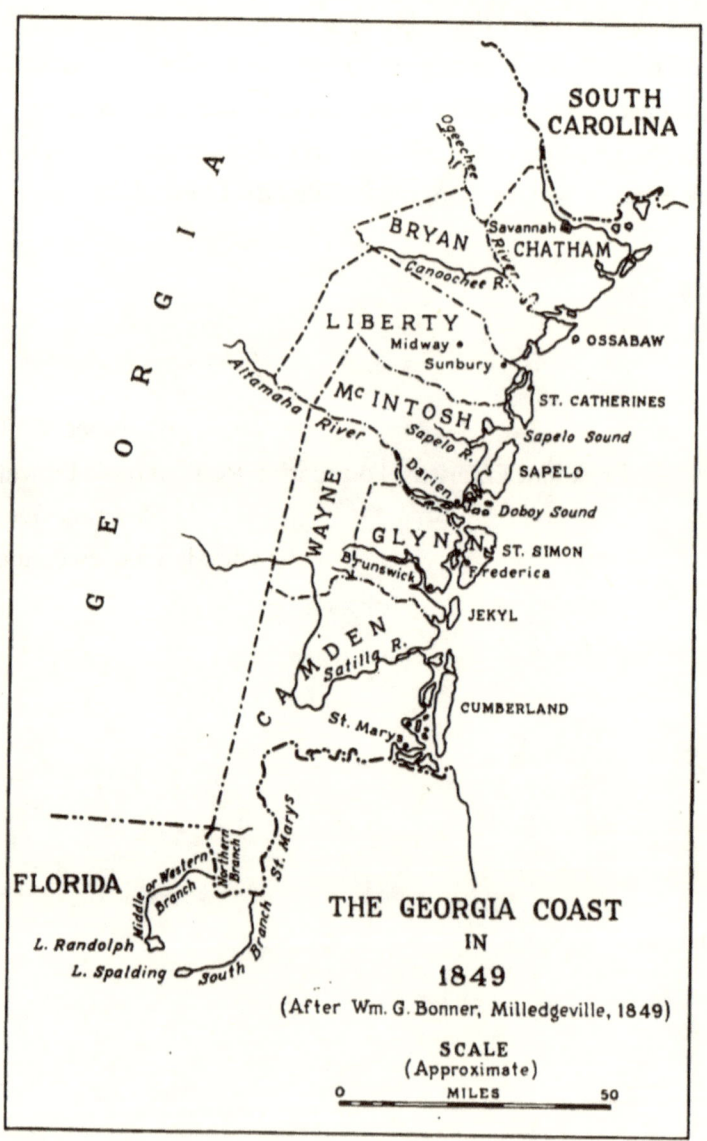

THE GEORGIA COAST IN 1849
(After Wm. G. Bonner, Milledgeville, 1849)

CHAPTER ONE

"A land without ruins is a land without memories—a land without memories is a land without history. A land that wears a laurel crown may be fair to see; but twine a few sad cypress leaves around the brow of any land, and be that land barren, beautiless and bleak, it becomes lovely in its consecrated coronet of sorrow, and it wins the sympathy of the heart and history. Calvaries and crucifixions take deepest hold of humanity—the triumphs of might are transient—they pass and are forgotten—the sufferings of right are graven deepest on the chronicles of nations."

~ *A Land Without Ruins* by Abram Ryan

26th of May, 1861

"Momma, we just can't gather up our belongings and desert our home," sixteen-year-old Sallie screamed. She flailed her white-knuckled, clenched fists above her head while stomping her heels into the pristine, sun-drenched sand on Nanny Goat Beach. Two nearby sea terns minding their own business at the water's edge flew off as tears cascaded down Sallie's flushed cheeks.

Fighting back tears of his own, thirteen-year-old Tom dashed down the sandy shore the instant he grasped the news his father shared. He plopped down just beyond the encroaching surf with his head slumped between his knees.

Randolph's wife, Mary, took their ten-year-old son, Bourke, by the hand. He appeared far more befuddled by what his father had told them than saddened or flustered like his older brother and sister.

They strolled hand-in-hand just beyond the water's edge while Sallie sloshed through the warm, ankle-deep surf mumbling to herself.

Randolph Spalding felt at a loss for what more he could say or do to lessen the sting inflicted upon his children. His bare feet felt imprisoned in the loose, sugar-like sand as growing pangs of powerlessness overwhelmed him. His eyes focused upon his oldest son flipping fractured shell fragments into the dissipating waves lapping at his feet.

With the sun to his back, he stared beyond the incoming surf to the distant horizon where the sparkling aquamarine ocean greeted the crystal blue sky. A bevy of towering, cotton-like clouds cast shadows as they floated high above the glistening Atlantic. The latest news of Lincoln's naval blockade, hell-bent on throttling the South's lifeblood—its cotton trade—captured his thoughts. He knew with each new dawn, the undaunted flotilla sailed farther south. It was only a matter of time before shallow-water merchant schooners and steamers, laden with Sapelo's cotton, rice, and sugar bound for markets in Charleston and Savannah, would run into the blockade.

He likewise feared both Northern and Southern blood would soon stain the land. Leaders in Georgia, like its neighboring Southern states, had ordered well-armed state militias to seize undermanned federal forts and armories throughout the state. Days after South Carolina's artillery assault on Fort Sumter, the call to arms resounded throughout the North and the South. War appeared inevitable.

Randolph recalled his last speech before stepping down from Georgia's esteemed state assembly in Milledgeville. As last fall's cotton harvest approached, he'd acknowledged the unstoppable political sway steering Georgia toward secession. His heartfelt speech that day affirmed his readiness to bear arms to preserve his family's legacy and livelihood. Though, he did offer one last plea for restraint over rebellion to his colleagues.

"I rise before this august body one more time as the elected voice for my beloved McIntosh County, but today my heart burdens my conscience. Many of you in this hallowed hall may well recall my father, the Honorable Thomas Spalding. After decades of exhaustive service to Georgia, he presided over the state convention tasked with deciding Georgia's position regarding secession in 1850. He urged Georgia to remain committed to our expanding nation at that critical time. Georgia's resultant decision disappointed other Southern states but appeased the rising fears among the coalition of northern states who sought to legislate their moral indignation against slavery. However, my father also remained steadfast regarding Georgia's constitutional right to self-determination to protect and preserve its economic lifeblood."

Randolph recalled the gravity of his appeal that regurgitated his father's similar speech a decade earlier: *"Gentlemen, I can never stand before you in my father's stead, but I am an heir to Thomas Spalding's celebrated legacy. Therefore, I beseech your indulgence while I read his last words before this noble assembly. His admonishment ten years ago staved off secession, garnering Georgia's support of the Great Compromise of 1850. Whereas today, Georgia appears destined to join our neighbor states in favor of secession."*

Before he'd continued, he had gripped the speaker's lectern as he sought his father's apparition among the imposing, ornate rafters and carved corbels overlooking the storied assembly chamber. Instead, he'd glanced upward at his older brother, Charles, likewise a former legislator from McIntosh County, seated in the gallery. His brother offered an unmistakable wink and encouraging nod moments before Randolph steeled himself and read aloud his father's succinct words:

"Gentlemen of the Convention: I thank you for the honor you do me in the chair of this memorial occasion. It is perhaps an appropriate—I feel it is a graceful—termination of my long life. From a small people, we have become a great nation under our Constitution—and rather than that Constitution shall perish, I would wish that myself and every human that has a drop of my blood in his veins should perish."

Randolph had ended his farewell address that day with his own portentous diatribe.

"Like Thomas Spalding before me, I stand unwavering before you. Georgia has the Constitution-protected right to determine its own course and destiny. Yet, I say, let us be mindful. Secession will dissolve us from the Constitution's protections and doom us all to accept, like our forefathers, what could become a red-stained course of action. Therefore, bearing in mind my father's foreboding admonishment, I will support whatever fate this assembly of leaders decides in the coming days."

Like his father, Randolph had become one of the most successful planters along the southern coast, yet he wondered about the South's economic future. Though cotton remained the predominant cash crop on Sapelo, sugarcane, corn, and rice were also cultivated. Over the past decade, he understood how the tyranny of cotton subjugated Southern planters unless deposed through agricultural diversity. As cotton's golden demand grew, so too did the cry for more laborers in the fields. Insatiable English and Northern textile mills craved all the cotton the South could produce. Indeed, Randolph embraced the prosperity he inherited and even parlayed over the past decade since his father passed. But, like his father, he grew disquieted over the paradox that arose because of the South's unrelenting reliance on slavery to harvest its crops while also sensing the wrongs the institution of slavery afflicted.

His older brother, Charles, and he wrestled with their father's ingrained solicitudes about the country's westward sprawl—an expansion that pursued the setting sun and provided new fertile lands to plow. By 1860, planters as far south and west as Texas pursued wealth by harvesting endless sunbaked fields of white gold. In but a few short years, cotton had deposed indigo, rice, and sugarcane as the supreme cash crop. As Thomas Spalding had forewarned, though, in cotton's wake the uncompromising, deplorable institution of slavery became like a millstone around the necks of planters throughout the sprawling south.

Now abandoned on the beach, Randolph dismissed further thoughts of a history he could no longer alter. He looked for his wife and children on Sapelo's pristine shore. They too now struggled with the unfathomable prospects of leaving their home and property with the winds of war blowing southward along the Atlantic seaboard. An icy shiver shook Randolph as though a mysterious anathema's dark shadow veiled his family's foreseeable future. Could he count on remaining for one more harvest on Sapelo? The question remained unanswered.

Though he had gained his father's South End plantation and its imposing mansion, *Big House*, filled with fond memories while growing up there, Randolph and his young family lived there only briefly after their home at Chocolate on the north end of Sapelo had burned down. In his heart, Randolph never felt his father's renown estate became his family's home. For that reason, they moved out of South End's grand tabby residence with its maze of genteel garden-lined walkways and lush green grounds.

They settled into a modest farmhouse estate he had built near The Ridge, a prominent residential community above Darien, where wealthier planters, merchants, and businessmen lived in lavish homes. Unlike many of the other coastal planters who only lived far removed from their vast lowland plantations during the sweltering, insect-infested months from June to September, Randolph's family lived year-round in their modest farmhouse overlooking the tidal creeks and marshes. Of course, as the celebrated master of Sapelo, Randolph continued to host grandiose social affairs and family retreats at South End, whenever such gala opportunities arose.

In recent months, Randolph and Mary had hoped the family could live unscathed by the harsh political realities, but Governor Joseph E. Brown's letter dashed their hopes. Randolph received a commission in Georgia's burgeoning militia like his brother and other prominent businessmen and landowners.

A scarcity of competent military officers hampered the state's rush to increase the ranks of its volunteer militia. Thus, Governor Brown reasoned that commissioning prominent men to lead their local militias would encourage the enlistment of volunteers.

Randolph's commission included orders to report to Brigadier General Alexander Lawton, commander of Georgia's coastal defenses, by June 7. Randolph welcomed being commissioned as a colonel and assigned as an aide-de-camp to General Lawton in Savannah.

Only time forestalled Northern blockade vessels from cresting the horizon Randolph glared at from Sapelo's sandy shore. He reasoned that before long, Sapelo Island and the busy port of Darien at the mouth of the Altamaha River would soon experience a Union blockade. With the governor's orders in hand, he and Mary decided they must tell their children what neither Randolph nor Mary fathomed themselves but deemed paramount to share.

Planters up and down Georgia's tidewater coast recognized the vital importance of the outcome of their upcoming harvests of cotton, rice, corn, and sugarcane to clothe and feed the burgeoning Confederate Army. On Sapelo, field hands continued to plow and sow acres upon acres of alluvium-rich sandy soil just as they had worked each springtime for decades, unaware of events unfolding.

Mary returned from her sobering walk along the water's edge, rejoicing in Sallie's playful laughter. "Randolph, please bring Tom up with you. Dinner will be ready shortly."

Sallie hollered, "Come on, slow poke," as she playfully corralled her younger brother, herding him up the path between the sea oat-topped sand dunes, and headed back to *Big House*.

Randolph abandoned his solitary spot on the beach and kneeled in the sand beside Tom. He picked up a piece of driftwood and flung it into the approaching waves. The splash broke his son's glum stare at the wet sand between his bare feet.

"Son, I'm sorry. God alone controls what the future holds. I'm just a mortal made of flesh and bones like you. I don't relish the idea of our family leaving here anymore than you. Your grandfather charged me to take care of this beautiful island. Whatever happens, I promise I will do everything I can to make it possible for you to become the Laird of South End like your grandfather wanted. And, when I am gone, you and Bourke will one day be the masters of Sapelo from South End to High Point."

"Pa, I understand why you have to leave us, but why can't I go with you?" Tom arched his back and sat two inches taller. "I'm fourteen, and—"

Randolph arched a brow.

"Well, I'm almost fourteen. Besides, I'm a sight taller and stronger than others my age."

"Yes, you are, son. All the same, don't be in such a hurry to grow up and leave your mom, sister, and little brother. I need you to take care of them. Besides—" Randolph stood and pulled Tom to his feet. He then pointed up and down the beach with outstretched arms. "South End will soon be all yours. Never forget that your grandfather chose you to preserve the Spalding heritage for future generations to come. Your uncle and I, along with the more than capable help of your older cousins, have sworn to do whatever it takes so you can fulfill the legacy promised you."

"But Pa," Tom blurted, gazing at the incoming white-capped waves.

"Listen to me, son. Let's pray President Lincoln realizes the Confederacy is very willing and capable of fighting for its independence. For the time being, let's stop bellyaching about what tomorrow might bring. Right at this moment, let's catch up to your mother. I bet Alma and Cecile have supper ready for the table, and they're just waiting on us."

Randolph then took off running. He yelled as he ran as fast as his thirty-eight-year-old legs could muster, "Come on, slowpoke. I'm hungry."

Tom hollered as he chased after his father, "Hey, no fair."

※ ※ ※

Mary was waiting on the top step of the tabby mansion's recessed portico seated between Bourke and Sallie by the time Tom raced up the walkway several strides ahead of his father. Sallie burst into an uncontrollable bout of giggles as she applauded the apparent winner of the race.

"Well, my dear, it appears Tom here has gotten a sight faster since you two last raced," Mary shouted with a whimsical smile as Randolph trotted up to the mansion's front steps.

Randolph nodded without looking up, hands on his knees to catch his breath.

"Father, is it true?" Sallie inquired, stifling her boisterous exuberance for her brother's feat.

"Is what true, Sallie?" her father said between gasps.

"Momma says Uncle Charles and Cousin William are not leaving? Neither are Aunt Elizabeth and her family leaving their home."

Randolph righted himself and glanced at Mary. "Yes, I guess it's true. Uncle Charles and Aunt Evie appear intent on remaining at Ashantilly, leastways for the time being. Besides, he's the commander of Georgia's First Cavalry Battalion stationed in McIntosh County, and your cousin William rides with Uncle Charles and refuses to leave Sutherland Bluff now that your Aunt Jane is dead."

"What about Aunt Elizabeth?" Tom asked as he sat on the step just below his sister.

"Your Uncle A.W. is the head of the Wylly family. He feels their home at The Forest will remain safe enough where they are located. Besides, the Wylly brood is darn near its own militia detachment with all them Wylly boys eager to join up. Your cousin Thomas is already a captain with the Berrien militia and will join me in Savannah. Why?"

Tom grumbled, interrupting his father and sister. "Pa, why should we get ready to leave our home if they're staying?"

"First, 'cause your mother and I believe it's the best decision for our family. Second, your uncle's and cousin's homes lie far removed from town. And third, Sapelo Island will be one of the first places the Yankees will want to occupy once their ships sail beyond Savannah. I've talked with your Aunt Katherine and Uncle Michael, and they will vacate the island when we leave. Uncle Michael has family in Milledgeville and already knows of a house for his family. He also arranged for a lease on a plantation with a house for us when the time comes."

"Why can't we stay in our own house? Uncle Charles and Aunt Evie live closer to town than us," Sallie begged with forlorn eyes.

Mary draped her arm around Sallie. "Let me add another excellent reason. They don't have irreplaceable, precocious children like you and your brothers. Your father and I will feel much better knowing that we can live far removed from any threat of Northern ships and guns when the time comes. Besides, your father is about to leave us for God knows how long. We chose Uncle Michael's offer to travel with them to Baldwin County when we all decide to leave."

"Here's one final and very pressing reason." Randolph huddled with Tom and Bourke and took hold of Sallie's hand. He looked each square in the eye. "I'd feel a lot better if I didn't have to worry about my family's well-being while I am away mustering soldiers to defend Georgia. Look, no one's going anywhere until it becomes vital. Your mother and I just wanted the three of you to be aware of what might happen."

"I guess it makes sense, but what about the workers and their families on Sapelo Island? Are we going to leave them behind if we have to go?" Sallie asked.

Randolph squeezed Sallie's hand. "Don't you fret. Your Uncle Allen knows, should that time come, what tools and equipment to bring along with our workers and their families. You'll see."

"What if those Northern blockade ships arrive before the harvest?" Tom blurted.

"Don't you worry about that either. We'll make sure everyone evacuates the island in plenty of time. Besides, Uncle Allen will make sure everything and everyone heads up the Altamaha River, even if a little earlier than we expect."

Sallie turned to her mother. "What about Cecile and her momma?

Will they come with us to the new house if we leave before everyone else?"

"No. When the time comes for us to leave, they'll be busy shutting down and packing up South End's *Big House* and tending to their own family needs before they can leave." Mary launched a broad, reassuring smile. "Now quit your fussing. They'll join us soon enough."

None of this made telling his children any less taxing, especially after Sallie learned Cecile and her family would remain at South End and join them later. Though Cecile, like her mother before her, was born a slave on Sapelo, she and Sallie had grown up together and had always enjoyed each other's company. Alma, Cecile's mother, had served as the housekeeper and cook at *Big House* during Thomas Spalding's later years at South End. Alma's own two children, Cecile and Jeremiah, had remained close to Sallie, Tom, and Bourke, even after Randolph's family had moved off Sapelo three years earlier. Josephine, an elderly widowed slave, became the family's cook and housekeeper after they left *Big House* to live in the farmhouse on the mainland.

As hard as it had been to leave Alma and her family behind on the island, Randolph honored his father's tradition of keeping his workers and family together on the land they lived and worked on.

Thomas Spalding's deep-seated belief of permanence and place remained enshrined in South End's sprawling mansion and barns, as well as in the duplex residences that comprised the island's slave communities near the fields where they worked. That practice remained engrained in how his sons, Charles and Randolph, managed their affairs and property. Randolph nudged all three children up the steps and into the large, central hall. Mary pointed to their bedrooms.

"Now, run along and change for supper. Alma and Cecile are setting the dining room table, so no dillydallying!"

Randolph barked, "You heard your mother. Now, scoot. I'm hungry, and supper smells mighty good."

"What did you tell Sallie?" Randolph asked Mary while in their bedroom changing his shirt.

Mary inspected her hair while seated at her dressing table. "Why do you ask?"

"Her tears had disappeared, and her inquiries sounded far more rational—a far cry from those foot-stomping outbursts on the beach earlier."

"When are you going to realize Sallie's a budding young woman? It's a young woman's prerogative to be victimized by capricious mood swings."

"But—"

"Oh my dear Randolph, Sallie is not a little girl anymore. Your sixteen-year-old daughter loves you and fears for you and the changes that the future is stirring. Remember, in the past few days she went from contemplating her first cotillion to being uprooted with no say in the matter."

Randolph walked behind Mary, who remained seated at her dressing table, staring into the mirror as they talked. He put his hands on her shoulders and kissed the back of her neck. "I can't change what the future holds, by God, but I can make sure she'll experience a proper and most memorable first cotillion. Why don't you tell her right after supper?"

"What about your orders? Don't you have to report to General Lawton in Savannah?"

"You let me worry about that. You get the word out to all our kith and kin in the county that the cotillion for Miss Sarah Spalding will take place at South End just as we planned on the first of July. Trust me. All this bombastic rhetoric and aggressive posturing is sheer poppycock. Mister Lincoln dispatched his navy to prove a point while testing the South's resolve and mettle. The spilling of blood in an all-out war comprises a price far too heavy to restore any hope of unity. A diplomatic resolution is still possible. There is ample room for two brotherly nations to coexist on this great American continent."

CHAPTER TWO

30th of June, 1861

After a month of scurrying about Savannah in his official uniform, Colonel Randolph Spalding stood in the foggy grayness on Savannah's moonlit wharf with his military uniform packed in travel bags at his feet. Joining him for the return voyage to McIntosh County, his nephew, Captain Thomas Wylly, likewise had packed his officer uniform. Eager to arrive home prepared and in time for his daughter's cotillion, Randolph visited one of Savannah's notable haberdasheries and treated himself and his nephew to new dress clothes for the occasion. Both wore their new light brown broadcloth trousers with matching brocade waistcoats for the trip home.

Deckhands of the *Northern Belle*, a twin-masted cargo schooner, scurried on and off the ship, manhandling the last of the burlap-wrapped bundles and dunnage items on the dock. Destined for ports of call along the Georgia coast, including Sunbury, Darien, Brunswick, St. Mary, and Frederica, Randolph arranged for passage. He knew Captain Stevens and his crew well, as they often sailed to Sapelo Island's High Point and Marsh Landing docks to take on and unload cargo. Though larger steamers had transported much of the tidewater's crops destined for markets in Savannah and Charleston in recent years, shallow-water schooners like the *Northern Belle* continued to traverse the treacherous tidal waterways better than the steamships loaded with cargo and passengers.

Brigadier General Alexander Lawton had signed their official orders, and Randolph had tucked them along with a supply of militia recruitment papers in his leather satchel. Lawton had granted them three days of leave before they were to recruit volunteers from McIntosh County for Georgia's coastal defense regiments.

In what felt like an interminable first few days after he reported to General Lawton in Savannah, Randolph discovered military life required him to draw upon the ingrained lessons he learned working under his father's scrutiny while growing up on South End. Although, since his father's passing, his confidence had increased, and he no longer looked over his shoulder while giving orders on his plantations.

Still, he toed the line as an aide-de-camp and remained in lockstep with the other staff officers beneath General Lawton. The general's often gruff command style came easier for Randolph thanks to the stringent discipline he experienced from his own father while growing up. In fact, he'd discovered early on how well-suited he was for obeying and giving orders. In no time, he embraced the esprit de corps and respect he earned being an officer in the Georgia Militia, now a part of the newly formed Confederate Army, far removed from the shadows of his father and his older brother that had hindered him on Sapelo.

Captain Stevens plodded down the gangplank and approached Randolph and Thomas on the otherwise deserted wharf.

"We're ready to get underway, Mister Spalding. We must leave on the tide to reach the narrow tidewater channel between Tybee Island and the mainland before daybreak. Beyond Ossabow, we should encounter nothing but smooth sailing before we drop Captain Wylly off at The Forest's landing on the Sapelo River. After that, good Lord willing, we should tie up in Darien before the sunset."

"Have you had any run-ins with blockade ships?" Thomas asked, sounding as though he relished the prospect.

Captain Stevens roared and then said, "For the time being, my dear brave Captain Wylly, they've shown little interest in bothering me and my crew. I reckon, until smaller gunboats arrive, their frigates are only interested in intercepting the daring ocean-bound blockade runners that still outwit and outrun them." He pointed to the cargo stacked on the deck. "Much of these supplies arrived only yesterday in the cargo holds of the *Sumter*. I just hope Captain Semmes and others like him keep those federal gunships preoccupied without getting boarded or, worse yet, blown out of the water."

"I can't agree more," Randolph said, grabbing his bags and heading up the gangplank. "We're indebted to you, Captain. My daughter's coming-out ball at South End is tomorrow. Neither the stagecoach nor railroad made sense with only three days of leave, before—" He raised his travel bag, "I must don my uniform again. I intend on making the most of what little time I have with my family."

※ ※ ※

As dawn's first light broke the ocean's distant horizon, the *Northern Belle* sailed beyond the mouth of the Savannah River into the treacherous tidewater channel, ever careful of the invisible, shifting muddy shoals and sandbars. Randolph relaxed atop a crate on the ship's foredeck as daybreak glistened across the lush green marsh cordgrass. He flavored his mug of coffee with McIntosh County's finest dark rum distilled from his own harvested sugar cane at The Thicket's sugar mill not far from his farmhouse estate on the mainland. The brown elixir anesthetized Randolph's lingering fears about the fate of his family's future on Sapelo Island. He also pondered the fate of Sapelo's field hands and servants. They knew little outside the daily grinds of plantation life.

Though South End would host his daughter's grandiose social affair, the burden of his father's legacy, one his father carved out from Sapelo's storied primordial woodlands, hammocks, and wetlands, weighed heavily upon him. Along with fields purchased over time, the Spalding family owned contiguous tracts of cultivated fields spanning from High Point on the north end of the island to South

End. The grand, tabby-built, estate mansion, constructed decades earlier at South End, with its picturesque tropical flower gardens, labyrinth of walkways, and lush green grounds, served as a fitting shrine to Thomas Spalding.

With his father's passing, Randolph became the laird, or master, of Sapelo's expansive plantation empire. The lone exception, Thomas Spalding gifted fifteen hundred acres along the Duplin River above Sapelo's Marsh Landing to his daughter, Katherine, and Michael Kenan, who married in 1832.

Randolph also felt overshadowed by his brother Charles, who was fourteen years older. Charles had inherited Ashantilly, his father's mainland mansion and the home where their mother, Sarah Spalding, lived before she died in 1843. Their father, after residing most of his final years at South End, took up residence at Ashantilly before he passed away in 1851.

Ashantilly became home to the Spalding City of the Dead, a community of tombstones beneath shrouds of funeral moss drooping from a guardian-like ancient oak. Their parents rested in peace side by side and surrounded by seven of their children who had died far too young, some at birth. Just three Spalding daughters survived into adulthood, married, and bore their own families.

Randolph's older brother, Charles, and his wife, Evelyn, had no children. Thus, Thomas Spalding bequeathed his beloved landholdings on Sapelo to his namesake grandson, Thomas Spalding II, Randolph's oldest son. Until Tom came of age, Randolph assumed the role of guardian of his father's indelible legacy.

# # #

The sun broached the horizon by the time Randolph and his nephew joined the crusty Captain Stevens in his cabin for breakfast whose tobacco-stained grin and unmistakable laugh belied his stern ebony stare. They reminisced about better days as they consumed their fill of cheese, bread, and hot coffee. Randolph remained seated at the scarred wooden table bolted to the cabin's floor, but his nephew, Captain Thomas Wylly, stood and headed back on deck after he had scarfed his breakfast.

Randolph rocked his chair onto its back legs, grinned, and said, "Thomas, don't be such a stick in the mud. Join us." He then shuffled the deck of cards Captain Stevens handed him as he egged his nephew into joining him and the captain for a few hands of poker to pass the morning away.

Knowing his uncle's reckless propensity to imbibe and gamble far too much, Thomas shrugged and returned to his chair. He snatched the rum bottle from Randolph's hand. "Don't mind if I do." He poured a finger of rum into his empty tin mug. With a half-cocked grin, he said, "Deal me in . . . on one condition."

"Pray tell. What?" Randolph said.

Thomas shoved the cork back into the half-empty bottle before placing it on the floor beside his chair. "I trust you and Captain Stevens will keep this a friendly game of poker to pass the time."

Randolph leaned forward in his chair and chuckled as he glanced at the two men while he adeptly shuffled the deck twice. "Sounds good to me. Ante up." Randolph slid the deck of cards in front of an unsmiling Captain Stevens. "Do you wish to cut the deck before I deal?"

Stevens tapped the deck with the tips of his fingers. "Randolph, just deal, my cocky friend."

※ ※ ※

The *Northern Belle* eased away from The Forest plantation's landing at the mouth of the Sapelo River after dropping Thomas Wylly off. The two-hour trip to Darien had drained the last glimmer of the rutilant sunset by the time Randolph bid farewell to Captain Stevens and his crew. He lugged his bags up Darien's lamplit riverside walkway, the ship's bell chiming eight times as the vessel sailed back into the coastal tidewaters, headed to Brunswick. The clock tower chimed eight times.

Thirteen-year-old Tom Spalding hopped down from their horse-drawn carriage with an exuberant smile, though it fizzled as soon as he ran up to greet his father.

"Is everything okay? You sure look mighty tuckered, Pa. Are the rumors true?"

"Whoa, son. Yes, I'm plum worn out. That's for certain." He patted Tom's shoulder. "Thanks for being here. I didn't relish walking home alone this evening." Randolph eyed the still dark livery stable next to the Mansion House on Broad Street—the primary thoroughfare in town lined with shops, warehouses, taverns, and other Darien mercantiles and businesses. Broad Street ran parallel to the riverfront in Darien until it wound northward and became Stage Road, the serpentine overland coastal road linking Savannah and Darien.

"Momma told Bourke and me to keep watch because you wrote you'd be arriving on the *Northern Belle*. When I recognized her sails, I raced to the edge of the marsh and waved. You couldn't see us, but I recognized you and Captain Stevens standing on the foredeck. We didn't want you to have to walk from town, so William hitched up Josie and Jackson as soon as he heard me yelling. They did the rest."

Randolph smiled at William, the Spalding's twenty-year-old mulatto ostler and farmhand. "Thank you, William. I sure appreciate you and my two boys coming to get me this evening."

William grew up as a misfit after his arrival on Sapelo as an infant with his mother. She had been noticeably ill-treated by her former master during one of Thomas Spalding's last trips to Charleston. She passed away not long before Randolph and Mary moved from South End to their farmhouse estate above Darien. William's freckled, caramel complexion and reddish, curly hair stood out among the far-darker field hands and servants on the island. He found a modicum of solace tending livestock at South End's stable until Josephine, an elderly servant, took him in not long after his mother died. She vouched for him when Randolph inquired about selecting someone to care for livestock on the new estate. Though younger than Randolph intended, Josephine's respectful cajoling and his tall-for-his-age stature earned William the position.

William fingered the reins. "Mister Spalding, sir, we sure glad to see you. Do you need a hand with your bags, sir?"

Randolph shook his head and motioned for William to remain seated as he tossed his bags in the back end of the carriage. He climbed in and sat between Bourke and Tom, stretching his arms behind their shoulders. "Tom, I don't know what rumors you're referring to, but I promise I'll discuss any rumors after we get home. Right now, I just wanna get home and hug your handsome mom and sister."

"They are dying to see you, too," Bourke said, snuggling closer to his father.

"Sit back and relax, Mister Spalding. We'll have you home in no time." William said as he slapped the reins. Josie and Jackson snorted and eased the carriage onto Broad Street.

Fluttering flames from Darien's streetlamps projected choreographed shadows off the overarching tree foliage lining the town's main road. Clopping hooves echoed against the vacated storefronts, accentuating the late hour as they left the otherwise bustling business district overlooking the river. By this time of the evening, only enterprising proprietors visible through store windows lingered beyond closing time sweeping or restocking their shelves.

They turned onto Cowhorn Road, a narrow, well-traveled carriage route leading to the elaborate residences at The Ridge and beyond. Primeval live oaks and magnolias lined the well-traveled sandy highway. The gnarly branches of the massive oaks offered a solemn drive with their moss-laden, shiny green, teardrop-shaped foliage. During the day, the arboreal canopy provided welcome shade but blocked the starlight and moonlight after nightfall.

Cowhorn Road led them away from the mouth of the river as

they turned northward. It skirted along the salt marshes and tidal inlets—nature's fertile buffer between the mainland, the navigable waterways, the shallower creek channels, and a labyrinth of coastal islands of which Sapelo reigned the largest.

Randolph stirred as they pulled into the drive leading to their house. He slapped Tom and Bourke on their thighs. "Will you two boys grab my bags, so William can put the carriage away and unhitch Josie and Jackson? I want to go greet your mother and Sallie."

Tom puffed his chest out as he lowered his father's leather travel bag and satchel to Bourke who grunted as he placed each on the ground. After Tom jumped down beside Bourke, William jiggled the reins.

"Don't worry, we got these, Pa. Sallie and Mom should be inside," Tom shouted, handing the satchel to Bourke before hoisting the heavier travel bag.

Randolph walked up the stone walkway to the porch where Sallie stood at the top of the steps with a smile as wide as her arms. Randolph hugged and kissed her forehead as he lifted her off her feet.

Mary rolled her sleeves down as she looked out the cookhouse doorway. "Josephine, Mister Spalding's back. Fix a plate for him at the supper table."

"Yes, ma'am," Josephine cried out with her familiar good-natured cackle as she shuffled about inside the lantern-lit detached kitchen. "I hears Mister Spalding's voice."

"Sallie, who's this strange man you're hugging on our porch? You know that ain't exactly becoming for a young woman," Mary said, her hands perched on her apron-wrapped hips. All three broke out in misty-eyed laughter.

"Oh, Momma," Sallie giggled.

Randolph lowered his giddy daughter and embraced his wife. After kissing both her cheeks, he turned his head toward Sallie and whispered, "How about giving Tom and Bourke a hand for me?"

As soon as Sallie scampered down the porch steps, he stared into

Mary's deep-blue eyes and gave her a long overdue passionate kiss.

"Randolph Spalding, what's gotten into you?"

"Can't a man enjoy kissing his wife after being away?"

"Of course." Mary placed her hands in his and stared into his travel-weary, indigo eyes. "But there's more, isn't there?"

"I'm afraid there's no turning back now. War's inevitable," he uttered, sadness tugging on his heart. "Though General Lawton believes the war will be brief, you and I should sit and talk further about what to do before Northern ships sail this far down the coast."

Mary masked her worry with a half-hearted rosy smile. "Well, what'll be will be, but nothing is gonna happen that can't wait until after our daughter's special day tomorrow. Now, come on inside and wash up for supper."

CHAPTER THREE

1st of July, 1861

After a restful night with his wife snuggled by his side, Randolph and his family, along with their twenty-year-old governess, Ada Northrup, stepped into their horse-drawn carriage. William maintained a tight rein on Josie and Jackson with his foot on the brake while the family got settled.

Randolph slid in beside his soft-spoken stable hand. Unless he was talking to his animals, William said little. "All right, son. Let's get a move on. We got a big day ahead," Randolph told him.

"Yes, sir." William freed the brake. "Git up, mules. The family's got a boat to catch."

Though still morning, the sun wasted no time stirring up the early summer humidity. The trip to The Ridge community dock would have taken less time had they walked along the edge of the marsh, but today was a special day—Sallie's coming out cotillion at South End—and everyone had dressed up for the occasion.

Mary, fretting as she preened her daughter's long blonde curls, sat across from Sallie. "Oh, fiddle-faddle. Now sit still. Use your fan and for Pete's sake, try not to perspire so much. We simply will not have time to fuss with your hair before you put your gown on at South End."

"Yes, Momma, but it's already so unbearably hot this morning. I'm doing my very best to not sweat." Sallie rolled her eyes as her fan flapped faster trying to cool her flushed cheeks.

"Young ladies don't sweat. We may perspire, but we definitely do not sweat," Ada whispered, leaning closer. She loosened her kerchief and used it to dab Sallie's forehead.

Bourke and Tom, facing one another, attempted to muffle their snickers with their hands over their mouths. Harsh stares from Ada and their mother failed to stifle their puckish laughter.

Randolph had named Sapelo's steam-powered launch the *Sarah Spalding* in honor of his mother and used it to shuttle supplies, mail, and guests to and from South End's dock. Charles and Evelyn Spalding waited patiently out of the sweltering morning sunshine beneath the vessel's red and green canvas canopy since a moderate tidewater breeze made sitting in the canopy's shade bearable.

As soon as Randolph's family stepped off the dock and onto the deck of the *Sarah Spalding,* Mary directed Sallie to sit between her Aunt Evelyn and Ada. Tom and Bourke wasted no time and jumped on board the vessel's afterdeck. Their coats lay folded over the back of a wooden bench near the stern rail. They shaded their eyes from the sun and glared skyward at an osprey circling overhead. Randolph and Charles left the women and stood side by side, gripping the foredeck rail as the vessel pulled away.

Two trusted South End servants expertly navigated the steamboat through the snake-like tidal channel and then followed the Darien River into the Doboy Sound. After its thirty-minute ferry, the crew docked at South End's private pier, just a short tree-lined walk to the mansion's rear entrance. Though Marsh Landing provided a deep-water dock near the mouth of Sapelo's Duplin River to accommodate larger passenger and cargo ships, visitors needed to travel one-and-half miles to visit South End's *Big House*. Sapelo had two other sheltered boat landings, the Kenan's boat dock farther up the Duplin River and High Point Landing on the island's far north end near Randolph's Bourbon and Chocolate fields.

As the morning progressed on the auspicious day, the sun drifted in and out of banks of billowing cumulus clouds, providing some relief from the summer heat. Friends and family began arriving early in the afternoon, and most would depart well before sundown to avoid the swarms of skeeters and gnats that came out from dusk to dawn during the summer months. For that reason, with rare exceptions, social gatherings at South End's regal *Big House* took place during the fall and spring months to allow guests to linger well into the late evening hours. Because of the uncertainty of the present circumstances, Sallie's cotillion became one of those rare exceptions. They would serve dinner on the grounds followed by music and dancing in the mansion's central hall after their daughter's presentation.

※ ※ ※

Cecile greeted Sallie as soon as the family stepped off the launch. "Miss Sallie, your new gown be laid out in your bedroom. You's gonna look mighty pretty in ya'r fancy white dress."

Sallie, doing her darnedest to restrain her bubbling giggles, looked back over her shoulder with winsome eyes directed at her mother. Before Ada said a word, Mary interrupted her conversation with Evelyn and said, "Oh, go on you two."

Sallie latched onto Cecile's hand. They scurried down the wooden boat landing steps and up the cypress and magnolia shaded walkway that snaked to the picturesque floral gardens adorning the lush grounds surrounding South End's grand mansion.

Ada placed one hand on the top of her yellow ribbon-adorned, sweet-grass sunhat as she walked faster to catch up to Sallie. Her long, dark curls bounced off her shoulders as Ada shrieked, "Slow down! Please try to behave like the dignified young lady you intend to be today."

Sallie giggled as she slowed to a suitable lady-like pace. Cecile mimicked Sallie's gait. With their heads held high, they squeezed their lips to stifle their snickers. Cecile's short legs struggled to keep pace with the accentuated, genteel gait of Sallie's lithesome strides.

"The two of you, stop this foolishness. Sallie Spalding, please act your age," Ada said, catching her breath. "And Cecile, if I end up needing to redo Miss Sallie's hair, I'll hold you accountable. Do you understand me?"

"Yes, Miss Northrup," Cecile said, giggling with Sallie.

The two girls continued working their way to *Big House's* side entrance. Tom and Bourke bumbled against one another a few steps behind their sister and Cecile, determined to pass on their father's instructions for Sallie to wait in the parlor for their mother. Ada kept pace a couple of steps behind them.

"The same goes for you two young gentlemen. No running," Ada said, sharing Mary's lighthearted smile. While Mary and Evelyn followed Ada, stepping off the dock, Randolph and Charles remained behind engaged in their own conversation.

Allen Bass, Mary Spalding's older brother and Randolph's overseer, stood with his son, Charlie, at the foot of the path. Allen nudged his son to run after Tom and Bourke. He swept his graying dark brown hair behind his ears just before he ceremoniously genuflected and produced a reassuring smile to his sister. Though nearly a decade older, Allen looked up to Randolph and his sister, and his gesture spoke well about the state of South End's preparations for Sallie's social affair.

After the death of Mary's and Allen's father, Sterling Bass, Sr., their mother handed the management of the Bass family's palatial estate in Russell County, Alabama over to the oldest daughter, Eliza, and her husband, Patrick Henry Perry. Allen moved his wife and son, Charlie, across the Chattahoochee River to Columbus where he became the railway agent. His wife died a few months prior to the lavish wedding of his niece, Miss Evelyn Livingston to Dr. Spalding Kenan, Michael and Katherine Kenan's oldest son. While attending the wedding held at the Bass family estate in November, Randolph invited Allen to move to South End and become his overseer.

Not long after Allen arrived on Sapelo Island with Charlie, then eight, his relationship with Randolph grew beyond that of brothers-in-law. Allen's years on his family's plantation proved invaluable. In no time, he embraced Thomas Spalding's paternal philosophy of working with the slaves on Sapelo carried on by Randolph Spalding. He also recognized the precarious future that lay ahead for the upcoming season's harvests with war looming on the horizon.

Shortly after the noon hour, Randolph greeted Michael and Katherine Kenan as they arrived in the first carriage with their twenty-five-year-old son, Dr. Spalding Kenan, and his pregnant wife, Evelyn.

Randolph offered his hand to his sister and said to his nephew, "Doctor Kenan, married life appears to suit you well. How is your medical practice coming along in town?"

"If you don't mind, I would like to talk to you and Uncle Charles about that a little later this afternoon. I received a letter from the governor offering me a commission in the state militia to serve as a surgeon." Spalding Kenan extended his hand to his wife, then asked Randolph, "Where's Allen? Evelyn wants to say hello to her uncle and share our good news."

"What good news, might I inquire?" Randolph smiled at Evelyn's reddened cheeks.

"Why, my dear Uncle Randolph, I would have thought Aunt Mary would have told you by now," Evelyn whispered with a coy twinkle in her eyes.

Spalding grabbed Randolph's coat sleeve. "You know this means you're going to be a great uncle before this year is out."

Uproarious laughter turned everyone's attention toward Lieutenant William Brailsford hopping down from the second carriage. Flaunting his tailored dress uniform, he bellowed, "Now, how is it I am the only one in uniform for my cousin's coming-out soiree?"

Randolph stepped away from Spalding and his wife. "William, have you started drinking already?"

"Oh, hell no. Not yet, leastwise. I'm counting on my favorite uncle to remedy that soon enough."

Thomas Wylly left his mother's side to corral his fun-loving but more often than not rambunctious cousin. He strong-armed William away from the scathing glares of Randolph and Charles. "Cuz, you ain't never gonna learn when to shut your big mouth." Though taller and brawnier, William Brailsford knew all too well not to ignore his cousin's stone-cold urging. William's mood noticeably changed, and he paraded from their brief heart-to-heart exchange with a scowl.

Four years earlier, Thomas Wylly had returned to his family's home in McIntosh County after eight years exploring the untamed West. He had left McIntosh County a naive yet ambitious eighteen-year-old and returned a frontiersman, Indian fighter, and soldier. His grandfather, Thomas Spalding, had supported his burning desire to join John C. Fremont's fourth expedition to California. Before he'd left on his bold adventure, Randolph's brother Charles gave his nephew a gold watch, and Randolph supplied him with a double-barreled shotgun. William McIntosh, another close relative, gave him a pair of dragoon pistols. He'd credited each gift as a timely lifesaver during his many harrowing escapades. On his return, he received a commission in Georgia's militia and mustered with the Berrien Minutemen.

Thomas Wylly's father, A.W. Wylly, said to Randolph and Charles, "I'm dreadfully sorry. We attempted to dissuade William from wearing his fancy uniform today, but you know how William can get."

Charles chortled. "No problem, A.W., as long as he's on our side in a fight, I believe we can forgive his boorish behavior."

"I'm glad William arrived with you last evening and stayed at Michael's and Katherine's house," Randolph said. "Do tell, how's he holding up since my sister passed away?"

"Holding up?" A.W. pondered a moment. "It feels much longer than a couple of months since Jane passed. What a pity. He gave so much of his life caring for his mother and managing Sutherland Bluff."

"My dear sister Jane. We all miss her," Randolph said.

"I still remember when that scoundrel Forbes bushwhacked his father right after Daniel fired him," Charles said, glancing at William, who remained preoccupied well beyond earshot.

"William and his sister, God rest her soul, were but children when they lost their father. Some folks believe Forbes killed Daniel because he flirted with his wife. Others claimed Daniel dismissed him for abusing his negroes," A.W. said.

"Whatever the case, Jane raised her two children and managed Sutherland Bluff with the help of a couple of overseers until William came of age," Randolph said, reflecting on his sister's struggles over the past twenty-eight years.

"If you ask me, the unexpected death of Jane's daughter a few years back," A.W. sighed, "extinguished the fire in her eyes. She prayed William would find peace and contentment with a family of his own, but he apparently had no serious interest in ever getting married. Of late, the women who have visited the Bluff are not the marrying kind, if you know what I mean."

Charles rested his hand on A.W.'s shoulder. "God help him. At least he's remained faithful to Jane. You and I know William has spewed his venomous anger out on anyone who happens along at the wrong moment, and that includes his negroes."

"Look, with Jane gone, Sutherland Bluff has become a miserable, lonely sanctuary for William," A.W. added. "I promise I'll continue to visit him as often as I can."

"I'll make it a point to keep a close eye on him too," Charles said.

Mary had disappeared into *Big House* to check on Sallie in her bedroom. Ada and Cecile had gone straight into Sallie's room to help her put on layers of undergarments and frilly petticoats, designed to reveal Sallie's blossoming female charms before she slipped on her gown.

Mary addressed the entourage of house servants hand-picked for this special occasion. They listened intently to her last-minute instructions. The male servants wore light-gray vests over high-collared, long-sleeve white dress shirts, charcoal gray trousers, and buffed black brogans on their feet. Alma and Cecile stood among the other female servants, earning an affirming smile from Mary as she inspected their white collared, gray cotton pleated dresses with white pinafores and uniform purple hair wraps.

"You all look extra special nice. Be sure to wear your best smiles around our guests this afternoon," Mary said. She then asked Alma, "How's Hector doing with the roasting of those hogs?"

"Missus Spalding, he be tendin' dem before da sun come up. And, don't you fret. He promised to put on that white apron you gave him before he serves the guests."

Mary nodded with pursed lips.

Evelyn arrived on the portico and took Mary's arm. She whispered, "How's Sallie?"

"She's getting dressed between giggles. When I left, Cecile had her sucking in her breath while she tied her corset. I declare, she seems to have grown up and out overnight," Mary tittered as she blushed.

"Sallie hasn't been a young girl for quite some time," Evelyn said, walking beside Mary and restraining her own joyful chuckle.

They greeted the string quartet recruited from among Sapelo's gifted field hands. "If they play as well as they look in those outfits, they will certainly keep your guests entertained this afternoon."

Though they dressed like the other male servants, they also sported loosely knotted red silk scarves around their raised shirt collars. They began playing as soon as Mary nodded her approval and began receiving her guests with Evelyn by her side. They continued playing from the portico as guests arrived and throughout dinner. After the meal, the quartet would resume playing in the grand hall for Sallie's presentation ceremony.

Hector, Cecile's father, tended two of South End's prized hogs roasting over a fire pit near the cookhouse. Smoke drifted overhead and carried whiffs of the succulent, slow-cooked pork across the grounds as the Spalding family greeted a stream of guests.

Alma instructed the servants where to stand with their practiced, gracious, tooth-filled smiles. They then took their positions behind tables covered with red and white gingham tablecloths loaded with an assortment of delectable fare.

By the time dinner began, Hector had put on a white bib apron. He carved portions of mouthwatering roasted pork at the end of the row of tables. The two boar's heads sported uncanny smiles, entertaining many of the guests as Hector filled their plates.

Cecile and Sallie nibbled on their dinners inside the confines of her bedroom while the family and guests feasted at tables set up on the manicured lawn on either side of South End's garden-lined entrance. Most of McIntosh County's notable families had arrived on their own boats or onboard the *Sarah Spalding*, which made several roundtrips between the landing at The Ridge and South End's dock.

※ ※ ※

While guests meandered the grounds or sought refuge in *Big House's* grand parlor, several of Randolph's closest male friends and family gathered in South End's renowned library, a spacious chamber off the main hall filled with Thomas Spalding's enviable collection of books, journals, and papers accumulated over the course of his illustrious lifetime. Only his love and devotion for Georgia and the nation held sufficient influence over the former elderly statesman to have pried him from the solace of his beloved library after his wife died. Sadly, after his fateful trek to Milledgeville in December 1850, he returned to Ashantilly, not South End, where he quietly slipped away with family at his side.

On this summery afternoon, Thomas Spalding's imperishable legacy extended far beyond the cataloged collections on the shelves. His life-sized painted portrait glared upon the guests from above the fireplace mantle. Randolph and Charles remained seated on opposing ends of the room, taking in the back-and-forth banter between family members and longtime friends. One after another stood to pontificate on the fate of the North's army should it march against the South. Each crescendo of bravado and cries of affirmation from the high-spirited circle of men stirred another to step to the center of the room.

Randolph, seated behind his father's mahogany writing desk, looked amused as he puffed on his cigar. When Charles left his seat on the Chesterfield at the other end of the library, Randolph leaned back in his chair and watched his brother struggle to mediate a bitter exchange between two of his bloviating guests.

Charles stepped between two men squabbling over the veracity of Lincoln's threats to preserve the Union. "Gentlemen, let us not fight among ourselves. Your lion-hearted convictions may, soon enough, require more than overblown prognostications. In this very room, my brother and I heard our father's innumerable admonishments against pursuing the spilling of blood to resolve conflict. He liked to quote the Prophet Isaiah, who said, 'The Lord shall judge among the warring nations. They then shall beat their swords into plowshares, their spears into pruning hooks. One nation shall not lift their sword against another nation, neither shall they learn war anymore.' He further impressed upon us that disproportionate outcomes never justify the pretentiousness of bloodshed war demands."

Randolph gulped the remaining dark elixir in his crystal tumbler as soon as the boisterous quests dismissed Charles's earnest plea. The grumbling grew, and he searched the room wondering whether the braggadocio of his friends and family soothed their waxing fears or further inflated their heartfelt pride. Though Randolph and Charles shared similar fears about the prospects of war, both steeled themselves to defend their property and lifestyle should the fight come to Georgia. However, Charles did so with more reverence for their father's legacy than Randolph.

Norman Gignilliat, a longtime family friend whose plantation neighbored Ashantilly, waddled into the middle of the room. His prodigious girth rivaled his compact stature; he looked like a balding hogshead that sprouted legs and arms. His coiffed, hoary beard made up for his balding head.

"Charles, my good fellow, if we cannot send an undeniable, robust response to these abolitionists invoking Lincoln's aggression, our families may all fall victim to a slave insurrection long before federal troops take a step on Georgia soil. Have you not considered an uprising among our darkies as an imminent, bigger threat?"

"Frankly, Norman, I haven't stayed up late worrying about such matters. Should your plantation slaves attempt to organize, which I highly doubt, and pursue such an ill-fated notion, the McIntosh Guard and Dragoons will squash their uprising," Charles said with a disparaging chuckle.

Randolph looked at his father's portrait perched above the mantle. The unyielding glare stirred him to his feet. "My dear Mister Gignilliat, I imagine if your overseer plied less lash you'd sleep better at night. Have you not heard a word my brother just shared about the futility of violence and bloodshed? Do you not recall our father's position on slavery?"

The rotund Gignilliat rocked back on his heels and glared with reddened cheeks at Randolph.

"If my dear friend imbibed less, he'd see clearer the threat to which I refer. Then again, his father, the great Thomas Spalding, made his misgivings about the future of slavery well known, and you and your family have continued to exhibit his coddling of your negroes."

"Pray tell, what are you trying to insinuate?" Randolph sneered as he stepped closer with a dark scowl.

"Come, come, my dear Randolph. It's no secret your father built Sapelo into a nigger heaven, and you still spoil your slaves like your father before you. Your slaves live in scattered communities on this island and in tabby houses with plastered walls and thatched roofs. You allow them to grow their own crops and raise their own hogs and poultry. But at least you had the sense to hire a proper overseer, unlike your father."

"What's your point?"

Norman Gignilliat looked around the room with eyes pleading support, but Randolph railed, "Our father taught us to not treat workers like cattle or chattel. Nearly all our servants and field hands were born on this island, as were their mothers and fathers before them. As long as a Spalding owns the land, Sapelo will remain their home, just as my father promised. He taught us to be mindful that all that we have has come from the labors of our negroes on our lands. Our position of privilege as the landowners comes with a responsibility to act generously and justly toward those less privileged who depend upon us and we them."

Gignilliat scoffed. "So, Mister Randolph Spalding, you have no fear of your workers turning on you and your family? What if Northern abolitionists threaten to stir a slave rebellion along Georgia's coast? There are growing rumors of Yankee sympathizers and spies instigating slave uprisings on plantations up and down the southern coast."

Unlike his father's hands-on superintendence and reliance upon a former slave named Bu Allah as his overseer, Randolph remained at arms-length with the day-to-day managing of his fields on Sapelo. He felt like a steward rather than the Spalding family's Laird of Sapelo and master of South End.

"My dear uncles," William Brailsford said as he staggered beside the much shorter Norman Gignilliat, placing his arm across his rounded shoulders. "Fear and a firm hand earn the respect of our slaves. My dear friend here fears his darkies because he coddles them too often and pretends to discipline them. As for me, my slaves receive fair treatment unless they choose to feel the sting of my anger."

Mary Spalding stood in the doorway of the library. "Gentlemen, I truly do not wish to bring your contentious confabulations to an end," she said, glaring with pursed lips at William, "but my dear husband is needed to escort his daughter for her presentation. The rest of you need to take stock of your talk. This is a joyous occasion, and I will not have it spoiled by all your fearmongering and cocksure boastings."

Randolph excused himself as the string quartet began playing processional music and the guests migrated into South End's grand central room. Mary stood between Charles and Evelyn and Allen Bass, who kept an eye on his son as well as his nephews, Tom and Bourke.

The guests applauded as Randolph and Sallie appeared arm-in-arm and briefly stopped before entering the throng of family and friends filling the grand parlor. Dabbing the sweat from his brow with his coat sleeve, Randolph took a deep breath, arched his back, and for one of the few times since his father passed, appeared as the Laird of Sapelo and South End's master like his father had before him. Sallie squeezed his arm, smiled, and said, "Thank you, Dad. I'll always cherish this memory."

"Thank me after all the guests and all your young suitors have exhausted themselves greeting and dancing with the prettiest young woman in all of Georgia. Like you, I will always remember this day." Randolph patted Sallie's gloved hand as it firmly clung to his arm while they walked to the center of the room.

※ ※ ※

Randolph and his family remained at South End after the last guests left. In the wee dark hours beyond the stroke of midnight, Randolph sprung from his bed when he heard Tom scream, *"Pa, the house is on fire! Help! Pa, the house is on fire! Everyone needs to get out."*

Wearing but his nightshirt, Randolph raced with bare feet across the slick tile floors in the dark silence. At the opposite end of the grand mansion, he stood in the doorway to his boy's bedroom. He caught his breath and listened but heard nothing before he unlatched the door. The one oval window on the far wall shed enough light into the room to recognize that his boys remained undisturbed in their beds. Both appeared fast asleep.

He opened the door further, stepped into the moonlit room, and stood beside Tom's bed. He leaned close and whispered, "Tom, are you awake?" His son remained motionless. "Tom, are you okay?" Randolph whispered louder.

Tom groaned. "Pa, is that you?" He raised himself on his elbows and squinted at the shadow of his father standing beside his bed. "What's the matter?"

"I heard you yelling the house was on fire a few moments ago."

Tom rubbed his eyes. "What are you talking about? I was sound asleep."

"I'm sorry. Go back to sleep. See you in the morning."

"Okay, good night, sir." Tom's head fell back onto his pillow, and he had drifted back to sleep before Randolph closed the door.

Mary awoke when Randolph climbed back into bed. "Anything wrong?"

"I don't think so. I thought I heard Tom having a nightmare, but he's fine."

"I heard nothing. Go back to sleep. We've got a busy day tomorrow."

Randolph draped an arm over Mary and lowered his head, but his eyes remained open until drowsiness subdued his thoughts.

※ ※ ※

The day after Sallie's cotillion, Randolph and his family returned to their home on the mainland. Randolph had the house built as a refuge for them well removed from Sapelo's plantation life. The two-story, wood-framed house faced the marsh-filled inland tidal waters. He and Mary loved how each sunrise glistened above Sapelo's treetops in the distance and illuminated their second-floor bedchamber most mornings from the elevated porch spanning the front of the home. Tall sash widows maximized the morning sunlight, allowing temperate sea air to fill every room. Ornate glass doors swung open onto the upper porch from Randolph and Mary's second-floor bed chamber while a single matching door provided access to the porch from the central staircase hallway. The roof overhang shaded both porch levels from the midday sunshine.

Beneath the five bedchambers and central hall upstairs, the main floor included a spacious parlor with an attached sitting room on one side of the hallway. A family-size dining room, serving room, and pantry spanned the other side of the central hallway. A brick walkway off the side entrance stoop led to the detached cookhouse and the three-room servant quarters. Unlike other properties up and down the coast with recognizable names like Ashantilly, Randolph Spalding's marsh front farmstead carried no imprimatur. For him and his family, their mainland home provided a private sanctuary away from Sapelo and his father's legacy at South End.

On this third morning since he departed Savannah, Randolph hugged his daughter on the lower porch. "I'm sorry I can't stay longer. We need to enlist additional volunteers for the militia. I promise to be back in a day or two at the most." With a spat of tears, Sallie buried her head into the breast of her father's blue officer's tunic as he fastened the last gold button. His black waist belt and crimson silk sash dangled from his hand while he looked at Mary.

Mary pulled Sallie to her side, and Sallie cried on her shoulder while Randolph wrapped his sash around his waist and buckled his belt over it. "Randolph, we've already said our goodbyes in case you cannot come back before you have to return to Savannah."

Randolph leaned over and kissed his wife's damp cheek before he put his hat on and adjusted the brim. "If you need anything, get word to Charles. If he's not at Ashantilly, he'll most likely be at Sutherland Bluff with William. They're busy mustering recruits into Georgia's First Battalion. For the present time, they will make certain you and the kids are safe."

Mary dabbed her teary cheeks with her free dress sleeve while stroking Sallie's blond hair with her other hand. With a contrived smile, she said, "If I'd known how dashing you look wearing that uniform, I would've gotten you to enlist sooner. Will you do me a small favor?"

"Anything, my dear."

"Try not to get any holes in it." She swept her fingertips across the double row of gold buttons on his chest.

Tom ran from the barn, arms waving. "Pa, a soldier just rode up. He stopped at the back stoop."

"Run and tell him to come to the front of the house." As soon as Tom raced off, Randolph chuckled. "Lord, I don't want Josephine to faint at the sight of a soldier knocking on that door."

Ada appeared at the doorway as a handsome lieutenant marched behind Tom with Bourke tagging along and gawking at the tall soldier. The young officer squared his broad shoulders and saluted Randolph at the foot of the porch steps. "As you were, Lieutenant. What's so urgent?" Randolph said, returning a half-hearted, perfunctory salute.

Sallie wiped her moist rosy cheeks with her fingers, blushing as she sported a kittenish smile. She stepped away from her mother and exchanged wide-eyed looks with Ada. The handsome lieutenant took notice and returned a chivalrous nod.

"Lieutenant, I know you didn't ride out here for no reason."

"No, sir. My apologies to you and your family. I've got an urgent message for you from General Lawton, sir." He removed a sealed letter from his leather haversack.

Randolph unfolded the handwritten dispatch. "Thank you, Lieutenant."

The soldier remained at attention, though the semblance of a smile appeared as Sallie and Ada stood next to each other near Mary. Randolph stepped back to read the correspondence from Savannah. He then took Mary by the arm and guided her to the far end of the porch.

"Would you like something to drink?" Ada asked the young officer, who looked uneasy as beads of sweat trickled down his face.

"Yes, ma'am. I'd appreciate a glass of water if it's not too much trouble."

"I'll get it," Sallie whispered.

Mary clung to Randolph's arm and looked up with sorrowful eyes. "Tell me. What's wrong?"

"General Lawton has ordered me back to Savannah straightaway. General Lee is arriving tomorrow to evaluate our coastal defenses."

"What about Captain Wylly?"

"He'll remain with Charles and William to continue the recruiting of volunteers."

"Colonel Spalding, sir, my commander instructed me to escort you to Savannah posthaste," said the lieutenant.

"Very well. My stable boy is saddling my horse. I already have a bag packed."

The lieutenant gulped down the water Sallie handed him. They exchanged regret-filled looks when he gave her the empty glass back. "Thank ya, Miss Spalding. Thank ya very much. I gotta go."

"What's your name, lieutenant?" Ada asked.

"My apologies, ma'am. I'm Lieutenant Archibald McKinley from Baldwin County." He doffed his cap.

Ada nudged Sallie. "This is Miss Sallie Spalding. I'm Ada Northrup, her governess."

Sallie's dimples deepened as she squeezed the empty glass with both hands. "Mister McKinley, by any chance, do you know the Kenans in Milledgeville?"

"Why yes, ma'am. They're all fine folks." He swiveled his head away from staring at Sallie's rubescent smile as soon as he heard Randolph say goodbye to Mary.

Randolph stepped beside his daughter and wrapped his arms around her waist. He eyed the lieutenant, who appeared hesitant with his mouth open. "Pardon my interruption, but I need to say goodbye to *my* daughter."

Lieutenant McKinley stepped back and returned his cap to his head.

"Sallie, I'm counting on you to help your mother with your

brothers. I don't know how long I'll be away, but as soon as I know anything, I'll get word to you and your mother." Randolph followed his young escort down the porch steps.

"Please be careful," Sallie whimpered before she bolted from Ada's side and caught up to Tom and Bourke at the foot of the steps. All three marched behind their father toward the barn.

Randolph secured his saddlebag while Sallie intently watched him cinch each leather strap. "Young lady, have you mentioned anything about our plans to anyone, particularly Cecile or her momma?"

Sallie's reddened eyes widened. "Not exactly."

"Not exactly? What does that mean?"

"I might've said something to Cecile about us possibly going away for a while and promised I'd ask about her coming with us. I said nothing more. I promise."

Randolph shook his head. "Please say nothing further to anyone. I'll be back as soon as I can. Your Uncle Allen has enough to handle on the island without having to quell rumors that could disrupt the work in the fields."

Tom handed his father the reins of his roan stallion, Zapala, the winner of many match races against the finest horses in McIntosh County. As their father and the lieutenant rode off, Tom and Bourke raced behind. By the time they ran onto Cowhorn Road, a cloud of dust surrounded them. They stood side by side and waved.

CHAPTER FOUR

9th of July, 1861

General Lee, escorted by General Lawton and his staff, toured Savannah for four days, inspecting the three fortresses—Fort Pulaski, Fort Jackson, and Fort McAllister—guarding the port city. While visiting Pulaski's artillery placements along the fort's parapets, General Lee recalled being a wet-behind-the-ears West Point lieutenant in the Army's Engineer Corps when he first came to Savannah thirty years earlier. In an unassuming, matter-of-fact demeanor, he recalled how he oversaw the planning and early construction of the fort after his commanding officer took ill. He appeared to take immense pride in describing the fort's formidable features, reverting to engineering jargon as he rambled on about the fortification's design and redoubtable massive brick construction.

Each evening, the staff meetings ventured well into the wee hours as the two generals discussed plans to expand Georgia's coastal defense. Lee impressed upon Lawton and his staff how Charleston or Savannah would likely soon face an assault by Northern ships and troops if the war continued its present course. Before Lee left, he articulated in no uncertain terms that the North's naval presence would certainly creep farther south along the coast to Florida. Growing reports of federal warships patrolling the waters near Tybee Island buttressed his proposition on the North's strategy.

By the time Lee boarded the *Savannah Albany and Gulf* train that would take him to meet with President Jefferson Davis in Montgomery, Alabama, the resounding thunder from Tybee

Island's artillery batteries echoed throughout the city. Savannah's genteel populous stepped livelier than usual while conducting its daily business. Families considered leaving their decadent homes behind to live temporarily in safer cities like Milledgeville, Macon, Thomasville, and Columbus.

When not trailing the generals and sitting through staff meetings, Colonel Spalding found refuge in a room on the second floor of a modest boarding house where several other staff officers quartered. On the city's outskirts, directly across the primary avenue bordering the Camp of Instruction's parade field, the boarding house served him well.

Two days after Lee departed, an orderly knocked on Randolph Spalding's bedroom door. An orderly saluted and handed him a handwritten note from General Lawton requesting him to report to Lawton's home.

Lawton's ostentatious mansion overlooked Forsyth Park and had hosted many of Savannah's most prominent citizens and visiting dignitaries. Earlier that year, Lawton went from the rank of colonel in Georgia's militia to brigadier general in the Confederate Army in command of Georgia's defenses. Standing at the front door of the imposing three-story white stucco residence with elaborate granite crowns and black shutters adorning its windows, the colonel reminisced about a summer day when he accompanied his father up the same shrub-lined granite steps to where two stone lions guarded the front stoop. On this visit, however, they appeared less fearsome than how Randolph recalled them two decades earlier.

After an exchange of routine salutes, General Lawton dismissed the orderly and escorted Randolph into the parlor. There, he directed Randolph's attention to the map of coastal Georgia pinned atop the room's garish floral wallpaper behind his cluttered desk.

"Colonel Spalding," Lawton said, stroking his graying dark-brown beard. He then swept his hand across the string of barrier islands that ran from Tybee just south of the South Carolina border to Cumberland Island above Florida's Amelia Island. Using his right forefinger, he circled Sapelo Island. "I've asked you here to discuss specifically fortification plans for your island."

"Yes, sir." Randolph had recognized Sapelo's strategic value long before participating in the meetings with General Lee that dealt with fortifying the barrier islands between Savannah and Jacksonville. Sapelo lay midway, and with its surrounding marshlands served as a coastal buffer for the Altamaha River delta and the busy port of Darien against nature's unpredictable storms. Sapelo would become a lethal deterrent for any intrusive enemy ships with strategically placed manned artillery batteries.

"I asked you here this morning because I realize General Lee's coastal defense plans may interfere with your plantation's harvest on Sapelo. The construction of the island's earthwork fortification and artillery batteries may require the labor of some of your slaves about the time your harvest gets underway."

Randolph swallowed the lump rising in his throat. "Yes, sir. My overseer, Mister Allen Bass, happens to be my wife's brother and, likewise, is a trusted friend. He boasted before I left that they had planted four thousand acres of Sea Island cotton along with some corn and sugar cane across Sapelo. As for my field workers, most live in communities near the fields, storehouses, or the sugar mill. I don't foresee a problem with them nor those who live and work in or around the house at South End. Likewise, I don't anticipate a problem supplying some workers to help with any earthwork construction. They'll want to help defend their homes as well." Randolph stepped up to the map and pointed to the island's Atlantic coastline. "Where exactly will our proposed battery placements be—"

"Colonel," the general interrupted, "besides constructing an earthwork fortification near the lighthouse and two additional artillery battery placements, we intend to station four militia companies on the island from a new regiment we are organizing to support the batteries and guard against Yankee troops stepping onto your island."

Randolph had not previously been aware of the decision to introduce such a large contingent force on the island. "General, is this why you wanted to meet with me? You certainly don't need my permission." As soon as his words came out, his mind raced. He knew every inch of the island and tried to visualize where their encampment would make the most sense.

Lawton lit a cigar and puffed. A billow of smoke hovered above his desk like a looming storm cloud before he sat in his chair. "Mind you, we won't bring them onto the island all at once. I imagine your fields will be 'white for the harvest,' as the good book says, long before all the militia units arrive on the island. At present, two companies of Berrien County volunteers are undergoing instruction under Captain Echols of the Confederate Corps of Engineers. They will be the first two militia companies to man the artillery placements on the island. Two additional units will receive similar training and arrive on Sapelo as well."

"General, I imagine most of these volunteers are quite unfamiliar with the tropical conditions, not to mention the infestations Sapelo hosts throughout the sweltering summer season."

"That's most likely true. What do you suggest?"

"If I may, sir? Sapelo's temperate weather arrives early in October. By that time, there'll be far less chance of our soldiers getting sick from either the miasmic heat or the summer swarms of insects. The plantation's workers will be busy harvesting by then, which should ease our mutual concerns about the extraordinary number of soldiers and slaves stirring up trouble on the island."

"Well, Randolph, excuse the informality, but that's exactly why I wanted to address you as the master of Sapelo and not one of my staff officers. I knew your father fairly well, and likewise have had the pleasure of chatting with your brother, Charles." Lawton puffed on his cigar, sizing Randolph up. "Take a seat, Mister Spalding."

"Thank you, sir. How can I be of service? I'll do whatever's in my power to facilitate defensive measures on Sapelo. My father's paradise, as he loved to refer to Sapelo, must not become subjugated to our abolition-minded enemy. General, I also made a promise to the intended master of South End on Sapelo, and I darn well plan to keep that promise."

"Pray tell. Who's the intended master of South End? I thought that would be you."

"My fourteen-year-old son, Thomas Spalding II. Before Father passed away, he charged me to manage South End until my son became old enough to take over. Outside of my sister Katherine and her husband, Michael Kenan, who live on a portion of the island my father gave them as a wedding gift, my father left South End, the southern half of Sapelo, to Thomas. I own the fields on the northern half of the island. Even with what I own, I am merely the caretaker of my family's legacy on Sapelo. No matter how you look at it, I'd rather not see either my sister and her husband, my son, nor I lose what is rightfully ours."

"Well, let's do our part to keep those promises."

"What do you wish me to do, General?"

"I would like you to get to know Captain Levi Knight and Captain John Lamb of the Berrien Minutemen. You're certainly going to see a lot of them and their men over the next few weeks and likely months. Captain Knight's company has been under General Styles's command at the 13th Georgia Volunteers in Brunswick before we ordered the Berrien companies to Savannah. Captain Knight is a most affable and seasoned military officer. His men respect him. I know little about Captain Lamb, but I am sure with Captain Knight's help, you will get to know him in short order. Also, introduce yourself to Captain William Echols. Your first order of business will be to introduce him to Sapelo."

"Certainly, sir. I sense there's more."

Lawton smiled. "Yes, Randolph. I had the pleasure of visiting your family's magnificent house at South End while your father was still alive. Quite an impressive home your father built on the island. Does any of your family still live there?"

"No, sir. We only stay at South End a few days a year anymore. My family lives yearlong on a piece of property along the coastline above Darien. Sapelo's not a desirable place to raise a family." Randolph's eyes widened. "Why do you ask?"

"I'm glad to hear that. South End's mansion will serve as the regimental headquarters, and our soldiers will establish a camp on the surrounding grounds. We'll designate it as Camp Spalding in your father's honor."

Randolph stared through the swirling gray cigar smoke at the map behind General Lawton. "Yes, sir."

"Fine. In return, I'll assign you to Camp Spalding as my staff liaison. You'll oversee all troop activity on the island to avoid any unduly interference with your plantation operations."

"Thank you, sir," Randolph stuttered, absorbing the general's comments.

"As soon as you and Captain Echols report back from your island inspection, I'll dispatch you straightaway back to McIntosh County. That should allow you a little extra time with your family while working out any changes you and your overseer will need to implement regarding your slaves on the island. Mind you, your plantation will be rendering us all a huge service when this season's cotton and sugar get shipped off the island. We certainly will need both in the coming months."

"General, thank you, sir."

"No, Colonel Spalding, thank you. Someday you'll be able to tell young Thomas the role Sapelo played in defending Georgia. You know, Randolph, I have raised three children myself right here in Savannah. What we do in coming days, we do for the legacy of our families' past, present, and future." Lawton rose from his chair and shook Randolph's hand before they swapped salutes.

During his walk back to the Camp of Instruction to meet Captain Echols, Randolph winced as booms reverberated over the city from cannon fire on Tybee Island and Fort Pulaski.

※ ※ ※

Two weeks later, Colonel Spalding placed his packed travel bag at the foot of his bed and walked in sock feet to the boarding house back porch. He stood above the preoccupied orderly who slipped a hand inside one of Randolph's boots and feverishly buffed the black leather.

"Soldier, my feet already appreciate your hard work."

The young, freckle-faced orderly looked over his shoulder. "Thank you, sir. This saddle soap ought to soften these new boots for ya."

"I admit, they didn't look this good when I first put them on."

The orderly applied another coat of saddle soap to the boot's instep and brushed again. "Sir, I think the other boot is ready for you. Do you want to try it on?"

Randolph scooted down the steps, sat beside the orderly, shoved his foot into the boot, and stood. "I should have done this a month ago. I believe you've saved my feet from any further needless suffering. Well done." Until this moment, the very notion of traipsing about Sapelo Island with Captain Echols and his men worried Randolph far more than the persistent toothache that now demanded regular swigs of rum throughout the day.

He then slipped his foot into the second boot. Not even the daily walking to and from staff briefings or chasing down Captain Knight's Berrien volunteers softened his shoe leather as well as the orderly had managed to that afternoon. He flipped the orderly a silver dollar.

"Thank you, sir."

An ever-present orange dust cloud hovered over most of Savannah thanks to the non-stop drilling and marching of infantry in training on sunbaked parade fields. After supper, Randolph slapped another day's worth of the orange dust from his uniform without too much grumbling. He appreciated his good fortune despite the late-night staff meetings and pre-dawn briefings. He relished sleeping in an actual soft bed in his own private room. Whereas, across the avenue, the Camp of Instruction hosted a sea of white canvas tents with soldiers trying to sleep on undersized cots or blankets on the hard ground.

Each day, sunset offered Randolph a respite when his mind could wander from the unceasing comings and goings of the camp, the railroad, and the roadways that cluttered Savannah. After supper, his thoughts drifted to how his family fared miles away from him. On the one hand, he breathed easier knowing Mary, Sallie, and his two boys would soon be safe and far removed from the coast. On the other hand, Randolph, much like his father before him, grew concerned about his slaves and his family's properties on Sapelo. Whereas most Southern planters recognized little or no difference among their property, livestock, and slaves, Randolph learned to know the difference.

As a youngster on Sapelo, he'd often sought after Bu Allah, his father's longtime black overseer. Bu Allah loved to spin mesmerizing yarns featuring barnyard, woodland, and marsh critters. Each tall tale always ended with Bu Allah revealing a profound morsel of wisdom. Born in West Africa, warring tribes sold Bu Allah to slave traders as a young man. After a stint on a Jamaican sugar plantation, Thomas Spalding purchased him while on a trading trip. Like many West African slaves, Bu Allah brought with him his Muslim traditions. Thomas Spalding gradually entrusted Bu Allah with overseeing all his slaves and running the daily operation of Sapelo's vast fields of cotton, sugar cane, and other staple crops. Because of Bu Allah, Thomas Spalding taught his sons to treat all his laborers as valued workers. Randolph repeatedly heard his family's plantations referred to as "Nigger Heaven" because of how they treated their slaves on Sapelo. He knew the derisive comment stemmed from jealousy because of his father's success and prosperity.

❦ ❦ ❦

As the number of federal gunboats and naval ships grew, so did his concern about the future. Randolph knew full well his brother's cavalry regiment could not defend Sapelo Island from Northern ships. Yet, he also dreaded the idea that life on Sapelo was about to be threatened by Georgia's own militia troops sent to defend it. As if Randolph needed an excuse, he soothed his toothache and rising fears each evening with healthy slugs of rum while he wrote his thoughts either in a letter to home or in the blank pages of his journal. However, his letters home always exuded optimism and hope while genuine concerns and fears filled the pages of his journal, a gift from Sallie before he left home.

CHAPTER FIVE

28th of July, 1861

After an uneventful night's rest at South End, free from the clamorous, nonstop comings and goings in Savannah, Randolph rose early and instructed Hector to hitch up a mule to a wagon while he and Captain Echols scoffed down one of Alma's hearty breakfasts. Dressed in borrowed shirt and trousers, William Echols climbed into the wagon with Randolph. Cecile raced from the cookhouse toting a burlap sack of ham and biscuits.

"Why thank you, Miss Cecile," Echols said, peeking inside the sack.

Randolph snapped the reins, and the old wagon creaked forward. He then looked over his shoulder. "Cecile, be sure to tell your momma to quit fretting about what she overheard at breakfast. I'll talk to her and your father later about the soldiers coming to the island."

"Yes, sir. Please tell Miss Sallie I be praying for her and your whole family, too," Cecile hollered, backpedaling out of the path of the wagon as it rolled past her.

"Come on, old gal, let's git!" Randolph cried out. The rickety buckboard jolted as the mule picked up the pace and headed to Sapelo's lighthouse on the island's southernmost point where Doboy Sound greeted the Atlantic.

A short time later, Randolph kicked the wagon's brake and wrapped the reins around it as he and Captain Echols climbed down in front of the lightkeeper's modest frame house. The lonely lightkeeper combatted the remote house's exposure to the sun, salt air, and blowing sand with an annual coat of white paint, but it took just a season before the wood clapboard siding returned to its dreary, weather-worn look.

Sapelo's longtime lightkeeper greeted them from his front porch. "Ahoy, Mister Spalding. What brings you out here today, and who might this be with you?"

"Captain Echols, this is Mister Alex Hazard, the most eligible yet reclusive bachelor I know. We would like to survey the island from the top of your lighthouse if you please."

"I think we can manage that for you. Captain Echols, are ya' afraid of heights?"

"Glad to meet you, sir," Captain Echols added, shaking his hand. "No, sir. I can't say I have ever been afraid of heights, but I have never climbed atop a lighthouse either."

The lightkeeper scrutinized Captain Echols as he stood beside Randolph. "Tell me something, if you will. I read militia from all across Georgia is being called up to protect us on the coast."

"That's a fact. There's militia already patrolling the mainland. Other units will arrive on Sapelo in a few weeks." Randolph said.

The unassuming lighthouse keeper's house stood a brief walk beyond the shadow cast by the towering, stark white brick lighthouse. Though the sun remained short of its midday zenith, their climb up the steep stairway inside the circular tower felt like a baker's oven until the lightkeeper opened the hatch at the top of the winding stairs. On the narrow metal catwalk atop the lighthouse, they would have a bird's-eye perch to identify ideal locations for Sapelo's proposed battery placements.

The spry lightkeeper gave Randolph and Captain Echols a hand as they climbed through the tight hatchway. "You gentlemen okay?" Hazard chuckled as Randolph and Echols climbed onto the catwalk. "That climb can make your legs pretty wobbly."

"You can say that again. Phew!" Echols said, catching his breath.

Randolph chuckled as he looked back at Echols, who maintained a death grip on the waist-high wrought iron rail. "Don't feel bad,

Captain. I recall the first time I climbed up here over twenty years ago. Trust me, the view from here will justify the soreness you'll feel later."

An unabated sea breeze swirled atop the lighthouse as they surveyed Sapelo's coastline. Alex Hazard pointed southward across Doboy Sound. "The safest channel for ships entering or leaving the Altamaha delta lies between these two beacons. Though a crow would fly less than five miles to reach Darien, ships must navigate those serpentine, murky tidewater channels to reach the docks there." The lighthouse keeper pointed to Darien.

From their lofty perch, they could see where the rush of the Altamaha River churned up the primordial sludge created by the tidal marshes until the thirsty blue waters of the Atlantic swallowed every drop of Altamaha's chocolate slurry. At the mouth of Doboy Sound, pods of dolphins surfaced, then disappeared, emerged, and disappeared again.

Alex Hazard anchored his hat with one hand as he pointed northward to sails cresting the distant horizon.

"I'd say that's likely a Northern warship, but so far they have shown little interest in sailing much closer and pestering our coastal merchant ships."

"We will not take any chances and wait until they decide to do so." Echols leaned over the rail, focusing on the grassy bluff abutting Nanny Goat Beach. He then turned his attention to the high ground with its unobstructed view of Doboy Sound on the same jut of land as the lighthouse.

"We'll construct the primary earthwork fortification on this point of the island. It will provide a clear view of Doboy Sound and deal with any unwelcome intruders. We will then add a beachfront battery to fend off ships approaching the shoreline from the ocean over there." He pointed to the sand dunes on Nanny Goat Beach.

"I agree. That will make those two artillery placements convenient to Camp Spalding." Randolph pointed to the creek inlet and the boat landing below South End's *Big House*.

"We still need to identify the best site for the third battery. It needs to be farther up the island near Blackbeard and Cabretta inlets. The location may not be convenient to the main encampment on this end of the island, but it will discourage venturesome gunboats from approaching the north end of the island," Captain Echols said, glaring up the shoreline to no avail. Sapelo's tall, dense canopy hindered their view even from their sixty-five-foot-high perch.

"We will need to head there before we sail back to Darien and enjoy dinner at my house with my family. The dunes on that end of the island should make a natural earthen redoubt for the battery placement there. There's a sizeable hammock near the inlet that can accommodate a detachment of militia. It's all of ten miles from where Camp Spalding will be to Blackbeard's inlet, but a wagon trail runs along the shoreline."

"Yes, Colonel, I agree with you. Are there any plantation fields or slave quarters between the main camp and Blackbeard Inlet?" Echols asked.

"If troops stay on the trail paralleling the beach and don't stray off into the woods, their coming and going should not disrupt the work in the fields or give them reason to bother them in their communities."

Back on the sun-drenched sand near the lighthouse, the sea breeze no longer offered any relief. Randolph wiped his brow on his shirt sleeve. "Captain, now you know why I advised against wearing our uniforms. Sapelo wallows in the sun well into December."

Captain Echols and Randolph waved at Alex Hazard as he walked back to his desolate house nestled between the creek and behind the lighthouse.

※ ※ ※

Dusk had marked the end of another long summer day by the time Randolph and Captain Echols landed at Darien's dock. They retrieved their horses from the livery stable and galloped off with moonlit, dark clouds overhead. The smell of rain filled the air followed by the rapid pattering across the supple spartina grass of the marsh moments later, drenching them before they could dismount and hand the reins of their horses to William in the barn. After washing up and a quick change of clothes, they joined Mary, Tom, Bourke, and Sallie at the dinner table.

"Captain, I hope your visit to Sapelo was fruitful and otherwise uneventful," Mary Spalding said with a gracious smile.

"Missus Spalding, the Colonel and I completed our inspection of the island today. By the sound of the downpour, not a moment too soon I might add." Echols paused and glanced at Randolph. "I've gotta confess. It's gonna be a real shame to see a portion of Sapelo's primal beauty disturbed when our soldiers arrive." Echols scratched the bug bites on his neck and forearms. "Of course, I wouldn't mind disturbing some of its peskier critters."

Randolph chuckled. "After dinner, Josephine can whip up a little of her special potion that'll help you forget about your skeeter bites. Until then, might I offer you a little tonic relief of my own while we dine?" He passed a dark bottle of Carnochan rum to his guest.

Mary's sparkling smile fizzled. "Randolph, might you save that for after dinner?" Her eyes flitted between him and their children.

"Mary, please. Our guest deserves a little during dinner for his malady. Besides, it dulls this nagging toothache of mine."

Echols shifted his eyes from one end of the table to the other. He then stared at the empty crystal ware before returning the rum bottle to the table. He turned to his hostess with a bewildered look, fearing his *faux pas*.

Sallie glanced across the table at Bourke and Tom, instigating a bout of giggles among all three.

"Well, seeing as my darling husband already poured himself a little, I don't see any harm in our guest having a drink during dinner." Mary signaled her change of heart by flittering her fingers toward her guest. Captain Echols tendered an appreciative nod and poured a shot into his glass, though with a sheepish grin.

Randolph raised his glass toward Echols. "To my darlin' wife, the belle of McIntosh County."

Captain Echols said, "Here, here." He took but a small sip, appearing to favor water until dinner ended.

Tom raised his glass of water, and Sallie and Bourke clinked their glasses against Tom's, causing youthful giggles that stirred their guest and parents to join the joyous outburst.

Sallie wiped her eyes on her table napkin, took a deep breath, and looked at her father with a sober countenance. "Father, when are you leaving?"

Randolph glanced at his wife. "In the morning, but—"

"You just got here," Tom blurted. "You have spent no time with us."

Randolph eyed the guilt-ridden look on Echols's face before he leaned back in his chair. "Whoa, son. You interrupted your father before he finished speaking. Right after Captain Echols and I report back to Savannah, we'll return straightaway. The general directed Captain Echols and me to survey the island before militia troops arrive."

"Will we be able to stay at South End with you, Father?" Sallie asked, aiming a giddy smile across the table at her mother.

"I'm afraid that'll be out of the question. Soon after we return, companies of militia will set up camp at South End," Randolph stared to get Sallie's attention, "but I'll be here as much as I can."

"What about Cecile and her family? What's going to happen to them?" Sallie muttered, afraid of the answer she might hear.

"Alma and Cecile will remain busy serving meals and tending to Captain Echols and myself. Her father and brother will continue caring for the livestock and chickens. The soldiers will require lots of meat and eggs, too."

"Please, let me come over to South End and stay with you," Tom pleaded, "even if just for a day or two."

Randolph smiled at Mary's fretful look. "Tom, I'll see what I can do, but no promises."

Following dinner, Mary walked into the parlor holding a folded copy of Savannah's *Daily Morning News*. "Please excuse me, gentlemen. I thought you'd like to hear the latest headlines." She eyed the front page of the newspaper and read aloud, "Beauregard had his horse shot out from under him while under terrific enemy fire, but he miraculously survived."

Randolph noticed the dread-filled expression on his wife's face. "Where did this happen?"

"A place called Manassas, Virginia. I'm not sure exactly where that is."

"Manassas is in northern Virginia near Washington," Captain Echols said. "I'm sorry for interrupting you. Please continue, Missus Spalding."

"The article also reports Colonel Francis S. Bartow of Georgia died while leading a magnificent charge on his horse with his regimental colors in his hands." Tears trickled down her cheeks. "So many lives lost in just the first battle of this war." She folded the paper and set it on the table beside her husband. "Did you know Colonel Bartow?"

Randolph nodded. "He was from Oglethorpe near Macon and was a friend of Charles as well."

"I've been hiding this from the children. Could war come here to Georgia?" Mary asked, trying to compose herself.

"Let's hope not, but that's why we decided on moving you and the children somewhere removed from the coast." Randolph sighed before swallowing the last of his rum.

"Missus Spalding, Virginia's Army will stop them from coming south, but Colonel Spalding may be right. This house is too close to the coast," Captain Echols said resolutely.

Randolph, desiring to alter the direction of the conversation, patted the cushion of the armchair beside him. "Come sit a moment. All this fretting does you no good. Besides, I've something to tell you that might ease your mind."

Mary sat on the edge of the chair's cushion and clasped her hands in her lap. "Are you gonna tell me Lincoln changed his mind?"

"Though that would be the best news we all could wish for, I have wonderful news pertaining to that young lieutenant who escorted me to Savannah."

Mary flashed a dubious glare at Randolph.

"Lieutenant Archibald McKinley just happens to be the son of Colonel William McKinley from Milledgeville. Though William is too old to serve, his son sure is most eager and ready."

Mary pursed her lips and shrugged.

"Come on, think back. We dined with Colonel McKinley and his wife, Anne, in Milledgeville. We served together in the Georgia Assembly."

Her eyelids flickered, and a modest, affirming smile appeared. "Yes, I now recall our visit. Anne was a wonderful and gracious hostess. They entertained us at their beautiful old home at Beulah, as my memory serves me. Are you telling me Lieutenant McKinley is their oldest son? He was just a shy, gangly young boy a little younger than Tom is now."

"Yes, we met the McKinleys at their Beulah home across the Oconee River from Milledgeville. It so happens, Michael Kenan spoke to William about leasing Beulah's twelve-hundred acres on our behalf."

"I don't understand."

"William built a much larger brick estate home called Barrowville to suit his large family. His new home abuts Beulah but gives him better access to the stage road between Sparta and Milledgeville."

"Yes, now I remember. His first wife, Patience Barrow, died giving birth to their fourth child. William almost lost everything after that, but then he met Anne, a widow. After they married, they moved into his former father-in-law's old home at Beulah and called Milledgeville home. Last I recollect, Anne bore William four more healthy children." Mary's eyes lit up, and she giggled after placing her hand over her mouth. "I would say he built Barrowville for the sake of their eight children."

"Thanks to William's need for a larger house, Beulah, with its fertile riverside fields, is available. I've already consulted with Michael. Beulah's land and beautiful home would serve our family well, and we've agreed to lease it."

"That's wonderful news, Randolph, but tell me about your conversation with William's son."

"Well, he graduated from Georgia Military Institute in Marietta a few days before he reported to Savannah as a new lieutenant."

"Oh, Randolph. He's so young."

"I know how you feel. I saw many eager young lads like him wearing their new uniforms strutting about in Savannah. Lieutenant McKinley is returning home under orders to help muster volunteers for the militias in Hancock and Baldwin County. Before he left, he promised to tell his father about our providential meeting and offered to visit after you and the children arrive with Michael and Katherine and their family."

"Thank you, Randolph, for sharing that good news, though I'm uncertain how it eases the dreadful news regarding those brave soldiers killed in Virginia. I'm afraid we will call upon them to sacrifice more blood in the coming days." Mary stood and squeezed Randolph's hand as she leaned to kiss his cheek.

"When I return from Savannah, we ought to sit down with the children again. We shouldn't mollycoddle them any longer. There's no way we can hide this from them."

# # #

The following morning, Josephine returned to the dining room as the family and Captain Echols finished breakfast. "Mister Spalding, sir. Your brother just rode up with Mister Wylly."

"I'll be right there, Josephine." Randolph gulped his coffee, wiped his mouth, and stood from the table. "Captain, please join me. I'd like you to meet my brother and my half-crazy nephew."

Randolph led the way onto the porch as Charles and Thomas tied their horses beside the water trough. They adjusted their Georgia militia blue frock coats and slapped flecks of mud from their blue trousers before walking toward the house. Randolph and Captain Echols waited at the porch steps, dressed in their red flannel shirts tucked in their uniform trousers. Charles and Thomas stomped their mud-caked, black leather boots on the granite steppingstones leading to the house. Randolph and Echols greeted them beneath the century-old sycamore towering over the front of the house.

"Captain William Echols of Alabama, please meet Lieutenant Colonel Charles Spalding and Captain Thomas Wylly. My brother is the regimental commander of the Fifth Georgia Cavalry here in McIntosh County. He and his charming wife, Evelyn, reside in that lovely home I pointed out last evening. My nephew is currently on staff with me in Savannah and is presently on a recruitment mission in McIntosh County. His family lives about five miles up the road from here."

After Echols exchanged handshakes, they went inside and joined the rest of Randolph's family in the dining room.

"Uncle Thomas, come sit down beside me," young Tom said with an eager look.

"We can't stay. We came to talk to your father," Charles interrupted. "Mary, please excuse us. We can't stay long."

Randolph motioned to the parlor. Charles, Captain Echols, and Thomas Wylly followed. Across the hall, Randolph closed the doors. "What's going on, Charles?"

Charles looked at the folded *Daily Morning News* on the corner table. "I presume you read about Manassas?"

"Yes. Mary made a point to show me the article last evening."

"Then you heard Francis Bartow died in the battle?"

Randolph peered at Echols. "It's a shame, too. General Beauregard whipped those Northern boys. The report said their entire army left the field in a fright."

"Let's not get too high and mighty. They had upwards of sixty-thousand men against our thirty-five thousand. They had us outgunned and outnumbered. We got lucky is all. According to the news accounts, Union troops panicked after their green officers lost their nerve."

Captain Echols stepped into the middle of the room. "What are you trying to say? They could've beaten us?"

"What I'm saying is that I've traveled north many times and witnessed their factories and crowded big cities firsthand. Exemplified by Lincoln's flotilla launched against our coastal port cities, this defeat will not deter the North. This first bloody battle embarrassed them and merely marks the beginning of many bloody battles yet ahead. Mark my words, it won't take long for Lincoln's armies to regroup and replace the wounded and those killed in action."

"But—," Echols began until Randolph rested a hand on his shoulder.

"My brother's right," Randolph said. "Our hope for winning this war rests upon the folks in the North losing the will to fight and seeking to keep their husbands, fathers, and sons from a senseless war away from home. The Confederacy must hold firm its willingness to fight. We have the most to lose. Northern homes and towns aren't likely to be threatened like our homes and towns."

"Uncle Randolph, I agree. We can't afford to lose. We have too much at stake."

Charles glared at Randolph. "How soon before we get reinforcements on Sapelo and Saint Simons? I'm of the opinion all this victory in Manassas has done is agitate a bull gator who'll not disappear for long but will circle back and fight even harder and smarter. Many a man has lost his life underestimating an angry bull gator."

"Captain Echols and I just left Sapelo. By early October, we will have no less than four militia companies camped on the island manning the fortifications and batteries to be constructed. General

Lawton has executed orders dispatching militia from across Georgia to defend the coastal islands and fortify the key port cities between Savannah and Saint Mary's," Randolph stated emphatically.

"Bull gators are the most dangerous when they're hungry, and they hunt where they have the advantage—in the water," Charles said.

"Captain Echols and I leave this morning to report back to Savannah. When we get back, we will get Sapelo ready to hunt gators."

"Thomas and I will use the news of Manassas to stir up volunteers for our regiment and other companies getting organized in McIntosh. Many of our McIntosh boys will soon head north to join the fight in Virginia. Either way, the advantage remains with us should the fight come to us." Charles put his hat on and patted Thomas Wylly on the shoulder. "We'll let ourselves out so you and the captain can finish up here and head up to Savannah as soon as you can."

"Thanks, Charles. I'll be back in a few days. It's not just my home and property I'm willing to fight for. It's our family's legacy that our father placed into our hands to pass on to future Spaldings. That's where my courage and resolve come from."

CHAPTER SIX

9th of August, 1861

"Aren't you tired of bellyaching?" Captain Echols carped, handing Randolph another mug of rum. "I know we are!"

"No sawbones is going to stick their grimy fingers inside my mouth," Randolph bellowed. His words became more slurred by the gulp.

"You heard the man," Lieutenant William Brailsford, Randolph's spirited nephew, snarled. "Whether you like the idea or not, you're not leaving camp until that rotten tooth gets removed. Now, drink up." William raised the mug to Randolph's lips.

Randolph guzzled the amber elixir, wiped his mouth with the back of his hand, and with a cockeyed grin spouted, "Who's gonna stop me from leaving, might I ask?"

"Your brother, my commanding officer, ordered me to restrain you if I must," Brailsford huffed menacingly.

William's mother, Randolph's oldest sister, Jane Martin, had passed away that spring at the age of sixty-four. William and Randolph grew up sharing a contentious sibling-like rivalry since only three years separated them. While watching his sickly mother slip away, William stewed in his loneliness. Many years ago, the tragic murder of his father and his sister's unexpected death in childbirth five years earlier embittered him all the more. Though they had grown close over the years, even inebriated Randolph recognized when to back off any time his nephew's eyes turned cold and distant. A powder keg of deep-seated, exacerbated emotions festered within his nephew, and his fuse grew shorter and shorter.

Lieutenant Spalding Kenan stepped into the tent ahead of Lieutenant Colonel Charles Spalding. Randolph downed more of his rum, hemmed in between Echols and Brailsford seated on the edge of his bunk. The camp's surgeon set his black satchel on the table across from his uncle and knelt on one knee. He examined Randolph's aimless, bloodshot eyes.

Randolph broke into an uproarious laugh, then glared from side to side at Echols and Brailsford. His laughter abruptly subsided when he stared open-mouthed at his brother. "You guys are pulling my leg. Spalding's your new camp surgeon?"

Charles maintained a stolid, arms-crossed posture to block the front of the tent. After an emphatic nod, he reached into his tunic pocket and cut a plug of tobacco to chew. He then said, "Lieutenant Kenan received his commission while you played soldier in Savannah." Charles glared at Randolph's dumbfounded and very sozzled expression. He asked his surgeon matter-of-factly, never losing his focus on his brother, "Lieutenant Kenan, can you help your uncle—I mean Colonel Spalding—with his tooth problem?"

The young doctor squeezed Randolph's lower jaw, gaining his undivided attention. "Open wide, please." The young doctor maneuvered Randolph's wide-open mouth up and down and side to side. He reached back, lowered his black bag by his side, and took out a probe. "Uncle, please hold still and try to keep your mouth open as wide as you can." Spalding firmly gripped Randolph's lower jaw.

Randolph jerked his head back, freeing himself from the young surgeon's vice-like grip. "*Owww!* Damn you, Spalding. Do you know what in Sam Hill you're doing?"

"Yep, you've allowed your decaying tooth to fester." Lieutenant Kenan wiped his probe on a towel. "Gentlemen, please pour my squeamish uncle all the rum he can drink."

Captain Echols obliged, emptying the last of the bottle into the tin mug. Randolph beseeched his brother for a reprieve, but Charles spat on the dirt floor and then inquired with a stolid look on his face,

"Lieutenant Kenan, can you extract the colonel's tooth from his big mouth?"

Lieutenant Kenan looked over his shoulder. "He'll feel a bunch better with that tooth removed, that's for sure. But—"

"But what?" Randolph blurted after he clamped his mouth shut, drool running down his chin.

The young doctor looked at Randolph. "I know what to do, but I've never extracted a molar from the back of someone's mouth before." The young doctor wiped his forehead and added, "But, I know it has to come out."

Randolph glared at Charles, unyielding. He then turned to Echols and Brailsford. With a half-hearted chuckle and smile—a sure sign his liquored-up senses had achieved the prerequisite anesthetic effect—he mumbled, "Whatever I might say to either of you in the next few minutes, please forgive me. I'm sure our young surgeon will require your brute strength to get this over with as quickly and pain free as possible." Randolph locked his eyes on his nephew's youthful face, gulped down the last drops of his rum, wiped the drool from his chin, and opened his mouth.

"Gentlemen, please grab him firmly with one arm interlocked in his and use your other hand to hold his head steady, if you please." Kenan stood over his uncle, holding a pair of dental forceps by his side, not allowing his patient to see the instrument before he slipped it into his mouth.

Randolph swallowed hard as he felt his head get tilted back. Echols and Brailsford flexed as they tightened their holds. After a couple of grunts, the young doctor stood between Randolph's flailing legs. He maintained a vice-like grip on the forceps as he removed the instrument from Randolph's bloody mouth and admired the intact molar held firmly between the forceps. Echols handed Randolph water to wash his mouth out. After rinsing, he promptly spewed blood and water onto the ground at the foot of his bunk before pointing to his footlocker.

Brailsford reached for another bottle of rum from Randolph's footlocker. A moment later, Randolph chugged a mouthful straight from the bottle before passing out on his bunk. Brailsford laughed, took a swig, and passed the bottle to Echols. A few minutes later, with his eyes still shut, Randolph touched the side of his jaw and moaned.

"Do you want to keep this as a souvenir?" Spalding Kenan asked, holding the tooth between his fingers.

Randolph blindly extended his hand and mumbled, "I think I oughta."

"Come on, let's take our conversating elsewhere and leave him to sleep it off," Charles growled, holding the flap of the tent open.

As they filed out, Randolph uttered succinctly, "Captain Echols, be ready to leave first thing in the morning."

※ ※ ※

Three weeks later, Captain William Echols and his detachment of engineers arrived on Sapelo Island. In front of South End's portico, a flagpole flew the colors of the Confederate States of America above Georgia's state flag. The grand tabby mansion became Camp Spalding's command post where Randolph remained available when not conferring with Allen Bass about the work on his fields or visiting his brother-in-law, Michael Kenan.

Each day, Sapelo's launch shuttled back and forth between South End and Darien. A recent dispatch from General Lawton's office in Savannah informed Randolph that the first two Georgia militia companies would arrive by the end of the month. The added manpower would come with the artillery and munitions to be placed behind the earthwork fortifications Captain Echols' men had built with Sapelo's workers handling much of the manual labor. Though the boat landing at the creek's mouth behind South End provided a convenient site to transport guests, supplies, and mail between Darien and Sapelo, Captain Echols's men supervised fortifying improvements to the deep-water wharf at Marsh Landing along the Duplin River. For decades, it accommodated the coming and going of merchant schooners and steamships. On the island's western side, its location provided less exposure and vulnerability to the prospect of prying enemy gunboats.

On this afternoon, Captain Echols and his men worked feverishly on the island's south end while Randolph rode with Allen Bass visiting the fields of white Sea Island cotton. After talking with Abraham and the other drivers supervising the workers in the fields, Allen assured Randolph that this season's harvest should yield two hundred bales of cotton and a ton of rice. They had already harvested twenty-five hundred bushels of corn. A portion remained in South End's barns for the livestock and consumption by the workers, but the workers would mill the lion's share to feed the soldiers.

Allen Bass expressed his relief and apprehension, knowing additional soldiers would soon arrive on Sapelo. Captain Echols' detachment of uniformed engineers and the construction underway already instigated growing chatter among the field workers.

"Randolph, there's but one of me," Allen Bass said. "We've had hardly a problem with dissension among our workers, but all the same, I'm worried what could happen if—"

"Quit your fussing, Allen. You and I both know that our negroes are loyal. Besides, we haven't had a runaway since you've been here. They trust and respect you."

"That may be true. I wonder how much they know about what has happened over the recent months. A handful has asked what Captain Echols's engineers are doing on the island. They will surely ask a lot of questions when the militia troops arrive."

"Allen, I know every one of our workers and their families. I want you to stay focused on the harvest. No doubt rumors may spread after the soldiers arrive, especially when they bring the artillery to the island. I reckon there'll be no way we can keep them from speculating. That's why I decided not to harvest the rice this year.

As soon as we get the corn and sugar cane milled and the cotton baled, I want our planting tools and supplies packed and ready to be shipped upriver to Baldwin County. The good Lord willing, we will transport our negroes off the island along with our tools and supplies right after the harvest."

"Until then, I hope you won't mind if I tote this with me." Allen reached in his saddlebag and pulled a revolver from its holster. "It ain't much, and I don't rightly intend to use it, but it sure makes me feel a mite better knowing I got my old Navy Colt with me."

"Just keep it tucked out of sight. One of my trigger-happy sentries might mistake you for a Northern sympathizer or something worse. Besides, you'd likely shoot yourself. Just act like you always have around the workers. Everything will be fine." Randolph chuckled as he rode away.

※ ※ ※

Two mornings later, Cecile ran into the dining room while Randolph ate breakfast with Captain Echols. "Mister Spalding, the boat be coming. I think your family's on it."

"Finish your breakfast, Captain. I'll be back in a few minutes." Randolph glanced at Cecile's solicitous genuflection as he donned his gold-braided, wide-brimmed, black hat. He inspected his double-breasted dark blue tunic before buckling his leather belt. He then addressed Alma with a light-hearted, self-approving grin. "Please keep Captain Echols company while Cecile and I walk down to the landing to greet our guests?"

Cecile looked up at her momma, earning a playful swat. "Go on, girl. Behave, you hear me?"

On the shaded path headed to the dock, Randolph quickened his gait to keep pace as Cecile scampered on ahead. The *Sarah Spalding* moored alongside the narrow plank dock. Two of the barefooted crew members jumped off the boat. One tied off the boat while the other received mail and supplies from the third crew member still on deck. William Brailsford and Thomas Wylly helped Mary and Sallie as they stepped gingerly onto the creaking, wooden dock. Randolph extended his hand to his wife as she stepped off the ramp. Tom and Bourke wore their going-to-church brown jackets and pants and lagged two steps behind their mother. Their smartly uniformed cousins escorted Sallie, who wore a bright yellow dress that complimented her light brown hair.

"William, what do I see? Please don't tell me they made you a captain," Randolph said, smirking.

Thomas Wylly said as serious as he could muster, "Captain Lamar accepted a promotion with the 25th Georgia Cavalry and headed off seeking glory and fame in South Carolina. Of course, I believe William egged Lamar into leaving and then wangled his own promotion before Lamar's dust even settled after he rode off."

"Ah, shut up. You're just peeved because Uncle Charles gave me Lamar's command."

Randolph walked between his two bantering nephews and placed a firm hand on each of their shoulders. "Captain Brailsford, congratulations. Remember the lives of those under your command now rest in your hands. May I also remind you, most of those men have McIntosh roots? Charles wouldn't have given you the command if he didn't believe you could handle it."

Sallie giggled. "Oh, father. I think William looks quite dashing as a captain. Don't you agree, Cecile?"

Cecile's playful spirit faltered. She paused, mindful of her place, and offered a brief nod, acknowledging Sallie's prodding smile.

"It appears, my darlin' cousin, the cat's got Cecile's tongue," William sniped with a stark look aimed at Cecile.

"Captain Brailsford, may I remind you, you're here on my invite to talk to me and not remonstrate for your ego's sake," Randolph said, exchanging a perfunctory tip of the hat with Brailsford. "You and Captain Wylly can go on up and wait for me in the library. Alma has hot coffee and breakfast waiting. I'll be along after I spend a few moments with my family."

Mary nudged Cecile. "Please see that Captains Brailsford and Wylly get some of your momma's coffee and her mouthwatering hoe cakes." She then put her arm around her daughter's waist as the gleam on Sallie's face evaporated.

"And ask Captain Echols to join them in the library," Randolph said. "Thank you, Cecile. We'll be up momentarily."

Randolph directed his family to a nearby willow where two benches allowed Randolph to sit between his two sons and face Mary and Sallie. A grim hush lingered as the family waited for Randolph to break the nervous silence. It became apparent to Randolph that Mary had prepared their children for the fateful decision they dreaded but knew was inevitable.

"Your Uncle Michael informed me our house in Baldwin County is ready. He and Aunt Katherine plan to leave in a few days with your two cousins, Catherine Clifford and Owen along with Evelyn, Spalding's wife. I want the three of you to help your mother finish packing so you will be ready when it is time to leave with them. Your Uncle Michael is arranging for all of you to make the trip by riverboat to Milledgeville."

Mary held Sallie's hand and pulled her closer to her side. "Your father and I are proud of the three of you. We wanted you to visit South End one last time before we leave."

"We will come back, won't we?" Tom spouted.

"Yes, son. This threat of war will not last forever. Sapelo belongs to our family, and just as I promised you, you'll be the Laird of Sapelo as your grandfather wished. No one can take that away from you."

"What about Josephine and William?" Bourke asked.

"Ada, too?" Tom added.

Randolph smiled at his two sons. "They'll be going with us."

A few moments later, they walked together up the path to South End.

※ ※ ※

In the library, Randolph leaned against the ornate desk as he read a dispatch from Savannah. He looked up, eyed the others, and said, "Captain Echols, they have ordered you and your detachment to complete your assignment on Sapelo posthaste. It appears two militia units under Captains Charles Rockwell and William Young from Thomas County will arrive along with ordnance for the artillery batteries on or about the sixteenth of September. Two other infantry companies from Berrien County should arrive by the first of October." Randolph looked at his younger nephew. "Furthermore, Captain Thomas Wylly shall report forthwith to Savannah for indoctrination training of the designated militia units assigned to Sapelo."

Captain Echols asked, "What about you, Colonel?"

"General Lawton has ordered me to assume command of Camp Spalding until such time our to-be-designated Georgia infantry regiment elects its officers."

Echols sighed. "Colonel, I think your island is growing on my men and me."

"Be careful what you wish for, Captain," Randolph said, now seated behind his father's former desk, staring once again at the dispatch.

"Sounds like I need to enjoy one last cozy evening with my family before I ride back to Savannah tomorrow," Captain Wylly grumbled. "Indoctrination training. I know General Lawton's making up for my too-good-to-be-true, home-based recruitment assignment."

"Enjoy your stay in Savannah, because if I get my way I'll get you assigned back here with me before my brother gets his hands on you again," Randolph said, one eye cocked at Brailsford. "If you go spouting off to my brother, I'll see you yanked off your gray stallion and given an infantry command."

For a moment, Brailsford measured Randolph's sincerity before they both swapped smirks.

Randolph then looked beyond the library entrance and into

the great hall. There, Sallie and Cecile hugged one another and exchanged sorrowful looks. Brailsford whispered, "Uncle Randolph, I don't get it. Sallie may wish it so, but Cecile will never be more to Sallie than what she is. Don't either of them understand what started this war in the first place?"

Randolph stared at the two girls. "William, I'm afraid you and I may never agree on why this war got started."

CHAPTER SEVEN

9th of October, 1861

Michael Kenan had arranged passage for both families and their belongings on the George M. Troup, a riverboat familiar with ever-shifting sandy shoals and mud banks up and down the Altamaha and Oconee rivers. Traveling by riverboat would take longer than by rail, but Michael Kenan and Randolph Spalding decided against exposing their families to the frenzy of military traffic on Georgia's rail system.

Bourke and Tom, with white-knuckled grips, held onto Randolph's uniform sleeves while Mary Spalding spoke with her brother-in-law, Charles. Josephine calmly stood beside William, but the young stableboy looked as skittish as an unrepentant sinner facing Judgment Day. They eyed the dock hands loading each of the family's final belongings. Ada and Sallie chatted with Evelyn Kenan, who appeared anxious with her baby due any day. Two ear-piercing blasts from the riverboat's whistle preceded Captain Robertson's call from the wheelhouse bridge for all passengers to board. Michael Kenan escorted his wife across the gangplank. Clifford and Owen broke up their sister-in-law's conversation with Sallie and Ada before escorting a tearful Evelyn onboard the steamboat. A rash of bedridden soldiers suffering from measles at Sutherland Bluff prevented Spalding Kenan from seeing his young and expectant wife off.

Above the churning idling steam engine, Captain Robertson barked orders to his crew as he leaned out the wheelhouse window. Randolph and his family appeared oblivious to the quickening activity of the boat's crew stirring around them as they shared their last goodbyes.

"Now promise me, Charles," Mary said, her eyes stressing her innermost fears.

"Don't you fret none." Charles stiffened and added, "You know, Randolph hated not making the trip with you and the children. He fears what'll happen to Sapelo with two added militia companies arriving this morning if he is not there. He's got his hands full right now. Look, Michael assured me you and the children will enjoy your time in Milledgeville, and he plans to introduce you to all their family's friends and neighbors."

"Yes, you are right." Mary looked along the river's edge. "I guess Allen kept Charlie with him on Sapelo." Mary sighed.

"When I last spoke with Allen, he felt it best for Charlie to stay with him."

"I just hoped—"

"Mary, you and the kids need to hurry and get on board," Randolph cried out above the rumble of the boat's engines. He took Tom by his arm before he ran off with Bourke and looked at him man-to-man. "I need to stay here for now, so I'm counting on you to take care of your mother, brother, and sister. You're the man of the house until I join you."

Tom wiped his eyes with his coat sleeve. "How soon before you can come see us?"

"You deserve a straight answer, son. I can't say exactly. I promise to get there as soon as the situation here allows me to break away for a few days. Until then, remember what I promised you."

"You will be with us for Christmas, won't you?"

"I sure hope so, son."

Sallie tugged on her father's arm. "Father, I almost forgot. I have something for you." She gestured to Josephine, who handed Sallie a brown paper-wrapped box she had safeguarded.

"This is for you Father under one condition," Sallie said, squeezing the hastily wrapped package against her chest.

"What is it? What condition?" Randolph said, extending his hands.

"Stationary and a journal. But you must promise to write us. When you can't write letters, scribble something in your journal."

Mary stepped beside Sallie and said, "Yes, dear. Please write to us as often as you can. Now, come on Sallie. We all need to get on board." Mary kissed Randolph on his cheek and then offered her hands to Tom and Bourke.

Randolph took the string-tied package from Sallie. "I promise. I'll pretend we're chatting on the porch every evening. Remember, we may be miles apart, but we will always share the same star-filled heavens."

Ada said, "Give your father a quick hug. They're waiting on us to board."

The *Sarah Spalding's* shrill steam whistle received a responding blast from the *George M. Troup*. A few minutes later, Allen Bass yelled as Sapelo's launch pulled along the dock, "Mary, I'm so sorry. I changed my mind. Please take Charlie with you. He'll be safer staying with you for the time being."

A deckhand scurried off the *George M. Troup* and retrieved Charlie's bags from Allen as he and his son ran up to Mary and Randolph. "You were right, Randolph. Charlie will be better off staying with your family in Milledgeville." He lowered to one knee and looked his son eye to eye. "You best mind your Aunt Mary and Miss Ada. I'll join you like I told you."

Charlie sniffled, and his lower lip quivered. "Yes, sir."

Sallie and Ada comforted Charlie as they joined Mary and their two sons on the boat's afterdeck. The captain yelled before he yanked on the boat's horn. After a loud, long blast, he shouted, "Cast off all lines."

Randolph yelled as the steamboat's wheel roiled hard against the river's swift downstream current. "Write as soon as you can. Tell us all about the house." He walked along the dock's edge with his brother-in-law a step behind, waving as the boat pulled away. "Mary, I'll get word to you as soon as I know when Allen will come to Baldwin County with the field hands and their families."

Allen sobbed as he waved at his son. "Randolph, this is the first time since Almira died last year that Charlie and I will not be sleeping under the same roof."

Randolph put his arm across Allen's broad shoulders as they watched the paddlewheel on the *George M. Troup* turn faster, leaving the dock in its wake. The captain sounded the riverboat's whistle when the boat reached the center of the river.

Charles caught up with his brother and Allen Bass. As soon as the steamboat disappeared beyond the river bend, he confessed, "Brothers, I gotta admit something. I'm jealous and proud of you." After a moment of dumbfounded silence, he asked, "I know you two gotta sail back to Sapelo, but Randolph, will you come with me to the family cemetery first? Allen, you don't mind waiting while I take your brother-in-law off for about an hour?"

※ ※ ※

A mile above town, Charles and Randolph dismounted their horses and left them tied to the wrought-iron rusted fence protecting the hallowed grounds. Moss-draped gnarled limbs of a time-defiant arboreal leviathan shaded the cluster of Spalding family graves. Inscribed tombstones memorialized the eternal slumber of deceased Spaldings. Some, like his youngest sibling, Randolph never knew. The sacrosanct bluff looked out on the winding tidal waters, lush marshlands, and, in the faint distance, Sapelo Island. This time of the year, the sea of green cordgrass began its annual transformation with much of the green leaves turning shades of brown and blending with the fertile, dark brown mud banks of the ever-winding tidal creeks.

"Brother, I invited you to come with me because we need to be reminded of our stake in this fight for Southern independence. Consider how many of our family sleep beneath this sprawling oak." Charles paused and pointed to a flock of snowy-white egrets roosted below a pair of storks in the giant tree's upper branches. "Look at the guardian angels God has provided to watch over our brothers and sisters whose lives ended well before their time. Every funeral carved deep scars into our mother's tender heart, and our father rued the fact he outlived far too many of his children. We can stand here knowing peace accompanies our family members reposed in eternal slumber. They no longer wince at the sting of death nor struggle with bloodshed's agony as the living will soon face."

Randolph's head sunk as he looked intently at his parents' side-by-side tombstones. "Charles, I get what you're saying. I pray it's true. Yet, I believe a curse remains over our family."

"Randolph, what the hell do you mean by a curse?"

"Stop and think back to our father's imprecation in his last speech to keep Georgia true to the Constitution. You were there when I repeated those portentous words in front of the state Assembly before I stepped down last year."

"Sure, I remember, but humor me," Charles groaned, his intentions for their visit waylaid by Randolph's supposition.

"He said, no he wished, rather, 'than that Constitution shall perish, I would wish that myself and every human that has a drop of my blood in his veins should perish.' I wonder if he died not long after that on account of he knew secession was inevitable, and—"

Charles folded his arms across his chest and growled, "Brother, I cannot believe you'd suggest such with us standing at the foot of his grave."

"I believe our father knew his philosophy of life reaped jealousy and scorn from others who did not understand him and his ways. I'm just glad he is not alive today. Since the Southern states answered the calls for secession, we have provoked the North into a war neither will win. It's clear to me that Georgia's unfettered rush into secession rejected father's appeal to support, not dissolve, the Constitution. As a result, father's blood curse surely will haunt us."

Charles stood silent, immersed in thought. Randolph scanned

the marshes and the waters that followed their serpentine course toward Doboy Sound and Sapelo Island before being swallowed by the endless ocean.

"Randolph, I brought you here to remind us of our cause in the fight that's brewing. You and I are placing our very lives on the line, and I believe we both do it willingly. We choose to do so, not because of our way of life. We choose so for the legacy passed down to us by our father. I've no children of my own, but we share the same legacy our father placed into our hands to preserve, protect, and pass on. My heart lies with Georgia, but I love our family's legacy even more so. I agree. Father's words sound foreboding to us now, yet he most assuredly professed what he knew would happen—a prognostication, not an imprecation. Nothing more, nothing less."

Randolph turned to his brother and cackled. "A prognostication. Now that's good. I'll try to remember that." He slapped his brother's back as they walked back to their horses.

"Almost forgot to ask, how'd it feel being called back to Milledgeville to represent McIntosh County once again?" Charles asked smugly.

"They couldn't find anyone else. It took me longer to get there and back. That's all I have to say about it. I did get to see Beulah, the McKinley property Michael arranged for me to lease. That made the trip worth the hassle sitting through the political foofaraw of another pretentious state convention with its outcome *a fait accompli*."

"Sorry I asked. By the way, I know you've got to stay at South End, but don't forget to check in with Evelyn and me. With so many families leaving their homes, we could use your droll company from time to time."

"I'll do that, and I invite you to visit me at Camp Spalding. Although, I suggest you not bring Evelyn with you."

The birds in the old oak remained unfazed and continued their lofty vigil. Charles rode to nearby Ashantilly to visit his wife before returning to his encampment at Sutherland Bluff. Randolph rode back to the docks to meet back up with Allen and sail back to Sapelo Island.

※ ※ ※

Shortly after he'd dined with the officers presently encamped on Sapelo in South End's dining room, Alma approached Randolph while he stood alone in the shadows of the mansion's grand portico.

"Mister Spalding, sir. Was supper good for you, sir?"

Randolph lit his cigar and blew a couple of puffs of smoke into the darkness. "Why Alma, your cooking is always good. In fact, everyone at dinner tonight left with contented smiles, full bellies, and empty plates."

"Well, sir, thank you kindly. But you, sir, hardly touched your plate. Is you okay, sir?" Alma said, wringing her kitchen-stained apron

."Thank you for asking, Alma. You and I've known each other a long time." Randolph puffed his cigar, focused on the sea of tents that surrounded South End.

Alma watched the puff of smoke rise in the night air as Randolph leaned against one of the portico's ionic columns, staring at the star-filled sky. "Yes, sir," she finally blurted. "Reckon that's a gen-u-ine fact. I can't rightly recall a time when I ain't taken care of you or helped care for your own family after you and Missus Mary came on the island. I remember when each of yo' three precious babies came into this world."

Randolph smiled. "Yes, you've always taken really good care of my wife and me. If I asked you and your family to leave Sapelo, how'd you feel?"

"Mister Randolph, me and Hector was borned right here, same as our mommas and poppas. We's lived nowhere else. It's our home, sir." Alma swept her hands across the wrinkles she had squeezed into her apron.

Randolph uncorked the rum bottle he had set beside him and refilled his glass. Before he took a taste, he studied Alma contemplating the harsh reality every person on the island would soon face. "You see all those soldiers? They're here because war is creeping our way. I've decided I'd rather lose the land than those who live on it."

Alma's eyes widened as Cecile stepped beside her. "Momma, are we leaving here?"

Randolph extended his hand and gestured for Cecile to join him. "Cecile, come here young lady."

Cecile slipped from her momma's grasp and stood, hands clasped, facing Randolph.

He brushed the dust from the granite step with his hand and sat. "Please, sit beside me a moment."

Cecile glanced at her mother, who offered a permissive nod. Randolph flicked his cigar stub into the grass beyond the steps and cupped his hands around his glass.

"Cecile, would you like to visit Sallie and her brothers?"

Cecile bobbed her head with a curious grin. "Yes, sir, but where's they staying now?"

"Well, it'd take nearly a week on a boat to travel there. It's a town far up the Altamaha and Oconee rivers."

Alma gnawed on her thumbnail while she watched and listened."

Sounds far, far away. I guess if Momma says so I'd like to go there and visit for a spell."

"What if your momma and your poppa went with you? What if you could stay there as long as my family stayed there?" Randolph tilted his head to look into Cecile's eyes.

Cecile began pinching the creases of her purple dress. "You mean we'd leave our home here?"

Randolph nodded with an affirming smile.Cecile looked at her momma, who broke her chary gaze. "Girl, Mister Randolph means to take us to his new house where Sallie and Thomas and Mistress Mary be staying. It be far enough away Poppa and me be going with you. Ain't that right, Mister Randolph."

"It won't be forever, but yes, that's right, Alma. Your whole family would make the trip together."

Cecile beamed but said nothing more.

"Come on, girl. Let's leave Mister Randolph be for now. He be telling us when we be leaving soon enough." Alma offered Randolph a modest, gracious smile. "Thank you, sir. I appreciate you telling us. I know you got lots on your mind. Do you need anything more before we leave?"

Randolph shook his head before swallowing the rest of the brown liquor in his glass. He pulled another cigar from his inside coat pocket, bit one end, and lit it. Though his mind drifted to thoughts far removed, his eyes scanned soldiers milling about and those congregating around campfires spewing sparks high into the night sky. He could not recall when so many souls ever stayed on Sapelo. Captain Echols and Captain Knight reported that nearly four hundred rank-and-file volunteers from South Georgia now called Camp Spalding home.

Before retiring for the evening, he stepped inside the library to make his first entry in the leather-bound journal Sallie had neatly wrapped. He picked it up from where it now waited inside his ornate wooden lap desk:

October 9, 1861
Camp Spalding
Sapelo Island, Georgia

The field of white canvas tents has grown farther and farther across South End's grounds, now designated as Camp Spalding. Still, there's spirited, light-hearted singing, whooping, and hollering each evening busting out from the maze of campfires. From South End's portico, Camp Spalding reminds me of Sapelo's harvest-ready Sea Island cotton fields with moonbeams reflecting off the lush green leaves while swarming fireflies flit about over the bursting white cotton bolls. Yet, I wonder how soon those fields of white will become blood-stained and snuff out the boisterous euphoria our troops exhibit as they naively ignore the enemy ships and troops already threatening Savannah. As abhorred as I am at the prospect of leading men into battle, my heart hardens at the thought of not being able to protect my family's legacy on Sapelo Island and the other plantations up and down the McIntosh coast. I know I can best serve the Confederate cause by defending our homes and lands. To that cause, I pray for my stouthearted nephews, Captains Thomas Wylly, William Brailsford, and Spalding Kenan, and my brother, Lieutenant Colonel Charles Spalding. God help any Northern troops who confront them and their valiant companies of Georgia militia. Lord, watch over and protect my family as the George M. Troup navigates upriver to Milledgeville. May they remain safe for the foreseeable future, far away from the sights and sounds the Northern gunboats will surely spawn any day now. I am also eternally grateful for the generous help and hospitality afforded us by my brother-in-law and trusted friend, Michael Kenan, and his wife, Katherine, as my family settles near their Baldwin County home. As I write this first entry in this exquisite journal Sallie gifted me, I confess I do not know when, if ever, my family will return to our beloved Sapelo Island. I fear life will never be the same, no matter what takes place in the coming months.

Colonel R. Spalding

CHAPTER EIGHT

18th of October, 1861

After dinner, the commanders updated Randolph on the status of each militia company occupying Camp Spalding. On this auspicious evening, the only medical officer stationed on the island, Captain William H. Way from Thomas County, reported favorably on the recoveries of those taken ill since their arrival. The most notable exception, Captain Levi Knight, remained bedridden, no thanks to an intolerable case of bloody piles. Randolph announced that Captain Thomas Wylly, who rejoined the Berrien company shortly after their arrival on the island, assumed command of Captain Knight's company pending his return to duty.

"Gentlemen, and that includes Mister Bass, may I have your attention," Randolph bellowed from the back of the candle-lit library as he rose from his chair, holding a half-full tumbler of his golden elixir. "Before Captain Echols provides his update—" He waved the latest dispatch from General Lawton over his head.

"I am pleased to inform you that your four companies, along with militias from Clinch, Chatham, Dougherty, Floyd, and two more from Thomas County, presently comprise a new Georgia volunteer infantry regiment. Headquarters requests company commanders have their rank-and-file soldiers cast votes for a regimental commander, second-in-command, and adjutant. Here is a list of all the qualified officers." Randolph saw his name and muttered to himself, "God, help us all," as he raised his glass.

Captain Wylly shouted as he jumped to his feet and raised his glass,

"Gentlemen, before we toast to the formation of our new regiment, let me assure you those remaining companies are just as eager as all of us. Captain Alexander's Floyd County boys underwent instruction at Big Shanty before they arrived in Savannah last month. They're champing at the bit, waiting for their orders. Scuttlebutt says two companies are coming to Darien while the others are to report to Fort McAllister." Thomas chuckled as he nodded at Randolph with his glass raised. "Let's share a toast to Georgia's finest no-name regiment."

Captain Echols asked, "Thomas, who do you think the other companies will want as their regimental commander?"

Wylly captured the attention of the others in the room with a cocksure grin. "Now, mind you, Captain Alexander from Floyd County has already strutted his stuff around Lawton's Camp of Instruction like the head rooster in a henhouse. Whether the rank-and-file soldiers want that highfalutin peacock as their regimental commander is a whole other question." Thomas broke into a belly laugh. "Then again, it wouldn't surprise me if he's already ordered a new uniform. In my humble estimation, he's nothing but a bona fide pompous arse from Rome who thinks us South Georgia boys are just a bunch of no-count, ignorant crackers." His colorful depiction ignited a round of uproarious howling among the other officers.

Randolph left his corner of the room, one hand raised high. "Here, here! Sounds as though Captain Alexander deserves a spell on our cozy island paradise, swatting bugs and dodging vipers and vermin, assuming he hasn't wet himself by the time our nightly malodorous miasma swallows him whole. Sapelo pays no mind to one's upbringing or breeding, nor accepts any bribe, and ignores all rank as I am damn sure all of you have already discovered. What say you, Mister Way, our overworked medical officer?"

The young surgeon looked every part an inexperienced doctor struggling with a shortage of help, adequate supplies, and sleep. "Colonel, I could not describe the combination of maladies on this island paradise better. Without a single shot fired, we lost two stout soldiers to bilious fever before I even arrived. I am uncertain which enemy we should fear most, Northern munitions or the island's miasmic swarm that reeks of death each night. Thankfully, we received an adequate supply of quinine to help those suffering from the fever. For what it may be worth, we are beholden to your experience and guidance, Colonel Spalding."

"Somebody, please pour our illustrious doctor another drink," Randolph said, standing in the middle of the room. He cast his eyes on each officer before nodding at Captain Wylly. "Gentlemen, let us take stock of the matchless charms of Sapelo. Where else can you witness the grandeur of our southern blue skies? They appear right after each awe-inspiring new dawn and continue until the next splendorous golden sunset heralds another unique moonlit and starry heaven—" Randolph interrupted his soliloquy and noticed the speechless, somber faces surrounding him.

Captain Echols held his glass out toward Randolph. "I'll toast to that. This paradoxical paradise of yours is most worthy of defending. Its mystical allure exceeds the legends of Homer's sea nymphs, the irresistible sirens in Greek lore. Thank you, Colonel Spalding, for proving to be a gracious host. We salute you and pray your family will return home soon."

"Captain, thank you. Of course, Homer's mythological sea nymphs drew unwary sailors to their doom. Let's not think Sapelo has that kind of lethal allure unless speaking about Union gunboats."

"I forgot about that part of the myth."

"Otherwise, please give a glowing report on the construction of the lighthouse point fortification and the other beach outposts."

Captain Echols set his glass aside. "With the cooperation of Mister Bass, just a little additional work remains on the fortification outer walls. However, the cannons are in place and ready for your men. We will continue training exercises as each detachment mans the artillery placements. If I and my men could receive the duty roster assignments each day, we would be most appreciative."

"Allen, thank you for making certain we could spare enough of our field hands to expedite the construction of the earthworks. How are we in the fields? The harvest going smoothly as well?" Randolph asked.

"Now that we have nearly all our workers back at our disposal to complete the harvest, we'll finish as planned," Allen Bass said, reluctant to step forward. He obviously felt out of place among the uniformed officers.

Captain Echols wrapped an arm across Allen's limp shoulders. "We understand the importance of this harvest for you and Colonel Spalding. As for my engineers and me, your slaves gave us an honest day's labor every day. They seldom fell behind stacking sandbags and setting timbers. We are grateful."

"Well, Mister Bass and Captain Echols, after that I'd like a chance to win back some of the money I've lost to both of you. How about another game of cards before we retire this evening?" Randolph said, scooting a chair out from under the library's round mahogany table they used for their late-night card games.

"Sure, why not? I'll be playing with your money, anyway. Who else will join Colonel Spalding and me? Come, come!" Echols let out a cocky laugh as he motioned for Allen Bass to join them.

"Cecile! Alma!" Randolph shouted loud enough to be heard well beyond the library doorway.

"Yes, Mister Spalding, sir?" Cecile said, arriving at the doorway in her bare feet.

"Bring us two bottles of my Carnochan rum."

"Yes, sir." Cecile disappeared as quickly as she had arrived.

Randolph settled into a chair at the table and handed a deck of cards to his nephew. "How about you shuffle and deal first?" He then lit a cigar.

Cecile returned and placed two bottles on the buffet. "Will there be anything else, Mister Spalding?" Cecile's ruffled shyness caused her to mumble as soon as she realized she had become the center of attention.

"Thank you, Cecile. That'll be all. Please tell your momma that both of you can go home for the evening. See you at breakfast."

Cecile nodded and shuffled backward toward the door as Thomas dealt the first hand of cards.

※ ※ ※

Three days later, sunbeams sparkled off Sapelo's murky waters, beginning another day. Alma had summoned Hector to check on Randolph. "Mister Spalding, sir. Is you okay?" Hector asked after rapping on his master's bedroom door. "Mister Spalding, sir, you's got two soldiers with Mister Wylly asking for you."

Extended moans and groans sounded just before Randolph opened the door and muttered, "Hector?"

"Sir, Mister Wylly is with two of your officers. They asked to speak to you." Hector shrank back into the hall when he saw Randolph barefooted and wearing his wrinkled, half-tucked, and unbuttoned red flannel shirt over his blue uniform trousers.

Randolph pushed his scraggly blond hair from his bloodshot and spiritless blue eyes. "Captain Wylly is here and asking for me? Why didn't Alma or Cecile wake me sooner?" He mumbled, attempting to clear his muddled senses.

"Mister Spalding, sir, they tried, sir. They asked me on account they was concerned you might be sick or something."

Randolph looked at his wrinkled shirt and pants and then noticed his tunic, hat, boots, and socks lying strewn across his bedroom floor. "Um, please advise Captain Wylly and the others I'll be with them straight away." As Hector turned away, Randolph grabbed his sleeve. "Have Alma or Cecile bring me some coffee."

After he closed the door, Randolph leaned over his washbasin and doused his head with a pitcher full of water. Ignoring the water spilled on the floor, he toweled his hair and face and put on a fresh red flannel shirt. Cecile's unmistakably timid knock caught his attention. "I'll be right there, Cecile. Hold a moment." He fumbled with the buttons and shoved his shirttails into yesterday's uniform trousers. "Come on in, Cecile."

She opened the door ever so slowly as Randolph yanked his boots on. "I got your coffee, Mister Spalding. It's still plenty hot too."

He motioned for her to hand him the coffee. "Thank you, Cecile."

"Are you well, Mister Spalding? You look like you got little sleep last night."

Randolph slurped Alma's extra-strong black brew. "I'm fine. I just had a hard time falling asleep last night, that's all." His frantic eyes searched the bedroom until he realized the empty rum bottle remained out of Cecile's eyesight. "Thank you, Cecile, for asking. Now, go on. Scoot! I need to finish getting dressed. I'm sorry if I caused you and your momma any worry."

Ten minutes later, Randolph paraded into South End's grand hall. Thomas Wylly chatted with Captain Levi Knight, who appeared to have color back in his cheeks. The young surgeon, William Way, stood off to the side reading a dispatch.

"Gentlemen, please excuse my tardiness this morning. I experienced a rough night but feel much better now." Randolph mustered a confident, strained smile, though his nephew recognized his uncle's droopy, reddened eyes.

Captain Knight removed his gloves and extended his hand to Randolph. "Congratulations, Colonel Spalding."

"Congratulations on what?" He reluctantly accepted Knight's handshake.

Thomas Wylly snapped to attention and saluted his uncle. "Headquarters sent this telegraph last night. After all the votes got tallied, you got elected as commander of our no-name regiment. I reckon that means we are standing in your regimental headquarters, at least for the time being. I wonder what Grandfather Spalding would say about that?"

Randolph slid his hand from Knight's grip but failed to return

Thomas's salute. "I didn't think—"

"It came down to Captain Knight and Captain Alexander before the men from Thomas County threw your name into consideration. Looks as though Levi here is now Major Knight, your adjutant and second in command on the island."

"Congratulations, Major Knight. I'm honored, but admittedly this news has caught me flatfooted." Randolph looked at his nephew. "And what about—"

"I'm Major Knight's replacement as company commander, assuming you agree," Thomas Wylly said.

"Of course, as long as Major Knight approves."

Levi patted Thomas on his back. "Then it's settled."

"While I continue to wrap my arms around being regimental commander today," Randolph cleared his throat, "Major Knight, please take charge. Report this evening on the status of our battery outposts and beach patrols." Though Randolph had served as a staff officer since June and learned much under General Lawton while in Savannah, his gut wrenched. Mixed feelings of gratification and trepidation stirred inside him as he mulled over the news.

After Thomas and Levi left, Randolph removed his hat and coat and walked beyond the dining room onto the covered walkway to the kitchen. He grabbed a biscuit and a cup of Alma's now lukewarm black coffee before stepping behind the cookhouse dependency rather than hiding inside the mansion. The late morning sun slid behind a swath of billowing white clouds. The added responsibilities—responsibilities in conflict with his desire to see his family—thrust upon him weighed heavily. He knew his liquor dependency had increased with his growing feelings of despair, disillusionment, and desperation. He tried to find comfort and solace in the memories of his youth and his family, but when he examined South End's scarred and trampled grounds, he felt the legacy his father had passed on to him for future generations of Spaldings slipping from his grasp.

Randolph's father had taught him how to treat others fairly

and honorably, emphasizing a high-minded life free of enmity. He lived out his sagacious lessons and demanded the same of his sons. Though Randolph battled his subterranean demons, he emulated his father's straightforward, quick-witted leadership style—when sober.

Before retiring that evening, he anesthetized his angst not with his usual brown elixir but with thoughts of his family. He took out stationary and the pen Sallie gave him and wrote to his wife:

October 23, 1861

My darling Mary,

I am truly sorry I have not written as I should, but I have been writing regularly in Sallie's journal. I find comfort knowing I will someday expound on my entries with the family when I see you. Until then, I pray you are finding your way around Milledgeville. How are you and the children adjusting? Have they enjoyed spending time with their cousins?

Adjusting to the daily regimen of army life remains a challenge for me. However, I remain resolved to do all I can to defend our beloved home and heritage on Sapelo. Of course, I am not alone in my resolve. Allen and the workers toil from dawn to dusk to complete the harvest. Hector, Alma, Jeremiah, and Cecile have faithfully provided me with comfort and familiar faces here at South End. Although the throngs of soldiers milling about South End disconcert Alma, they know to distance themselves from our servants and the workers.

I confess, I am glad you are not here to witness the sacrifices we have made on Sapelo to accommodate all the troops who occupy our once beautiful grounds around South End. The gardens lining the walkways lay trampled. Campfires that flicker in the night along the rows of canvas tents have scorched what little grass survives. Soldiers wander about the grounds when not marching off to an outpost or an artillery battery. But you would enjoy listening to the gay music these soldiers have brought with them. It soothes the sting of the sacrifice South End has had to make. Each night I wander among the young men, many not much older than Tom. They congregate around their fires, some strumming banjos and guitars and others blowing their harmonicas or plucking a mouth harp, as singing and storytelling fill the night air. There's one company that even prefers listening to the wail of bagpipes in their camp near the beach. That would be the only music my father would have tolerated.

What I have realized among these young and old soldiers is they are mostly farmers, merchants, and tradesmen. A handful owns slaves, and for most, our negroes are the first black men they've interacted with. And when they hear our negroes speak among themselves, they shake their heads. Their stake in secession has to do with independence and their love for Georgia. They have eked out a life worth going to war to protect. I confess, I am jealous in so many ways. Major Knight is from Berrien and has two of his sons in uniform on the island. He is older than Charles and fought Indians in the Wiregrass swamps of south Georgia. I admire his example, steady hand, and calming voice by my side.

I have good news to share with you. Today they made me the commander of our yet-to-be-designated new Georgia infantry regiment. Though I did not seek it, Mary, my dearest, I believe it will give me the needed authority to protect our land and our negroes while we remain here. They continue harvesting our cotton fields and soon your brother will pack up the essential tools and supplies required in Baldwin County.

Garrisons of infantry and cavalry presently protect the coastline from Savannah to Jacksonville. All the while, more and more of our friends and acquaintances have left their homes, closed their businesses, and moved farther inland. Of course, Charles and Evelyn remain at Ashantilly, as do many others on The Ridge for the time being.

Oh yes, our nephew, Captain Thomas Wylly, has taken command of the Berrien Guard. His presence provides yet another familiar face besides Allen that I can rely on among the myriad of strangers occupying our island.

I regret to include some sad but not unexpected news. My brother-in-law, William Cooke, passed this week. After his funeral in Darien, Charles buried him beside my sister Hester at Ashantilly.

O' how I miss sitting beside you on our porch. I miss sharing my bed with you all the more. It is late, and I have a staff meeting first thing in the morning. Send my love to Sallie, Tom, and Bourke. Until I am back with you, I embrace each of you in my nightly dreams.

Your loving husband,
Randolph

CHAPTER NINE

23rd of October, 1861

An unexpected late October warm spell enveloped the island. Randolph grabbed a scarlet cotton shirt and gray trousers from his personal wardrobe rather than wear his uniform. He garnered little notice from soldiers milling about as he strode through Camp Spalding and headed to South End's stables. His scraggly light brown hair made him feel and appear younger than his thirty-nine years as he climbed atop his chestnut stallion, Zapala. He then rode off for an impromptu inspection of the island's fortifications before catching up with his brother-in-law overseeing the harvest in the remaining cotton fields.

Three-man gun crews supported by an infantry detachment manned the five batteries on the island. Company commanders ensured every soldier under them pulled their share of tedious sentry duty and sleep-deprived overnight patrols if not assigned to one of the artillery batteries. Unsettling rumors floated among the troops on the island concerning the size of the North's naval fleet. The consensus feared an assault on Georgia's barrier islands while a blockade tightened their grip on the well-defended port cities. Letters from home added to reports about a growing number of runaway slaves, and some stories purported bloodshed. Nearly all the soldiers on Sapelo had known little about slaves before their arrival on the island. The realization that almost as many slaves as soldiers occupied Sapelo added to their increasing uneasiness.

Since the first militia units pitched their tents, both rifles and cannons remained silent. Sightings of federal blockade ships far out to sea became commonplace. One gunboat ventured close enough to raise the alarm but sailed back into deeper waters before coming within range of the sixteen-pounders at the Lighthouse Point batteries. The young lieutenant on duty at the time reported that his gun crew had rammed home powder and ball and ordered the muzzle raised to maximize its range, but the order to fire never came, much to the dismay of his eager gun crew. Captain Wylly congratulated the lieutenant's prudent actions for not needlessly revealing the island's battery positions. As long as enemy gunboats did not enter Doboy Sound or threaten Sapelo's shoreline, the artillery placements would remain silent behind their earthen installations. However, raucous cheers reverberated across the island, perking ears back at Camp Spalding when a Southern merchant paddle-wheeler bravely skirted northbound across the mouth of Doboy Sound under a full head of steam.

After visiting the three battery emplacements at the earthen redoubt on Lighthouse Point, Randolph stopped to chat with Alex Hazard, the lightkeeper. His unassuming whitewashed frame house backed up to the sand dunes a short walk from the lighthouse and opposite the manned fortification guarding the mouth of Doboy Sound. Alex was puffing on his pipe with his feet propped on his weathered porch rail when Randolph arrived.

"I didn't expect to see you out here."

"To be honest, neither did I," Randolph said, dismounting. "Since they went and made me commander of all these homesick volunteers, I figured it would be a good idea to get a firsthand look at what our boys are accomplishing on Sapelo."

"From what I can tell, you said it right. Most of your soldiers look like a mishmash of wet-behind-the-ears schoolboys and shiftless wire-grass farmers. Then again, they's been considerate enough toward me."

Standing just off the porch with the reins of his horse still in his hands, Randolph held a grateful grin. "I am pleased to hear you say that. Tell me if any of them give you a hard time."

"Surely will, Randolph." Hazard tapped his pipe against the edge of his wooden chair seat. "I just wish they'd not relieve themselves against my lighthouse. I'm not looking forward to painting over them pee-stained bricks."

"I'll remind them the lighthouse ain't a privy. And don't you worry. They'll do the whitewashing for you."

Hazard laughed. "Much appreciated. What can I do for you?"

"Seen any ships lately I might be interested in knowing about?"

"Their masted blockade gunships stay well out at sea. In fact, I rarely see two navigating the same horizon. Of course, I've noticed Captain Stevens's merchant schooners weaving their way below Wolf Island from the Altamaha. I gather they are pretty much limited to running cargo and supplies to the towns and plantations between Sunbury and Saint Mary."

"Old Captain Stevens is the one shipmaster ornery enough and experienced enough to sail the shallower tidal channels. Should a federal gunboat ever try to chase one of his schooners, they'll surely wind up beached on a sand or mud shoal. As for those bigger blockade warships, let me know if you see any snooping where they ought not. Of course, my guess is the North's Navy has its sights on assaulting either Savannah or Charleston. At least that's what some reports say, anyway."

Hazard stood and scraped the burned tobacco ash from his pipe's bowl with his pocketknife. "Randolph, be honest. Do you think this island will ever be the same again? I heard your family left with Mister Kenan and his family to Milledgeville."

Randolph fidgeted with the reins in his gloved hand. "Alex, my friend, I wish I had an answer I believed to be true. In another couple of weeks, Mister Bass will wrap up this season's harvest. I'm afraid it's the last on Sapelo until this infernal war ends. Shortly after that, our planting tools and supplies will travel with our negroes up the Altamaha to property Michael and I leased near Milledgeville. We've been fortunate so far with all the soldiers on the island. Not a morning passes when I wonder what would be worse, keeping idle soldiers here to defend the island or evacuate. I read the Union Army has begun conscripting any runaway slaves they run across. If that's a fact, I'd rather not see that happen should they land on Sapelo—"

The sudden sound of rifle fire and boisterous yelping froze Randolph until two additional shots echoed in the distance. Sentries atop the lighthouse battery turned their attention to the sounds coming from somewhere farther up the trail that skirted the shoreline. Randolph climbed on his horse and yanked the reins. Zapala snorted before carrying Randolph up the path. It had been four years since he last rode his horse that hard and fast. A sentry at the crossroad from Camp Spalding waved him along, and another shot rang out, followed by a violent squeal, cheers, and then laughter. In the distance, Randolph noticed a handful of soldiers running into the thick woods on the inland side of the trail. A wide-eyed teenage soldier bolted in front of Zapala, nearly causing Randolph to make an unwelcome dismount as his horse swerved underneath him. Regaining a firm seat in the saddle, he heard inharmonious cussing, screaming, and laughter-filled cheers. He dismounted, left Zapala behind, and followed the sounds into the woods.

The ongoing ruckus led him to a clearing where dozens of animated soldiers stood shoulder to shoulder goading two of their own who had their rifles pointed upward beneath a sprawling giant oak. Randolph noticed splatters of blood on the dirt near the base of the tree before he looked up. Jeremiah, Hector, and Alma's teenage son cowered in the upper branches hugging the tree's trunk. Randolph shoved his way through the raucous but otherwise oblivious gathering.

"Lower your weapons . . . NOW!"

After being pushed aside by Randolph, one soldier yelled, "Who the hell—" and shoved Randolph's shoulder as he bulled his way undeterred through the throng of soldiers.

The two soldiers with upward-pointing rifles peered over their shoulders when they heard the commotion and then the immediate hush. They relaxed their rifles but not their anger. A scruffy dark-haired trooper snarled, "That nigga' knocked me down and kicked Elias square between his legs when we tried to wrestle him down to the ground."

"Both of you, shut your mouths," Randolph seethed as he stepped closer to the centuries-old oak. Jeremiah remained crouched high overhead, nearly invisible with his head tucked behind two moss-laden limbs. "Jeremiah, come on down. No one's gonna shoot you."

"Mista Spalding, sir. They shot Poppa's boar. Please, sir. I jus' try to keep 'em from killin' Poppa's boar."

At hearing Jeremiah identify their interloper as Mister Spalding, the two startled soldiers lowered their rifles. Their shoulders and heads followed.

"I believe you, Jeremiah. Now climb down, and let's talk about it." Randolph looked at the trail of blood splatter and figured it must belong to the hog since it led into the dense, briar-infested underbrush.

Jeremiah dropped in front of Randolph, his head and eyes downcast. "Where's your Poppa's hog now? None of this blood is yours, is it?" he asked, eying Jeremiah closely.

"He likely bleed out by now, Mista Spalding, sir." Jeremiah pointed to the edge of a stagnant black pond beyond the dense thicket.

Randolph pointed to the young soldier who'd reacted to his brusque entrance and shoved him in the back. "You and your two buddies, go retrieve the hog."

"Yes, sir," grumbled the gray-haired corporal who was standing beside the defiant red-haired private. He snatched the private by his suspenders and growled, glaring at him and the other dumbfounded private on the other side. "Come on, you two. Colonel Spalding didn't ask if you wanted to or not!"

Both wide-eyed privates stopped abruptly on the other side of the tree and gawked at the maze of briars and thorns. The hot-tempered, red-headed trooper looked back and pleaded, "You expect us to find the hog through there?"

The wily corporal snatched both men by their sweat-stained shirt collars. "The Colonel gave us an order, boy. Now follow me, and both of you quit your bellyaching."

"Thank you, corporal," Randolph muttered, returning his attention to the two soldiers who'd instigated the incident. He examined Jeremiah's busted lip and gash above his right eye. "Are you sure you're okay? How d'you get these?"

"Ain't nothin', Mista Spalding, sir," Jeremiah said, gritting his teeth.

"By the looks of your forehead, I'd say you tangled with the butt of a rifle. Which one did this to you?"

Tears welled in the corner of Jeremiah's eyes, but he uttered not a word. Randolph understood Jeremiah's fear-laced reluctance. He then glared at the two soldiers now leaning on their rifles, sharing uncertain, exasperated looks. Randolph barked, "What are your names and your outfits, soldiers?"

The two soldiers snapped to attention, yanking their rifles tight along their side, displaying proper military posture. Both looked straight ahead as they sounded off. "James Blackshear, sir. Ochlocknee Light Infantry, sir." The other answered, "Private Elias Beall, sir. Ochlocknee Light Infantry also, sir."

"Well, Privates Blackshear and Beall. Does either of you have anything you wish to say about the shooting of the hog, or why this young man has a gash on his forehead from a rifle butt? I presume—"

"Elias, I got—" a private shouted as he raced as fast as he could around the gaggle of soldiers still caught up in the events unfolding beneath the old oak. He jolted to an abrupt halt and gasped for air. Clutching a coil of rope, he failed to absorb what had happened.

Blackshear gawked at the private. Elias Beall shook his head with a fearful look.

"Colonel Spalding, where do you want this hog?" the corporal asked between grunts as he and the two younger privates dragged the five-hundred-pound carcass of Hector's boar by its legs into the clearing.

Randolph shook his head in disbelief. He put his hand out.

"Thank you, private." Randolph reached for the rope in the startled, freckled-faced youngster's hand. "I'm sure you intended to use it to haul the dead hog back to camp?"

Blackshear gawked at their befuddled blond comrade and blurted, "Thanks, Willie. That rope will work just fine to haul that hog." His bug eyes caught Randolph's attention, as did Willie's confused look and dropped jaw.

Randolph gesticulated again for him to hand the rope over with a look that caused the young soldier to stutter, "Yeah, yes, sir."

"What's your name, son?"

"William Jones, sir."

"I assume you're from Ochlocknee too and friends of these two privates?"

The young blond soldier nodded and sighed, "Yes, sir."

Randolph handed the rope to Jeremiah. "Would you help these three tie the hog up so they can tote it back to camp? Then, see that your Poppa knows what happened and tell him Privates Blackshear and Beall will have their pay docked to cover his loss." He then turned to the remaining curious soldiers still standing around. "Unless y'all want to help these three men lug that hog all the way back to camp, I suggest you skedaddle back there yourselves."

※ ※ ※

Row after row, acre upon acre of withered, picked-clean cotton plants greeted Randolph as he rode Zapala to the other side of the island. He headed for the tabby ruins of his family's former mansion at Chocolate on the northern end of the island. The impressive home had burned to the ground two years after his father had passed away. For decades, the once beautiful estate home looked out upon seven-thousand acres of picturesque woodlands, marshlands, and tended fields of sugar cane and cotton on the island's north end. Chocolate Plantation had been a wedding gift from his father to Randolph and

Mary, but now the charred ruins left scarred memories of better days. Mary's once meticulous gardens and manicured grounds, where Sallie and Thomas played as young children, had long since succumbed to the plow for the sake of reaping additional cotton.

Randolph entered the skeletal tabby remains of his former home, recalling happier, innocent days on Sapelo. Back then, his father occupied South End and managed its grand plantation while Randolph's sister and brother-in-law raised their family on their portion of the island along the Duplin River. Charles and Evelyn Spalding lived on the mainland at Ashantilly but enjoyed their roles as uncle and aunt to Sallie, Tom, and Bourke, spoiling them as well as the Kenan children during their frequent visits to the island.

A broad smile emerged as Randolph recalled the look on his brother's face when he once strutted up the footpath from Mud River with young Tom toting a bucket of shrimp. They had spent the morning casting their nets off Chocolate's wharf, a short walk from the house. Randolph chuckled as he recalled that Hector and his young son Jeremiah had followed close behind with their own catch. Randolph could still hear the giggles from Sallie and Cecile as they peered into the buckets of shrimp their respective brother had lugged home.

"Randolph, I thought it was you when I saw Zapala out front of the old house. Is everything all right?" inquired Allen Bass sitting atop his unmistakable spotted gray mule. Two ox-drawn wagons brimming with cotton waited on the cart path.

"I wanted to catch up to you. We have to talk."

Allen waved for the wagons to continue and hollered to Abraham, his lead driver, "Y'all hurry on and get offloaded before it gets too dark."

"Yes, sir, Mista Bass." Abraham, a soft-spoken and meek giant of a man, tipped his hat with a pleasant smile when he recognized Randolph. "Good evening, Mista Spalding, sir. We sure pleased to see you, sir."

Randolph waved and said, "Thank you, Abraham, and all of you, for working extra-long days to get this harvest completed this season. I am the one most pleased." In his heart, he knew change was coming. This likely would be their last harvest on Sapelo for the foreseeable future. He also knew his field workers had no inkling about how their lives were about to change as well. Both drivers and the boys riding on the tail of each wagon waved with great big grins.

Randolph and Allen sat on the remains of Chocolate house's front steps and discussed the harvest near its completion. After Randolph told Allen about the incident with Jeremiah and the soldiers, they discussed Allen's suggestion of transporting their cotton bales to Darien's warehouses until they were sold and shipped to alternative markets. The buyers in Savannah and Charleston no longer could afford to invest in further loads of cotton since the blockade virtually choked off both ports from nearly all merchant ships. Allen had devised a plan to broker the cotton to other inland buyers over the coming weeks.

They likewise agreed that the relocation of the workers and their families would happen in stages, since transporting all the island's slaves two hundred miles inland at one time would be impractical and far too risky. Allen accepted the responsibility of organizing their gradual evacuation after their baled cotton was off Sapelo and either sold and headed elsewhere or stored in Darien's waterfront warehouses. Randolph agreed.

"Allen, we can work out a handsome broker's fee for all the cotton you can sell to other markets. As much as I would prefer you help your sister handle our affairs in Baldwin County, having you here for a while longer to manage matters is more pressing. I suggest you inform the workers as you see fit, but assure them we will keep their families together, no matter what. Is that understood?"

"Yes, Randolph. I understand."

"And please make certain they know, under no uncertain terms, they are to stay far away from the soldiers. I do not wish for another altercation like today. It's all the more reason to get our workers off

Sapelo before something unfortunate happens. Removing them from their homes—the only place most have ever known—will unsettle them enough."

Allen climbed back on his mule and headed to the storage barns.

Randolph mounted Zapala and trotted off as dusk swallowed the last remnants of an orange sunset. Tired and hungry, his body and spirit longed to be sated with food and drink. On the ride back to South End, he dwelled upon his reminiscences after visiting Chocolate and sharing them with his wife.

CHAPTER TEN

30th of October, 1861

Hackneyed routines trudged on without further incident in the immediate days following the run-in between Jeremiah and the three enlisted soldiers. Hector shared the slaughtered hog with well-deserving families on the island, though Alma made certain extra thick, fried slabs of bacon appeared with Randolph's morning fare of biscuits and coffee.

Even though life on the island had found a relatively uneventful pace, Randolph couldn't shake a paradoxical wariness that had begun festering when he became regimental commander. Word had spread among the rank-and-file about his unorthodox punishment of the three soldiers while excusing Jeremiah's assault on them. Further grumbling was already brewing over the cramped, damp, and filthy living conditions at Camp Spalding while slaves on the island slept each night in warm, dry, tabby-walled houses. Discontent extinguished many of the laughter-filled huddles around the campfires. Quarrelsome rumblings displaced much of the camp's gay tunes and songs of better days back home. None of this went unnoticed by Randolph.

After daily staff meetings with company commanders, Colonel Randolph, accompanied by his nephew Captain Thomas Wylly, rode off in full uniform to make his rounds about the island. Randolph's father had taught that leadership comes with deciding matters fraught with misunderstanding by the individuals those decisions affect. On an uneventful Wednesday, Randolph visited the lone battery on the north end where Blackbeard's inlet divides the shoreline. A detachment from Captain Wylly's Berrien militia company manned that isolated battery and security outpost. The hour-long ride allowed Randolph to gain valuable insight into his reputation among the troops.

"Randolph, I know why you handled those pig-ignorant farm boys the way you did, but just about every soldier on this island feels you oughta've handled it differently. Let's be honest, these volunteers know nothing about Grandfather Spalding's legacy on Sapelo. To them, slaves are but a rich man's property subject to the whims of their owners and overseers. Heck, there are some plantations right here in McIntosh where livestock gets treated better. Only a fool would rip away the hide of a boar or a bull headed to market. I heard when I visited my family at The Forest . . . well, let's just say my headstrong cousin had a handful of his slaves run off because of his cold-hearted, harsh treatment—"

"Yes, Thomas, I heard. I wish William and others like him would recognize our slaves are not the crux nor cause of this war for Southern independence. Our earthbound heritage bears far more responsibility for igniting the fuse of this irrevocable conflict. Why must we treat those who work our fields with such contempt? Do we not bleed the same red blood, breath the same air, and thirst for the same water? Yet, we judge them as inferior because—"

"I understand. What I saw out West proved to me we all are victims of a destiny dependent upon the fruits of what others long before us instituted. What you confessed is true. A threat of force can't undo this heritage of ours any more than brutality can earn the respect of our slaves. Yet, prosperity has enslaved us—and them. I dare say, in due course, industry as well as divine providence will bring about slavery's undoing. Until then, barring this war tearing us asunder, lasting change begins in the hearts of men like us. Just don't expect everyone else to accept the reality of the change we believe will inevitably come."

"Thank you, Thomas. I shall rely on forbearance rather than forthrightness while Mister Bass begins the evacuation of all the workers and their families in a few days since it appears our military presence will continue into the unforeseeable future. We will not glean the fields further. I do not want to risk more run-ins between the soldiers and our negroes. These rambunctious volunteers are itching for a fight, and, for the moment, the North's Navy doesn't appear eager to scratch that itch."

"Colonel Spalding, one observation if I may."

"Colonel Spalding?"

"When you are away from the fields and around the regiment, you are best seen as our regimental commander, not the Laird of Sapelo and not my uncle. I suggest you remain in uniform for their sake whenever you are out and about."

Randolph ran his gloved hand across the front of his double-breasted coat. He then nodded. "Point made. Thank you Captain Wylly."

Not long after, Randolph stood atop a dune that hid the artillery placement and scanned the horizon. "Captain Wylly, look to the south. What do you see?"

"I reckon we might be in for a storm tomorrow by the looks of those black clouds."

"My thoughts, too. Maybe it'll stay offshore, but I'd keep an eye out throughout the night. I'm going to head back to camp to set up a weather watch patrol."

※ ※ ※

Jeremiah, no worse for wear, greeted Randolph when he rode up to the barn.

"Where's your pa?"

"He's at the house finishing the dinner that Momma brought over, Mister Spalding, sir."

"How are you feeling? Does your head still hurt?"

'Nah! I be fine, sir." He instinctively touched above his eye. "It be just about good as can be."

"Brush Zapala down for me and give him a little extra feed. I may need to go back out later this afternoon."

Behind the barn, nestled among a grove of cedars, Hector sat on the back stoop of their family's modest tabby-built house. Randolph's father had it built for Hector and his family years ago. It had a sitting room with a fireplace, two attached bedrooms, and a loft where Jeremiah climbed into each night to sleep. A small covered front porch remained cool in the shade beneath the tall cedars towering over the house.

"Mista Spalding, sir," Hector said as he got to his feet.

"Sit down, Hector. I wanna ask you something, and I want an honest answer."

"Yes, sir, Mista Spalding. I do my best."

"Next week, Mister Bass will begin loading the first group of our folks headed to the plantation far inland up the river. As much as I'd like for you and your family to remain with me here for a while longer, would you like to be on that boat? With all the work needed at our new place, I know you'd be a big help when the livestock arrives."

Hector stroked his scraggly gray beard. "Mista Spalding, we be where you want us to be."

"Until last week, I'd have agreed with you. You know how much I love Alma's cooking." He patted his belly. "But I figure it'd be for the best if Jeremiah gets off Sapelo. I'd also feel better if Cecile left as well. I'm sure she'd like to see Sallie."

Hector removed his hat and fingered the brim, preferring to inspect his sweat-stained sweet-grass hat. "Mista Spalding, who gonna tend the hogs and chickens and milk the cows? Who gonna cook for ya?"

Randolph picked a piece of brown pine straw from the black ostrich feather that stuck out of his gold-banded, black hat. "Hector, they made me their commanding officer, so I reckon I can scrounge up a few able-bodied volunteers who might prefer to tend the animals you will leave behind. If I'm also lucky, maybe, just maybe, there's a decent cook among all those militia boys, too. In either case, they can never replace you and your family, but, well, what do you say?"

"Mista Spalding, being you put it that away. We do what you think best," Hector said, examining Randolph's crestfallen look.

Randolph tendered a half-hearted smile as they both resigned themselves to what neither wished was necessary but knew otherwise. "I'll tell Mister Bass. He'll stop by to discuss what all you and Jeremiah will need to get ready for the trip. I'll let you break the news to Alma and Cecile."

"Yes, sir, Mista Spalding. I don't know what I'll say, but I surely will talk to her. Thank you, sir."

※ ※ ※

As soon as Randolph stepped into South End, Charles spoke up from the library. "I thought you'd never get back. I saw you ride up."

Randolph tossed his hat on the table and unbuttoned his coat. "What in blue blazes brought you here today? Not enough trouble on the mainland to keep you busy, so you came here looking for some?" He bit the end of a cigar and lit it before pouring himself a drink. He then topped off his brother's glass between puffs.

Charles reached inside his coat and pulled out a letter from Mary and exchanged it for his glass of rum. Randolph sat and read it without saying a word. Charles kicked his brother's calf and said, "I thought you'd at least thank me for delivering your mail."

"Yes, Charles. Thank you. Give me a moment." He sat across from Charles in the matching leather armchair, slumped with his legs crossed at the ankles. A puff or two of cigar smoke rose above the stationary before his eyes perked up. He carefully folded the letter and slid it into his coat pocket.

"A love letter from Mary, I presume."

Randolph looked flustered with an awkward cat-got-the-canary grin. "How would you know what she wrote?"

"Randolph, my dear younger brother, I did not just get off the wagon. I smelled her perfume as soon as the postmaster handed it to me when he heard I was heading to see you. The rest of your mail is on the table beside your hat."

"So, how might I serve you this afternoon?" Randolph sipped his drink and puffed on his cigar as he slouched back in his chair. "Is this official or social?"

"A little of both. I surmise you heard about the slaves that ran off from Sutherland Plantation?"

Randolph nodded and motioned with his cigar to continue.

"Norman Gignilliat also lost a dozen of his field hands as well. They overpowered the overseer at his Belford estate when he tried to stop them. Thankfully, he merely got roughed up. No blood got spilled."

"Charles, I don't understand. Norman may be a blowhard, but he's never had problems with his slaves before."

"I agree. What happened is a fact. I've assigned a patrol to remain on alert up and down the road along the marsh inlets. We got word that abolitionist provocateurs are stirring up unrest on some plantations. Ever since General Styles ordered the McIntosh Guard to Brunswick, my patrols became stretched thin from Sutherland Bluff to Darien."

"How's Evelyn? Any problems at Ashantilly or on the Ridge?"

"Everything is fine with Evie and up at your place, except we have a bigger potential problem. William led a patrol looking for some runaways when he heard reports of them hiding out on Saint Catherine's Island."

"What happened? Did our firebrand Captain Brailsford find them? If so, I dare ask what happened?"

"The slaves purportedly had guns and fired at William and his men when they encircled their encampment."

"Anyone get shot?"

"No one but William and his men returned from the island."

"What did William say happened?"

"He argued he could not ignore the fact that slaves attempted to kill a white man. His men returned fire, and then they left the bodies in the marsh grass as a message."

Randolph gulped down what remained in his glass and wiped his mouth. "Damn that hot-headed ape. As if we don't have enough to worry about with Lincoln's armada on the prowl. Lawton believes they have targeted somewhere between Savannah and Charleston or along Georgia's southern coast to launch an assault. We don't need to be watching our backs while bracing for an attack. Damn that fool. The sooner I get all our workers and their families off Sapelo, the better. What about your plantation? What are you going to do?"

"For now, I am negotiating land in Brooks County. I can evacuate my slaves a lot easier than you can on Sapelo, though. My cotton's nearly all baled and in our storehouses."

Randolph stood. "I'm facing another immediate problem. Remember how father used to tell us that 'Boredom is the agent of sin'?"

Charles raised his glass and took a sip. "Father was a wise man, that's for sure—"

"Yes, and I'm facing a boredom problem with nearly four hundred soldiers itching for a fight that so far has not manifested itself. Not that I am looking for a fight myself, but I broke up an altercation between Jeremiah and three hot-headed Ochlocknee lads. They wanted to kill one of Hector's stray boars while Jeremiah wanted only to stop them from harming the hog before he could catch it. You can guess how that almost ended up."

"So? I saw Jeremiah. He looked no worse for wear to me."

"Trust me. I'll feel much better once Jeremiah and his family get off the island along with the rest of the slaves on the island. Eventually, a powder keg will blow, and Northerners will have had little to do with it, just like William and his merry misadventure. Sin is knocking at the door waiting for boredom to invite it in."

"Brother, let me know what I can do to help you. I agree it's a good idea to get all your black workers off Sapelo as soon as you can."

"A steamer will pull in next week at the Duplin wharf to be loaded. I've arranged for them to make as many round trips needed to get our people, livestock, and equipment to Baldwin County." Randolph pulled his letter from Mary back out. "Mary sent good news. Michael is eager to help her when the boat arrives in Milledgeville. Why don't you stay and enjoy dinner with me? That way, you can post my letter to Mary for me in the morning."

"You read my mind, little brother. Pour us another. I can see the bottom of my glass."

CHAPTER ELEVEN

31st of October, 1861

Frantic rapping on Randolph's bedroom door in the pre-dawn darkness woke him from a rum-induced slumber. "Colonel Spalding, sir. Colonel Spalding, sir."

Randolph rolled over to the edge of his bed and sat up. He wiped his face with both hands to clear the blurriness. "Yeah, who is it?"

"Sorry to disturb you, Colonel. This is Corporal Hopkins, sir. There's something happening that Mister Hazard wants you to see."

"Damn, son. The lightkeeper, Mister Hazard, sent you?" Randolph grabbed his trousers and yanked them on as he shuffled to the door. Adjusting his suspenders, he said, "Enter, Corporal."

The lanky soldier opened the door but remained in the doorway holding a rigid salute.

"Relax, son. It's far too early for all that. Were you on storm watch?" Randolph's brain exited the dense fog that cluttered his senses.

Still standing at attention, the corporal said, "Yes, sir. Some nasty-looking black clouds appear to be headed our way. The wind and the tide are rising all along the shore. I wasn't sure what to do until Mister Hazard found me and instructed me to wake you. He wants you to meet him at the lighthouse."

Alma, wearing her housedress and apron and holding a lantern, scurried from the shadows and into the hallway. "Mista Spalding, is you all right? I heard someone screaming yo' name and making a God-awful racket all the way from the cookhouse."

"Thank you, Alma. Would you wake my brother? Inform him to get dressed and meet me on the portico."

"Your brother is up," Charles barked from across the hall. "What's going on?"

"Charles, get dressed. Meet me out front. Alex wants me to meet him at the lighthouse. Sounds like there's a nasty storm headed our way. Now hurry. I'll have a couple of horses saddled and waiting out front."

"That doesn't sound good. I'll be right behind you."

Randolph raced out of the house and across Camp Spalding. Jeremiah stepped beyond the darkness inside the barn toting a stool and a bucket of milk. "Mista Spalding, sir. What might ya need this time of the morn', sir?"

"Put that bucket and stool down. Saddle a horse for my brother while I saddle Zapala." Jeremiah looked confused. "Now, son! Hurry!"

"Yes, sir."

The milk bucket nearly toppled as Jeremiah set it atop the stool inside the barn before he raced into the stables. Randolph had tightened Zapala's cinch just before Jeremiah had a chestnut mare saddled for Charles. Randolph mounted his horse and snatched the mare's reins from Jeremiah's outstretched hand.

When a bewildered Charles grabbed the reins of his horse at the foot of *Big House's* portico steps, he said, "You mind telling me why we are riding to see Mister Hazard in the middle of the night?"

"I figured you oughta ride out to the lighthouse with me. Alex obviously is concerned enough to have me rustled out of bed." Randolph pointed to the caliginous clouds darkening the starless, pre-dawn sky. "What do you make of that?"

Charles stared once again at the black storm clouds approaching from the Atlantic. "Little brother, you likely don't remember the storm of twenty-four. You were barely walking. I helped Father and Bu Allah when that hurricane tore across the island. It wiped out a full season of crops that year. I pray this won't be like that, but I won't lie to you. That nasty pitch-black sky, and the sound of the surf concerns me too. Being as Alex summoned you, we best not waste any time speculating." Charles snapped his reins and dug his heels into the sides of his horse.

Randolph yelled at the sentry. "Find Major Knight and Captain Wylly. Tell them to report to me at the lighthouse, posthaste." Zapala reared, spun past the startled sentry, and galloped off close behind Charles on his horse.

※ ※ ※

"Alex, what do you think? How bad might this storm get?" Randolph asked, standing with his brother on the leeward side of the lighthouse as gusts of wind rattled the surrounding treetops. The roar of the crashing waves required that they yell at one another.

"Randolph," the lighthouse keeper said, anchoring his hat with one hand, "we'll know how bad it'll get after morning breaks. My guess, like most storms barreling up from the south this time of year, the worst will remain out to sea, but that doesn't mean we'll escape damaging gale winds and blankets of rain cutting across the island. I'd say batten down the hatches and expect the worst by this evening." Hazard pointed to the barely visible churning waves at the mouth of the Doboy Sound. Through the early dawn's dimly lit grayness, the worst of the storm appeared farther out to sea. "I dare say, we ain't gonna have to worry about any ships navigating these waters while this storm hangs around."

"Randolph, by your leave," Charles said. "I think I would like to grab my stuff and hitch a ride back to the mainland while I still can. If this storm comes any closer, Evelyn will worry, and our rambunctious nephew Captain Brailsford might actually think he's in command." Charles shook Alex's crusty hand. "Until tonight, keep one eye on this storm."

Hazard smirked. "Mister Spalding, if the storm gets too bad, I'll seek safe shelter in the lighthouse. I suggest you leave the island while the getting is good. Even now I suspect you'll have a pretty bumpy boat ride."

After Charles rode off, Major Knight and Captain Thomas Wylly rode to advise that the troops already on duty should batten down and remain at their stations until relieved. Randolph's nephew volunteered to ride to the northern outposts with the news. Major Knight returned to Camp Spalding to order the company commanders to have Camp Spalding's tents prepared for a long day full of rain squalls likely to get worse before the day ends.

Randolph then found Allen Bass. They checked and secured all the barns and storehouses on the island. Both knew, though they hesitated to say it aloud, that this storm would mark a soggy end to the cotton harvest. Protecting the crop already harvested and everyone on the island became paramount.

A drenched Randolph rode back to South End just before nightfall swallowed any remaining daylight. There would be no glimmering golden sunsets. Camp Spalding's city of tents struggled throughout the day, coping with windswept downpours. Rain-soaked soldiers pounded extra stakes into the saturated ground, desperately trying to anchor their waterlogged, wind-blown canvas shelters. Darkness reigned across the camp with no fires, no music, no songs, no boisterous laughter. Only the slapping and smacking of discordant tent flaps drowned out the mumbling of soldiers huddled beneath their soaked canvas dwellings. Whirling winds rustled through the surrounding treetops as nightfall's bleakness added to the misery the storm inflicted.

Jeremiah ran from the barn as Randolph dismounted Zapala. "Mista Spalding, sir. You need me to put your horse up?"

"Thank you, Jeremiah." He handed Jeremiah the reins. "Did my brother get home all right?"

"Yes, sir. Surely did, sir. Poppa and me took him ourself. We bounced around a bit in them waves, but we took him straight to Ashantilly like he ask us. When we got back, sir, Poppa told me to tie the boat real good at the Duplin wharf. He thought it best not to take the *Sarah Spalding* back to South End's dock."

"Very good. Your poppa is a mighty smart man. We are likely to catch more squalls throughout the night. You and your poppa did right securing the *Sarah Spalding* at the Landing. Make sure you rub the horses down good and keep the barn doors closed so the wind won't spook them too bad tonight."

"I will, Mista Spalding. Poppa ask'd me to stay in the barn tonight. Animals don't like all this wind and rain."

"Neither do I, Jeremiah. Do you need anything?"

"No, sir. My sister said she'd bring me supper later."

※ ※ ※

Rain-soaked field officers ventured into *Big House's* dining room and reported on the conditions in Camp Spalding while they supped on spoonfuls of chicken and rice and gulps of hot coffee. Major Knight had ordered the rank-and-file soldiers to report to South End's cookhouse with their mess kits. Beneath a canvas canopy erected behind Alma's kitchen, regimental cooks ladled heaping portions of chicken and rice and hot coffee to the enlisted men. They huddled shoulder to shoulder against the grand house's leeward sturdy, tabby walls while scoffing down their warm supper beneath the eaves.

Bands of rain continued well into the night dumping buckets of water. Sapelo's towering pines and sprawling oaks offered some protection from the worst of the ocean gusts. Beyond South End's portico, pitch darkness swallowed the sprawling city of canvas. Flickering kerosene lamps inside a few of the officer's tents and the windows and doorway of *Big House* offered some comfort from the utter darkness on Sapelo. Any semblance of rest for soldiers shivering in their tents grew increasingly futile by the hour. Camp Spalding's grid of grassless, trodden paths between the once meticulous rows of tents became an oozing quagmire resembling the muddy marsh banks that surrounded much of Sapelo. South End's once lush green grounds upon which prim and proper, gaily dressed guests sashayed arm in arm during previous grand affairs lay bare and drown beneath standing water.

Later in the evening, Cecile cleared the dining table after Randolph and Major Knight adjourned to the library. Randolph lit a cigar and grabbed a fresh bottle of his favorite dark rum. "Levi, would you like to warm your innards a bit?" Amid a hearty laugh, he poured two glassfuls. "Major Knight, a toast to Sapelo. She weathers storms better than poor mortals like us."

"Here, here, Colonel Spalding. I am jealous. Sapelo has certainly revealed herself as a strange yet enchanting paradise over the past month. Though, it has tried to dissuade us from our mission. It's a shame that we mortals have spoiled the legacy your father established here."

Major Knight hoisted his glass, toasting the portraits of Thomas Spalding and Sarah Spalding hanging on opposing walls in the library. The French artist had painted Randolph's attractive mother with a demure smile, but his father's portrait glared down from above the fireplace with a stern, austere look that his family knew well.

"Colonel Spalding, I would like to toast to you, sir. May your family's legacy and Sapelo's untamed natural beauty outlast mortal man's propensity to cause death and destruction."

"I second that toast. May neither lose its appeal." Randolph hoisted his glass to the life-size painting of his father. "Yes, Father, we salute you and pray you are watching over your island. May I survive to witness your legacy handed over to the next generation of Spaldings here at South End's grand house on your beloved Sapelo." He downed the last in his crystal glass and hurled it into the fireplace as if he wanted to alter his father's sneer.

Thomas Wylly entered the library. "Come outside. You won't believe it."

Randolph and Levi Knight followed Thomas to the front portico.

"Listen!" Thomas said.

"Listen for what?" Major Knight said, staring at Captain Wylly as though he had gone stir-crazy.

"The wind and rain stopped." Thomas looked at his uncle.

"By God, I think you're right," Randolph replied. "It seems our storm has blown itself up the coast and remained out to sea. If that be the case, may it blow all the harder when it reaches the federal fleet and sinks their ships, blowing the Yankees back whence they came. Major Knight, Captain Wylly, this deserves another toast. Come on back inside with me. There's little we can do further until morning. We can examine the damage from the storm after the sun comes up. How about a game of cards before we call it a night?"

"By your leave, Colonel. I think I will head off to bed. I suspect we have a big day ahead tomorrow," Major Knight said, stretching his arms and ending with a drawn-out yawn.

"Sounds good to me, too. I think I'll check on the men before turning in as well," Thomas Wylly said before he walked off the portico and headed into the darkness.

Randolph sat alone in the library lost in thoughts of family and better days before he drifted off, his mud-caked boots stretched out as he slumped back into a leather armchair.

※ ※ ※

"Mista Spalding, Mista Spalding, sir. Come quickly, sir. Hector be hurt." Alma stood beside the chair Randolph had fallen asleep in. Her tear-filled eyes reflected the urgency in her plea as she waved her arms.

When Randolph awoke and jumped to his feet, Alma snatched him by the elbow. "Please, Mista Spalding. Hector be in the cookhouse and be bleeding bad. He ain't making no sense at all either." Alma tugged Randolph with one hand and hiked her skirt with the other as if she was about to run across the great hall.

Randolph sensed the panic in Alma and took her by the arm.

Hector sat slumped over in a chair next to the cookhouse rear door pressing a rag to the back of his head. Randolph pulled Hector's hand away and dabbed the blood with the rag. The back of his neck and collar were soaked in blood.

Hector mumbled and shook his head back and forth. "My boy. My boy. They's take my boy."

"Who's taken your boy? What happened?"

"Them soldier boys." His mumbles worsened. "I gotta find my boy."

Alma wiped the caked mud from Hector's cheeks and forehead with a wet cloth. Randolph rinsed the bloody towel in a basin of water on the counter and set it back over the open gash atop the swollen lump on Hector's head behind his right ear.

Levi Knight stormed into the cookhouse. "Colonel, what can I do?"

"Mister Knight, can you roust the surgeon out of bed for us?"

Hector winced and swiped Alma's hand away. "Woman, let me be. We's gotta find the boy," Hector growled as he tried to stand.

Randolph pushed him back into the chair. "Hector, you're going to sit right here until the surgeon gets here. Quit your fussing! I'll look into what happened to Jeremiah. Now tell me, how did you get hurt? Did they hit you?"

"Mista Spalding, sir." Tears poured down Hector's cheeks. "I walked into the barn to check on my boy. Them soldier boys be standing over Jeremiah lying in the dirt. I asks 'em what happened and knelt down to check on Jeremiah. Next thing I knowed, they's gone and my head done got busted."

Major Knight and William Way, the camp's surgeon, then came through the door that led to the dining room. "What happened, Colonel?" the surgeon asked, examining the severity of Hector's injury.

Randolph shouted in frustration, "It must've been those Ochlocknee boys who busted Hector's head open and took Jeremiah. Hector said he walked in on them with his son lying on the ground in the barn." He looked at Major Knight. "Levi, go round up Captain

Young of the Ochlocknee company, and the two of you locate those three soldiers before they do anything more to Jeremiah."

After Captain Knight left, Randolph looked at Alma. "Where's Cecile?"

Alma squealed, "Sweet Jesus! She went to bring Jeremiah and Hector their dinner." Her eyes gaped wide. "Hector, was Cecile at the house before you went to check on Jeremiah?"

Hector shook his head. "I thought she be here with you."

Randolph placed his hand on Alma's shoulder. He felt the tremble of a mother's worst fears. "Keep your husband here. The doctor will need you to help him. I'll bring both of your children back. I promise."

Randolph bolted out the cookhouse back door and raced through the mud straight to Hector and Alma's house. His heart skipped a beat when he saw a lantern burning from their front window, but the door was ajar. He looked inside and called out, "Cecile! Jeremiah! Please be here." When no answer came, he grabbed the lantern from the table and strode straight into the barn. Inside, he stooped down and inspected the blood-stained straw and dirt. There were signs that a struggle had taken place. He shined the lantern into the shadows and saw two broken plates with clumps of rice and chicken strewn across the ground.

Oh, God! Please, not Cecile too. Help me, Lord. Not for my sake, but for Alma and Hector's sake and my own children's sakes. Please let nothing happen to them. Please, God. Randolph's silent pleas tried to calm his panic.

Major Knight entered the barn with Captain Young and two of his men from the Ochlocknee company. "Colonel, what did you find out? What do you want us to do?"

"Hector said they were the same three soldiers who killed his hog and damn near shot Jeremiah, too. Captain Young, do you know where those three are right now?"

"I assume, sir, you are referring to privates Blackshear, Beall, and Jones. Sir, I have not seen them since the storm hit," Captain Young said, his eyes darting at the blood on the ground and the broken dishes.

"Dammit, man. Get your men out searching for them. From what I can tell, they have kidnapped two of my servants. I'm afraid they mean to do them harm. Don't report back until you find them. Do you understand me?" Randolph snarled.

Captain Young and his two men turned and double-timed it back into the darkness.

Levi Knight placed his hand on Randolph's shoulder. "Colonel, where do you want to look? I'll go with you."

"No, you stay here in case those three come traipsing back into camp. They couldn't go too far in this darkness. I know every inch of this island. I'll find them. Inform Captain Wylly and ask him to help organize a search. He knows the island better than any of you."

CHAPTER TWELVE

1st of November, 1861

Blood on Zapala's stall door piqued Randolph's deepest fears. Zapala stirred, but there were no other signs of a violent struggle. Boot prints intermingled with those of bare feet led Randolph out the back of the barn and beyond the corral. The tracks took him onto a pitch-dark, muddy path leading away from Camp Spalding and South End and winding through densely wooded undergrowth.

Dressed in his hastily buttoned tunic over his red flannel undershirt and trousers, the colonel knew his best chance of finding Jeremiah and Cecile depended on him not wasting valuable time. He carried a lantern through Sapelo's woods and knew the pathway behind the barn led onto the wagon trail connecting South End and the docks at Marsh Landing.

Randolph sloshed through endless mud puddles and shoved aside rain-soaked undergrowth, stopping every few minutes to listen for foreign sounds. He broke free from the gauntlet of sharp cabbage palm leaves and thorny brambles that narrowed the muddy footpath, standing tall in a small clearing at the edge of the woods to catch his breath. He scoured the road's edge for footprints like the ones that led him into the woods, but they had disappeared along the soggy path. Raising his kerosene lantern, he bent over and scoured the soggy ground along the road and between the deep wheel ruts. He mumbled prayers for any signs where the soldiers and their captives had exited the woods. He turned and faced South End and Camp Spalding but saw nothing. He then turned back around and looked toward the

Duplin River and Marsh Landing with the same grim result.

Soaked to his skin, he felt the chill in the air. He set the lantern down in the middle of the road. Randolph believed the three desperate and likely scared soldiers also exited the woods and were lost, drenched, and chilled as well. They would not dare risk trekking farther in the bleak, moonless darkness, especially if they still had Jeremiah and Cecile with them. They had to be desperate and seeking a way off the island before dawn.

Randolph banked on the lantern catching the attention of search parties sent out from Camp Spalding. He bent over, hands on his knees. *Think, Randolph. Think! Lord, don't let any harm come to Jeremiah and Cecile. Lord, please help me find them.* Thoughts of Sallie, Tom, and Bourke surfaced as he sought divine illumination to help him locate Jeremiah and Cecile. He would let the three Ochlocknee boys escape if he could find Jeremiah and his sister, safe and unharmed. The images of his own children spurred Randolph to walk faster along the edge of the road. He grew more frantic with every step.

A frail shriek brought him to an abrupt stop. Faint whimpering followed. "Cecile! Where are you? Jeremiah, call out." He stumbled and fell to his hands and knees in the rain-battered ruts in the road, but each time he got back to his feet and ran up the road to where he could make out what had to be Cecile's whimpers coming from beyond the undergrowth. He pushed aside bush limbs as Cecile's muffled moans and indecipherable muttering grew louder.

"Cecile! Jeremiah! Keep talking. I'm coming."

Randolph followed her voice deep into the impenetrable treed darkness, forging a path through the tall grass and undergrowth, calling out in a cautious voice, "Cecile, please keep talking to me."

He found himself in a clearing that surrounded a centuries-old, moss-laden oak. Randolph felt something soft rub against his face as he ducked under a low-lying branch. He tugged on it until it fell from the tree limb. He fumbled with the dripping-wet cloth until he realized he held Cecile's dress. "Cecile! Where are you?"

Her sniffling and incoherent murmuring drew him to the base of the giant oak. He felt in the darkness until he touched her sopping wet hair and face. Quickly, he realized she was lying naked and curled up in a fetal position between two monstrous tentacle-like roots at the base of the tree trunk. He removed his coat and draped it over her shivering body.

"Cecile, it's Mister Spalding. You're safe now."

Randolph promptly eyed the clearing as best he could. He could see neither hide nor hair of the soldiers or Jeremiah. "Jeremiah, where are you? Say something."

She sobbed louder as she mumbled, "They kilt him."

Cecile rolled her head and, with fear widening her eyes, stared at Randolph's colorless shadow kneeling beside her. She raised her right hand and pointed upward.

Randolph looked up and saw the rope tied to the tree trunk. He felt the steep angle and tautness of the strand of rope. He tugged on it before he noticed the lifeless shadow suspended from an upper tree limb. Randolph got to his feet and touched the limp, mud-caked bare feet. He screamed, "O God, no!" and fell to his knees. He pounded the sandy ground. "Oh dear Lord, why?"

Cecile wept uncontrollably as she pulled herself into a tighter fetal position and squeezed her eyes shut.

A voice called out from the road, "Colonel Spalding, sir? Are you all right?"

"Levi, we're back here. Follow my voice."

Major Knight appeared with Captain Thomas Wylly and two soldiers from the darkness holding lanterns as they pushed the undergrowth aside until they found Randolph at the giant tree's base.

"They hanged Jeremiah. Those backwoods bastards couldn't leave well enough alone. They lynched Jeremiah and assaulted his sister. How am I going to tell their momma and poppa?" Randolph stammered, returning his focus to Cecile. He tucked his coat around her naked body and hoisted her into his arms. Cecile buried her tear-soaked face into Randolph's chest. "Cut Jeremiah down, Major." He then glared at Thomas Wylly with an unmistakable look of rage. "Thomas, find those three monsters before word gets out about what happened. I imagine they have high-tailed it for the docks to steal a boat. If they are stupid enough to hide on the island, they'll be dead men."

Major Knight removed his service revolver and fired two shots into the pre-dawn darkness. "You two, take the body down. One of you, stay here with Colonel Spalding. The other, run back and tell Captain Young what happened and that Captain Wylly and I will head to the boat landing. Then, fetch a wagon for Colonel Spalding."

Major Knight then stared at Randolph. "Colonel Spalding, what else can we do? My signal shots will have every patrol headed this way. Please wait here until the wagon arrives to take you back to camp."

"Levi, no, thank you. She's almost like a daughter to me. No one but me will take her back to her momma and poppa. The walk will help me find the words to tell Alma and Hector what happened to their son and daughter."

"Uncle Randolph, I'll make sure we find them or their bodies. As soon as we get to the dock, I'll send a boat to tell Uncle Charles and William what happened and to be on the lookout. Those three murderers can't hide for long, and they will not head back home to Thomas County."

"Captain Wylly's correct. If they get off the island, they will head for God only knows where, but we will find them. You can count on that."

After Randolph began the long walk back to South End, cradling Cecile in his arms, the two enlisted soldiers returned and placed Jeremiah's body on the wagon and followed him back to camp.

※ ※ ※

The following morning, Captain William Way knocked on the closed library doors. "Colonel Spalding, may I come in, sir?"

"Go away! I don't need the services of a surgeon, Mister Way."

"Sir, I thought you wanted to know about the young girl you asked me to check on, the one sleeping in your—"

"Enough, man. Come on in. I'd prefer you report to me, not every soul in earshot."

The young surgeon entered the dimly lit room that reeked of the island's malodorous marsh mud. Randolph remained sprawled out between two oversized upholstered chairs, his feet propped on one while he slouched back in the other. The surgeon stood near the door as if fearing Randolph's wrath.

"Well, Mister Way, how is Cecile? What is the extent of her injuries?"

"Sir, she suffered multiple bruises and abrasions on her legs and arms. Her momma helped me clean her up and bandage her serious scrapes and cuts. She suffered one gash under her jaw that will leave quite a nasty scar."

"Had she been—?"

The young doctor nodded. "I'm afraid it appears so, sir."

"Did she say anything about what happened?"

"No, sir. She hasn't spoken a word, not even to her momma. Anytime either of us touched her, she jerked her head back and forth, curled herself up into a tight ball beneath the blankets, and began crying again. I'm afraid she's still in a state of shock."

"How long will she be like that?"

"Hours, days. It's hard to say precisely. I can diagnose and treat Cecile's physical wounds, but her biggest wound afflicts her mind and soul. There's little I can do to help her heal that wound. I recommend she get plenty of rest for now. Her momma can offer Cecile far better recuperative care than I can give her."

"Thank you, Mister Way." Randolph draped his forearm over his eyes and sighed.

"Colonel, with your permission, sir—"

Randolph groaned. "Yes, Mister Way?"

"Your well-being is also my concern. You look and smell as

though you have been wallowing in the mud, sir."

Randolph lowered his arm and propped himself onto his elbows, inspecting his filthy undershirt and trousers. He fingered his scraggly light brown hair. Flecks of caked mud fell onto the floor.

"Sir, as the acting regimental surgeon, I prescribe hot water with lots of soap along with you changing into some clean, dry clothes."

"I will take that under advisement, my dear surgeon," Randolph moaned with his forearm shielding his shut eyes from the slivers of sunlight chasing the shadows into the corners of the library.

"Sir, you oughta know, Major Knight and Captain Wylly have been asking to speak with you."

Randolph sat upright, his bloodshot eyes squinting. "Why did you not say so sooner? Ask Alma to fetch me some hot water and a change of clothes. I'll use a spare room to scrub up and change."

"Sir, may I remove those bottles for you?" The young surgeon pointed to the two empty rum bottles on the table beside Randolph.

"Yes, thank you." With a sheepish grin, he said, "They helped me catch a little sleep." Randolph wiped his eyes and planted his sock feet squarely on the floor. "How are Alma and Hector?"

"Hector's head injury will be fine. I bandaged his nasty gash, and Alma got him settled into his bed. Otherwise, he's gonna tote a mighty big headache for a couple of days."

"That is great to hear, but how are they coping with Jeremiah's death and Cecile being raped."

"She's a tough old woman. She spent last night at her daughter's bedside, except for twice when she disappeared to check on her husband. I believe she got less sleep than any of us. She whispered to her daughter loud enough for me to hear words I could understand while stroking her cheeks and holding her hand. Other times, she mumbled portions in a strange language. I figured she meant for me to hear her prayers, even if I could not understand all of what she said."

"What did you understand?" Randolph asked, rising from his chair.

"Well, she begged God to curse all those responsible for the evil that happened to her son and daughter."

"She's Geechee, a mighty superstitious and deeply religious people. They have lived on this island for decades. It wouldn't surprise me if a divine curse didn't fall from heaven upon us after all of this. I just hope the curse doesn't arrive aboard any federal warships."

Dressed in a clean uniform but showing the lingering effects of a long, sleepless night, Major Knight rapped on the open library door. "Colonel, may I have a word?"

Randolph looked at the young surgeon. "Would you excuse us, Mister Way? Let Alma know I'd like to talk with her when she brings me a change of clothes to the guest bedroom."

The surgeon squeezed past Major Knight before Randolph gestured for the door to be closed. "Whatever you have to tell me, please keep it brief. I'm certain we can discuss whatever you have on your mind further during our staff meeting and after we have some breakfast."

"No, sir, you need to hear this before the meeting."

Randolph nodded.

"One boat at the Duplin River docks is reportedly missing. The sentries on duty said they saw no one, but one skiff definitely disappeared during the night."

"Are they sure the storm didn't cause a skiff to come untied and drift off?"

"No, sir. The sentries never checked the dock until first thing this morning."

# # #

The following evening after dinner, Randolph smoked a cigar on the portico steps. He stared into the cloudless, starlit sky while his puffs of smoke dissipated into thin air and wondered why his feelings of guilt could not do likewise. His tormented mind tried to consider how to write such a tragic letter to Mary and his children.

He contemplated not writing but knew the news would make its way to his family in Baldwin County. It would be but a matter of time.

The soldiers at Camp Spalding still trudged through the thickening mire that surrounded their tents, but campfires returned as did the boisterous chatter across the grounds. Randolph wondered how the soldiers could carry on as usual just two days after the storm wreaked havoc across the island and three of their own brutally killed one of Sapelo's servants and raped another.

Alma spoke hardly a word while serving dinner. Before he left the dining room, their lone conversation pertained to Cecile returning to her own bed in their house. Randolph stressed to Alma that Cecile could remain in his bedroom for as long as she needed. Alma insisted she could provide better care for Cecile and Hector under one roof. Her sorrow and grief remained inward after losing her son and for the irreparable harm done to her daughter's innocence. Randolph noticed that Alma's trademark pleasant smile had lost its luster as did her energetic gait. Though Randolph could sleep in his own bed that night, he resigned himself to find refuge in the library's solitary confines. He found the words to write to his family, but his hand struggled to pen the letter without trembling.

CHAPTER THIRTEEN

3rd of November, 1861

"Feeling sorry for yourself, little brother?" Charles Spalding bellowed, waking his younger brother from his late morning slumber.

"Who in the blue blazes—" Randolph snarled as he rubbed his bloodshot eyes awash in beams of sunshine and rose from his makeshift bed on the library's upholstered Chesterfield. "What are you doing here?" he grumbled before he realized his brother was not alone. Standing in the doorway were Major Levi Knight and Lieutenant Colonel Thomas Alexander, second in command to Randolph and acting commander of the militia companies ordered to Camp Security on the outskirts of Darien.

"Colonel Spalding, these orders and dispatches arrived late last evening from Savannah," Alexander said, stepping forward. "A courier hand-delivered them with word from General Lawton to deliver them to you first thing this morning. Charles and I rode together on the launch from Darien."

Randolph set the letters beside him and glanced at Charles. "Well, I reckon you deserve a hardy thank you, brother," he said while sliding his sock feet into his mud-encrusted boots.

"I wanted to check on you anyway and offer any help." Charles reached inside his tunic and pulled out a string-tied bundle of letters. "Besides, I thought you'd like these. The postmaster said they arrived just before the storm." He flipped through the letters, selected the one from Milledgeville, and sniffed it. "Yep. This is definitely from

Mary. Do you want me to open it for you?"

Randolph unceremoniously leaped up and snatched the letters from Charles's outstretched hand. The letters remained unopened beside General Lawton's dispatches while he tucked his stained flannel shirt into his trousers. As soon as he adjusted his suspenders and sat back down, he motioned for the three to find a seat. "Charles, any chance you saw Alma before you barged in? I could sure use some coffee while I read over General Lawton's correspondence."

"Colonel, when I got up this morning, there were no signs of Alma in the dining hall," said Major Levi Knight. "But I stumbled across a cloth-covered bowl of warm biscuits and a pot of hot coffee on the stove when I checked the cookhouse. Do you want me to scrounge you up some coffee and a biscuit?"

"No thank you, Levi. Please have the sentry grab the coffeepot and some cups. I would rather hear the latest regarding our three murderous deserters and read over what General Lawton sent so urgently."

Randolph opened and read over the sealed dispatches. Still staring at the letter, he spouted, "Gentlemen, it appears Lincoln's military brain trust decided bottlenecking our ports is not enough. They want their forts back. General Lawton has ordered all available militia companies back to Savannah. We are sending reinforcements to bolster South Carolina's defenses around Beaufort. Intelligence reports a massing of the North's naval fleet between Tybee Island and Port Royal Sound."

"Colonel Spalding, are we vacating Sapelo Island?" Major Knight asked.

"No. Not yet, leastwise. Lieutenant Colonel Alexander, you will march your companies to the railhead at Walthourville where you will board the train to Savannah. For now, companies on the island are to heighten their watch." Randolph looked at his brother. "Charles, it appears your cavalry troop will need to expand your patrols to replace the garrison in Darien."

"Is that all, Colonel Spalding?" Charles replied with a smirk. "We've already stretched our patrols pretty thin."

Randolph snarled at his brother. "We'll send additional troops from Camp Spalding to shore up the garrison at Darien as soon as we can." He turned to Lieutenant Colonel Alexander. "I assume none of your patrols found any signs of our three deserters?"

"No, Colonel."

Charles blurted, "Before you ask, neither have any of our patrols."

"Captain Wylly and his men have not returned yet from searching the north end of the island. He believes they are still on the island," Major Knight added.

Randolph sighed. "At this point, I don't care if sharks or gators feasted on them, or they hanged themselves from a tree. I want them or what's left of their bodies found."

"Excuse me, Colonel Spalding. Where do you want me to place this?" The room went silent. A freckled-faced, sandy-haired soldier stood at the library doorway holding a coffeepot in one hand and four mugs gripped by their handles in the other.

Charles motioned to the table near Randolph.

A moment later, Randolph slurped on a mug of lukewarm coffee while he unsealed the second dispatch from Savannah.

"Gentlemen, Savannah requests updated muster rolls for each militia company under our command. Our rag-tag volunteer regiment is officially the 29th Georgia Infantry Regiment assigned to the Confederate Army under General Robert E. Lee. Levi, I will leave it to you to get the muster lists of each militia unit at Camp Spalding. Tom, get the remaining muster rolls directly to headquarters after you arrive in Savannah. Otherwise, you have a thirty-mile march ahead of you. You need to catch the midnight train that will transport you and your men from Walthourville to Savannah. You will receive further orders once you arrive."

"Are you not going with us?"

"Mister Alexander, I will follow you in a day or two. You wanted to lead, so I am giving you the chance to assume command of half of our regiment. Now, let's not waste any more time." Randolph's sternness softened as he turned to his brother. "Charles, you don't mind if I send him on ahead? I'll make sure the launch returns to shuttle you back later this afternoon. We have a few things to talk about."

He wrote a brief letter to General Lawton and signed it *Colonel Randolph Spalding, 29th Georgia Infantry Regiment.* Charles excused himself and ventured into the cookhouse shortly after Alexander and Knight left, allowing Randolph time to read the letters from his wife and Michael Kenan.

By the time Charles returned with a plate of biscuits and piping hot coffee, he found his brother wearing a calico shirt, a vest, and brown tweed trousers. Randolph had washed his unshaven face and combed his wet, shaggy brown hair.

Charles laughed. "What has gotten into you?"

Randolph scoffed, "I need to wash my uniforms. Besides, we're heading to the fields." He put on a tan duster and grabbed his hat. "Come on. Let's talk while we ride to find Allen. He's at Hanging Bull, Barn Creek, or Chocolate. We harvested nearly two hundred bales, but over half remains stacked in our storehouses. Crane and Graybill in Savannah continue to buy what they can squeeze onto their ships bound for England. When I last saw James Graybill in Savannah, he told me his family's ships fly English colors. So far, they've evaded the blockade, allowing much-needed raw cotton to feed their hungry textile mills in England. Allen has also been negotiating a deal for some of our cotton to be shipped to yarn mills in Columbus. He found out the army issued contracts for plain and red-dyed Osnaburg to replace the army's standard issue flannel shirts and undergarments. He is unabashedly calling in family favors. How about you?" Randolph grabbed a biscuit and slurped hot coffee as he headed out of the library, leaving his brother in a lurch.

Charles gulped down his coffee. "We sold a hundred bales, below market, mind you, to Steven Waldrop. Hey, Randolph, wait up!"

"Keep up! We have no time to waste. I want to stop in on Hector and Alma before we saddle our horses."

※ ※ ※

Restless, subtle voices disturbed the otherwise eerie stillness that had settled over Camp Spalding. Soldiers milled about or huddled in small groups near their campfires as they engaged in curious chatter. The morning sun rose above the treetops with a cloudless blue sky overhead. Sapelo's fertile, sandy soil wasted no time lapping up the storm's watery remnants. But the storm left behind a balminess better suited for an early summer day.

Charles struggled to keep pace with his younger brother as they made their way to Hector and Alma's cozy quarters near the barns and livestock pens. Two sentries snapped to attention as Randolph and Charles walked past, though they gawked at Randolph looking like a respected planter rather than their commanding officer. His wide-brimmed, black felt hat alone offered a reminder of his regimental rank.

"Mista Spalding, sir. Can I help you, sir?" Hector inquired, pushing a wheelbarrow of corn toward the hog pens.

"I thought Alma wanted you to stay in bed for a couple more days?"

"Mista Spalding, ain't no one else gonna tend them animals. Sides, that old woman ain't stop cryin' since we put our boy in the ground. I needs to git outta that house."

"How's your girl?" Charles asked.

"Thank you kindly for asking, Mista Charles. I don't rightly know for sure. She ain't talking, just sleeping most of the time."

"Before my brother and I saddle a couple of horses, I need to sit down with you and Alma for a moment," Randolph said, looking eye-to-eye with Hector.

"I reckon, sir. Let me go git her to come outside for a moment."

A minute later, Alma stepped through their front door, her eyes burdened and grief-stricken. She smoothed the wrinkles from her soiled apron to avoid eye contact with Randolph or Charles.

"Alma, I missed you this morning, but then again, I missed a lot this morning until my brother woke me."

Alma glanced up as a light smile struggled to survive the sadness that weighed upon her.

"How's Cecile? I need to write to Sallie and Missus Spalding and hoped you could tell me what to say."

Alma's wide-eyed stare begged Hector to answer. He remained nearby, fidgeting with the brim of his sweetgrass hat with both hands. Hector nodded with a shallow shrug of his shoulder.

Charles spouted, "Alma, I am so sorry about what happened. I remember how much my father liked your poppa and his pa. Your family has been a part of South End from its earliest days. My brother and I pray we will never feel the pain you are experiencing right now."

Alma lost the glimmer of the smile she tried to hold. Hector stepped closer and said, "Thank ya, Mista Spalding, sir." Hector turned to Randolph and added, "I believe you come to talk to me about us leaving our home. Mista Spalding, sir, iffin it be all the same to you, your father promised we would never have to leave this place. It's our home. We buried our boy beside our family at Behavior." Hector shuffled the dirt at his feet, losing eye contact.

"I understand how hard this may be for both of you. I imagine your daughter needs a little time, but I need to keep y'all safe along with all the other families. There's a war headed our way. That's why all these soldiers are here."

Alma peered at Randolph. "Your war done touched our family, and death ain't done wit' us. The great owl hooted from our rooftop last night. More death be coming soon."

"Mister Spalding, sir, she speaks the truth," Hector begged. "Jus' this morn', she throw'd salt and Jeremiah's old shoes into the fireplace." The whites of his eyes jutted as if they were about to pop out of their sockets, captivating Randolph's full attention.

"That's nonsense. Maybe the owl wanted you to know more death will come if you choose to stay. I want your family on the next boat that will take you and others up the river to where Missus Spalding and Mister Kenan are waiting. Once you get there, you'll understand why I am insisting."

"But—"

"No, Hector. It's for your own good. Mister Allen will make sure someone will take care of the livestock after you leave. Major Knight recruited a cook and orderly to take care of my needs at the house."

Alma wiped her tears with her soiled apron. Hector patted her shoulders. "Go on, git back inside. I be along shortly."

Randolph and Charles walked with Hector back to the barn. Hector fed the hogs while Randolph and Charles saddled two horses and rode off.

※ ※ ※

"Allen, you've been one stop ahead of us since we left South End looking for you," Randolph said, leaning down from atop Zapala as Allen stepped from inside Chocolate's barn.

"Funny, I sensed you shadowing me. I got a telegram from Graybill's office. The good news is he's dispatching a ship to stop at High Point on the high tide tomorrow evening to pick up another twenty-five bales."

"What's the bad news?" Charles piped in atop his horse, looking down at Allen with a dubious smirk.

Randolph's incredulous stare required no words.

Allen pulled the telegram from his coat pocket and handed it to Randolph.

Randolph scanned the brief message that followed the good news:

We expect this will be our last order. Sorry. Advise Randolph to visit us when in Savannah.

Randolph took stock of the stacked baled cotton inside Chocolate's barn as he handed the telegram to Charles.

Charles glanced at it, folded it, and returned the message to Randolph. "Well, we both sensed the inevitable. Damn Mister Lincoln. Damn all those Northern hypocrites. Where do they think all those New England textile mills are going to get the cotton needed to feed their looms? It does not take a genius to know Mister Lincoln's blockade will shut down the North's textile industry. Folks are sure to lose their jobs and livelihoods once the supply of quality Southern cotton can no longer get to market. Worse yet, nothing will stop England from looking elsewhere once our cotton can't reach them. Prices are sure to go sky-high, too."

Randolph nodded. "Damn those ignorant Yankee abolitionists. They are too busy pushing their ideals without considering the consequences. Father predicted the slave trade would end, but not this way. He talked about new scientific agricultural methods and innovation eventually displacing the need for cheap slave labor, but intolerant partisan idealism and stupidity make a dangerous combination. It does more harm than good."

"Amen, Randolph," Allen said. "You can add greed to that as well. Such an ill-conceived concoction claims no boundaries. Planters, such as your father, strived to make life better for all who had a hand in their prosperity, but far too many Southern landowners succumbed to either insatiable greed or unrelenting frustration. They inflicted pain and suffering on the very souls who brought about the bounty of their fields. They reaped the wrath of those Northern bleeding hearts seethed all the more by abolitionist propaganda promoting the worst tales to stir partisan outrage."

Randolph crumpled the message from James Graybill and tossed it to the ground. He pointed at the bales of cotton stacked inside. Tears of defeat swept over him.

"Brother, I do not know what you think, but I believe Sapelo blessed us with its last harvest. Once we remove the last of our workers off the island, Sapelo's rich fields will remain fallow. Only memories sown by the wind and rain will remain on Sapelo after that day."

"You paint a fatalistic vision of the future, brother," Charles said, staring at Randolph, who remained fixated on the barn.

Allen grabbed Zapala's bridle, stirring a snort from his flared nostrils. Randolph instinctively tightened his grip on the reins as he broke his trance.

"Are you all right, Randolph?" Allen asked.

"Yeah," Randolph uttered. How could he confess to his older brother and his brother-in-law the depth of the disappointment weighing on him? He thought about his father and his son, Tom.

"If this will cheer you up, Michael's negroes from Kenan Fields will be ready by the time he arrives to escort them up the Altamaha and Oconee to Milledgeville next week. We moved what little cotton and other crops left from the Kenan Fields to South End and Chocolate."

"That is good news. Charles brought me a letter from Michael this morning. He'll be on board the *George M. Troup* when it docks in Darien on the tenth."

"Why the long face, brother?" Charles asked. "Did you write to headquarters yet requesting leave to visit Mary and the kids?"

"No, not yet. There have been more pressing matters to attend to. And of this morning, I'll be able to address the question face-to-face in a couple of days."

The sound of horses interrupted Randolph.

"Uncle Randolph, am I glad we found you here with Uncle Charles and Allen," Captain Thomas Wylly said after his horse pulled alongside Zapala. "We now know without a doubt the three Ochlocknee deserters absconded a boat at High Point. They hornswoggled two of our dock workers. They told them you ordered them to take a bateau and patrol around Blackbeard's Island."

The four other mounted soldiers with Captain Wylly watered their horses in the trough near the barn while he reported to Randolph and Charles.

"They must have been pretty convincing," Allen spouted. "Word has spread like wildfire up and down the island about what happened to Jeremiah and Cecile. I would not give you a sack of rocks for the lives of those three if anyone realized who they were."

Randolph snarled, "God almighty! Thomas, did the boys on the dock have any idea where they're really headed?"

"They inquired about Saint Catherine's Island before they rowed away," Wylly chuckled.

"What's so funny?"

"The dock hands wondered if they could handle the bateau without capsizing or getting caught in the current and washed out to sea. As soon as we get something to eat, do you want me to take the *Sarah Spalding* out to see if we can find them?"

"Good idea. Maybe you can drop me off at the Ridge before you circle back," Charles said, staring at his brother and nephew.

Randolph and Charles joined their nephew and his men and headed back to South End. Allen Bass returned to loading cotton bales on wagons to be hauled to High Point's dock and loaded on Graybill's ship when it arrived.

CHAPTER FOURTEEN

4th of November, 1861

Randolph awoke well before sunrise with a primal sense of urgency. What if the report of the federal warships massing off South Carolina had been but a ruse? Had the day Randolph feared arrived when Georgia's troops no longer needed to travel north? Had the war arrived on Georgia's doorstep?

He climbed out of bed and opened his door. "Orderly! Orderly! Go tell Major Knight to report to me out front as soon as he gets dressed."

Minutes later, Randolph buttoned his double-breasted, blue uniform tunic as he stepped out onto the portico. Major Knight greeted him along with the four company commanders on the island.

"Major Knight, you've got the most experience. What do you make of the report about Port Royal?"

"Colonel, all I can say with any certainty is I cannot comprehend the Union fleet launching a head-on assault against Savannah. Forts Pulaski, McAllister, and Jackson would wreak havoc on their ships. I speculate the target may in fact be Port Royal with Beaufort as its prize."

"I agree. Have any of our outposts reported seeing any Union ships?" Randolph asked, surveying each of the captains whispering amongst themselves.

"No, Colonel. I would recommend reinforcing the batteries and stepping up our patrols as a precaution?"

"Yes, let's do that first thing this morning, Major. Instruct the patrols to stay off the beaches, and the batteries are not to open fire unless fired upon. No sense in instigating a fight. In the meantime, dispatch a courier to sail straightaway to Darien to catch any news coming across at the telegraph office. I'll give him a letter he can give to my brother."

"Very well, sir," the grizzled major said like a resolute, battle-hardened veteran.

"Captain Wylly, please give me a moment before you head off," Randolph said he watched the other officers follow Major Knight, who looked like a father instructing his sons about to join him on their first hunting adventure. Whenever Levi pointed, one of the overeager captains left his side. As a chiseled veteran of the Seminole campaigns along the Georgia-Florida border two decades earlier, Levi Knight also had the sway and confidence of a wily, revered politician.

"Thomas, I have not had the opportunity since you got back from searching for those deserters to ask about your family. How're they doing?" Randolph asked once they stood alone.

"Johanna's proud British heritage argues that England will not abandon their ties with the South. She understands the significance of our cotton getting to their textile mills. Otherwise, she knows she can do little to change what's happening and keeps busy caring for Lilly. I'm sure you recall how pampered four-year-old daughters can behave. As for Mother and Father, they appear to be holding up but are growing uneasy. This news will certainly add to their concerns over what the future holds."

"Were they able to get their harvest to market?"

"No. Our barns are just as full as everyone else's, making my brothers anxious about volunteering to fight. They figure they can single-handedly drive the Yankees back to where they belong. I will not repeat their colorful opinions of Mister Abraham Lincoln, either."

"Didn't your brother A.C. already enlist?"

"He's riding with Captain Newbern and the Coffee Revengers. So Mother is trying to convince William to wait a while longer, but I'm pretty sure he'll wind up in uniform if the fighting threatens Georgia. He thinks being nineteen makes him a full-grown man."

"I reckon he's a lot like his older brother," Randolph said, laughing.

Thomas grinned, swaying his head. "God, I hope not. Anyhow, William heard what happened on the island with Jeremiah and Cecile. He shared his anger over it and promised to take our launch out and spread the word amongst the planters along the Sapelo River."

"Thanks, Thomas. You best get with your men. I'm going to see if Alma left any coffee for me in the cookhouse. This is going to be a long day, a very long day. I wonder how Lieutenant Colonel Alexander and his companies made out. They should have their orders by now and are likely headed to South Carolina."

※ ※ ※

Randolph visited Camp Spalding's mess tent to grab some coffee after discovering neither hide nor hair of Alma, Hector, or Cecile at their house or South End's barns. Randolph saddled Zapala, preparing to ride out to the lighthouse and visit the artillery batteries and outposts along the shoreline. The soldiers guarding Sapelo no longer moped and meandered about with heads hanging from the tireless monotony that had plagued Camp Spalding since shortly after they'd arrived. The sobering realization of why they occupied Sapelo Island showed on their faces.

Detachments headed out from Camp Spalding prepared to sleep under the stars rather than beneath their tents' canvas roofs. Tin mess kits clanged as militia units scurried into formation while platoon leaders barked, "Fall in!" Junior field officers shouted instructions above the stomping and clanging as they readied their units to march to their designated posts. Wide-eyed privates did their best to mimic the calm, unwavering appearances of the older soldiers the moment they heard, "Platoon, forward, march!" Randolph watched, perched in his saddle beside Major Knight on his. He had previously watched soldiers march in formation at the Camp of Instruction in Savannah, but today had nothing to do with mindless drills.

"With your permission, Colonel Spalding, I'll follow the men north and report back if enemy gunships appear. Would you mind watching over the men getting settled out on Lighthouse Point? Mister Hazard might get rattled with all the activity going on out there," Major Knight said, though his eyes remained trained on each platoon as they marched out from Camp Spalding.

Randolph patted Zapala's neck with one hand and gripped the reins tightly in the other. He watched one company march toward the mainland side of the island.

"Where are they headed?"

"Captain Rockwell has orders to disperse his platoons to patrol the landings along the Duplin River. Captain Wylly and his company will march to the north end of the island to secure High Point and to patrol from Mud River to the back inlet on Blackbeard Island."

Randolph nodded his approval. "I'll check on Mister Hazard and see about climbing to the lighthouse catwalk." Zapala snorted and clopped his hooves when Randolph pulled on the reins. "I hope the courier we sent over to Darien brings back some news before nightfall about what's happening. Looks like it'll be pretty lonely tonight around Camp Spalding."

"Our surgeon and his men will keep you company if you wish. They will be in camp tending the sick. Captain Lamb assigned one platoon to handle sentry duty at South End. My son, Lieutenant Knight, will remain behind and be at your disposal," Major Knight said, grinning through his gray-streaked beard.

※ ※ ※

At dusk, the courier arrived back from Darien with an urgent telegram from Savannah and the latest news about a possible naval assault on Port Royal. The courier stammered as he apologized for his delayed return. The telegraph office in Darien bristled all day with unsettling reports about troops headed to shore up Port Royal's defenses as the fleet of Northern gunboats and warships anchored just beyond the mouth of the Broad River.

"Colonel, sir, I stayed as long as I could. Lieutenant Colonel Spalding of the First Cavalry and some of his officers waited like me outside the cramped telegraph office along with a congregation of curious citizens. He gave me this dispatch from Savannah and told me to tell you, 'Sapelo can take care of itself.' He said you'd understand and ordered me to return." The dog-tired older corporal handed Randolph, who had collapsed with buckled knees on South End's portico steps, the dispatch before he saluted then begged his leave.

"Of course, Corporal. You did well. Go get some chow and hot coffee. Stay in camp. I may need you later." Randolph returned his salute, though his attention turned to the dispatch from Savannah.

General Lawton's letter informed him of what he already had known to be true. General Robert E. Lee was now commanding all Confederate forces defending South Carolina, Georgia, and Florida. Also, Brigadier General William Henry Talbot Walker took over as the commander of Georgia's army assigned to defend Savannah. Randolph knew little of Walker other than his reputation as a no-nonsense firebrand. Though he hailed from Augusta, he was a career army officer and West Point graduate. After his controversial resignation from his command in Virginia, though, Governor Brown had given him a commission in the Georgia Army beneath General Lawton.

Lawton wrote:

> *Situation at Port Royal, to my personal regret and loss, growing untenable without added Georgia reinforcements. Come immediately with two companies from the complement of your regiment still on Sapelo. Expect further orders upon arrival in Savannah.*

Randolph growled out loud as he crumpled the letter. "Father, what am I supposed to do?"

A salvo of cannon and rifle fire sounded across the island. Randolph jumped to his feet. Soldiers in the camp grabbed their rifles and looked toward the beach, their heads on a swivel, glancing at Randolph as he walked among them equally startled. Major Levi Knight rode his horse at full gallop from the beach road into camp. Randolph raced up and grabbed the horse's bridle as an out-of-breath Levi dismounted. "Colonel, my apologies. A Union gunboat cruised too close to Cabretta Island. The lads at the north end battery opened fire. The gunship returned fire before turning tail and heading back into deeper water."

"What about the rifle shots?"

Levi began laughing. "As soon as that Yankee ship turned about, several of our brave lads ran whooping and hollering onto the beach and discharged their rifles."

"Anyone injured in the exchange?" Randolph asked. His look let Levi know he saw no humor in the incident.

"No, Colonel. Though, I believe it rallied the spirits of the men to feel finally engaged in this war."

Levi's attempt to soothe Randolph's obvious annoyance failed. Randolph blurted, "You realize Sapelo is now going to be a target of future incursions by Yankee gunboats and warships to determine our strength and positions on the island?"

"Begging the Colonel's pardon, the men have been on pins and needles since early this morning. With few exceptions, our ranks are full of young men who have never fired their rifles in anger, much less in a war. For the first time, they saw the faces of their enemy manning the decks on that gunboat. They felt in imminent danger. They acted pretty darn well if I say so myself."

Randolph huffed. "I did not ask your opinion, Levi, but I understand your point. My apologies. General Lawton ordered me to bring two companies immediately to Savannah as Fort Walker on Hilton Head needs reinforcements."

"Randolph, what the Sam Hill is happening?" Allen Bass hollered as he rode his ornery gray mule.

The sight of Allen gasping with his dark, wide eyes glaring back caused both Randolph and Levi to burst into laughter, breaking the tension of the moment. "Allen, give me a second," Randolph said, holding one hand up. "Major, please return to the men at the Cabretta battery. Tell the gunners that their actions were understandable and commendable, but please only fire when they can see the colors of the enemy's eyes in the future. We do not want any unnecessary lives lost by hasty actions on our part. I'll get word to Captains Rockwell and Wylly to have their men ready to leave tonight."

Major Knight mounted his horse and galloped off.

"Allen, get down and walk with me. Today has reminded me how urgently we must get everyone off this island."

His brother-in-law tied his mule to a nearby post. As they meandered back to *Big House*, Allen told Randolph he'd found another cook and a couple of workers to handle the livestock in South End's barns for the time being. He also shared that he had not seen or heard anything about Hector and his family. He then gave Randolph the list of names of who would join Michael Kenan for the trip to Milledgeville. They were all from either the Kenan estate or South End and included Hector, Alma, and Cecile.

Randolph reminded Allen to make sure none of the island's negroes were to wander anywhere near the beaches or boat landings. Allen informed Randolph of the restlessness growing among the workers on the island. Rumors had spread about the war coming to Sapelo. Some pondered whether they would be better off staying on the island rather than leaving.

Allen shook his head and said, "Some argued they'd be free and could leave the island on their own if Northern soldiers arrived on Sapelo. Others feared the thought of Yankees coming to the island if they stayed."

Randolph nodded, absorbing how his orders from Savannah would affect their plans. "Allen, do you think you can manage without me here to pester you?"

"What in the blue blazes are you saying?"

Randolph told him about his orders to report to Savannah and that he was unsure how long he would be away. Allen reluctantly agreed after Randolph assured him Major Knight would be in command of the remaining militia on the island and would help when Michael Kenan and the boat arrived to load the designated workers and their family members.

※ ※ ※

That evening, Randolph ate a hardy supper alongside the two companies of soldiers who would accompany him to Savannah with the prospect of facing the enemy on Hilton Head Island in South Carolina. They asked a lot of questions, though he averted aggravating their obvious growing fears. He yearned to temper his own apprehensions with a stiff drink or two but instead washed the cook's hoecakes and bean soup down with plenty of coffee.

Randolph, for the first time, felt a burning desire to get to know each of the soldiers. Most hailed from small yeomen farms that had sprung up throughout the barren Georgia-Florida Wiregrass flatlands. A handful boasted of wives, and fewer still boasted of children. Most talked about their parents and sweethearts back home.

An emboldened, taller-than-most, blonde sergeant spoke up when Randolph asked how they felt about the sounds of the cannons they had heard earlier in the day.

"Colonel, if I may speak plainly, it's been hard not knowing what's happening up north. The mere thought of fighting going on everywhere but here makes my blood boil all the more. Why are we stuck here while others face the thick of battle?"

All eyes turned to Randolph.

"A much bigger plan is underway. You, me, and all the men on this island are but a part of that plan. Like you, my blood boils from time to time. My blood gets riled when I think of my family being uprooted and miles away. My blood gets riled when I wake up each morning and stare at the trampled state of my family's home and all the mud and dirt where once flowered, green grounds existed. My blood gets riled knowing each of you has had to leave your homes and loved ones. My blood boils over knowing how engrained pride and prejudice started this war." Randolph stared into the darkness and seethed before composing himself.

Two quick blasts of a ship's horn rang out from Marsh Landing. He stiffened his jaw, rose to his feet, and said, "Captains Rockwell and Wylly, gather your men. Two steamboats are waiting to take us to Hilton Head Island before daybreak. Once ashore, we will join Colonel Styles's Brunswick Regiment and head for Fort Walker."

※ ※ ※

Right after daybreak, Randolph and his two regimental companies scurried along a wagon trail that skirted Hilton Head's exposed unharvested cotton fields on one side and dense undergrowth beneath tall pines on the other. Each step brought his men closer to where cannon shells from circling Union warships and gunboats bombarded Fort Walker's earthen walls. The pungent smell of sulfur hung in the smoke-filled air, hovering like a foul-smelling morning fog across Hilton Head Island.

Colonel Spalding and his men spread out on the edge of the open, untended cotton fields that separated them from the suffocating barrage of cannon fire unleashed by the Union ships cluttering Port Royal Sound. They could see that Fort Walker's artillery no longer returned fire. Instead, soldiers from Fort Walker scurried out from the battered earthen fort across the barren and exposed cotton fields. Colonel Styles and his men cheered and waved the survivors toward their position in the thickets along the road beyond the Union Navy's cannon onslaught that began at daybreak.

Lieutenant Colonel Alexander and his men from the 29th Georgia Infantry remained dispersed and dug in behind the grassy sand dunes. Yankee longboats ferried soldiers toward the shore. When Alexander's men opened fire with their rifles, gunboats hurled mortar rounds at their positions. Randolph led his two militia companies closer but kept them hidden along Hilton Head's dense wooded undergrowth, though they maneuvered closer to where Alexander and his men remained pinned down.

The gunboats ceased launching mortars among the sand dunes as soon as dozens of Yankee longboats came ashore near tattered Fort Walker. Alexander stood and ordered his men to leave their positions. They ran across the open fields as Yankee soldiers opened fire from the beach. Mortar rounds landed behind Alexander and his men, sending clouds of sand high into the air.

Skirmishes broke out as more Yankee soldiers arrived on shore and advanced toward Fort Walker. Colonel Styles and his men kept the enemy soldiers busy while Colonel Spalding and his two companies provided cover fire as Alexander and his men raced for cover. Many of the frightened young soldiers left their haversacks and bedrolls behind and scooted through the cotton fields like scared rabbits.

Hunkered down behind a sprawling oak tree, Captain Thomas Wylly whispered, "Randolph, stay low, and for God's sake stay behind me." He pressed down on his uncle's shoulder with one hand as he peered at Lieutenant Colonel Alexander's men bolting helter-skelter past them. "We do not need to be shot by our own soldiers."

Randolph shoved his nephew's hand off his shoulder. He stood and ordered Wylly's Berrien Militia to continue providing cover fire while Captain Rockwell and his Thomasville Guard created a perimeter along the road to collect the retreating soldiers. Randolph found a grave Lieutenant Colonel Alexander sitting at the base of a pine tree, his attention fixed on his blood-stained hands.

"Are you wounded?" Randolph asked, kneeling beside Alexander.

Alexander looked at Randolph with a blank stare. "Sergeant Culver."

"What about Sergeant Culver?"

Alexander wiped his cheeks with his coat sleeve. "A mortar

round got him. He was kneeling beside me when it landed. I had to leave him behind."

"Was he dead?"

"I couldn't stop the bleeding. I think so."

"Sorry to hear that. Was he from your hometown?"

Alexander nodded, staring at the blood on his hands.

Following the brief exchange of fire with the Union troops who pursued the retreating Confederates, Randolph's other officers reported mostly superficial casualties among the ranks in his regiment. The Yankees pulled back and appeared content to occupy Fort Walker while more longboats offloaded men and equipment.

The Union assault against Fort Walker repelled him and his regiment the entire length of the island before they were rescued. His harrowing, miraculous escape inducted him into the bloody reality of battle. Like the soldiers under him, he had loaded and fired his Enfield rifle almost blindly during the regiment's hasty retreat. The smell of death etched itself in Randolph's memory that day.

Instinctively, he fingered the frayed blue fibers of the bullet hole in the bottom flap of his tunic. He couldn't recall when or how it happened, but he thanked God Mary wouldn't have to don black like the so many women who'd lost sons, husbands, or fathers that day.

Randolph earned renewed respect from his men when he fired his Enfield rifle during several brief rounds of cover fire while the regiment retreated to safety on the southern end of Hilton Head. By midnight, the wounded were receiving medical care on board a small flotilla of crowded steamboats.

Randolph and Thomas Wylly sat with Alexander near the water's edge chewing on their rations of hardtack, the first bite they'd had to eat since arriving on Hilton Head. They swapped details about their perilous day. Alexander described the events of the Union's initial naval artillery assault that began before daybreak and, for all intents and purposes, ended not long after Randolph arrived with his two companies from their regiment.

"Our regiment had arrived early yesterday and took up positions along the shoreline. By late morning, the non-stop shelling obliterated Fort Walker's walls. We found ourselves helpless and exposed as they began shelling the beach. We lost several men, but it could have been much worse. When word came that the fort had been vacated, I ordered a retreat. That's when Sergeant Culver got hit. I cannot remember ever running so fast after that happened."

Thomas Wylly said, "by the sounds of it, you and your men were very fortunate."

"Thomas," Randolph said, patting Alexander on his shoulder, "what happened at Port Royal over the past couple of days should not dishearten nor discourage but, instead, ignite the fires of unconquerable determination within every man, woman, and child who reads about the harrowing accounts of this battle. There'll be far more victories than setbacks in the weeks and months ahead."

By daybreak, a bevy of steamboats headed back to Savannah and sailed past Fort Pulaski, leaving the handful of dead behind. Lieutenant Colonel Alexander and most of the 29th Georgia Infantry Regiment remained in Savannah while Randolph returned with the two companies he'd brought up from Sapelo. Though the stench of battle clung to their hair and uniforms, Randolph had discovered courage he'd previously doubted he could muster. Coming face to face with death on the battlefield sobered him. He knew he had to do more. The North would soon be treading upon Georgia soil.

CHAPTER FIFTEEN

12th of November, 1861

A day later than expected, Allen Bass handed Michael Kenan the list of names for those due to make the first trip up the Altamaha and Oconee Rivers to Baldwin County. The *George M. Troup* arrived after offloading regular passengers and cargo in Darien before docking at Sapelo's Marsh Landing dock. Nearly one hundred passengers, along with sundry planting tools and supplies from Kenan's property on Sapelo, stood in line to board the first of three such contracted trips to take place over the next two months.

Captain Roberson observed the orderly but glum queue of slaves dressed in their best threadbare clothes for the journey from his perch in the wheelhouse as they made their way onto his boat. The line crept forward as each worker and family member slunk one-by-one across the narrow gangplank when Allen Bass called out their names. Michael Kenan confirmed their names as they stepped off the gangplank onto the steamboat's foredeck. After he checked their name off his manifest, he instructed each to take their bundle of clothing and move toward the rear along either side of the main or upper deck. Most of the wary-eyed passengers had been born, worked, and lived their entire lives on Sapelo. While the children laughed and giggled among themselves, their mommas and poppas appeared circumspect about leaving the only home they had known. The oldest workers who remembered the promises Thomas Spalding made to them or their parents held long faces, some filled with tears from sad, reddened eyes. Thomas Spalding's promises of permanence and place on Sapelo for the workers who'd invested their lives through daily toil in its fields meant little any longer.

Captain Thomas Wylly and Colonel Randolph Spalding stood behind Michael Kenan and watched the orderly loading from the rail of the boat's foredeck while Kenan accomplished his diligent task unabated. Randolph admired Michael's calming and reassuring presence as he welcomed each man, woman, and child on board with their varying degrees of anticipation and trepidation. Randolph's return after experiencing a taste of the war brought about a noticeable change in him. He arrived back stone-faced and expounded little when asked about the bloodshed he'd witnessed for the first time in his otherwise cocksure, sheltered life. When not engaged with others, he appeared far removed in thought and locked in a dark, distant gaze.

Tobacco smoke swirled above the surly old captain's head as he puffed on his pipe when not barking orders to his crew. He kept a keen eye on the tide, wanting to shove off long before it changed. Reports of the island's recent run-in with a Union gunboat added to Captain Roberson's vigilant watch. Shade, Elex, and Moses, his experienced crew of three, unloaded and secured four ox-driven wagonloads of tools and supplies on the afterdeck. Allen Bass had carefully identified each barrel, bundle, cask, and crate on the separate manifest that Shade, Captain Roberson's pilot, diligently checked. All three crew members were slaves themselves, belonging to Freeman Rowe, one of the boat's principal owners. Elex served as the cook while Moses kept the boiler fired when underway. Otherwise, all three shared on-deck duties.

With the last passengers checked off the manifest, Randolph and Thomas followed Michael Kenan across the gangplank and back onto the dock. Thomas and Michael greeted Allen Bass with hardy handshakes and congratulatory smiles.

"It appears Hector, Alma, and Cecile remain unaccounted for," Randolph said, sounding remorseful as he rested his hands on Allen's and Michael's shoulders. His words reflected dejection, not a sense of relief at seeing the first boatload of the island's innocent residents ready to depart Sapelo.

"I'm sorry, Randolph," Allen said. "Sapelo's secrets remain Sapelo's secrets when these folks wish to protect Sapelo's secrets. Hector and his family just ain't gonna leave until they are good and ready to do so."

The afterdeck's cargo boom hoisted the rear gangplank from the dock just as Captain Roberson shouted after two long blasts from the ship's whistle, "Prepare to cast off as soon as Mister Kenan boards."

Randolph waved at the captain. He then looked at Allen and said, "I understand about Sapelo swallowing its secrets. It's been that way for as long as I can remember. My father said the same thing whenever something or someone turned up missing for a spell on the island. He rarely got upset when everyone went mum or played ignorant to protect others. So, I should respond likewise. I got nobody to blame but me. Hector'll make his whereabouts and intentions known when he's good and ready, not a moment sooner." Randolph sighed as he glanced up toward the main road that led back to South End.

"Uncle, don't be hard on yourself. What happened was not your fault. The way I look at it, what took place could have turned out far worse if it wasn't for you," Thomas Wylly said.

"From what Allen shared, Thomas is right," Michael Kenan interjected. "You could not have known the hate boiling in those three boys' hearts. What they did went well beyond the pale. Nonetheless, I hate to say this, but being a hunted army deserter is far more serious than killing a negro boy or brutally raping a negro girl. Hell, Randolph, they're likely to get hanged or shot either way," Michael Kenan growled in disgust.

"Be that as it may, getting executed for desertion offers no justice for Jeremiah's death or for what they did to Cecile. Nor will it bring peace to Hector or Alma nor my conscience," Randolph seethed.

"Justice will not come until Hector and Alma say those three miscreants got what they deserved for inflicting the loss and pain they brought to them."

Michael Kenan stared into Randolph's tired, dark eyes. "Listen to me. On top of the bloody horror you just went through on Hilton Head, you have been carrying far too heavy a burden on your shoulders. You have wangled yourself into a real quandary. You want what's best for your family's legacy on Sapelo and for the workers and their families who have spent their lives on it, and now you're serving as commander of the soldiers sent here to defend it. All the while, an invading enemy's army and navy threaten to destroy it all. Worst of all, you're trying to live in the shadow of Thomas Spalding."

Michael straightened his back and folded his arms across his chest. "Though you and I are brothers-in-law, I've known you since you were running around in knickers on South End. Allen here has known you since before you married his sister. Likewise, Thomas might be your nephew, but he's not much younger than you, and the two of you are like brothers. So, take our concerted, brotherly advice. Remove yourself from Sapelo's grip while you still can. Spend time with Mary and your children. Whether our glorious Confederate States of America prevails in this God-forsaken struggle or not, your family is a sight more valuable than all the harvests this cursed island may ever produce."

Before Randolph could say a word, Michael pounded his chest and added, "And there's not a living soul on this island or the mainland who carries Spalding blood who'll say differently. Your father and mother, God rest their souls, found strength in their love of family. That is the legacy you should embrace and preserve."

Allen patted Michael's back. "Here, here! I wish I had said that."

"Uncle Michael, you need to head back on board," Thomas shouted above another blast from the steamboat's horn as he looked up at Captain Roberson's scowl in the wheelhouse.

Randolph embraced Michael. "Give my wife and sister a hug for me." He reached into his tunic and pulled out a letter. "Lord, I almost forgot. Please give this to Mary. Tell them I will do my best to be there before Christmas."

"I will tell them." Michael Kenan slid the letter into his coat's side pocket and adjusted his hat. "Captain Roberson will return in three weeks. Then, if we are lucky and our defenses keep the Union forces bottled up on the South Carolina coast, the third and final trip will bring you to Milledgeville before Christmas."

"For what this is costing us, let us not neglect Allen. He needs to see Charlie as well." Randolph shook Michael's hand before his brother-in-law hopped from the dock onto the deck of the *George M. Troup*. A moment later, the boat's paddlewheel churned the muddy water frothy white as the steamboat eased away from Marsh Landing's pier. The trek up the Altamaha and Oconee Rivers would require a week to reach its destination in Baldwin County.

※ ※ ※

"Uncle, I brought the latest copy of the newspaper from Savannah," Captain Wylly said as he entered *Big House's* dining room. "I see you've a new cook and housekeeper," he added as he glanced at the elderly female servant.

"Lord, yes in deedy. I sent the mess cook back to the camp's mess tent. His biscuits could've been better used as cannonballs, and his grits could be plaster on tabby walls," Randolph said. He then offered a half-hearted chuckle before gulping his coffee. "Have a seat and join me for a little breakfast."

The new cook, who Allen had recruited from the slave community at South End, poured coffee for Captain Wylly and fixed him a plate of biscuits with fried slabs of bacon on the side. "Mister Wylly, sir, can I gits you anything else?"

Thomas waved her off with an obliging smile. He waited while the cook exited the room and headed back to the cookhouse. His lighthearted smile disappeared as he said, "My family's in big trouble. Father's unable to raise enough money to pay the back taxes he owes. To make matters worse, Billy enlisted. Though he'll ride with Brailsford's troop at Sutherland Bluff and be under Uncle Charles's watchful eye, all the same, that leaves James, my youngest brother, to help father and mother. How much help can a ten-year-old boy be? The cotton harvest hasn't reaped enough money to cover the taxes."

Randolph rocked back in his chair. "Have you heard from your other brothers?"

"Last I heard, Alex and his regiment headed off to join the fight in Virginia. Charles is somewhere in South Carolina."

"How's your wife and daughter fairing?"

"Johanna is trying to help where and when she can, but she's got her hands full with Lilly. Johanna wants to take her away if I can't be around to take care of them and help my parents. I think her stiff upper lip English upbringing is failing her. My sister Sarah even begged me to stay before I rode off last night. She told me how mother cries herself to sleep every night while my father broods all alone by the fireplace worrying over the family's future."

"Thomas, between Charles and me, we can help with your family's tax debt. Beyond that, we all are facing uncertain times. Lilly's younger than Bourke. I understand Johanna getting upset with you for your daughter's sake. You can do more by defending your family's future right here for the time being."

Thomas leaned forward, put his elbows on the table, slurped his coffee, and gazed blindly at the far wall. "Read the front page of the paper I brought you."

Randolph fell silent as he scanned the articles.

"As long as the blockade keeps Savannah and Charleston bottled up, the cotton merchants will not accept any further shipments. Their storehouses and docks are overflowing. How in heaven's name can any of the planters up and down the coast recoup what they've invested in this year's harvest?" Thomas huffed.

"Listen to me," Randolph said, looking up from the paper. "We are all in this together. Allen already told me as much about our cotton harvest. However, it's a little harder to swallow when I see many of our longtime business acquaintances listed in the article supporting this cotton embargo." Randolph rattled the pages of the paper to break Thomas's fixed look. "Did you see where they wrote about General Robert E. Lee arriving back in Savannah?" Randolph hesitated to find the date of the article. "Let me see . . . three days ago. The report also tells of Brigadier General William H. T. Walker's commission from Governor Brown to aid in Georgia's defense."

"How's that news going to soothe the nerves back home at The Forest?" Thomas snarled.

"Robert E. Lee's return to Savannah sounds like change is coming with him. I think I'm going to run back up to Savannah and see what I can find out before I request Lawton's approval for a few days to visit Mary and my family in Milledgeville. While there, I'll do my best to catch the direction of the wind before it blows our way again and Lieutenant Colonel Alexander and the rest of our regiment get redeployed around Savannah." Randolph folded the newspaper and dropped it on top of his half-eaten breakfast before he rose from his chair.

"What can I do?" Thomas asked, also rising from the table.

"Find Major Knight. Tell him I am going back to Savannah and want him to stop to see me this afternoon."

"Where's he now?"

"This is an island! Somewhere with the men along the coast, I imagine."

CHAPTER SIXTEEN

2nd of December, 1861

"Randolph! Is that you in there?"

"Yes, it's me. Put your pistol away." Randolph opened the back door to his house below the Ridge. "William, what are you doing here?"

"I was about to ask the same thing of you?" William holstered his sidearm.

"This is still my house, last I recollected," Randolph said, tugging on his leather suspender straps.

"Uncle Charles told me to check here. He figured you might have stopped here before heading back to Sapelo. Not to mention, Major Knight reported you were three days overdue arriving back from Savannah." Captain William Brailsford snarled, "Damn, Randolph! My entire troop has been out looking for you since yesterday. There have been reports of Yankee spies between here and Savannah. We thought you might've got bushwhacked or something."

"Well, I needed an extra day or so before getting back to Sapelo. I brought back a lot to sort out in my head. Since I arrived well after midnight, Zapala and I both deserved a break."

William turned and whistled loud enough that Zapala whinnied and snorted from the stable. A moment later, Lieutenant Billy Wylly, Thomas Wylly's nineteen-year-old brother, rode from the back of the house to where Randolph and William stood on the porch.

Billy tipped his hat and grinned but remained on his horse. "Uncle Randolph, I sure am glad to see you, sir."

"Enough of the pleasantries, Billy. Go find Uncle Charles and tell him we found Randolph."

Young Wylly yanked on his horse's reins and galloped off, headed to Ridge Road.

Randolph smiled at William. "How about some coffee?"

"Sure, and maybe you can tell me the latest goings-on up in Savannah. We hear Yankee troops have taken Tybee Island."

Church bells rang out in the distance from the Ridge as they sat and drank coffee in the parlor. Randolph told his nephew how upset General Lawton became over the news his childhood hometown of Beaufort fell so quickly into Union hands. He also talked about meeting Brigadier General Walker while accompanying General Lawton and General Lee at Fort Jackson. Walker had recently resigned his command in Virginia and returned home to Augusta before he received the command of the Third Georgia Brigade and military commandant of Savannah Defenses. He told Brailsford how the three generals whooped and hollered seeing the English steamship *Fingal* sail past while on the ramparts at Fort Jackson. The ship maneuvered undaunted through the Union blockade and slipped past the North's artillery now occupying Tybee Island. Later that morning, the ship had offloaded much-needed military munitions, arms, and supplies.

After talking in detail about his meetings with the generals, Randolph's mood changed. He turned serious. "William, you'll hear about this soon enough. General Walker talked with me at great length about finding available staff officers. Before I left, he asked me to join his staff as his adjutant on Lawton's recommendation."

Brailsford glared at Randolph. "What did you tell him? What about Sapelo and Camp Spalding and your regimental command?"

"After listening to the generals for three days, it's only a matter of how soon the militia abandons the barrier islands. Savannah's defenses are the priority with the Union moving men and artillery closer to the city. With Port Royal in the hands of federal forces,

General Lee expects Savannah and Charleston to be their next targets. Lee also fears Port Royal provides the Yankees with a strategic deep-water base to ramp up their naval presence up and down the southern seacoast."

"You did not answer my question."

"The way Walker put it, it was not if I accepted but how soon I could resign my regimental command. Walker understands my conflicting situation on Sapelo Island. He gave me written orders to join him in Savannah at the end of the month. I conceded that will allow sufficient time for Allen and me to finish what needs to be done to evacuate Sapelo and still spend Christmas with Mary and the kids in Milledgeville."

"So, what now?"

"I need to talk to Charles and Allen. While in Savannah, I learned the *George M. Troup* is due to be commissioned into the Confederate Navy. We won't have time to find another steamer. We're going to have to manage with the *George M. Troup* making one last run."

Lieutenant Billy Wylly returned. "Uncle Randolph, Uncle Charles requested you meet him and Major Knight at Ashantilly. Aunt Evelyn is setting an extra place for you to have Sunday dinner with them. He also said he has news about the missing soldiers."

"Billy, did Uncle Charles say what kind of news?"

He hesitated to answer Brailsford's inquiry.

"Billy, what did he say about the soldiers we've been looking for? Did they find them?" Randolph pleaded.

"I think so, sir. Well, kinda."

"What do you mean, kinda? Billy, what did Uncle Charles tell you?" Brailsford snapped.

"Uncle Charles said he dispatched a boat to Saint Catherine's Island to check out a report of what sounded like High Point's missing bateau on the beach. The crew found the bodies of two soldiers near where the boat lay upside down in the sand," Young Wylly said.

"What about the third soldier?" Randolph asked.

Billy Wylly shrugged. "Sorry, but that's all Uncle Charles told me before I left."

"Gentlemen, it sounds like I am headed to Ashantilly for dinner," Randolph said. "Captain Brailsford, take charge of your cousin. Thank you for checking up on me."

※ ※ ※

Milder than usual temperatures continued under overcast cloudy skies on this early December afternoon. The noon-hour dreariness offered little in the way of a sense of urgency for Randolph as he rode Zapala to Ashantilly. The horse's slow, steady gait along the sandy road suited Randolph. Overarching moss-filled branches shaded the faint sunlight at its midday zenith. Randolph dwelt on the scenes of panic among the citizens in the streets, still fresh in his mind from his trip to Savannah. Refined carriages and wagons cluttered virtually every avenue and boulevard as the city's residents of even the grandest houses surrounding Savannah's celebrated squares added to the pandemonium. By the time Randolph left Georgia's most elegant and oldest city, the military presence exceeded the civilian population. Residents who could afford to leave their homes did so to seek refuge in cities like Thomasville, Augusta, Macon, and Columbus. Prominent families filled the otherwise empty seats of outbound railcars as fast as the incoming ones transported soldiers to town.

To accommodate the swelling ranks arriving daily, Generals Lawton and Walker had discussed moving the army's camp from the city's edge to larger and more accessible grounds near the railroads beyond the city's outskirts. Randolph had grieved when he left the fabled city he had grown to love, trying to recall how it looked when he had tagged along with his father as a young boy.

As he neared Ashantilly, Randolph patted Zapala's broad neck and contemplated what war might bring. *Will McIntosh County survive this war unscathed? Darien offers no military threat like Brunswick. I wonder what Mary and others in Milledgeville are thinking about the news of Port Royal's loss and now Tybee Island?*

Beaufort had provided Mary and Randolph with many memorable summer excursions whenever they sought a romantic getaway removed from Savannah's all-too-familiar, formal social circles. Beaufort, like Darien to Savannah, had rivaled Charleston's history and wealth. However, the fervor of secession at social affairs when attended by Robert Barnwell Rhett or his son, Robert Jr., soured their recent memories of the quaint port city. The elder Rhett had vocally opposed Thomas Spalding's efforts during the Compromise of 1850 deliberations. Spalding had successfully fostered Georgia's support and upset Rhett, a firebrand newspaperman and politician who vehemently opposed the Compromise. As much as Randolph rued Beaufort falling into the hands of Union forces, he recognized the political significance of Port Royal's defeat beyond its strategic offerings to Lincoln's assault forces. The occupation of Beaufort, the seat of Southern secessionism, served as a notice to all the port cities in the South.

Zapala snorted as his gait changed when Randolph jerked the reins. They left the main road and went up the carriage trail leading to his brother's home at Ashantilly. Private William Washington Knight greeted Randolph with a salute at the foot of the mansion's front portico steps. Evelyn Spalding waved with a cheery smile from the top step. "Why such a long face, Randolph Spalding? You look like you could use some of Maddie's home cooking. You get any skinnier, you'll need a whole new wardrobe."

Randolph kissed Evelyn on both cheeks. "Since Alma disappeared to Sapelo's hinterland with Hector and Cecile, good meals have been few and far between. So, what's old Maddie dishing up for us this afternoon?" Randolph looked back at Major Knight's son. "Thank you, William. We can leave Zapala tied beneath that oak tree."

"Walk with me to the veranda. Charles and Major Knight are

waiting." Evelyn took Randolph's dust-covered, gold-braided black hat. "Maddie's been cooking up a storm since she heard we were having guests on the veranda for Sunday dinner. She's preparing one of our favorite shrimp dinners. Please, tell me the latest news from Mary."

"The last news I received arrived two weeks ago with Michael Kenan. She and the children are finding their way around Milledgeville, thanks to the Kenan family. I plan to break Sapelo's hold on me so Allen and me can spend Christmas in Milledgeville."

"I wish Charles and I could join you, but he feels he can't afford to leave. He's told me he wants me to move me to a plantation he bought way down near Thomasville. I dare not argue with him about it. He grows more cantankerous by the passing of each day."

"Is he not going to leave with you?"

"Absolutely not. Not now that the ladies of the McIntosh Relief Society of First Presbyterian Church hailed him as the guardian of McIntosh. They told him how sound they slept at night knowing he and his troops patrol the county roads."

"Just what Charles needed, toplofty affirmations from all those well-meaning old biddies." Randolph tugged on Evelyn's arm at the doorway to the veranda. "How is it Major Knight and his son are joining us?"

"Charles ran into them this morning headed to church not too long before Billy—I mean Lieutenant Wylly—told him you were back at your house. How was it for you staying at your house all alone? Mary and the kids left over a month ago."

Randolph paused and then offered his arm to her. "Let me say it this way. I never knew how noisy the house could be with only me there. I had a hard time sleeping with all the sounds an empty house can make."

Evelyn giggled and hooked her hand onto Randolph's arm as they stepped onto the shaded veranda. It offered a nearly unobstructed view of the tidewater salt marsh islands separated by dark brown mud banks. The mid-summer, supple, lush green leaves had transitioned into rustling foliage donning their late autumnal shades of reds and browns.

"Charles and I wanted to take advantage of this unseasonably warm weather and eat outside this afternoon. I hope you don't mind," Evelyn said.

"Suits me fine. This time of the year, the only winged creatures have feathers and do not swarm."

Major Levi Knight, wearing his dress uniform, stood the moment Randolph approached the table. Randolph motioned for him to return to his seat. "I think we can forgo the formalities, Levi, at least for this afternoon." He then glanced at Charles, who wore brown tweed trousers, a tan silk waistcoat, and a chestnut-colored cravat that decorated his silk shirt. Randolph brushed the dust off his blue uniform tunic and adjusted his belt buckle.

"Charles, you look comfortable."

Charles sat at the head of the table with his chair out far enough to cross one leg over a knee enjoying a chaw of tobacco. Despite his attire, his fifty-three-year-old wrinkled smile contained brown drool. He glanced at Evelyn, preparing to spit before he grabbed a bronze spittoon at his feet. Then, after returning the ornate receptacle to its place on the granite tiles, he reached into his waistcoat and offered Randolph and Levi a portion of his tobacco. Levi pulled out a pocketknife and carved a piece from Charles's plug. Randolph dismissed the offer with a wave of a hand before pulling a panatella from his coat pocket and lighting it.

"While you men sit out here and confabulate with one another, I'll go see what I can do to help Maddie. Whatever she's fixin', it smells mighty good. I'm certain she'll have dinner ready to serve shortly," Evelyn said, disappearing into the house.

"Missus Spalding, would you ask William to join us?" Levi Knight said. "I imagine he's admiring Colonel Randolph's horse."

Major Knight captured Randolph's attention when he reported that another young soldier from his Berrien County militia had died after contracting measles. "Our young assistant surgeon, Mister Way, appears to have his hands full with six new cases since yesterday morning. It seems that battling sickness and boredom has become Camp Spalding's biggest threat. We have lost three good men so far—"

"Make that five, maybe six," Charles interjected. "We found the bodies of two of your three missing soldiers on Saint Catherine's. One appeared to have drowned. The other, bludgeoned to death."

"What do you mean bludgeoned to death?" Randolph asked, sitting taller in his chair, his eyes glaring at Charles. "Any signs of the third murderous deserter?"

Charles leaned over and spat before answering. "No. He likely drowned, too, but his body did not make it to shore. No telling."

Major Knight added, "If two drowned, who killed the third?"

"I'm merely sharing with you what we found," Charles said. "If the third soldier survived, he alone likely knows the answer to your question."

"If one of them survived and had a hand in what happened to the other two, then he'll forever have to look over his shoulder," Randolph said. "I have important news to share that affects us all. Levi, your days are numbered at Camp Spalding. I expect all remaining militia units occupying the barrier islands from Ossabow to Amelia will receive orders to report to Savannah."

Major Knight peered at his son. "So, the news we heard about federal forces on Tybee Island is true?"

"Yes. The Yankee army took Tybee Island right after we removed our troops. By the time I left Savannah, far more than the sight of blockade ships caused the citizens in the city to panic. General Lee ordered General Walker to shore up fortifications protecting Savannah," Randolph said, staring across the tidewater.

Charles sat upright. "Randolph, what else do you know? Is Lee abandoning the militia forces guarding ports like Darien?"

"Not that I'm aware. General Lee believes we have no choice but to abandon the barrier islands and reinforce our defenses around Savannah. If Savannah falls, the Confederacy will not prevail in what likely will be a drawn-out and costly war. He sent similar orders to South Carolina's coastal militia to defend Charleston."

"What about the remaining workers and servants left on Sapelo?" Charles asked, drawing curious stares from both Major Knight and his son.

Randolph puffed on his cigar for a moment. "The *George M. Troup* can only make one last trip to Milledgeville before our navy commissions her. Our fledgling Confederate Navy needs river steamers like her to counter the growing number of Union gunboats."

"Does Allen know yet?" Charles asked.

"No. We have to find out how many additional passengers we can cram onto the *George M. Troup* for the next load."

"What about those you cannot get on board?"

"Charles, I don't know yet." Randolph's shoulders slumped. "Any suggestions?"

Charles explained he had purchased a plantation in Brooks County and planned to transport his workers by train on the Brunswick to Thomasville rail line. He suggested he might finagle the same arrangement for any remaining workers on Sapelo Island since the railroad lost much of its inland freight business.

"It will require getting them from the island to Brunswick, but that is a far sight easier prospect than any options going through Savannah."

Evelyn brought two bottles of Madeira to the table, placed them in front of Charles, and took her seat at the opposite end. Charles smiled as he uncorked the wine.

"Major Knight, I know you and I imbibed a little Madeira when we served together in Milledgeville years ago. What about William? Would you like a taste during dinner?"

"Thank you, Mister Spalding. I'm actually not much of a wine drinker, but I'll try a glass."

"Madeira is no ordinary wine, my dear William," Randolph said. "It is the golden nectar of the gods. It comes from the enchanted island of Madeira, but beware. Its sweet taste can quickly make a fool of the heartiest soul."

After dinner, Randolph walked with Charles to the water's edge where he revealed his intent to resign his regimental command and join General Walker in Savannah at the end of the month. After thanking Evelyn for inviting him to dinner, he left Zapala behind in the care of Ashantilly's stable hand. Charles took Randolph, Levi Knight, and his son to Darien's dock. On the trip back to Sapelo, Randolph considered telling Major Knight about the orders he carried in his coat pocket but decided to wait until he spoke to Allen. Instead, he contemplated the challenges ahead before he could travel to see his family in Milledgeville for Christmas.

CHAPTER SEVENTEEN

14th of December, 1861

"Allen, we might as well eat breakfast together. Our fields are empty, and there's no room for the remaining harvest to leave with us tomorrow," Randolph said, pouring molasses on a biscuit. When he set the jar of molasses back on the table, he added with a queried look, "It just dawned on me. You and I can count on one hand the times we've eaten breakfast together since you moved onto the island."

"That very well may be a fact. These last few months have kept both of us preoccupied with the changes we both have had to handle," Allen Bass said with a mouthful of grilled ham.

"Do you think Charlie will recognize his Pa when you get home?" Randolph scratched his day-old stubble.

Allen grinned as he ran his fingers through his own unruly, dark beard. "You might be right, but all the same, I kinda like my beard. Not to mention, it beats stropping a razor every morning."

"You might want to think about it after we get you to Baldwin County. It has been nearly two years since Almira passed away." Randolph's smile widened.

"Whoa!" Allen blurted. "I plan to be quite content being a hardworking father. Besides, I've no intentions of courting again."

Randolph laughed. "Okay. I am just suggesting that Father Time might get in the way if you wait too long. There are apt to be several eligible widows in Milledgeville who might take a shine to a good-looking widower."

"I appreciate you placing that prospect into my head."

"I gotta tell you a dream last night spurred me to say that. I dreamed about Mary's and my wedding at your family's grand home in Russell County. It was so real to me. I believed I could actually smell the newness of the wallpaper and coats of varnish on the stair rails."

"What stirred that memory?"

"Our eighteenth anniversary. I realized Mary's and my anniversary date almost slipped by."

"You'll be with her and the kids within a week."

"I hope so. I gotta tell you something funny about my dream. Your father called me Randy. He always told me Randolph sounded too pretentious for his liking."

Allen laughed. "The old man liked you and your parents until you took Mary away to live in McIntosh County. After that, he referred to you as Mary's husband until the day he passed away."

"You know you're right. When we visited before your father passed away, that's how he referred to me. Stopping to think about it, I don't recall him ever calling me Randy after our marriage."

"Do you think we can leave memory lane long enough to talk about getting to Milledgeville?"

Randolph's expression returned from sullen to cold stone. "Did you draft a new manifest? Did you keep Hector, Alma, and Cecile on it?"

"Yes and no."

Randolph arched a brow. "Why no?"

"One of my drivers told me Alma and Cecile refused to leave until Hector returns."

"Where's Hector? Are Alma and Cecile okay?"

"He didn't say anything further about Hector and pleaded that I not ask him where Alma and Cecile stayed."

"I dislike it, but I understand. Be sure to get word back to them. They can return to their home at South End whenever they feel like it once we leave. I'll be sure Major Knight sees to it no one will bother them."

"I'll take care of that this afternoon." Allen unfolded the manifest identifying one-hundred-and-twenty-five names who were ready to leave. "I understand not bringing additional tools and supplies allows added room for passengers, but are you certain about leaving our cotton, corn, and sugar behind?"

Randolph sighed. "Yes, Allen. I'd rather get our people off the island. The Yankees can have our harvest, just not our negroes. I've heard horrible stories about the Union Army conscripting slaves they run across. I'm not sure what they do with the women and children. Orders will arrive any day. The militia will leave the island headed to Savannah."

"What about the remaining workers and their family members? Some wanted to stay but a number are afraid and want to leave."

"Charles promised he'll arrange one final exodus for those left behind wanting to leave. I don't know how or if they will travel to Milledgeville, but they'll get off the island."

Allen thumped his fist on the table. "Why leave so much of our hard-earned crops for the Yankees to confiscate?"

"Do you really believe I'd do that? Meet me after dark." A smirk appeared. "I have a message in mind the Union will understand."

※ ※ ※

Later that morning, Randolph met Levi Knight at Alex Hazard's house near the lighthouse. He broke the news about his decision to Alex and that orders would soon arrive for the militia to leave the island.

Alex puffed on his pipe, contemplating the news.

"I suspect you'll be told to shut the lighthouse down when Major Knight gets his orders. No sense in making it easy for any Yankee ships."

Alex groused, "I got orders to that effect yesterday." The lightkeeper turned to Levi Knight. "I could use the help of a couple of your men when the time comes. I have orders to remove the lens when I leave. Without it, the Yankees will sail blind if they attempt to navigate the Doboy at night. I'll be ready to leave with the major."

Levi offered his hand to Alex. "Whatever you need from me, just tell the duty officer to tell me."

※ ※ ※

Randolph gave Major Knight orders as soon as they returned to Camp Spalding. "I understand, Colonel Spalding," Levi said and saluted. "Do whatever you need to do tonight. I'll alert the company captains." He then shook Randolph's hand.

Rather than head to *Big House,* Randolph walked out onto the beach and stood at the water's edge. Pillows of white dotted the sky. He stared at the Atlantic Ocean's nearly seamless horizon. Masts with unfurled sails remained far out to sea. Randolph accepted the reality they likely flew Union colors. His thoughts rushed back to the unfathomable one-sided exchange of cannon fire and endless volleys of rifles and muskets on Hilton Head. He felt indebted to God for his survival and looked forward to visiting his family before reporting to General Walker in Savannah.

Randolph realized he stood near two sandpipers pecking at the wet sand near the foam-lined water's edge, oblivious to the events threatening the island. Observing God's tiny creatures, he again began to contemplate:

Sapelo owes no debt to me or my family nor those who had ever claimed to own a portion of the island. Long before men stepped foot on Sapelo, it witnessed the birth of the innumerable ancient oaks, sprawling cedars, and towering pines that populated the island. Long after man leaves, this primordial rich sandy soil would nurse new trees and reclaim the deforested fields man claimed as his own. Men can purchase Sapelo, but they will never own it. The pipers, terns, gulls, egrets, herons, eagles, ospreys, and all the other wildlife on Sapelo know what men will not accept—we are but transitory tenants.

His walk back to South End's mansion prepared him for what he knew he had to do before he could leave the island.

※ ※ ※

The regimental officers gathered in South End's main hall shortly after dinner. Colonel Spalding handed Major Knight the orders from General Walker. Major Knight glanced back at Randolph after reading them.

"Gentlemen, I have ordered you here to meet with you one last time as your regimental commander. As of midnight, my resignation from the regiment will be official. I will send word to Lieutenant Colonel Alexander and the remaining regimental companies in Savannah about my decision as well. Major Knight will assume command of the companies remaining at Camp Spalding. Expect orders to arrive for you to depart Sapelo Island for reassignment in and around Savannah. I'm joining General Walker as his adjutant. You all should expect to see me at your new posts in Savannah. I wish you and the entire 29th Georgia Infantry Regiment Godspeed in the coming days and weeks. General Lee expects, with your help, to push the Union forces who now occupy Georgia soil at Tybee Island back from whence they came. He has a plan to drive every one of them out of Beaufort and back out to sea."

A round of rallying shoutouts resonated from among the cadre of officers in South End's grand hall. Randolph raised both arms to regain their attention.

"Before I share a special farewell surprise, there are two announcements I wish to make as your regimental commander. Captain Wylly, please step forward for a moment."

His nephew approached him and Major Knight.

"Captain Wylly, I have your new orders, signed by General Lawton. Effective as of midnight, you are to report to Lieutenant Colonel Charles Spalding for further orders. You'll assume command of the McIntosh Light Dragoons, a troop assigned to Georgia's Cavalry Command south of the Altamaha River."

Thomas accepted his orders and shook Randolph's hand as rallying cries came from the other officers.

"Gentlemen, as a parting gesture aimed as a message for any prying Northern eyes, I and Mister Bass will torch the remaining cotton stored in the island's barns and storehouses tonight. Please advise your men to not get alarmed. I refuse to leave anything behind the Yankees may want to confiscate after you leave the island."

"Do you want a hand? We will gladly assist you, Colonel Spalding," Captain Young shouted, instigating uproarious laughter from the others.

"Thank you, Captain Young. Mister Bass and I have well enough in hand to handle this task. I suggest you kick back and enjoy the sky getting lit up. This war for our independence has just begun. I suspect those of you who believed we would lick them Northerners handily now realize, thanks to the latest news, they have no notion of walking away from this fight either. This war will require sacrifices from all of us before it is over. What I do tonight is just the beginning of the sacrifices my family must make. Now, if you will join me in the library, I have provided ample libations for all of you to partake."

A few minutes later, Randolph stood before the officers congregated in the library, glasses raised. "To family, friends, and better days ahead."

Allen Bass arrived and stood beside Randolph during the toast. Instead of savoring his drink with the rest of the men, Randolph set his glass down, prompting Allen to ask, "What's the matter? I've not known you to ignore a glass of liquor."

With a wry smile, he gazed at the young men, engrossed in their conversations. He lit a panatella and turned to Allen whispering, "Tonight, I want to keep a clear head so I can remind myself later why I did this. Yep, God bless the Confederate States of America. May it not be in vain."

※ ※ ※

The clock inside *Big House* had struck midnight when Allen and Randolph climbed atop the mule-driven wagon waiting by South End's barn. The unmistakable smell of turpentine from the casks loaded in the wagon's bed filled the air. Allen and Randolph traveled first to the storehouses along Barn Creek on Kenan's property. The thick tabby walls served as a chimney as flames shot upward, razing the roof and consuming the stacked bales of cotton inside. The night dragged on for Allen and Randolph as they traveled up High Point Road to Chocolate and Bourbon and repeatedly sent flames roaring into the nighttime sky. They stopped to calm the fears of the few remaining workers who ran out of their houses to watch in stunned silence.

They arrived at the final storehouse not long before dawn. Exhausted and hungry, Randolph doused the barn nearest to South End House, struck a match, and watched the upper half of one of the oldest outbuildings on the island collapse upon itself within minutes. Then, satisfied the flames posed no further danger, Randolph joined Allen atop the wagon when the screech of an owl caught his attention. Randolph wondered if they had inadvertently destroyed the owl's nest, as it likely had been in the rafters of the old barn. Then he recalled the gyrations Hector and Alma went through to ward off their superstitious belief about how an owl's presence portended death to those beneath the roof of a house where an owl alighted.

Allen noticed Randolph was lost in his thoughts. "You all right?"

"Yeah. I just recalled what I hope was Geechee poppycock about owls. Let's call it a night."

CHAPTER EIGHTEEN

15th of December, 1861

Pillars of gray smoke rose above the smoldering storehouses in the pre-dawn twilight as Randolph and Allen hopped down from the wagon at South End's barn. They unhitched the two mules and washed the soot from their faces and hands in a nearby water trough.

A lone sentry saluted Randolph as he and his brother-in-law walked across Camp Spalding. After a change of clothes, they sat for an early breakfast they could hardly eat. Though dog-tired from their all-night, fiery mission, sleep for the two arsonists had to wait. They knew rest would not come until Sapelo Island lay in the wake of the *George M. Troup* as it headed up the mouth of the Altamaha River.

※ ※ ※

Onboard the crowded afterdeck of the *George M. Troup*, Randolph clutched Allen's hand as they shook. "Are you sure about this?"

"Yes, Randy, old boy. Don't worry about me. I'll more than likely arrive a day or two after you. Captain Stephens and I have it worked out. He'll transport the remaining negroes willing to leave for Brunswick. As soon as I get them on their way, I'll scramble onboard the next train out of Brunswick to Macon and then onto Milledgeville. Tell Charlie I promise to be with him before Christmas. Now, let go of my hand so I can disembark before Captain Roberson shoves off. Here's the manifest. Don't lose it."

Allen hopped down from the gangway a moment before Elex,

the boat's deckhand, hoisted it from Marsh Landing's wharf. Michael Kenan weaved his way through the huddles of Sapelo's refugees and found Randolph at the afterdeck rail, gazing at the marsh-lined mouth of the Duplin River. Thin wisps of smoke still rose above the island's treetops. Michael rested his hand on Randolph's shoulder. "I know this is hard for you, but Sapelo will still be here when this war's over, and we can plant cotton again."

"I know you're right," Randolph said, still sulking as he looked squarely at his brother-in-law. "I'm not sure why this came to mind standing here, but my father used to quote Caesar at watershed moments like this. I believe my father would say this is my Rubicon moment when Caesar declared *'Iacta alea est*—I have cast the dice. What now happens cannot be undone. What will be, will be.'"

"Sounds far too foreboding to my liking. Listen to me. Thomas Spalding would be proud of what you accomplished these past months."

Randolph stared at his brother-in-law with sad, bloodshot eyes. "Then why do I feel like such a failure? Ashes are all that remains of our last harvest. I fear I will not see another on Sapelo."

"What you need is some well-deserved sleep," Michael said, glaring back. "We have five long days ahead. That ought to allow you to get caught up on some much-needed rest." Michael reached into his coat pocket and handed his brother-in-law a letter from Sallie. "Here, I almost forgot. This should take your mind off things you cannot change while I rustle up something for us to eat and drink before you collapse from exhaustion."

"Thanks, Michael. I cannot shake the notion I will never step foot on Sapelo again. For Tom's sake, I pray I am wrong.

※ ※ ※

Before the sun had risen too high on the fifth day, the *George M. Troup* tied up at Beulah Plantation's wharf, downriver from the landing at Milledgeville. Tom, Bourke, Owen, and Charlie waved their arms high over their heads and danced back and forth as they screamed, "Pa, Pa, Pa!"

Captain Roberson shouted instructions to his crew and the handful of Sapelo workers who had made the first trip upriver. While the crew secured the *George M. Troup* mooring ropes and gangways lowered at each end of the boat, Mary and Sallie eagerly looked on, clutching hands with Katherine Kenan and her teenage daughter Clifford.

Extending from the bare red clay at the river's edge and up the sun-drenched grassy bluff, the first of Sapelo workers and servants to arrive at Beulah formed a funnel of welcoming cheers. With hesitant shuffling of feet and wide-eyed stares, the boatload of new arrivals disembarked from both ends of the boat. Fears abated as, one by one, they recognized familiar faces eager to greet them.

The moment the gangplanks cleared, Tom, Bourke, Owen, and Charlie raced onboard and found Randolph and Michael Kenan talking with Captain Roberson. Tom and Bourke latched onto Randolph's coat sleeves, and Owen Kenan held his father's hand. Charlie's cheerful laughter turned to tears when he couldn't find his father among them. Michael Kenan pulled him to his side and told him that his father would arrive as promised in a couple of days. He then hoisted Charlie and Owen into his arms and stepped onto the dock where he greeted his wife and daughter.

Captain Roberson's shoulders slumped as he turned and walked away from Randolph and his sons. He realized this trip from Darien marked his last trip aboard the *George M. Troup* before he relinquished the vessel to an expectant Confederate Navy crew waiting across the river at Milledgeville's dock. They had orders to retrofit the steamboat into a warship. It would then return to coastal waters carrying soldiers and guns to combat Union gunboats.

Randolph's two exuberant boys dragged him by his coat sleeves toward the gangway and onto the dock. Sallie ran from her mother's side to greet her father, squeezing his waist and squealing, "Oh, Father! I'm so glad you are finally home. We missed you something awful."

Peeling her tight embrace so he could look at his daughter's face he said, "Sallie, I missed you too, sweetheart." Randolph wrapped his arms around his daughter's narrow waist, hoisting her off her feet. After a lively, full circle twirl, he set her down. "My darling, please hold on to that smile and keep an eye on your brothers for a few moments. Your mother needs a proper greeting too." He then kissed Sallie's forehead as he released his embrace.

Mary dabbed her teary eyes just before Randolph placed his arms around her. She sniffed and then whispered as he bent closer with puckered lips, "Randy, behave yourself." She then offered her rosy cheeks to kiss.

"My sweet, Mary, how I have dreamed about this for so many excruciatingly long weeks. I feared I would never hold and kiss you again." He then lifted her off her feet and cackled so loud heads turned as he spun her around.

"Randolph Spalding, you put me down this very instant," she shouted amidst her own stifled laughter. She pecked his moist cheek and whispered, "Wait until you see the view we have of the river from our bedroom." She then grabbed his hand. "Come on, let me show you around Beulah."

"Please, lead the way my darling."

Michael grabbed Owen's and Charlie's adolescent hands just as Katherine said, "We'll meet you up at the house after you two take your stroll on the grounds. I'm most certain Josephine has her hands full with Evelyn—her baby is due any day now." She turned to her daughter, Clifford, and Sallie. "You two come with me. Let them spend some time alone before you pester them with the incessant questions I know you two young ladies are dying to ask."

Michael looked at Bourke and Tom standing near their parents. "That goes for you two as well. Scoot! Run and tell William to hitch up a carriage for your ma and pa."

The recent arrivals disappeared up the bluff, chatting with and escorted by the others already settled in their new quarters on Beulah. Like those before them, Sapelo's newest displaced workers and servants would discover Beulah had but one central slave community a short walk along a rutted red clay cart path from the main house. Two rows of weather-worn wooden shacks with cramped three-room slave quarters on either end with a shared red brick fireplace in the center of the common wall.

Though not the sturdy tabby-walled homes they lived in on Sapelo, the solidly built wooden shacks provided adequate protection from rain, wind, and winter's cold. A wrought iron strap-hinged wood plank door anchored each end of the two-family shacks. Each three-room dwelling included a large room with a pine table and benches in front of a red-brick fireplace. Two attached narrow rooms served as bedrooms. A single shuttered window on the opposite wall from the door allowed daylight to fill the main room. The windowless back rooms had either crude wood pallets or narrow stacked bunks along opposing walls to accommodate as many slaves as possible. Twenty-four shacks faced each other in two equal rows. The newest Sapelo slaves, like those who preceded them, would need time to adjust to their new cramped living conditions at Beulah.

Josephine and William shared a room in the rear of the brick cookhouse. Two glass-paned sash windows offered light and welcomed ventilation in their otherwise spartan quarters off the kitchen. On the other side of the red-dirt cart path that led to the fields, a modest two-story brick overseer's house waited for Allen to arrive in a few days.

Randolph would learn on his walk with Mary that Beulah offered a compact layout with its carriage house, barnyard, and blacksmith nestled convenient to the large main house among a grove of winter-barren sycamore and pecan trees. The front of the two-story framed house had an unobstructed view of the Oconee with Milledgeville's heaven-seeking church spires and glistening cupolas rising just above the treetops in the faint distance. Upstream, a bridge spanned the Oconee and connected the bustling capital with stage roads from Sparta to the east and Augusta to the north. Randolph recalled taking many stagecoach rides across the river during his previous years in the Georgia Assembly.

※ ※ ※

Mary found Randolph brooding on the front porch not long after they had returned to the main house. "My dear, what is wrong?"

"Nothing, really."

"Well, then what has caused you to sneak out here with such deep furrows across your forehead."

Randolph sighed. "I cannot quit feeling like I let down the whole family."

"Why, Randolph Spalding, what in tarnation are you talking about? If not for you, we would not be sitting on this fine porch looking out over the river. Beulah may be nothing like the mansion at South End, but it is not too different from our house at the Ridge. Of course, I'm surprised William McKinley and his wife, Anne, raised such a big family in this house before they moved to their new home. There are days I have chased the children outside, so I could get a little peace and quiet. Otherwise, we have adjusted fairly well in my estimation."

"Please do not misunderstand me. I'm indebted to Michael and especially to William McKinley for providing this place for us."

"Then why are you so glum and out here all alone?"

"I reckon Beulah will suit us just fine for the time being, but I'm concerned about Allen and Charles getting our remaining workers off Sapelo. I'm also worried about what will happen to Hector, Alma, and Cecile. They would be right here with us if it had not been for my hot-headed foolishness."

Mary joined Randolph on the bench that sat on the porch beneath the parlor's double windows. "What happened to Jeremiah and Cecile was not your doing."

Her response drew a cynical chuckle from Randolph. "Now you sound like your brother."

"Oh, pshaw!" She held his hand and stroked his forehead with her fingertips, trying to unfurrow his brow. "Now, listen to me. General Lawton placed you in the impossible position of commanding the militia he placed on Sapelo while you dealt with the evacuation of your family and our negroes to a safer place. You did not instigate this war, and I know full well that taking up arms to resolve the growing divide between Lincoln's abolitionists in the North and the Confederate secessionists in the South bothered you from the beginning."

His long face grew longer as he shook his head. He mumbled, "I wish a bunch of those glory-seeking snollygosters could have joined me on Hilton Head." Randolph's eyes went dark and cold. "They might've thought twice before voting for secession to gain Southern independence. Francis Bartow paid the ultimate price in the first battle of a war we started. Before this war ends, I'm afraid many other notable friends will lose their lives."

"Randy, my dear. Do you believe the South will not win this war?"

"What I'm trying to say is both sides will lose countless lives before one side declares victory. I witnessed with my own eyes men being shot and left dying in their own blood. I realized on Hilton Head both Union and Confederate soldiers spill the same red blood on the battleground. Thinking about Jeremiah and Cecile makes my heart ache all the more. I fear hatred is our real enemy."

Mary pulled her handkerchief from her sleeve and dabbed her husband's tears.

"Mary, the worst of the fighting had already taken place by the time my men and I took up positions on Hilton Head. And, before you get to fretting too much, my nephew displayed enough grit to keep me safe when the shooting started. We defended the retreat of my regiment's brave soldiers after they held their ground while Fort Walker's ramparts crumbled, like a sandcastle against the waves when the tide rises, from the Union Navy's overwhelming cannon fire. Afterward, we ordered our soldiers to fall back as soon as the Yankees landed wave after wave of soldiers on the island and fired on our infantry until they turned tail and occupied Fort Walker."

"Pa, did you and Uncle Thomas shoot any of them?" Tom said, poking his head up from the porch steps and staring at his father with his jaw hanging.

"Young man, that is not a proper question to ask. How long have you been listening to us talking?" Mary chided.

Randolph patted Mary's hand before he stood and walked to the edge of the porch. "Tom, I do not know exactly all you heard, but I will answer your question. Your Uncle and I fired our rifles, but did I shoot anyone? I really do not know. Fact is, I believe them Yankee soldiers were about as scared as I was and their aim likely as poor as mine, too."

Tom sat beside his father. "You were scared?"

"Son, a man who says he is not scared in battle is either a liar or a fool. Your Uncle Thomas is the bravest man I know, and he will tell you how scared he was that day." Randolph pulled his son close and looked him in the eyes. "War always sounds glorious before blood stains the battleground. I pray you never have to take a man's life, but if you must, do so to defend life, liberty, and your property."

"Yes, Pa," Tom muttered with his elbows propped on his thighs and his chin cradled in both hands. "Uncle Thomas scared? If that don't beat all."

"Thomas Spalding, go on inside and wash up for supper. Smells like Josephine roasted a ham, and—" She sniffed the air with a pleasant smile. "My oh my, and I think she baked us a sweet potato pie, too."

Randolph nudged Tom through the front door. He held it open as Mary rose from the bench. "Do you miss having Ada around to help with the children?"

"Sometimes, but she needed to join her father and brothers in Atlanta. Being here has helped me get closer to Sallie, though. After we eat, will you help me and the children collect some mistletoe and holly to decorate the house?"

"Of course. That reminds me. I hope Allen will be here before Christmas Day."

CHAPTER NINETEEN

21st of December, 1861

Winter in Baldwin County arrived with frost on the ground and a chill in the air, a rarity along the coast. Randolph helped Evelyn Kenan, well into her ninth month of pregnancy, step up into the carriage and slide in beside her mother-in-law, Katherine, who sat behind Michael and their two children. Owen squirmed, his arms tucked tight by his sides, between his father and Clifford, his sister, on the front seat. William, the Spalding's stableman, tied a rope across the Kenan's luggage on the back of the carriage. Mary, her shawl pulled over her shoulders, exchanged goodbyes with Katherine and Evelyn. "Promise to get word to me the minute that baby of yours decides it's time."

Evelyn nodded nervously as she lay a blanket over her lap.

"Mary, I promise we will, but what about you? Will you be all right out here after Randolph leaves?" Katherine said, adjusting her daughter-in-law's blanket.

"Quit your fretting. We'll be just fine." Mary looked at Randolph with a coy smile. "We intend to make the most of the time we have before he leaves."

Katherine reached across Evelyn and squeezed Mary's hand. "You and the children are always welcome to stay with us. Our house has plenty of room."

"That certainly is mighty generous of you. My brother will be here long before Randolph leaves. Besides, if I need anything, the McKinleys live just down the road."

Randolph shook Michael's hand. "I promise we'll come see you Christmas Day. Thanks again. I cannot imagine myself standing here without you."

"See you in a couple of days, then." Michael flicked the reins. "Get up!"

Michael eased the two-horse team down Beulah's bare dirt drive toward the narrow wagon road that meandered along the river to Sparta Road. There, they would safely cross over the rapidly flowing Oconee. On the other side of the bridge, the tree-lined road became Stage Road and continued into the center of Milledgeville.

Randolph blew into his bare hands before he took Mary's and Sallie's hands. "I believe I will throw another couple of logs onto the fire. Sallie, see if Josephine can rustle up something hot for us to drink while we get warm by the fireplace."

Mary laughed. "Sounds good to me. The boys won't want to stay outside long without their overcoats."

"Momma, why is it so cold here?" Sallie asked, squeezing her crossed arms tighter.

※ ※ ※

A day later, two red tarp-covered wagons rambled into view along the river's edge. Both wagons bore large, fancy, dark-blue painted letters across their white-washed sideboards.

"Pa, look! Two wagons are coming," Bourke hollered, standing at the front door. "They got the name *Jacob Gans and Company from Milledgeville* painted on them."

Mary grabbed her shawl and draped it over her shoulders as she headed to the door. "Randolph, this must be the blankets and coats we ordered."

Randolph slipped on his coat and hat. "Mary, stay inside with the children." He stepped onto the broad front porch and greeted the older man in the first wagon.

"Might you be Colonel Spalding? If so, Missus Spalding ordered these flannel blankets, osnaburg shirts, and coats. They arrived on the train from Macon yesterday evening. My son and me figured you might appreciate us bringing them straight out here for you. You mind if I ask what ya gonna do with all these?"

"Yes, I'm Randolph Spalding. Why not climb down and step inside for a minute?" He extended his hand as they stepped onto the porch. "And you might be?"

"My apologies, Mister Spalding. My name is Jacob Gans, and this here's my son, Jake." Mister Gans pointed to the painted sideboards with a proud grin. As soon as he saw Mary standing with their two sons in the doorway, he removed his cap from his balding gray head. He pulled the invoice for the shipment from his coat pocket. "I suspect you be Missus Spalding?"

"Why yes, I certainly am. We've been expecting you. Please come inside, Mister Gans," Mary said. She took a step back and scooted Tom and Bourke from blocking the doorway. "You two boys go find something to do while we talk with Mister Gans."

Jacob Gans stomped his brown brogans on the porch floor before he stepped inside. A stern look over his shoulder sent an obvious message to his son. Jake hesitated, checked the soles of his boots, then wiped the tips against his pant legs.

Jacob and his son stepped inside the parlor. He held onto his cap and the invoice with both hands in front of him. "Colonel Spalding, the whole town is talking about you and Mister Kenan moving your darkies here from McIntosh County. The word is you've come here with a larger number of them than either Mister McKinley or Mister Barrow ever had at Beulah."

"Mister Gans, is that a problem?"

"Oh no, sir. Most folks seem pleased you moved here and intend to bring Beulah back to life." The merchant's eyes lit up. "It'll be good for business all around." He tightened his grip on his cap, scrunching the invoice.

Mary returned to the parlor. "Josephine will have some hot coffee for us in a few minutes. Please have a seat."

"May I see the paperwork?" Randolph asked, pointing to the rolled-up invoice.

Mister Gans unfolded the wrinkled handwritten invoice and passed it to Randolph. Jacob and Jake then sat in the two chairs facing Randolph and Mary who sat together on their plush, upholstered Chesterfield. Jake Gans consumed the awkward silence by inspecting the parlor and stairwell while Mary and Randolph looked over the invoice. Jacob dangled his cap from his fingertips between his knees.

Randolph listened as Mary explained each item on the order to him. "Don't you agree that three hundred blankets, shirts, and coats will keep our workers warm and help them adjust after leaving their homes on Sapelo? The winter here will be much colder than what they've been used to. Besides, we need them to cooperate with all the work needed here to get the fields cleared and plowed."

Josephine poured hot coffee for Mister Gans and his son.

Randolph sighed as Josephine handed him and Mary coffee. He held the coffee cup in both hands and stared briefly out the window. He then leaned toward Mary and whispered, "Of course, my dear. You should know Michael approached me weeks ago about the idea and offered to pay his fair share as well." He pointed to the bottom of the invoice. "We have James Graybill to thank for getting these items for Mister Gans."

"Then why the long face?" Mary whispered back.

"It makes me think of how much cotton Allen and I destroyed before I left Sapelo. Graybill's mills could've easily filled this order by milling the cotton we torched. Let's not forget there's a war underway. The army may soon find blankets, shirts, and shoes in short supply."

Mary took her husband's hands in hers and kissed the back of each one. "You did what you had to do. Let's pay attention to what lies ahead for us here and not back at what we left behind."

Randolph sighed and stared once again at the invoice before he raised his eyes to Jacob Gans. "Is everything accounted for in the wagons?"

Mister Gans nodded.

"Give me a minute. I will write you out a bank draft for the balance we owe you."

"Yes, sir. That'd be fine. I want you to know that after I sent your order to Crane and Graybill Company as your wife suggested, he wrote straight back and promised everything would arrive before Christmas."

Randolph slumped back with a subtle smile. "I will thank James when I visit him in Savannah."

Jacob looked at his son. "Yes, sir. Please tell him my family will have a nice Christmas thanks to this order. With all the uncertainty in the coming months, we all need something to feel good about."

Jake Gans slurped down the rest of his coffee, then glared over his shoulder at Josephine. "Old woman, I'm done," he snarled, holding out the empty cup.

Josephine cowered and took a step back as she looked at Mary.

Mary stood with her arms folded and scowled at the younger Gans. "Mister Gans, we have found a little civility goes a long way. The old woman's name is Josephine."

"But—" Jake muttered. His head slumped.

Jacob Gans slapped his son's arm. He then turned his attention to Josephine and, avoiding eye contact, said, "Thank you, Josephine. I think we are both done. Please, forgive my son. His momma and me taught him better. I blame his poor manners on the young men he hangs out with in town."

Randolph stood beside Mary and said, "Josephine, thank you. Would you round up the boys?" He then looked at Jacob and his son and said, "I'll write out a draft while you offload your wagons."

※ ※ ※

After Mister Gans and his son drove off, William and Tom waited on the front porch until Randolph and Mary stepped out from the parlor and took stock of the neat stacks of coats, blankets, and shirts that covered much of the porch floor.

Bourke ran up to the porch with his cousin Charlie one step behind. "Pa, what are all these for?"

"They're Christmas gifts for the workers. Would you like to give us a hand?"

The young boys nodded in unison, keeping their eager eyes fixed on Randolph.

"Go find Abraham for me. Tell him Mister and Missus Spalding want everyone gathered by the well but say nothing about the Christmas gifts. You two understand?"

Once again, as if their noggins were one, they bobbed their heads.

Mary clapped her hands. "Good. Now come straight back after you find Abraham, and no dillydallying."

The two youngsters raced up the grassy hill toward the gravel path leading to a village of weathered wooden shacks where all the Sapelo workers and their families lived. In the middle of the two rows of dwellings, a water well served as the meeting place for community gatherings. A brass bell mounted above the well signaled the workers to and from their assigned tasks during their workdays and tolled everyone to any important gatherings at the well.

By the time the two boys ran back down the hill to the main house, William, Tom, and Randolph had loaded their hitched wagon under Mary's and Sallie's watchful eyes. When the brass bell chiming began, Randolph helped Mary climb onto the front seat beside him while their children and Charlie scurried into the back of the wagon and sat on top of the bundles of coats, shirts, and blankets.

A fine layer of orange-colored dust from the trampled barren red clay hovered around the well as each worker stepped to the back of the wagon and received their clothing and blankets. Mary and Randolph watched and nodded as each of them looked up with expressions of gratitude before stepping aside.

Randolph stood in the wagon's rear and called out to Abraham. As he had been on Sapelo, he continued to be the head driver. He stepped forward, cradling his three neatly folded items in his thick mahogany arms. "Yes, sir."

"Mister Bass will be here in a day or so," Randolph said, loud enough for all to hear. "He stayed behind to make certain everyone who wanted to leave Sapelo could do so before he joined you. What Missus Spalding and my family have given each of you today can never soothe the uncertainty you are feeling. Neither are these houses meant to replace the homes you left behind. We, too, share the same longings. But I want to assure you I intend to keep my father's promise to you. We all will return to Sapelo one day. Until then, consider Beulah your new home. I only ask that you obey Missus Spalding and Mister Bass while I am away. Until Mister Bass arrives, do what you must to get settled. Some of you may have to make room for others, but there are enough beds for everyone. It may not be what you are used to, but we ask you to cooperate with each other. Abraham, if there's anything we need, let us know. As soon as Mister Bass arrives, he will see to it we replace the animals and supplies of rice and cornmeal left behind. Abraham, we will need the barn and fences repaired for the time being."

"Yes, sir, Mista Spalding, sir. Thank ya." Abraham backed away until he was among the slaves gathered. Some whispered among themselves in their familiar Geechee tongue while others surrounded Abraham with questions. He listened and responded like Solomon, sharing words of wisdom. Unlike Solomon, though, Abraham's broad shoulders slumped, and his balding gray head hung, hiding his sad, weary eyes.

Randolph lowered his head as he climbed back to the front of the wagon and took the reins. "Kids, climb in or walk back to the house," he said, choking back the roiling emotions rising within him. He stared straight ahead as he drove back to the house with Mary's arm wrapped in his and her head on his shoulder.

※ ※ ※

By Christmas Eve, daylight waned in favor of longer nights. Oconee's cold, damp air claimed the bluff overlooking its banks like an invisible fog, and the coral-streaked sunset faded. From Beulah's main house, the Spaldings could see the twinkling of Milledgeville's city lights through the distant, winter-bare treetops. On this crisp night, the sound of creaking carriage axles and horse hooves on the gravel announced the Spading family's arrival at Barrowville for a holiday dinner with the McKinleys.

Mary McKinley and her younger sister, Sarah, the teenage daughters of William McKinley, greeted the Spaldings at the door of their unpretentious red-brick country home. The main entrance hall served as a large reception foyer. Two ornate paneled parlors with tall ceilings and matching windows adjoined the central entrance hall on either side. Randolph and his family removed their coats, scarves, and gloves and joined William McKinley, surrounded by his family, in the west parlor.

Randolph craned his neck, admiring the elegant details and exquisite architectural wainscot paneled walls with matching crown molding around the ceiling. "William, it's been a few years. I must confess, Barrowville suits you and your growing family well."

William spread his arms wide with a proud father's grin. "Anne has blessed me with another four wonderful but sometimes rather loud, fun-loving children. That's Guy in Anne's lap. Next are Andrew and Will, and the shy, fair-haired young girl hiding behind her mother is Julia."

"Anne, thank you again for inviting us this evening," Mary said, her hands guiding the three young boys to stand in front of her. "This is Thomas and Bourke, our two sons, and their cousin, Charlie. My brother is due to arrive on the train tonight—at least we hope so."

"I'm sure he'll be here soon," Anne said with a congenial twinkle in her eyes. "Our oldest son, Archibald, promised to join us as well.

He stays in the city most of the time recently. He remains rather busy mustering in another new militia unit—"

"The Baldwin Independent Volunteers, my dear," William blurted with his chin raised and chest puffed.

"Good for him. I enjoyed traveling to Savannah with him a few months ago. He appeared to have a level head on his shoulders, which will serve him well," Randolph added as Tom giggled beneath his hand-covered mouth.

Mary glanced at Tom before she said to Anne, "Will your older daughters and their husbands also join us this evening?"

"No, they plan to visit with us tomorrow."

Across the room, seated together on a gold upholstered Chesterfield in front of the roaring fireplace, Sallie whispered back and forth with Mary and Sarah.

Anne turned to the three giddy teenage girls. "Behave yourselves. Show some manners and respect."

The McKinley's manservant stood at the rear doorway of the parlor. "Mister McKinley, sir. Master Archibald has arrived and brought some other gentleman with him."

"Where are they now, Scott?" William asked.

"Right here, father," Archibald said, wearing a pale-blue, dust-covered militia uniform. He hung his cloak and tossed his leather gloves and matching wide brim hat on top of the mahogany hall tree in the entrance. Behind him, Allen Bass stood looking the worse for wear as he ran his fingers through his dark hair.

"Pa!" Charlie screamed, running into Allen's open arms.

William laughed. "Scott, would you make certain we set an extra place at the table? And show Mister Bass and my son where they can wash up for dinner."

"Yes, sir. Mister A.C., you and Mister Bass can follow me. I will get you a wash basin and towels for y'all," Scott said, shaking his head and mumbling to himself.

A.C. smiled as he pranced up behind Scott and wrapped his

arms around his servant. "What would I do without you, Scott?" A.C. looked back at Allen's confused look. "Scott has been picking up after me and keeping me out of trouble since I can remember. When we get orders to leave Milledgeville, I reckon old Scott will have to come with me. Am I right, Scott?"

"Mister A.C., you be right, if Mister McKinley lets me go," Scott said, peering at William, who nodded his wrinkled forehead.

"Oh, fiddlesticks! It's Christmas Eve. No more talk of such things tonight. Sarah, please play us a tune on the piano, a Christmas carol we all can sing." Anne set her toddler son down and cackled aloud with Mary as the younger children gathered around the piano and, one by one, joined in the singing of *One Horse Open Sleigh*.

※ ※ ※

Later that evening, Allen lifted his exhausted son from the carriage and entered Beulah's main house. Sallie took Charlie by his hand after he hugged his father and led him upstairs where he slept with his cousins. Mary then nudged Tom and Bourke up the stairs to their beds. Randolph stoked the smoldering ashes in the fireplace and added slivers of pine kindling before laying logs over the rising flames. Mary got out a bottle of rum and offered Allen and Randolph a nightcap before she excused herself to go upstairs to bed.

"Mary, why not sit with us?" Randolph begged. "I'm certain your brother would enjoy your company before we all head up to bed."

"You two can stay up a while longer if you wish, but this has been an endless day. Tomorrow will probably be no different, I'm afraid. We have to be up early to drive into town. After church lets out, Michael and Katherine expect us at their house for Christmas dinner. Josephine knows we plan to leave first thing in the morning and will have breakfast ready early." She took two steps up the stairs and stopped. "Allen, I am truly glad you found your way here for Christmas. I look forward to talking tomorrow and showing you the cottage house for you and Charlie. Good night."

Randolph and Allen echoed, "Merry Christmas and good night."

Amidst the glow of the roaring fire, Allen shared how Charles had arranged for forty-four of the workers and their family members to be taken by rail to property in Brooks County near Thomasville. He had purchased, at a most fair price, a suitable plantation from a family who found themselves in debt. Charles felt it best to include the forty-four Sapelo negro family members with the workers he'd inherited from their brother-in-law on his Harris Neck plantation off the Sapelo River. Randolph knew Allen's decision had been for the best, and after seeing the cramped living conditions his workers faced at Beulah, he sighed a little relief.

"I'm sorry, but Hector, Alma, and Cecile were not among those we got off the island before we left. Like a handful of others who vanished on the island, I reckon they had their reasons."

Randolph refilled their glasses. "So, you did not even get to talk to them either?"

"No, and no one spoke a word about them when I asked."

Allen and Randolph stared silently into the flames.

CHAPTER TWENTY

25th of December, 1861

After breakfast, Allen climbed aboard a mule-drawn wagon with Tom, Bourke, and Charlie. The three youngsters appeared impervious to the damp chill reddening their cheeks amid puffs of adolescent laughter and chatter. Randolph goaded the team of horses pulling his family's carriage onto the wooden bridge. Mary and Sallie snuggled close, sharing a gray and blue flannel blanket across their laps in the carriage's rear seat. Allen and the boys followed close behind as they drove across the wooden bridge. Once across the rushing frigid waters of the Oconee, they entered Milledgeville.

Families dressed in their finest crisscrossed bustling Statehouse Square in the center of the city, exchanging pleasantries and well-wishes as they walked to either the Baptist, Methodist, Episcopal, or Presbyterian churches. Since Christmas fell on a Wednesday, the capital's otherwise teeming thoroughfares and tree-lined walkways appeared far more congenial than usual. This Christmas, the Spaldings and Kenans ambled into church like all the other folks in Milledgeville, hoping to listen to a holiday message about peace and joy. Like the other churches, the Presbyterian pews overflowed.

Inside the Gothic red-brick place of worship, Michael Kenan stood at the end of a pew box where Clifford, his teenage daughter, and eight-year-old Owen sat between his wife, Katherine, and Spalding Kenan. Spalding's wife, Evelyn, glowed next to him with a look of peace, even though they expected the birth of their baby any day. Michael directed Randolph and his family to the empty pew behind his family. Somber processional music hushed the congregation as the solemn holiday service began. Randolph squeezed Mary's hand when they realized their nephew, Spalding Kenan, had arrived unexpectedly from Darien.

Charlie held a boyish smile, his eyes fixated upon his father's grizzled beard. Allen, his son's small arm wrapped around his own arm, latched the pew box's door after they squeezed in beside Randolph.

Randolph held a modest grin while he watched the acolytes in their black-and-white gowns walk up the aisle. The white-haired pastor in matching vestment watched the acolytes light the ceremonial candles one by one. Out of the corner of his eye, he noticed Allen's head arch upward, his lips moving and his thankful eyes welling.

At that moment, Randolph failed to recall an instance when he had looked at his father and received such an endearing grin. He cherished few memories of his own father ever expressing paternal fondness to him.

He glanced at his two sons and then saw Sallie lost in her own thoughts while Bourke and Tom squeezed their lips tight, stifling their boyish silliness. Mary held Sallie's hand while she intently watched the service unfold. Randolph and Mary ignored their two sons squirming in the bare hardwood pews ill-suited for young boys.

The pastor's Christmas homily failed to compete with Randolph's ruminations of Christmases long ago when he, too, no older than Tom or Bourke, squirmed in stiff wooden seats with feet dangling. He peered at Katherine, the youngest of his older sisters, nestled beside Michael. He struggled to visualize any of his siblings sitting next to their mother and father during church services. All his older siblings had either passed away or left home before Randolph turned ten. Even Katherine, the closest to Randolph in age, was twelve years old by the time he was born.

Their famous father took advantage of his well-earned celebrity and traveled extensively as a politician and acclaimed agriculturist.

He had turned fifty by the time Randolph learned to walk. His mother, Sarah Spalding, celebrated her forty-fourth birthday right after the birth of Randolph, her fifteenth and last child.

Randolph felt empty at moments like this, feeling ill-prepared to become the father he yearned to be. Yet, he bore no grudge toward his parents. His older siblings adored and idolized them but experienced different, yet also the same, father and mother.

The Christmas sermon ended with an impassioned prayer seeking God's judgment to fall upon the North's intruding army and a swift end to this war for Southern independence. The pastor's voice hardened. "Lord God Almighty, I beseech you to smite our enemies and return peace to our families, our homes, and our land once again. Until then, may the righteous indignation of Jesus Christ, the Lion of Judah, lead and protect our sons, husbands, and fathers as they enter the battlefields against our enemy. Amen!"

※ ※ ※

After church, the Spaldings, along with Allen and his son, drove their carriage and wagon two blocks to the Kenan's house on the corner of Green and Liberty Streets. Two teenage mulatto servants scurried from a carriage house behind the two-story house where Michael's father had lived until he passed away. Since returning to Milledgeville, the Kenans had obtained from Michael's brother, a prominent lawyer in town, two younger servants along with Augustus, a gray-haired manservant and a cook.

A sprawling wraparound porch stretched across the front of the elegant, but not garish, two-story house, making it appear grander. Sleek black shutters framed every window of the stark white house. Yellow, orange, and green decorative stained-glass side panels adorned the large black front entry door. A bronze cast gavel served as the door's knocker, a reminder of Mister Kenan's tenure on the bench.

The governor's mansion towered above the surrounding

neighborhood made up of the city's well-to-do families. The other nearby stately homes, mostly built long after Mister Kenan constructed his house, overshadowed the unassuming, original Kenan family home. Yet, it suited Michael and Katherine and held many cherished memories of Michael's boyhood years. In many respects, the house reminded them of their home on Sapelo Island.

While the boys remained preoccupied on the porch, Clifford led Sallie upstairs to her bedroom. Evelyn, with her husband, disappeared after the young surgeon said, "Please pardon us. My expectant wife needs to follow her doctor's advice and get some rest before dinner."

Harmonizing aromas of a lavish Christmas dinner filled the Kenan household by the time Augustus walked around the parlor with a tray of elegant crystal glassware filled with warm Christmas punch. Michael stood in front of his armchair. "To my dear family. May this Christmas bring love, joy, hope, and peace into each of our new homes. May we also toast our brave Georgia boys who have joined their South Carolina brothers to send the Yankee intruders back from whence they came, or to perdition if Mister Lincoln persists in his folly."

Michael stepped beside Randolph with his glass still held high. "Likewise, let us toast to my brave brother-in-law, Colonel Randolph Spalding. He will soon return to Savannah and offer his wise counsel to the generals leading Georgia's army." He then turned to his son, "And to Doctor Spalding Kenan and all the surgeons called into service, may their skilled hands and sharp minds save lives in the coming days." His thoughtful mood fell silent as he closed his eyes for a moment. When he opened them again, they sparkled with a jubilant, celebratory guise. An uproarious laugh ensued, and he said, hardly containing himself, "What am I saying? Enough of such thoughts. This is Christmas Day. Let's toast to God's gifts of love, joy, hope, and peace on this most sacred day and to our family gathered here today."

Randolph rose from his seat beside Mary and raised his glass.

Michael walked over and stretched his arm around Randolph. "I want to make sure you have my good ear."

Randolph looked at Michael with a huge grin. "To you, Michael, and my charming sister, Katherine, thank you. Mary and I are eternally grateful." He looked at Allen, who nodded his affirmation. "We all have left lands and houses we hold dear in McIntosh County, but God willing, we'll gather there again to celebrate many more Christmases with all our family. Until then, Baldwin County is our home this Christmas, thanks to you. Merry Christmas, Michael and Katherine." After gulping down his punch, Randolph looked at Augustus. "May I have a refill?"

After the family enjoyed the succulent Christmas feast, Spalding Kenan asked his uncle to join him for a walk. During their stroll around the grounds, he handed Randolph a letter. "Uncle Charles said this letter was important and I should give it to you at the earliest convenience. He also said to tell you, 'Merry Christmas.'"

Randolph opened the sealed letter.

22 December 1861

Randolph,

> *I received word the missing Ochlocknee soldier involved in the killing of Jeremiah and rape of Cecile is under arrest and facing court-martial on desertion charges in Savannah after confessing to leaving Sapelo with the other two Ochlocknee soldiers found dead on St. Catherine's. He claimed a slave he knew as Hector from South End attacked them, and he escaped by hiding in marsh grass while the slave bludgeoned one with his own rifle and drowned the other. A fishing boat found him and brought him to Sunbury where they arrested him. The crew said they found him delirious and half-starved on the beach.*

I knew you would want to know about his arrest. His claim that Hector followed them off Sapelo and then killed the other two soldiers on St. Catherine's strikes me as dubious. I will get word to you if I learn more.

Zapala awaits your return before you report to Savannah. See you soon. Your negroes are safe and among those I sent to Brooks County.

Merry Christmas,
Charles

Randolph tried to mask his pent-up emotions, but on their return to Beulah that evening, Mary asked why he returned so glum for the rest of the afternoon after talking to his nephew. He shared what Charles told him and said he needed to leave right away.

※ ※ ※

Two days later, the Spalding family sat together in the dining room at Beulah and ate the breakfast Josephine had prepared. Scooting chairs on the bare wood floor and clinking forks, spoons, and knives while they ate broke the silence. Their downcast faces replaced unspoken words and hid the tears they'd promised not to shed. Colonel Spalding, dressed in his uniform, his official orders tucked in his coat pocket, left his plate untouched and pushed his chair back from the end of the table.

Allen wiped his mouth with his napkin. "Charlie, please stay here with your Aunt Mary and finish your breakfast."

"But Pa!" Charlie wiggled in his chair, aiming to follow his father.

"No, son. I need you to stay here. I'll be right back. Uncle Randolph and I need to meet with Abraham and the rest of our workers this morning."

Allen grabbed his jacket and hat and joined his brother-in-law on the back stoop. "Randolph, are you okay? You ate nothing at breakfast."

Randolph buttoned his cloak and then slid his hands into his leather gloves. "I've got a lot on my mind is all. Come on. Let's get this meeting over with."

An unfettered layer of frost covered the ground. Swirls of smoke from the chimney rose above the house's icy roof and drifted into the low-lying drab clouds. Smaller swirls of smoke floated above the two rows of small red brick chimneys warming the shacks from which the negro workers assembled at the well had emerged.

As soon as Randolph and Allen started their walk from the main house, Abraham rang the bell at the well. Negro men and older sons had congregated around an open fire. They all looked alike in their new clothes and coats. The women stood in front of their houses wrapped in a blanket, their children close by bundled in extra layers of clothes. All eyes fell upon Randolph and Allen as they arrived from the main house.

"Abraham, is this everyone?" Allen asked.

"Yes, sir, Mista Bass, I's afraid so," the burly chestnut-skinned driver stuttered, his eyes darting to the ground at his feet.

"Abe, who else left?" Allen asked.

"Jane and her four child'en, sir. After James done ran off, she be crying a river of tears ev'ry night. She told her folks she wanted to go home and wait for her husband there."

"Allen, who else has run off?" Randolph asked, his arms folded across his chest.

"Beside Jane and her four children, just two. Abraham told me James and Moses disappeared Christmas night."

Randolph stepped beside Abraham. Though his arms remained crossed, his right hand stroked his chin as he examined the faces of the men staring back at him from the gathering around the fire. What he saw appeared foreign to him. Their faces could no longer hide their fear and uncertainty. Their eyes begged for answers about their future. The familiar sights, sounds, smells, and routines they once counted on no longer existed. They had left the only homes they had ever known. They had no way of knowing how far they had traveled from the familiar and certainly had no notion of how to find their way back to Sapelo.

Randolph patted Abraham's broad shoulder. "I can see in your eyes how unsettled you all are. I wish I had the answers to ease all your fears, but I can promise you this—my father, Mister Thomas Spalding, promised you, and your poppas and mommas before you, you could always live on Sapelo. None of you has done anything to deserve to be removed from your homes on Sapelo and brought to Beulah. Look around here." Randolph pointed to the rolling hills lined with tall green pines rising above leafless oaks, poplars, and sycamores surrounding Beulah's barren but fallowed fields. He then looked toward the Oconee River's rushing waters. He reached down and scooped up a fistful of Beulah's orange dirt and let it fall through his fingers. "This land is not Sapelo. There are no rising and falling tides nor waves stirring the salt air along the shore. Where are the marsh inlets teeming with all the shrimp, crabs, and fish you can catch in your nets? Sapelo's gray-bearded giant oak trees hold their green leaves even in the harshest winter. And yes, the soil appears strange to us. But I promise you, this land will grow whatever we plant on it. Until we all can return to our homes on Sapelo, I am asking you to trust me. I promise, neither my family nor any of you will go hungry. While I'm away, Mister Bass will keep Missus Spalding apprised of anything you need for your homes, your clothing, or your doctoring."

The fearful looks and furrowed brows among the faces gathered around relaxed as Randolph spoke. They remembered the promise they knew so well about Sapelo, their home. They also knew that promise required their cooperation and hard work to cultivate the land. Beulah's hardened red clay soil would be more difficult to plow than the sandy moist dirt on the island, but there would be no cotton or sugarcane crops to labor over. Until they returned to Sapelo, they heard Mister Spalding speak of growing corn and other food crops along with raising livestock.

The men surrounding Randolph, Allen, and Abraham chattered amongst themselves until Abraham raised his huge hand and shouted, "Does anyone here need to say anything to Mista Spalding?"

Heads swayed back and forth.

"Listen to me," Randolph said. "If any of you feel you want to leave here, Mister Bass won't come after you. But if you stay and work hard for him and Missus Spalding, they'll be sure you have plenty to eat, clothes, and a roof over your head as long as we are here. When it's safe to return, all who stay will see your homes again. I promise. I'm leaving for Savannah to help our brave soldiers put an end to this fighting. Some of you may have heard that Northern folks want to give you your freedom from a life as a slave."

All eyes became glued to Randolph. From the back of the gathering came a rush of shushing.

"I'll tell you the truth about freedom. Freedom allows you to choose your master. The war the South is fighting is over independence, not freedom. Independence has no master. My father understood the innate need for freedom that resides in all men, but he also knew freedom comes at a price. A price that cannot become a burden for others. He taught me that freedom will not feed you, clothe you, or put a roof over your head. Freedom will not allow you to break laws established to protect and preserve how we must live amongst others. Your freedom does not remove me from my responsibilities and obligations to each of you. My father gave you and your parents before you the freedom to live and work on Sapelo or choose to become the slave under heavy-handed masters who my father turned his back on, masters who mistreated and abused their workers. He foresaw a day when agricultural diversification and advances would provide independence for every man willing to work and sacrifice to attain it. I ask you to decide if it is freedom you desire or independence."

Glimmers of hope filled their eyes and eased some of their fears. Cautious smiles stared back.

"Until I return, listen to Abraham and Mister Bass. I told them to allow you a couple of days before we build a new barn, add fencing for livestock, construct a grist mill, and then set our plows to the fields."

※ ※ ※

Not long after Randolph and Allen returned to the main house, Randolph hugged Mary, standing beside the carriage out front. Allen consoled Sallie, Tom, Bourke, and Charlie at the foot of the porch steps.

Mary ran her fingers across the stitches she'd carefully applied to repair the tear in the flap of Randolph's tunic, a token from his brief but harrowing experience on Hilton Head. "Please take care of yourself and write when you can." Her lip quivered as she locked her eyes on his.

"I will," he mouthed as he caressed her cheeks. "Now, for the sake of the children, no more tears. Allen will handle what needs to be done around here. Let him deal with Abraham and the other drivers to till the fields we will need for planting this spring. You mind the children."

Mary dabbed a tear from the corner of her eye with her fingertip. "I am grateful Allen is here. With him, these barren fields will soon be ripe with endless rows of cornstalks, and our gardens will reap fresh sweet potatoes, squash, greens, peas, and beans." She turned her head toward the huddle of children surrounding her brother. "I think Charlie agrees with me, too."

Randolph laughed. "Yes, I confess I feel far better about leaving you and the kids here knowing Uncle Allen is here with you. Funny, this will be the first time in my lifetime that cotton will not be in our fields. Then again, in his final years, my father promulgated the need for crop diversity to offset the South's blindsided dependency on cotton. I bet he smiles on our choice of crops this year." He gently squeezed her cheeks and kissed her lips. "My dear darling, the stagecoach will not wait for me."

"William, you be sure Mister Spalding gets on board that stage," Mary said, looking up at William's anxious gaze trained on the carriage's two-horse team.

"Yes, ma'am. I most assuredly will get Mister Spalding and his bags on that coach. I will not head back until then."

Just then, A.C. McKinley galloped up the drive, dressed in his uniform. "Good morning, Colonel Spalding." He then tipped his hat at Mary. "We heard you were leaving today. My mother and father asked me to ride out here to assure you that our family will keep a watchful eye on Missus Spalding and your family while you are away."

"Why thank you, Lieutenant McKinley." Mary tendered a rosy-cheek smile. "Will you be around, too?"

"Not for long, ma'am. Our company is waiting for orders to arrive any day. Word is we'll be headed north for Tennessee to defend the rail lines."

"Lieutenant, Godspeed. I pray you and the Baldwin Volunteers will send any Yankees that come your way back home with their tails between their legs."

"We'll do our best, sir. May I ride along with you?"

"Tie your horse to the back and grab a seat. I'll enjoy the company until I have to board the coach."

Lieutenant McKinley walked his horse to the rear of the carriage and cinched the reins to the back end. The looks Sallie and the dashing lieutenant exchanged did not go without notice. Randolph climbed in just before William snapped the reins and the carriage jerked forward down the barren, stone-lined drive. Tom and Bourke raced to the bottom of the hill, waving as the carriage traveled farther down the rutted red dirt road until their father no longer waved back and turned his attention to Lieutenant McKinley.

※ ※ ※

Randolph's return to Darien required four days of travel. During a coach transfer in Dublin, he said goodbye to a most loquacious, yet entertaining, coach companion, Mister Sydney Lanier, a recent graduate of Oglethorpe College. Randolph swapped stories about his time at Oglethorpe twenty years earlier. Sydney went on to Savannah, intent on enlisting in the nascent Confederate Navy.

On the long journey from Dublin to Darien, Randolph enjoyed the solitude of being the lone passenger. He pondered what waited for the Ochlocknee soldier who had allowed his hate to seal his fate. He also contemplated the dubious accusation the soldier made about Hector killing the two soldiers on Saint Catherine's Island. Randolph felt a growing urgency to learn of the details before he, too, would head to Savannah and report to General Walker. He read the latest newspaper accounts describing the growing number of Union forces occupying Tybee Island following the Georgia militia evacuation. The encroachment of the Northern forces onto Tybee posed an imminent threat to the city of Savannah.

CHAPTER TWENTY-ONE

31st of December, 1861

On the last day of 1861, Colonel Spalding's coach pulled into Darien. Randolph stepped down, placed his hat on his head, then looked up and down Broad Street. He struggled to recognize the once prosperous port city his family had helped build. Though the stage arrived in the middle of the day, just a handful of the shops and mercantile stores appeared open with many having shuttered their doors and windows.

Below Broad Street's once bustling business district, dockworkers offloaded cargo from the lone merchant schooner moored alongside the city wharf. Most of the city's prominent citizens had closed their businesses and moved their families far from the coast. Georgia's second oldest town and vital port looked like a ghost town except for raucous droves of enlisted soldiers wandering in and out of the handful of establishments still open. The owners of the two taverns and the town's lone open hotel welcomed the high-spirited young soldiers.

Boisterous singing caught Randolph's ears. With his bag in one hand and his satchel in the other, he followed the sounds into the crowded watering hole he had visited many times in the past. Standing in the doorway, he noticed his nephew, Captain William Brailsford, hovering over the shoulder of the piano player, a nimble-fingered soldier with a first-rate, polished tenor voice. He entertained the roomful of soldiers, young and old, privates, corporals, sergeants, and officers of various other ranks.

William scrambled away from the piano as soon as he recognized his uncle. A hearty laugh erupted from the center of his scraggly brown beard. "Welcome home, Uncle!" He embraced him in a bear hug.

"William, it's nice to be back. What's going on?"

"Ah, come and join us. I'll buy you a drink. You look as though you could wash down the dust. We are all here to celebrate the coming new year when the South will finish the fight the North began this past year."

William's harsh growl cleared the way as Randolph followed in his wake, toting his bags to a table across the smoke-filled room. The piano player began playing "Dixie" once again. By the time William sat down beside Randolph, he sounded like a bear growling when he joined in on the final stanza. *"In Dixie land, I'll take my stand to live and die in Dixie. Away, away, away down South in Dixie. Away, away, away down South in Dixie."*

Major Levi Knight left his chair beside the roaring fireplace across the room as the music ended. "Colonel, I thought you'd still be enjoying a few extra days with your family. What brought you back to Darien? Last I heard, General Walker was in Savannah."

"I'm just passing through to visit my brother before I pick up Zapala at his stable. I received word that soldiers in Sunbury arrested the third deserter, and he's facing a court-martial in Savannah. What's with all the soldiers being here?"

"We had a measles outbreak at Camp Spalding and lost a couple of young men right after you left. Colonel Alexander agreed to move the militia from the island. We moved all but a duty garrison that gets shuttled back and forth from Camp Security. From what we hear, General Lawton's about to recall the entire regiment to Savannah. The Union took Tybee Island."

Randolph leaned closer to Levi Knight as the music began again. "I heard. That's another reason I left sooner than planned and am just passing through on my way to Savannah."

"Randolph, listen to this song. You may like it."

"What is it?"

"It's titled 'The Bonnie Blue Flag.'"

After the tenor-voiced piano player sang a few bars, the clamorous chatter came to a prompt end. Every head turned and listened.

"We are a band of brothers, And native to
the soil, Fighting for the property We gain'd
by honest toil; And when our rights were
threaten'd, The cry rose near and far, Hurrah for
the Bonnie Blue Flag, that bears a Single Star!

Hurrah! Hurrah! for Southern Rights Hurrah!
Hurrah! For the Bonnie Blue Flag, that bears a
Single Star!

As long as the Union was faithful to her trust,
Like friends and like brothers, kind were we
and just; But now, when Northern treachery
attempts our rights to mar, We hoist on high the
Bonnie Blue Flag, that bears the Single Star.

Hurrah! Hurrah! for Southern Rights Hurrah!
Hurrah! For the Bonnie Blue Flag, that bears a
Single Star!"

An ear-to-ear smile spread across Randolph's stubbly face as he listened to the lone highland lilt of the piano player accompanied by the roomful of spirited soldiers joining in with each chorus of hurrahs. As soon as the music subsided, he leaned closer to Levi Knight and said, "That song sums up well what instigated the North to start this war, and we just want to preserve our God-given rights. Yet, the big Northern newspapers continue to kowtow to the ardent cries of the highbrow abolitionists. Not one of these young soldiers has drawn his sword or fired his musket to preserve slavery. They left their homes, their farms, their families, and rallied to the call of patriotism."

Levi nodded. "I could not agree more. The North has staked this war upon something these brave young men have little stake in fighting over. Slavery's not why the shooting began and bloodshed followed. This war started over the supreme and sacred right of self-government. The notion promoted by Northern abolitionists that Southerners would place their lives, fortunes, and their sacred honor in the balance for the sake of preserving slavery is absurd. These young farmers, merchants, and mill workers are sons, fathers, and husbands and have proven their willingness to endure the hardships of the march, extended tedious camp life, and the perils and slaughter of battle. Yet, I venture to say nary a one owns a slave back home."

"They sing out of love for what they hold most dear, their God-given right to defend family and property. No different from you and me," Randolph said.

Levi looked Randolph square in the eyes. "Would you ever free your negroes so they might live and work as they choose?"

"Yes, in time. I believe many of the planters already understand what my father professed years ago. Slavery and cotton are detrimental to the future of agricultural progress in the South. We cannot continue to risk our economic future on cotton alone. Allowing our negroes in due course to earn the right to self-determination for themselves and their families and to reap benefits from their hard labor is in the South's best interest. Let's be honest, Northern abolitionists shoved slavery into the headlines to justify the war, but it is a paper ruse."

Randolph looked across the table at his nephew staring back with inquiring eyes. "Before you say anything you may regret, William, I know you understand what I am saying. Spalding blood runs through you, too. But, has the way you have treated, or should I dare say, mistreated, your servants and field hands helped you sleep well at night? Is their fear of you the deterrent you're counting on? How many of your negroes have run off while you have been patrolling the roads keeping an eye out for runaways and Yankee spies?"

The windows to Brailsford's soul turned red. "Them good for nothin' niggras of mine. Those who ran off weren't worth chasing. As for sleeping well—" He placed his service revolver on the table. "They don't fear me, Uncle. They fear this."

Levi Knight shook his head as Charles, who had heard most of their fiery conversation, walked over and stood behind Brailsford. Levi then said, "He's your nephew, Randolph."

"He's my nephew, too!" Charles laughed, his hands resting on William's shoulders. "Randolph, I didn't expect to see you for another day or so."

"After I read your letter, I knew I had to head to Savannah straightaway. I'm merely passing through."

"Major Knight, I suggest you and Captain Brailsford enjoy the rest of the afternoon singing and drinking. As for Captain Brailsford," Charles tightened his grip on his nephew's brawny shoulders, "he better not forget he needs to report back to camp by midnight. Major Knight, I'm glad to see your lads are making the most of this afternoon too." Charles handed Levi a telegram from General Lawton in Savannah.

"He has ordered you to shut down Camp Spalding, remove all the artillery and munitions off the island, and be ready to march to Savannah within the week."

"But, what about—" Randolph said.

"Come with me. We have no time to waste if you want to leave first thing in the morning," Charles said, grabbing Randolph's bag and clearing the way across the crowded room.

# # #

Charles and Randolph sat beneath the canvas-covered roof of Ashantilly's steam launch as it headed up the Doboy Sound. Both raised their coat collars and sat with their backs to the bow as water sprayed aft when the boat rebounded with each wave. The bitter watery chill turned their cheeks bright red. They exchanged icy puffs between them as they shouted above the steam engine and constant slapping of the waves against the launch's hull.

"So why are we going to the lighthouse first? I would've preferred tying up at South End's dock," Randolph hollered.

"Orders! We have orders."

"What orders?"

Charles patted the breast of his coat. "General Lee is abandoning our island defenses. He ordered all the lighthouses disabled."

"How are we going to disable Sapelo's light? We aren't going to blow it up like they did on Tybee?"

"No! Alex has orders to dismantle the light's Fresnel lens and destroy the tower's reflector. I reckon they figured blinding the lighthouse would suffice, thus saving the gunpowder," Charles said amidst an icy chuckle. "They got the same orders over on Wolf Island to destroy the beacon on their side of the Doboy."

After tying off the launch, Charles and Randolph made their way up from the water's edge. Captain William Young, commander of the Ochlocknee company, accompanied by a small detachment, approached them en route to the lightkeeper's house. Saluting Randolph, he said, "Colonel Spalding, sir."

When Captain Young hesitated, his jaw gaping, Randolph said, "Captain, just the man we needed to talk with. We have what I believe you will receive as good news for you and your men. Major Knight has orders to remove all militia units from Sapelo."

"Yes, sir. That's mighty fine news, sir. Do you know where we might go next, sir?"

"My guess is Savannah with Colonel Alexander to join up with the rest of the regiment."

The youthful captain stepped closer to Randolph. "Begging your pardon, sir, why are you here? Can me and my men be of any assistance to you?"

Randolph peered at Charles, who remained aloof, arms crossed, behind him. "After we talk with the lightkeeper, you and a couple of your men might make yourself available to lend Mister Hazard a hand. He has to disable the lighthouse before you can leave."

"Of course, Colonel. As soon as we get back, I'll speak with Mister Hazard."

"Get back? Where are you off to?" Randolph asked, also crossing his arms.

"We received word that the runaway niggar, along with his wife and daughter, are at Barn Creek."

"He's my responsibility, not yours. Captain Young," Randolph blurted.

"Begging the Colonel's pardon." Captain Young reached into his jacket and showed Randolph the communique sent out from General Lawton's headquarters.

After Randolph read what he already knew, he handed the paper to Charles who handed the communique back to Captain Young and said, "As Colonel Spalding said a moment ago, the referenced runaway slave is none of your concern."

"Sorry, sir, but the three lads accused of killing that nigga boy and raping that gal were from my company. I knew them and their families back in Ochlocknee. That niggar murdered two of my men in cold blood, and the third faces a firing squad for desertion. My apologies, sir, but this identifies your runaway slave as the one who killed the two soldiers. It doesn't mean a hill of beans that they were deserters and likely did what they were accused of doing. Your niggar had no right of perverting their right for a fair trial. From where I am standing, sir, your runaway slave is a dead man walking."

Randolph's jugular veins popped. "Captain, I will see that you and any of your men are brought up on charges if I learn my runaway slave died on account of either you or your men. Do you understand me? If you find him, he's to be brought to Savannah. If he did murder those two soldiers, he'll face the consequences. Do I make myself perfectly clear?"

"Yes, sir! But, if he threatens my men when we find him, you cannot hold my men responsible for defending themselves, sir."

Charles stepped in front of Randolph and got into the face of the indignant captain. "If you arrest this runaway, he is to be brought to me personally at my headquarters. I know you know where my headquarters are located. There best be far more blood on you and your men than on him . . . or else. My men will transport him to Savannah to stand trial. You are dismissed, Captain. Do what you feel you must do. Just remember what Colonel Spalding and I have advised you."

Captain Young snapped a hard salute.

Randolph smirked. "And Captain, don't forget to check in with the lightkeeper when you get back."

"Yes, sir." The red face commander barked at his detachment of soldiers, "Fall in!" A moment later, they marched away, headed back to their post at the Lighthouse Point fortification.

Charles looked at Randolph as they turned to visit with Alex Hazard. "I guess he heard us loud and clear. If I were you, though, I'd get word to Hector to get off the island. That hot-headed captain might just get lucky and stumble into Hector and his family before he leaves Sapelo for good."

"My thoughts exactly. A handful of our negroes remain on the island. It shouldn't be too difficult to get word to Hector."

※ ※ ※

As dusk slowly crept into an icy darkness covering the coastal marshlands, Charles huddled with Randolph on the aft deck of his launch as they made their way back across the black water that separated Sapelo from the mainland.

"I'm sorry we didn't have time to check on the house at South End. However, I locked it down several days ago. Outside of needing a good cleaning, whatever you left behind is safe behind the locked doors."

Randolph chuckled. "I can always count on my older brother. Thanks. What did you think about Alex's reaction when we told him the news?"

Charles puffed on his hands. "Look behind us. Is the light still flashing?"

"I wondered why it seemed darker than usual. I guess he figured he didn't need to fire up the light any longer."

"I imagine he didn't want to waste the energy hauling buckets of kerosene up them winding steps one last time. Did you see his eyes when I suggested he could move into the cottage on Ashantilly for the time being?"

"I sure did. I bet he's already packing his belongings. Where do you think they want him to store the lens?"

"Beats me. I've got greater concerns to fuss about," Charles said, blowing on his fingers. "I meant to tell you the latest news that came out of Savannah. This should warm you up. Captain Olmstead had his artillery crew test firing his newest toy, a rifled, long-range cannon, at Fort Pulaski. The news account says four Union soldiers stood on the parapet of the redoubt fortification we abandoned on Tybee Island. Well, I guess they felt invincible, not to mention out of range from our sharpshooters and artillery. Olmstead ordered the gun crew to test the range and accuracy of his new artillery piece. He had them aim at the Union soldiers flaunting about in full view. A moment after the cannon fired, one of them Yankees swallowed the artillery round while the others leaped from the parapet clean out of sight. The reporter wrote that the gunners atop Fort Pulaski cheered while Captain Olmstead strutted away, his chest puffed out."

Randolph's initial smirk sobered. "I wonder if abandoning Tybee like we did was a good idea. I'd feel much better with them Yankees under our guns and hunkered down around Port Royal, but it looks as though we allowed them to get beyond just a toe in our door."

"You worry too much, brother. We both will feel much better

warming ourselves by the fireside, savoring some warm rum after supping with Evelyn. She's eager to hear about Mary and the kids before you leave in the morning."

"Sounds good to me. However, I cannot get over the feeling nagging me, brother, that I am responsible for what happened to Hector and his family."

"Listen to me. You are not responsible for the hatred that haunts the souls of men. Cheer up. We will get warmed up shortly."

※ ※ ※

At dawn, following a restless evening, Randolph stood beside Zapala in front of Ashantilly. "Thank you, Evelyn, for your most gracious hospitality. I hope all this fuss will be over sooner rather than later, and we can return the favor to you and Charles."

"I do declare, Randolph. You know Charles and I would love nothing more. Here's something to munch on while on the road today."

Randolph hugged Evelyn. "Would you see that my brother posts these letters today?"

"Brother, I will be sure to personally hand them to the postmaster this afternoon. At least our mail delivery is more dependable than in Savannah," Charles said, retrieving the letters from Evelyn. "Are you still intent on arriving in Savannah tonight? You can always stay the night at the Brailsford place in Bryan County."

Randolph stroked his horse's straw-colored mane. "Zapala has had plenty of rest and can use the long ride. James Graybill and his wife have offered for me to room at their house in town. Until General Walker orders me differently, that's where you can find me."

Charles opened both arms wide causing Randolph to take a step back before the two brothers embraced each other. Charles then gripped Randolph by the shoulders. "Don't fret about South End or your house up the road. If I hear anything at all about Hector and Alma, I'll let you know. My guess is Hector and his family are staying with the handful of negroes who refused to leave Sapelo up on the north end of the island."

"If I fret any, it will be over you, Evelyn, and the Wyllys, especially Thomas and his family."

Charles slapped Randolph's shoulders. "I already talked with Alexander and Elizabeth. We will not allow family to falter with their harvest still in the barns." Charles clutched his brother's gloved hand, and they locked eyes. "No heroics. You hear me? I'll look you up the next trip I make to Savannah."

Randolph tucked Evelyn's cloth-wrapped ham and biscuits into his saddlebags and mounted Zapala. "You tell William for me that if anything happens to you, I will hold him personally responsible. Leave the fighting to the younger warriors." He tipped his hat to Evelyn as he spun around, rode off, and yelled over his shoulder, "I'll expect to see you in Savannah real soon."

CHAPTER TWENTY-TWO

1st of January, 1862

A starless cold and rainy night slowed Randolph's arrival into Savannah. Once Zapala sensed their destination was near, his gait quickened. His hooves sloshed in and out of puddles, stirring a half-asleep Randolph in the saddle. The city's lamplit, muddy avenues guided them to Oglethorpe Square, two blocks off the crowded riverfront overflowing with bales of cotton stacked from the water's edge to the streets and alleys surrounding the warehouses.

Randolph dismounted and tied his horse to a hitching post in front of the winding stairs of Graybill's two-story townhouse off the stately square. He knocked twice before noticing a flicker of light in the stained-glass transom. Then he heard footsteps just before the handsome red door cracked open. A young woman's face appeared, lit by her raised lantern. Her other hand gripped the ends of her dark green, knitted shawl tightly draped across her shoulders.

"Who might you be, sir? What might be your purpose for calling this time of the evening?" She squinted as she pushed the lantern toward Randolph's face.

Her Irish brogue raised a grin. "My apologies for arriving at this late hour. My name is Randolph Spalding. Mister Graybill is expecting me." Rain dripped from the brim of his hat as the lass inspected Randolph's sopping cloak, no longer keeping his uniform dry.

"Who is it, Margaret?" James Graybill called out from the upstairs landing.

"A soldier, sir. He says he is Mister Randolph Spalding."

"Well, Margaret, for goodness 'sake, let him in," James shouted, descending the stairs as he cinched a crimson robe over his buttoned white shirt and black trousers.

Randolph removed his drenched hat and unbuttoned his caped greatcoat after he stepped inside the foyer. "My apologies for arriving at this ungodly hour. The weather slowed me and my horse down."

"Where's your horse?"

"Tied out front. May I take Zapala to your stables?"

"No, please. My brother will be happy to lend a hand." James yelled down the hall where a lantern illuminated the library. His younger brother appeared in the doorway. "Louis, would you take Colonel Spalding's horse around to the stable and get him settled?"

"Mister Spalding, we are pleased to see you again. Nasty night though," Louis said, pulling on his coat. "I'll make sure to wipe him down and leave fresh fodder and water in his stall."

"Much obliged, Louis." Randolph stood holding his hat and gloves with his greatcoat draped over his forearm. Water dripped onto the floor tiles beneath his feet.

James grabbed Randolph's soaked overgarments and handed them to Margaret, their young Irish housekeeper and nanny. She disappeared down the hall carrying Randolph's wet items, mumbling in Gaelic and leaving a trail of water drops on the floor.

"Please, come sit by the fireplace," James said after a hardy handshake. "May I get you something to eat or drink?"

"Is that Randolph Spalding's voice I hear?" Mary Graybill cried out as she came down the stairs wearing a regal blue house dress adorned with frilly white lace on the collar and cuffs. Her dark brown hair was pulled up in twin braids and pinned neatly on the back of her head. Her matronly appearance made her look older than her twenty-five years.

"Mary, I apologize and beg your pardon for arriving at this time of the night." Randolph accepted and gently kissed the back of Mary's hand at the foot of the stairs. "I hope I didn't wake your toddler."

James cackled. "Henry has gotten used to the sporadic booms and whistles of artillery fire. I doubt your arrival has disturbed his sleep."

Randolph ventured into the parlor and shared the latest news from Milledgeville and Darien about his family. James filled Randolph in about the stiffening of the Union blockade ever since the Yankees took possession of Tybee. His company's blockade runners had sailed unthwarted across the Atlantic carrying raw cotton to England and returned with vital goods and supplies—but no longer. In recent days, James had tried hauling their raw cotton to Fernandina by rail since the Union blockade thinned the farther south their ships patrolled. But James admitted the sparse flow of cotton reaching England from the South would certainly get worse if Union ships and the Yankee army advanced farther.

Margaret returned and hung Randolph's hat and caped overcoat on the coat rack and placed his gloves on the nearby tabletop. Mary asked, "Margaret, thank you for taking care of Mister Spalding's coat and hat. Before you go up to bed, would you bring a board of cheese and bread for our guest?"

"Yes, ma'am," the red-haired young housekeeper muttered and retreated to the kitchen.

Mary returned to the parlor with a bottle of Madeira port wine. James had uncorked the bottle by the time Margaret brought the board of cheese and bread. Not long afterward, Randolph thanked James for supplying the blankets and clothing he had ordered for his workers. Their conversation made it clear such favors would not be possible again. The Confederate Army had already issued his family's business orders it struggled to fill from their textile mills in the state.

James showed Randolph to his room upstairs. "Randolph, I read about the deserter who got arrested from your regiment. His tale about escaping off Saint Catherine's Island after a runaway slave murdered his two comrades has been the talk about town. The mere notion of runaway negroes killing soldiers rattled many of the city's already skittish residents, especially the wives. Is that why you arrived earlier than you wrote in your letter?"

"Partially. Thanks for allowing me to board with you and Mary. See you in the morning."

※ ※ ※

Margaret, the Graybill's housekeeper, interrupted Randolph and James Graybill at the morning breakfast table. "Colonel Spalding, this just arrived for you." She handed him a sealed letter from the Adjutant General's Office.

> *Headquarters. Dept. of Georgia*
> *Savannah, January 1. 1862*
>
> *Colonel R. Spalding*
> *Adjutant, 1st Georgia Brigade. Savannah*
>
> *Colonel*
> *I have the honor of receiving you as adjutant and request your prompt arrival. Please report forthwith to headquarters.*
> *Further, Colonel Styles, ad hoc judge advocate for the court-martial trial of Private Beall, requires your attendance at the tribunal, morning of January 9.*
>
> *W. H. T. Walker*
> *Brig. Gen'l Commanding*

"It appears General Walker received my telegram. I'm afraid I must report straight away to headquarters. Of greater importance to me, Private Beall's trial is next week." Randolph folded the letter and stood to leave. "By your leave, I must excuse myself."

James rose from the table. "If you can offer any support in kicking them Yankees back to whence they came, then, by all means, you have my blessings. Will we see you for dinner?"

"Something tells me the answer is no. I suspect General Walker has other plans."

※ ※ ※

Several days passed as dreary, overcast skies persisted. During his first week as Brigadier General Walker's adjutant, Randolph found his gruff exterior and high-handed reputation well-earned when addressing military matters. Yet, Colonel Randolph soon discovered the general's sedate, paternal side. Whenever their hectic schedule of endless staff meetings and traveling on horseback to inspect the ever-increasing number of fortifications, supply depots, and militia encampments surrounding Savannah allowed, William Henry Talbot Walker rambled on about his family back home in Augusta. When not talking about his family, he sympathized with Randolph's frustration and fears about leaving his own family's heralded home and property in McIntosh County.

Walker expressed an unusual interest in the upcoming court-martial of the young soldier who'd deserted Randolph's former regiment. But Randolph's disappointment had weighed on him ever since he'd learned the court ignored the murder and rape charges. Tomorrow morning, the court-martial tribunal headed by Colonel Styles as judge advocate and Major Knight as provost marshal would decide on the willful desertion case against Private Beall from Ochlocknee. Walker, a proud West Point graduate with a long and distinguished service record, responded often to ease Randolph's disappointment. "The poor lad faces a firing squad either way. It may be hard to swallow, but the sentence for a conviction of willful desertion will be swifter and just as severe. Dead is dead, all the same."

Randolph sighed. "I reckon that's a fact all right, but it won't be justice for what he and the other two did to Jeremiah and Cecile."

"Assuming I understand you right, their pa exacted his own

justice on two of them."

"Now General, not once have I made such a claim as that being God's honest truth. I merely repeated the rumors about what happened to those two other Ochlocknee boys," Randolph said.

Walker eyed Randolph, stroked his black beard, and said, "Well, dead is dead, just like I said before."

Later that bleak evening, Randolph scurried after General Walker outside of Lawton's headquarters when their early evening staff meeting with Generals Lee and Lawton ended early. Lee, with his masterfully calm voice, had just silenced the back-and-forth raucous exchanges of ardent opinions in the room when he rose from his chair and said, "Gentlemen, please. Let us be mindful that each of us has the same common purpose for being here. We shall never defeat our enemy as long as our headstrong opinions exceed the dire importance of our meetings. I think we can all agree that we are all tired and hungry. Let us resume our discussions tomorrow afternoon."

General Walker stormed out of Lawton's headquarters with a scowl on his bearded face, grumbling to himself. Randolph knew Generals Lee and Lawton respected Walker's battlefield experience against the Yankees in northern Virginia, but his adamant, fiery passion and unceremonious manners during staff meetings was also bothersome. However, Walker never expected his opinions and invaluable insight to be dismissed with a patronizing nod. As a Georgia militia brigadier general, his sway remained confined to Savannah's defense. On broader discussions involving tactical maneuvers and strategies to counter the creep of Union forces threatening Savannah and the entire Georgia seacoast, Walker's insistence on aggressive offensive maneuvers to drive the Yankees back into the sea fell on the deaf ears. General Lee often left such heated meetings with Lawton quelling Walker's infuriating outbursts. He wanted to avoid ill-fated offensive campaigns against well-equipped and dug-in Union forces, but he could not dodge General Walker's obstinance, which often bordered on insubordination.

Before Randolph and Walker mounted their horses, Randolph suggested a favorite hotel nearby where they could grab a drink and have dinner. After shaking the rain from their cloaks and wide-brimmed hats, they stepped into the grand foyer of the Marshall House, an establishment Randolph had frequented during his many business and pleasure ventures to Savannah. Throughout the ornate lobby, local merchants, factors, and prominent businessmen mingled with uniformed officers. A handful engaged in serious parleys, without a doubt, posturing for handshake favors, a quasi-social activity Randolph himself had often engaged in. However, most appeared caught up in genuine, good-natured palavering. Their bellowing laughter and light-hearted chatter extended beyond the lobby into the elegant dining room.

With a highbrow sophisticated English accent, the maître d' escorted Randolph and Walker to a vacant table in the back of the dining room. Randolph's idle conversation attempted to further mollify Walker's stubborn mood. After their waiter brought two crystal-stemmed goblets of warm mulled wine, Walker savored a mouthful while his eyes darted around the room. A minute later, he shoved his chair from the table and stood, scanning the roomful of diners preoccupied with their light-hearted table talk. Hardly a head took notice as he glared at each table from the back corner of the dining room.

He crossed his arms over his chest, his dark, deep-set eyes glazed over, and he scoffed loud enough to be heard across the room. "I beg your pardons! I cannot help to notice how everyone here tonight seems to be ignoring the fact that our enemy, Lincoln's unwelcome intruders, is threatening this fine city. Yet, all I have heard this evening is laughter and devil-may-care chatter. Do you not care Yankees occupy Tybee Island and threaten to occupy Georgia soil farther down the coast?" Walker spoke brusquely, expounding on the dire reality Savannah would soon face. His stern, loud inquiry disrupted every conversation in the dining room as well as most in the nearby lobby. With all eyes on him, he concluded his diatribe declaring in no uncertain terms that as the commanding general in charge of defending Savannah, he planned to fight the Yankees in the streets before surrendering even if that meant seeing homes and buildings reduced to rubble. Before he'd even finished and sat back down, the carefree patrons wore scowls and fearful grimaces with almost everyone staring at one another, jaws hanging and lost for words.

After the mood of the restaurant settled with quieter, sober, unsmiling conversations, Randolph felt the curious glances while they dined. Then the glances became fixed gazes after a reporter from the *Savannah Daily News* walked up to the table. He interrupted General Walker mid-bite into his steak dinner. The general appeared unfazed by the reporter's questions. He lowered his fork and smugly looked up at the reporter. Walker slid the vacant chair next to him out and invited the eager reporter to have a seat. The reporter's flattery earned a gratifying smile from Walker. He sought the general's insight on the city's situation, all the while taking fastidious notes. Randolph listened while he finished his steak and washed every bite with his mulled wine. The newsman sensed General Lawton and certainly General Lee might take exception to Walker's forthright opinions when his words appear in print in tomorrow morning's edition of the newspaper.

CHAPTER TWENTY-THREE

9th of January, 1861

Private Beall's court-martial convened beneath the mess tent at Camp Davis following breakfast. Judge Advocate Colonel Styles from Georgia's 13th Regiment and Provost Marshal Major Levi Knight from Georgia's 29th Infantry Regiment sat at a bare mess table. Private Beall stood facing the table, head bowed, hands and ankles in chains and shackles. Two armed soldiers stood on either side of him at attention with their Enfields at order arms.

Colonel Randolph sat on a front-row bench off to one side. With the court's decision a foregone conclusion, he took part as an interested observer. His sole duty before the court came with his affirmation of the charges read at the opening of the court-martial against Private Beall. After Colonel Styles announced he struck the names of two deceased soldiers discovered on Saint Catherine's Island from Colonel Randolph's original charges of desertion, he had Randolph stand. "Colonel Spalding, before this court announces its verdict and passes sentence on Private Elias Beall of the Ochlocknee Light Infantry, do you wish to say anything to this court?"

Randolph glanced at the well-groomed, shaven, young man. His fresh, clean uniform made him appear like so many other wet-behind-the-ears, callow volunteers who joined their local militias and traveled far from their homes across Georgia. But Randolph knew that Private Beall's engrained, ignorant hatred instigated the events that led to this fateful morning, and he grieved briefly for the boy's ma and pa. He then looked straight ahead and said, "Colonel Styles, I have nothing further." He returned to his seat on the bench.

"For the record, Colonel Spalding declined to say anything. Major Knight, would you read the findings of this court-martial?"

Major Knight stood, made brief eye contact with Randolph, and turned to Private Beall. The young private sobbed openly, his eyes begging Randolph for forgiveness. "I'm sorry, Colonel Spalding, for what we done to those two niggars. I now wish they's pa had killed me too the night he killed Willie and Jim."

Randolph's back straightened and his neck stiffened, but he remained silent. He refused to make eye contact, and his lip quivered. He knew Private Beall's utterance pronounced a death sentence on Hector if arrested.

Major Knight cleared his throat and read the findings of the court. "Before this general court-martial, convened at Camp Davis on this 9th day of January in the year of our Lord 18 and 62, and in concordance with General Order Number 58 of the Georgia 1st Brigade issued by Headquarters, Savannah and of which Colonel Styles, 13th Georgia Infantry presided, Private Elias Beall, Company B 29th Georgia Infantry, on the sole charge of desertion, this court-martial finds you guilty. It is the decision of this court you shall stand before a firing squad tomorrow morning and be executed. May God have mercy on your soul."

Colonel Styles rose and motioned to the two sentries. They shouldered their Enfields, grabbed the sobbing Private Beall by his handcuffed arms, and escorted him away. The few soldiers who witnessed the proceeding left the mess tent talking amongst themselves in somber voices as they returned to their tents. Randolph and Colonel Styles exchanged halfhearted salutes before Styles pulled his overcoat on and exited the makeshift courtroom.

Major Knight shook Randolph's hand. "Thought you would like to know the last detachment at Camp Spalding will leave the island by the end of next week. A security detachment will remain in Darien along with a handful of men too sick to travel. The rest of the twenty-ninth are assembling here at Camp Davis waiting for further orders. Colonel Alexander heard the companies of the twenty-ninth are to be divvied up and stationed at Fort Jackson and Fort McAllister."

"I believe I can verify that rumor to be likely true. How are you and your sons fairing?"

"My sons are eager for some action. Me, I'm realizing how old I really am every morning when I clamber out of my bunk. What about you? I hear you're hobnobbing with the generals and dining pretty good."

"What do you mean? Being General Walker's adjutant ain't no stroll through the park. He's a stringent taskmaster and becomes rather surly when our days drag well into the night."

Knight smiled. "So, do you regret resigning to take General Walker's offer?"

"No. I can do more good right here to stop the Union Army from gaining any more Georgia soil. If they encroach much farther down the coast, I'm afraid I'll end up breaking a promise to my son and never see another harvest on Sapelo. But enough gloom and doom thoughts. I confess I miss chewing the fat with you, puffing on a good cigar, and sipping rum." Randolph untied and mounted Zapala. "Levi, look me up in Savannah. You bring the cigars, and I'll break out a bottle."

"Count on it." Levi said, walking away.

"Hey Levi, anyone heard more about Hector or Alma? I'm afraid what'll happen if—"

Levi raised his hand. "Hector did what I would've done. Leastwise, I don't suspect he'll poke his head up until the last of our troops desert Camp Spalding."

"I sure pray you're right, my friend." Randolph saluted. He rode off, headed back to headquarters for another long day sure to feel even longer. He expected General Lawton's reprimand to fester like a burr under General Walker's saddle. The promised article about the fiery incident at dinner the previous evening, along with the general's colorful comments afterward, had made the morning edition of the *Savannah Daily News*.

The early morning rain subsided, leaving a fine, chilly mist beneath an unrelenting, thick gray blanket overhead. Randolph slacked his grip on the reins and slouched in the saddle. Zapala's gait responded as they poked along the waterlogged city streets. Randolph sulked over Private Beall's fate and then grieved for Hector, Alma, and Cecile. All the while, he dreaded the likely tenor of the staff meetings that awaited his arrival.

# # #

Randolph's uniform felt damp and cold after his ride from Camp Davis when he removed his soaked frock coat and hung it with his hat in the entry of Lawton's headquarters. The laughter and lighthearted chatter coming from the staff meeting underway in the parlor quelled much of the burden he felt. Governor Brown puffed a cigar at the head of the conference table seated with Generals Lee, Lawton, Jackson, and Walker engaged in jovial conversation. Other staff officers sat or stood around the room, adding to the laughter whenever the generals found humor in their back-and-forth banter, a far cry from stress-filled staff meetings to strategize and organize the defenses to thwart the Union's troop and naval activity on and near Tybee Island.

"Colonel Spalding, we have been waiting for you to join us," General Lawton said, puffing on his cigar. "The governor arrived this morning wanting an update on our plans to defend Georgia, specifically Savannah. I trust the court-martial went as expected?"

"Yes, General." Randolph turned to Governor Brown. "An unexpected but welcome surprise to see you, Governor."

"Randolph, my friend. I'm sorry I did not get to visit with you and Mary while you were in Milledgeville for Christmas. I spoke with

Michael Kenan just before I made this trip, and he told me your family moved to Beulah along with your slaves from McIntosh County."

"Yes, Governor. Until we bid these Northern invaders a final warm farewell and their ships leave our coastline, I felt it best to send my family inland."

"Understandable. Tell me, Colonel Spalding, how's your brother?"

"He's as ornery and cantankerous as always. I dare say he's far more like our father than I'll ever wish to be," Randolph jested.

"I beg to differ. Charles's stodginess comes from all those impressionable years he spent getting an education in Edinburgh. And I will grant you, your brother still shares the same stiff upper lip as your father. But Randolph, like your father and brother, your heart and soul belong to Georgia."

"Thank you, Governor. That's why I'm here. I made a promise to my father on his deathbed, and short of my own grave, I intend to honor that promise." Randolph eyed the generals around the table.

"Colonel Spalding, I'd like to introduce you to Colonel Charles Olmstead, commanding officer at Fort Pulaski," General Lee said, inviting Olmstead to greet Randolph with the wide sweep of his hand.

Randolph cracked a grin as they shook hands. "I heard rumors about your artillery crew and how they, under your orders, reminded the Yankee soldiers on Tybee's shores they are not out of range of Pulaski's cannons."

"We have had a demonstration or two to that fact, but it will not be long before the Union adds their own bigger cannons," Olmstead said, maintaining a somber tenor.

General Lee stood. "Gentlemen, the hour is getting late. First thing tomorrow we all will meet at Fort Jackson. The *Ida* will sail us downriver to Cockspur Island for a visit to Fort Pulaski. The Governor wants to see a sample of what the State of Georgia purchased to defend Savannah."

"Here, here!" General Lawton barked. "Might I suggest we wrap up our session here before we all head over to the Marshall House for dinner? Does that suit you, Governor?"

General Lee returned to his seat and invited Colonel Olmstead to sit next to him. General Walker waved and nodded to Randolph to take the empty seat between himself and General Jackson. The meeting continued as Lawton discussed the newest fortifications and batteries along the Savannah River, and the expansion of Georgia infantry numbers at Camp Davis. During the discussion about the latest intelligence reports, Lawton and Walker highlighted the slow encroachment of Union forces across the river in South Carolina. General Walker asked Randolph to assess the Union threat along the South Carolina side of the Savannah River.

Randolph thought a moment before pointing to Jones and Turtle Islands on the map. "Generals, Governor Brown, I know these waters very well. They are not unlike the marsh islands surrounding Sapelo Island. Northern soldiers will end up swimming in a chest-deep slurry of mud as soon as they agitate the quagmire beneath the tidal grasses. Even the smallest men stomping across the marsh flats will find their efforts bogged from advancing. The recent rains and high tides serve us—not them. Men walking over the precarious marshland, supported by the fragile roots of marsh reeds and grass, will sink at least six inches with each step until they break through and get sucked down waist-deep, sometimes deeper. It will force their engineers to wait weeks, maybe months, hoping for better weather before they can make any threatening headway. I contend, short of sailing up the Savannah past Fort Pulaski and Fort Jackson, they will need to gain a foothold farther up the river to threaten the city with sufficient men and artillery to be a viable threat to the city."

General Walker patted Randolph's back. With a confident smile, he rocked back in his chair and said, "I agree with Colonel Spalding's assessment and suggest we discuss plans to go on the offensive against the Yankee troops entrenched on Tybee Island before they get reinforcements, and the bigger guns Colonel Olmstead fears are coming."

Governor Brown turned to Lee. "What do you think, general?"

"Governor, it is not in my disposition to comment until I have had time to sleep on it after enjoying a splendid dinner. Let us adjourn, if you please, Governor?" General Lee looked at Lawton after a subtle nod to Randolph and Walker.

Lawton shoved his chair back. "Gentlemen, let us retire to the Marshall House. Governor, your carriage will be out front shortly."

※ ※ ※

In the predawn glow of candles and a lantern, Randolph entered the dining room to eat breakfast before riding to Fort Jackson. Louis Graybill, wearing his captain's uniform, sat with his brother James. Margaret poured coffee for Randolph after she handed him a plate with a stack of griddle cakes and fried bacon. "Mista Spalding, top of the morn' to ya. Might I fetch you anything else?" the spirited housekeeper asked with shiny rose-colored cheeks and locks of her bright red hair dangling wildly in her face.

"This looks just fine, Margaret. Thank you," Randolph said before gulping his coffee.

James left the table and returned with a letter and a telegram for Randolph. "These arrived yesterday afternoon."

"Gentlemen, what can I get any of you before I head upstairs to take care of Master Henry before he wakes Missus Graybill?" Margaret asked, pushing the unruly stray hairs from her face.

Randolph smiled as he sniffed the envelope from Mary and tucked it inside his coat. "I think I'll read this a bit later." He then unfolded the telegram, and his disposition soured.

"Colonel Spalding, anything the matter? Is it unexpected news?" Louis asked.

"I'm not exactly sure as of the moment. My brother says Captain Young and a detachment from his company apprehended my servant, Hector, along with his wife and daughter just before they escorted

Mister Hazard, the lightkeeper, off Sapelo. He expects Captain Young to send word to Lieutenant Colonel Alexander, acting regimental commander at Camp Davis, seeking further instructions. In the meantime, they are under guard at Camp Security. He says he will try to see Hector and his family and send another message as soon as he can find out anything."

"What do you think will happen? They accused your man of murdering two soldiers. It will not matter that those two may have had a hand in killing his boy and raping his daughter. He won't receive a fair trial," James said.

"I'm afraid you're right. If I write out a response to my brother, would you see it gets sent first thing this morning? I'm going to be walking in the shadows of the governor and the generals most of the day."

Louis blurted, "Colonel, I'll have it sent as a priority telegram to your brother from the telegraph office at the train depot."

"Thank you, Louis. It'll be brief and worded not to draw attention. I need to find out what will happen to Hector. Charles may find out long before I can break free and talk to my regimental replacement at Camp Davis."

※ ※ ※

The sun finally broke through the gray clouds, but a stiff, cool breeze swept across the Savannah River as the steamer sailed from Fort Jackson to Cockspur Island. Randolph left the other staff officers and found a quiet spot on the leeward rail of the *Ida*. He pulled Mary's letter from his coat pocket and gripped it firmly as he read it, afraid a gust of wind would blow it overboard.

Mary wrote about the repairs to the fencing and the hog pens surrounding the barn and about how loud the passel of pigs squealed, and sows and boars snorted in the morning. Their ruckus reminded her how sorely she missed Hector and Jeremiah, and she wrote that

Sallie continually asks about Alma and Cecile. She added that Allen still intended to add a couple of milk cows, a bull, a flock of chickens, and a rooster. Thanks to Michael, Beulah's barn held enough rice and cornmeal to get them through the winter. She bragged how Abraham and the field hands started clearing several acres in the fields nearest the barn, but Abraham confessed they could not plant crops until early spring. The workers just wanted to stay busy. Baldwin County remained wet and cold, and it snowed to the delight of the children two days after he had left, although it melted as soon as it touched Beulah's dark red ground.

A solitary smile rose when Randolph read how Mary had arranged for an elderly schoolmaster, Mister Brinkley Babb, to visit once a week to tutor Sallie, Tom, and Bourke. He'd earned Mary's approval after she met him and received Anne McKinley's glowing recommendation about his demanding Socratic teaching philosophy tempered with a likable, sagacious wit.

He then read the words Mary penned on a separate page:

My loving husband, Randolph, we parted in silence; we parted at the break of day beside the banks of that lonely, icy river far removed from the tidal waters we call home. In the frigid air here since you left, no birds flutter and sing their tune as they did on our coastal shores. I stare into a foreign night sky and listen for the stars overhead telling touching stories of friends and family long passed to the kingdom of glory, but these stars away from home remain silent. We parted in silence, our cheeks wet with tears past controlling. And now I look at this midnight sky, my heart full of weeping, each star a sealed book full of tales long forgotten. But when we stand together again, the fragrance and bloom of those memories we left behind shall fill the silence and tears that keep us apart now. Come back to me soon. I pray we can return home again. Almost forgot, Evelyn and Spalding named their newborn

Michael. He arrived two days after you left.

Your dearest wife,
Mary.

"By the look on your face, I'd say you received good news from your wife," General Walker said, finding Randolph alone while the other staff officers mingled near the governor and the generals.

Randolph folded the letter and slid it into his coat pocket. "Yes, General. Very pleasing news."

"Come with me, Colonel. We should get ready to disembark with the others. General Lee is eager to give Governor Brown a tour of Fort Pulaski."

Randolph straggled behind the entourage of staff officers who huddled within earshot whenever General Lee and Colonel Olmstead stopped during the tour of Fort Pulaski to point out the formidable features of the fortress. When the gaggle of officers halted atop the fort's ocean-facing parapet, Colonel Olmstead ordered his artillery crew to fire one of the new English Blakely rifled cannons. The governor applauded when the round exploded on the nearest tip of Tybee Island and sent three Yankee sentries scurrying.

General Lee puffed his chest and told Governor Brown, "They will surely make it very warm for Colonel Olmstead and his men with shells fired from that point on Tybee Island, but they cannot breach this fort's thick walls from that distance." Lee then instructed Olmstead to continue adding sandbag traverses around the parapet guns to protect the gunners from bursting shells, and to erect wooden blindages covered with several feet of earth over the exposed colonnades below to protect the barracks and storerooms.

Randolph walked alongside General Walker on the return to the *Ida*. Walker looked at him and said, "If we do not attack the Union emplacements, Fort Pulaski will soon find itself under a warmer siege, thanks to the Yankee guns. I would dare say Satan himself will dance among the flames that will rain down within the walls."

"What did General Lawton say about your suggestion to mount an offensive against Tybee?"

"Nothing."

CHAPTER TWENTY-FOUR

18th of January, 1862

"Colonel Spalding, there's an army officer at the door asking for you. He says he's got word from your brother," Margaret squinted with pursed lips. "Shall I let him in?"

Randolph folded the newspaper and jumped up from the armchair in the parlor. "No, Margaret. Don't bother. I'll go see who it is. Thank you."

"Mister Spalding, were you expecting anyone this time of night?" Mary Graybill inquired from the sitting room across the hall.

"I'm not sure who it is, but I am expecting to hear from my brother Charles. You two return to whatever you were doing. I will take care of it," Randolph said, glancing across the hall. Mary returned to her knitting while Margaret sat back down and started winding yarn by hand, though she kept one eye on Randolph.

A raucous exchange of laughter erupted as soon as Randolph opened the door. "Come in, come in, Thomas. What brought you here tonight? The housekeeper said you have word from Charles."

His nephew stepped inside and removed his cloak and hat. "Pardon my calling this late." His eyes drifted to the sitting room. "Excuse me, ladies. I realize the hour is late, but it is important I talk with my uncle."

"Mary Graybill, this is my nephew, Captain Thomas Wylly, from McIntosh County."

Mary set her knitting aside to greet her guest.

"Mary, you do not need to get up. Thomas and I can retire to the parlor. He has some news I have been looking to hear."

Margaret took Thomas's cloak and hat. "Might I get you anything, Captain?"

"Margaret, might you have some additional coffee for my nephew?"

"Yes, sir. I think we might still have some on the stove. Would you like a cup as well?"

"Yes, that'd be fine. We'll be in the parlor."

Randolph pointed to the matching armchair across from where he had been sitting. "Grab a seat." He stooped down and added a couple of pieces of wood to the fire. "Thomas, you are certainly a sight for sore eyes," he said as he sat down beside his nephew. "What news did you bring with you?"

"Those folks who haven't already left their homes from above the Sapelo River to Glynn County below the Altamaha are getting more and more skittish by the day. Uncle Charles removed all the negroes he could from Harris Neck and loaded them on wagons headed to the Brunswick rail yard. He said to tell you that makes nearly sixty additional workers headed to his plantation in Brooks County."

"Excuse me, sirs. I brung your coffee," Margaret said in her Irish brogue tongue. She smiled at Thomas as she placed their mugs on the table between him and Randolph. Thomas offered a polite smile back, but his eyes darted to Randolph.

Randolph cleared his throat. "Thomas, tell me about Johanna and my darling niece, Lilly. Are they doing well?"

"Johanna's stiffening her British backbone and refuses to join in the hysteria the local women have gotten caught up in. And my precious Lilly, God bless her soul, she's behaving more like her mother every day."

The red-headed housekeeper lost her smile just before she disappeared back to the sitting room with Lilly.

"Uncle," Thomas continued, "I gotta be honest with you. The last of the twenty-ninth received their marching orders and will join up with the rest of the regiment at Camp Davis by the end of the month.

General Mercer also ordered all the artillery and munitions removed from Saint Simons and Jekyll Islands and sent to Savannah. Is it that bad here?"

"Union troops landed on Tybee Island and now occupy our former positions along the mouth of the Savannah, and there are reports of them maneuvering artillery on the South Carolina side. Blockade runners risk getting blown out of the water navigating past Tybee Island. Then again, we're sixty-thousand strong around the city, and Fort Pulaski, Fort McAllister, and Fort Jackson are well-armed and manned. Every day railcars bring more soldiers from all directions. There are nearly as many being sent to South Carolina to keep them Yankees hemmed in around Beaufort as there are those being dispersed around the city. Intelligence reports tell us Union ships sail in and out of Port Royal freely, bringing additional men and supplies. There're even tales of slaves being conscripted into the Union army on Hilton Head."

"Sounds like you and the generals have this war pretty well under control. The way you describe it, there's a giant chess match underway." Thomas sipped his coffee.

"We are doing our best to thwart further encroachment of Yankee soldiers on Georgia's sovereign soil. Let us not forget, Northern soldiers are not risking their homes and heritage. We are! We risk far more than our fortunes—the fortunes of those who follow us. This is a chess match we cannot afford to lose. Now, tell me about Hector, Alma, and Cecile."

"Uncle Charles went and retrieved Alma and Cecile. They're at Ashantilly for now. I saw them before I left. They are obviously scared but safe."

"What about Hector?" Randolph leaned forward and slapped Thomas on his knee. "Tell me about Hector."

"Captain Young received orders to bring Hector to Camp Davis for a trial. Since Hector stands accused of murdering two soldiers, they will try him in Savannah. I suspect Major Knight and Lieutenant Colonel

Alexander know about that. Uncle Charles couldn't find out anymore."

Randolph stood and braced himself with one arm on the mantle. He stared into the flames. "I just sat through Private Beall's court-martial. He's now buried in an unmarked grave like his two comrades. The look on his face after Major Knight read his death sentence turned my stomach."

"My father told me death lingers on the lips and in the hearts of the living. What happened on Sapelo and Hilton Head changed you. Death changes us all. It does not matter the cause, it sobers the best and the bravest," Thomas said.

His uncle slouched, his arm still gripping the mantle. He sighed and said, "Your father has lived long enough to witness his share of death's sting on those left behind. I used to find comfort and solace in my drinking, but now every sip stings going down as if death festered an open wound inside me." He turned and faced his nephew. "I'm afraid the grim reaper will harvest many more souls torn from their mortal hosts, struck down by hatred, ignorance, and blind patriotism. God, I wish I could wash away the taste and smell of death. Every night I wake in a sweat trying to bring the dead back to life."

The happy-go-lucky voices of the Graybill brothers disrupted Randolph and Thomas.

"Mister Spalding, I am sorry we disturbed you and your guest," James said, his brother by his side.

"Actually, your arrival is quite fortuitous. This is my nephew from McIntosh County, Captain Thomas Wylly. He brought me news from back home." Randolph glanced at the three others in the room, staring at each other. "Thomas, this is James Graybill of Crane and Graybill Mercantile here in Savannah and his brother Captain Louis Graybill, although he prefers you call him Lou. I believe they have been at a militia meeting this evening."

After James invited Thomas to spend the night and had his horse taken to the stable, the four sat around the fireplace, sipping port wine and chatting about better days. Randolph coaxed Thomas into sharing several mesmerizing tales from his adventures out West after Mary and Margaret retired to their bedrooms. By the time Randolph followed Thomas upstairs, his dark mood had brightened after Thomas egged him into spinning some tales of his memorable high-stakes card games, horse races, and boating regattas.

※ ※ ※

Early the following morning, Randolph waved at Thomas as they rode off in opposite directions. Thomas headed back to McIntosh County with a promise to get word back to Randolph with added news about Hector and his family.

The sun broke through the wintry clouds by the time Randolph dismounted Zapala in front of General Lawton's residence. Lawton had summoned him and General Walker to discuss deployment of the latest Georgia regiments arriving from the barrier islands and coastal ports. General Lee ordered the last units reallocated to Savannah's defense before he left to report to President Jefferson Davis in Richmond. General Walker once again argued vehemently for an assault on Tybee Island.

"General Lawton, we cannot afford to tuck our tail and cower behind our brick walls and redoubts waiting for the Union Navy and Army to attack. If we do nothing, they will have time to increase their forces on Tybee Island and entrench new artillery."

General Lawton rocked back in his chair behind his desk. "General Walker, this discussion cannot continue. General Lee considered your advice and believes our defenses provide a tenable deterrent against an attack on Savannah. He believes the North's intentions are not to get bogged down with a long and costly siege on Charleston and Savannah. From Port Royal, he contends, the North could launch a campaign inland to capture the rail lines."

"Begging your pardon, General Lawton," Randolph said, "Lincoln needs money to appease the Northern states. It makes far more sense that he plans to strengthen his grip on our key southern ports of Charleston, Savannah, and New Orleans. Before Lincoln commits his armies to an expensive and very bloody campaign, my bet would be on his army and navy robbing the South of its cotton, clogging the docks and warehouses of our major seaports. Unless we can get our cotton removed off our docks and out of our warehouses, the South will suffer the longer this war continues."

General Walker scratched his beard. "Your assessment is sound, Colonel. Why wouldn't they be happy corking up the mouth of the James, Savannah, and Mississippi Rivers? They have the naval advantage and enough troops to occupy the positions they have already gained."

"I would like to hear your response to General Walker's question," Lawton said as he lit a cigar. Randolph walked to the map on the wall behind Lawton's desk.

"A long siege costs money. Lots of money. Northern factories need the cotton for their textile mills. The North cannot afford a stalemate strategy. They know the South will ship the cotton straight to England, and the North will never see another bale as long as this senseless war continues. They need to go on the offensive to get their hands on our cotton. Lincoln knows it would cripple us financially. General Lawton, whether we adhere to General Walker's aggressive plan or not, I contend as far as it concerns Savannah, the North will not remain satisfied just bottling our merchant ships. They want our white gold."

Lawton puffed his cigar and stared at Randolph standing in front of the map. "Until we figure out what those Yankees are up to, we must trust General Lee's faith in Fort Pulaski."

Walker huffed, and his dark eyes glared at Randolph. "Colonel, I have something to show you." Lawton laughed as he handed Randolph a letter.

"I don't understand, General."

"General Cooper is behind on the recent changes. I did not want to stir a hornet's nest. Until the twenty-ninth regiment names new commanding officers, your name remains as regimental commander. My response simply affirms your old regiment's readiness. I will forward the names of the new commanding officers in a few days. I expected the regiment's last companies to march from Darien by the end of the week, and Lieutenant Colonel Alexander has orders to hold elections forthwith."

"Thank you, General Lawton. I like where I am at the moment, serving you and General Walker."

"And we intend to keep you here with us, too."

"Yes Randolph. You are where we need your talents the most. I'm afraid we all are going to have our hands full around here over the next few weeks."

※ ※ ※

Randolph returned to the Graybill's house just before sunset. He unsaddled Zapala and brushed him down in the stables behind the house. He walked into the back of the house, startling Margaret preparing dinner in the kitchen.

"Colonel Spalding, will you be joining us for dinner this evening?"

"Yes, Margaret, if it would not be too much trouble. Is Mister Graybill home yet?"

"I believe he just got home a little while ago. He and the Missus might be in the parlor."

Randolph stepped through the dining room into the hall by the front door and removed his cloak and hat. He noticed a telegram on the table beside the coat rack addressed to him. He grabbed it and stepped into the parlor where Mary and James sat with little Henry at their feet on the floor near the fireplace. Randolph smiled at the tranquil image.

"This is a pleasant sight to come home and see. With all the talk about this war, seeing you two with Henry is refreshing. May I join you?"

James stood, and Mary hoisted Henry into her arms, preparing to leave the two men to talk by themselves.

"Mary, please stay," Randolph said.

Mary sat with Henry in her lap, distracted by his mother's sparkling necklace rather than paying attention to the adults in the room. James invited Randolph to sit in the armchair beside him and placed a log on the fire before he returned to his seat.

"Where's Lou tonight? Another militia meeting?" Randolph asked.

"Yes. He's quite busy recruiting. It's getting harder to find eligible and willing volunteers. He even placed an advertisement in the newspaper to see if that will help catch the attention of a few eager young men in the city," James said.

"Randolph, did you see the telegram that came for you? I had Margaret place it on the table in the hall," Mary said.

"Thanks, Mary. I have it right here." Randolph held the folded telegram out. "I guess I should read it."

Randolph looked concerned as he read.

"Anything wrong?" James asked.

"Is it bad news from your wife?" Mary asked.

Randolph shook his head. A curious smile appeared. "No. This is news from my brother, Charles in Darien about Hector, the negro I told you about. Hector disappeared while being transported to Savannah for trial."

"That's good news?" Mary asked. "Didn't he murder a couple of soldiers?"

"After they killed his son and raped his daughter."

Mary pulled Henry's head to her bosom. "How dreadful."

James leaned over and patted his wife's knee and then stroked his son's long, dark hair. "If they find him, he may not live to stand trial this time," James said. "What do you think will happen now? Where can he go?"

"I am not sure. Most assuredly, he will not risk going to my brother's place at Ashantilly. That's where his wife and daughter are right now. My brother says he'll keep me informed if he hears anything."

Margaret stood in the doorway. "Mister Graybill, dinner is ready, sir."

CHAPTER TWENTY-FIVE

6th of February, 1862

The long hours took their toll on Randolph. Rumbles of cannon fire became less frequent as Confederate supply ships accompanied by gunboat escorts skirted the marsh shallows of Daufuskie and Turtle Islands on the South Carolina side of the Savannah River to avoid detection by Union forces entrenched on Tybee Island.

General Lawton feared reports of Northern troop activity approaching Jones Island. Pilings, placed recently by Captain Echols and a team of engineers, clogged the shallow mouths of the Wright River and the Mud River bordering either side of the three-sided marsh-filled island almost directly across the river from Savannah. Farther up the Wright River, they scuttled the hulk of a Confederate-masted warship to block Union gunboats and troop ships from using the narrow serpentine marsh river channels from Port Royal on the Savannah River to reach Jones Island.

"Gentlemen, General Lee remains confident the North will engage in an offensive campaign as soon as the weather breaks. He contends they intend to sever the rail lines and cut Georgia off from the Carolinas and Virginia. However, I do not wish to get caught with my pants down. General Walker, it may be prudent to consider Colonel Spalding's premonition about General Thomas Sherman's sights on capturing Savannah. I do not trust the feeling haunting me lately. After taking Tybee, we have received no reports of further troop and supply ships from Port Royal sailing there," General Lawton said.

He walked to the map on the wall in his office. Holding his cigar between the first two fingers of his right hand, he circled Tybee Island, then slid his hand down the mouth of the Savannah River to Fort Pulaski on Cockspur Island. He placed his cigar between his gritted teeth and grunted. His fingers calibrated the distance from Jones Island and Tybee Island to Cockspur Island. He then used his forefinger to tap Fort Jackson's and Fort Lee's locations along the Savannah River. "Should Fort Pulaski fall, the Union Navy would launch a siege on Jackson that Lee could not withstand, and the battle for Savannah would be nothing like when the British took her back in 1778. This time, I believe that Colonel Spalding's assessment is correct. The North would not hesitate to level the city to capture its prize—the cotton clogging our docks and riverside warehouses."

General Walker stood and looked at Randolph seated beside him. "Does that mean we should proceed with my plan to make sure the Union cannot use Tybee Island to launch an assault on Fort Pulaski, if not stage a land-based campaign against the city?"

"Not yet, at least until we can find out what they plan to do on Tybee Island. I am quite concerned at the moment about reports of their movements across the river. If they manage the impossible and move men and artillery across the river, they could bypass Fort Pulaski." Lawton glared at the map again. "Damn it all! We are waiting to hear from General Lee. Let's hope he intends to order an offensive against Port Royal."

"By God, General, somebody needs to order an offensive before they do. Would you allow me at least to organize some nighttime reconnaissance missions?" General Walker said.

Lawton gesticulated his approval with his arm. He then looked at Randolph. "Colonel, I have some information here you may be interested in seeing." He searched the top of his cluttered desk and handed Randolph an official letter.

Randolph groaned as he read the letter from General Jackson.

"I thought you'd be pleased. Captain Young will receive a

promotion to colonel as the new regimental commander. At least, his men in the regiment seem to think so."

The thought of Captain William Young, the arrogant company commander of the Ochlocknee Light Infantry, Company B, becoming the new regimental commander tore at Randolph's stomach. Captain Young's militia unit had brought the three soldiers who killed Jeremiah and raped Cecile onto Sapelo. Captain Young had fulfilled his boast to Randolph and Charles Spalding and arrested Hector when he led the last detachment off the island with Alex Hazard, the lightkeeper. There was good news in the correspondence, though, with the appointment of William P. Clower as the regimental surgeon. Randolph wondered how many lives an experienced surgeon like him could have saved had he arrived earlier to work with the young assistant surgeon, William Way of Thomasville.

"Oh, yes sir. I assume Lieutenant Colonel Alexander and Major Knight will support him with a steady hand. Young's election just caught me off guard," Randolph said.

"Colonel Spalding, with the General's leave, how about you and I grab some dinner and a couple of drinks to cheer you up," Walker roared.

"Yes, General Walker. Colonel Spalding is looking like he could use a good steak and a little libation." Lawton lit another cigar. "Randolph, that's an order," he added with an ear-to-ear smile.

That evening at the Marshall House, Colonel Spalding washed down his steak with a mug of mulled wine and later shared a bottle of Jamaican rum with General Walker. For a brief time, both drowned their longings for family and the return of days the past held fast. The two staggered to the livery stable next door where Randolph needed Walker's help to mount Zapala. The cold, moist air vaporized each burst of laughter as they rode off in separate directions, Randolph promising Walker Zapala would get him to the Graybill's house safely.

Sometime after midnight, Margaret woke Lou and the two went to the stable and found Randolph out cold on a bed of hay in Zapala's stall, his horse still saddled. Lou tended to Zapala while Margaret got Randolph onto his semiconscious feet and wrapped his arm around her neck. She assisted him into the parlor by the fire. By the time Lou caught up to them in the house, she had helped Randolph out of his tunic and hung it with his cloak and hat.

"Mister Spalding, you had a bit too much to drink this fine evening," Margaret said, yanking off his boots.

Randolph slurred, "No, darling, I had far too much to drink tonight, but I loved every drop, too! My good friend General Walker and I both got loaded tonight. Lord, I hope he got home all right."

"Colonel, how about I help you get upstairs to your room?" Lou said, then shushed him.

"Yes, we shouldn't wake the family. *Ssshhh!*" Randolph snickered with a finger to his lips.

Margaret handed Lou two envelopes mailed from Milledgeville. "Put these where Mister Spalding will see them when he wakes in the morning. Thanks, Mister Louis."

James met his brother struggling to get Randolph upstairs and helped get Randolph into bed. "He doesn't look good, Lou. Tell Margaret to cook up one of her special breakfasts in the morning for him. We can let him sleep in a bit, too. This damned war can just hold its horses and let Mister Spalding get a little extra rest for one morning. Would you mind riding to see General Walker in the morning? If the colonel doesn't get some needed rest, he'll wind up under a doctor's care."

Louis nodded before heading back downstairs to his bedroom.

※ ※ ※

Margaret brought Randolph's breakfast to his bedroom the next morning. Between his gigantic hangover, nausea with a temperature, the smell and mere thought of eating ham and eggs made him feel like retching.

She lay her hand on his flushed cheeks and forehead. "Mister Spalding, darling, you ain't goin' no place. You looked rather peaked to me before you went to sleep. This morning, there's no doubt about it, you're one sick man." She pulled his blankets up, leaving his arms free. Before she took his breakfast back to the kitchen, she slid the bedpan from beneath the bed. "If'n you feel like retching whatever you ate last night, please grab this." She eyed the two envelopes still on his nightstand. "Maybe these will make you feel a wee bit better. Now, stay in this bed. Mister Graybill's brother is riding to see your General Walker this morning. He'll inform him of your present state and need for some rest."

"But—"

"No buts about it. If you get out of this bed before you feel better and your fever is broken, you'll risk winding up in the hospital under the care of one of those know-nothing surgeons. You just leave it to me. You'll be back good as new in no time. Now, read your letters and get some rest. I'll be back to check on ya' in a wee bit."

Randolph scooted up in bed and sipped a little coffee, but quickly set it aside on the nightstand. He wiped his forehead and eyelids with the top edge of his sheet before considering which letter to open first. He recognized Sallie's script on the first envelope:

28 January 1862
Beulah

My dearest father,

We are all doing most well in our new home. Of course, it is not really our home, and we all wish soon to return to McIntosh County. Beulah in the winter is so bleak and colorless, except for the ample red dirt that stains our shoes and our clothes. Father, we saw snowflakes. I never knew it could snow in Georgia. Well, at least we never saw it snow in Georgia.

Tom and Bourke miss you almost as much as I do. Momma's staying busy and travels with Missus McKinley to the Southern Ladies Relief Society. She says it makes her feel like she is helping you and all our family and friends who now are serving in our army. As for Tom, Bourke, me, and even Charlie, Mister Babb comes each week like clockwork. We enjoy the stories he tells after we do our lessons. Tom spends every day reading the novel Mister Babb gave him by James Fenimore Cooper, Last of the Mohicans. I am reading The Personal History, Adventure, Experiences and Observation of David Copperfield the Younger of Blunderstone Rookery by Charles Dickens from England. Despite such a long title, Mister Dickens's story makes me appreciate the life we have. I cannot wait to ask Uncle Charles about his time in England.

Uncle Allen and Charlie eat dinner with us every evening. During the day, Charlie stays with us while Uncle Allen directs our workers fixing fences and building a new shed and chicken coop. Yes, father, we now have a flock of cackling hens. At least the boys enjoy chasing them around the barnyard.

Father, Archibald McKinley and his servant Scott marched off together with the Independent Militia from Milledgeville. I hope he stays safe. He promised to write to me when he can. I hope you do not mind that he does.

Please write back soon. I miss you. Stay safe. You are the only father I have.

Your loving daughter,
Sallie

Have you heard any more about Cecile, her ma, or her pa? I shed tears every day thinking about what happened.

Randolph carefully folded the letter, inserted it back into the envelope, and closed his eyes as his mind's eye pictured the faces of his children before opening the letter from Mary. He felt guilty for not writing to her sooner and for not being faithful to his promise to write regularly in the journal Sallie gave him.

He sniffed the letter from his wife, producing a meager smile on his otherwise pallid face:

28 January 1862

Dear Randolph,

I pray you are well. I imagine the weather in Savannah is no better than what we have endured since you left. Rain, ice, and even snow have sent chills through this old house. William totes chopped wood every morning from the stable to feed the fireplaces. Allen has been a blessing. We eat dinner and chat every night. Of course, I would rather chat with my husband instead of my brother.

When I get into town, I purchase the newspaper for the latest news. I cannot believe Yankees are on Georgia soil, even if confined to Tybee Island. That just concerns me so. Please tell me you are safe, my love. Have you heard anything about Hector, Alma, and Cecile? I worry about them, and I know Sallie does as well. What happened to their family haunts both of us. She asks if Cecile can join us here. Would that be possible?

You would be proud of the children. They appear to enjoy the company of Mister Babb. He is a top-notch storyteller, too. The children know that if they complete their assignments each week, he will spend a little extra time with them around the fireplace in the parlor and spin a tale or two that leaves them thinking about tales of King Arthur instead of the present reality of war with the North. I confess Mister Babb's stories help me as well.

I am a bit concerned for Josephine. This weather has been hard on her, though she dares not show it. I hope you will not mind if I inquire with Allen to recruit another housekeeper to help Josephine. William tries his best, but cooking and cleaning require a woman's touch.

I know you most likely are very busy keeping up with those generals in Savannah, but take care of yourself and write to tell me you are well. I have no intentions of mending any bullet holes in your dashing uniform.

Your adoring wife who misses you every day,
Mary

Sallie is writing her own letter to you. I hope both arrive at the Graybill's address at the same time. I will stop at the postmaster office in town tomorrow before I attend the Ladies Relief Society meeting with Anne McKinley and your sister, Katherine.

Randolph placed Mary's letter on top of Sallie's on the nightstand, sank back under the blankets, and drifted off to sleep.

※ ※ ※

General Walker arrived with an army surgeon from the hospital the next day. Upon examining Randolph, the doctor said, "Colonel, unless you have a death wish, I prescribe plenty of bed rest at least until your fever breaks."

"Randolph, stay in bed as the doctor ordered. I will inform General Lawton the surgeon confined you to your quarters for the next few days." Walker glared at Randolph sitting up in bed.

"General, but—"

"That's an order, Colonel Spalding. Get back under those blankets."

The surgeon looked at Margaret and Mary Graybill standing in the hallway just outside his room. "Missus Graybill, his fever is not contagious. His illness is because of extreme exhaustion and extended exposure to this cold, wet weather. Two or three days of bed rest should get him back on the road to a full recovery. As soon as the colonel feels up to it, he could benefit from eating some good home cooking."

"Don't ya' worry. The missus and I will make sure Mister Spalding stays in bed and gets some of my cooking. We'll help him get his color back in no time," Margaret said, keeping one eye on Mary Graybill. Both shared confident smiles.

General Walker grunted. "That settles it. Colonel Spalding, I remit you to the care of Missus Graybill and her housekeeper." He looked over his shoulder at Mary and Margaret. "Ladies, if he gives you any trouble, have Mister Graybill or Captain Graybill get word to me." He watched Randolph settle back under his blankets. "I mean it. We need you back as soon as you are fit as a fiddle again, not a day sooner."

"Yes, General. Thank you, doctor." Randolph knew how sick he had allowed himself to become. As soon as Margaret closed his bedroom door, he glanced at the two letters on the nightstand. He knew the ache in his heart would not heal until he could be back with his family. *No more broken promises. This war cannot last forever. Damn you, Lincoln.*

CHAPTER TWENTY-SIX

16th of February, 1862

Colonel Randolph Spalding stood on the ramparts atop Fort Jackson overlooking the Savannah River. Colonel Anderson, the commanding officer of the river defenses, pointed beyond narrow Elba Island to the faint marsh shoreline of Jones Island.

"Colonel Spalding, we all are pleased to see you back with us again. I understand you allowed yourself to get pretty sick for a spell."

Randolph adjusted his sagging waist belt. "Thank you, Colonel Anderson. I'm glad to get out from under those blankets and all the fuss Missus Graybill and her housekeeper poured over me for the past week."

"Now Colonel, we have been getting reports from our river batteries of nighttime activity on Jones Island across the river. Use this and look where I am pointing." He handed Randolph his spyglass.

"It looks unoccupied. Then again, I imagine they are concealing their activity under the cover of night. Have any of your reports pinpointed where the Union forces might be? I thought we had the Mud River fairly well obstructed?"

"Randolph, if I may be so casual—"

"Please, go right ahead." Randolph nodded and then turned his attention once again to staring across the Savannah River through the spyglass.

"Randolph, while you have been recuperating, the *Ida* and her gunship escorts have come under increasingly heavy Union Navy gunfire on her daily runs back and forth. So far, the guns at Fort Pulaski and our forward river batteries have prevented their volleys from reaching their target. I feel them Yankee bastards are up to something."

"What makes you think that?"

"They only maneuver against our ships during the day. They remain beyond the reach of our guns. At night, the firelight up and down the river mainly emanates from our positions. There is hardly a flicker on Tybee or the islands across the river."

"I gather you think they are moving men and munitions at night. Have we sent reconnaissance patrols to Tybee and across the river?"

"The weather has made it difficult for the past few nights. After one patrol failed to return from Tybee, we paused further patrols for a few days waiting for the weather to break. General Lawton and General Walker agreed that the terrible weather affects them worse than us. We should sit tight."

"I sense a but—"

"Them Yankees may get bogged down but not deterred. Their ships control the waters between Port Royal and Tybee Island. The last word we received indicates they now have in the vicinity of fifty-thousand men with ample munitions and supplies at their disposal, and we seem inclined to wait and see while they reinforce their hold on Port Royal."

Randolph looked up at the gray clouds sweeping overhead. "Colonel Anderson, begging your pardon, but I believe we should head back to your office. I just got over being sick and would rather not test my luck."

"Of course."

Headed across the parade ground to Anderson's headquarters, Randolph stopped. "Colonel, just a moment please. I just recognized one of my young officers from the twenty-ninth."

Randolph walked toward Major Levi Knight's young son, Lieutenant William Knight, overseeing the unloading of a wagon of supplies. "Lieutenant Knight!"

William snapped to attention and saluted. "Good afternoon,

Colonel Spalding. How are you feeling? My father said you were pretty sick."

"Tell your father I am back and fit as a fiddle again."

"I shall do that, sir. What brings you here?"

"General Walker asked me to ride out here to get caught up on what's been going on across the river. Are you and your Berrien boys stationed here?"

"Yes, sir. It sure beats camping under the stars, that's for certain. Don't get me wrong, Colonel. My time on Sapelo Island sure was interesting and pretty memorable, but all the same, three squares and a real bunk at night suit me just fine."

"No problem, William. Tell your father to stop by when he's in the city. I'll treat him to dinner. Hey, I heard today Captain Young got promoted to regimental commander. Is your father pleased?"

"I reckon. He figures in the army commanding officers come and go. He says he's too old and ornery to get frazzled about it. Now, Lieutenant Colonel Alexander is a horse of a different color. He ain't too pleased. He thought for sure he'd fill your shoes after what happened on Hilton Head. I think he's trying to get transferred to an outfit headed north."

"There's too many of you South Georgia Wire Grass boys in the twenty-ninth. You just stuck with who you knew best this time. Either way, I think your father will help your new regimental commander like he did for me. Carry on, Lieutenant." Randolph saluted before he headed to Anderson's office.

By late in the afternoon, Randolph agreed with Anderson's assessment. *The North will probably gain some advantages over our defensive placements before we make significant changes to oppose them.* But by the time he rode back to the city, he wondered if he shared the same abiding confidence Anderson expressed that whether by land or water, Northern invaders would soon either be buried beneath Southern soil or be driven back in disgrace. Surely, rendering such a devastating defeat upon Lincoln's army could put an end to the war. Walker's argument for pushing for an offensive campaign weighed on Randolph. *The longer we wait, the stronger their grip.*

※ ※ ※

The next afternoon, Randolph reported to Lawton's headquarters. Inside, General Lee stood with arms folded staring at a map of the city and the Savannah River rolled out on the conference table. Across from General Lee, Generals Lawton, Walker, and Jackson grumbled amongst themselves, each pointing to various locations marked on the map added since Randolph last took part.

Walker eyed Randolph in the doorway. "Colonel Spalding, come in, come in. What did you learn from your visit to Fort Jackson? Any news from Colonel Anderson or his staff?"

"Thank you, General." He joined Generals Walker, Jackson, and Lawton on their side of the table and examined the markings on the map.

Lawton said, "Colonel, the *Ida* took heavy cannon fire a couple of days ago. It appears, against your assessment about the soggy marsh conditions on Jones Island, Union artillery fired several rounds from near the river shoreline. We've received no further reports of shots fired, but we cannot risk sailing the *Ida* and her gunboat escorts to Cockspur Island until we know more."

"Begging the General's pardon, Colonel Anderson and I talked about some nighttime movement the sentries at Fort Jackson and some of the river batteries have reported. We scanned the shoreline. Nothing, sir. If they fired on the *Ida*, it came from a small gunboat or barge. But this afternoon we could not find any trace of activity."

General Lee pointed to the mouth of the Mud River that ran along the upriver side of Jones Island. "How would you explain a gunboat firing on our supply ship without being seen?"

"I'm sorry, General Lee, I'm not sure. It would seem to me they would need the aid of the high tide to maneuver a gunboat loaded with cannons. For a gunboat to fire on our supply ship and its escort gunboats without being seen seems highly unlikely. My next guess is they constructed a raft and floated it at night near the mouth of the river. It could be difficult to see tucked behind the cordgrass. However, would a raft remain stable enough for artillery to be fired accurately, even if it bottomed out at low tide?"

"So, gentlemen, we now face two concerns. Neither sits well with me." Lee smacked his hand on Cockspur Island. "It appears that until we know exactly what and where the Union is up to on Tybee Island, and now Jones Island, we cannot risk the *Ida* sailing to and from Fort Pulaski. I suggest we get word shuttled over to Colonel Olmstead. He and his garrison may be in for a long siege and cut off from supplies and reinforcements. He has ample supplies and munitions to hold out for months if needed. Order two additional regiments to reinforce the batteries along the river and at Fort McAllister on Wilmington Island. We must make the Union commanders think twice about advancing any farther."

General Jackson cleared his throat and said, "I'll see to moving the rest of the twenty-ninth and twenty-fifth infantry from Camp Davis to reinforce the batteries under Colonel Anderson. General Wilson can bring up the twenty-first regiment to report to Major Gallie at Fort McAllister."

"Very good, then. Let's find out what the Union is doing that we cannot see," General Lee said, grabbing his hat from a nearby chair. "Gentlemen, I do not know for certain what your plans are for this evening. However, Missus Lawton invited me to dine with them." He glanced at Lawton, "Shall we?"

Lawton patted Randolph's shoulder. "Glad you recovered as well as you seem to have done. By the look of your uniform, a few home-cooked meals will do you some good."

Randolph instinctively adjusted his sagging belt. "I plan on it, General. Thank you, sir."

General Walker grabbed his hat and turned from talking with General Jackson. "Colonel Spalding, do you wish to join us this evening? We are talking about dining at the Marshall House."

Randolph smiled. "General, sir, if it's all the same to you, Missus Graybill's housekeeper promised to cook her Irish version of shepherd's pie this evening."

Walker grinned through his dark brown beard. "Go on then. Eat your fill."

※ ※ ※

Randolph returned to the Graybill's house. James and his brother greeted him while he hung up his coat and hat.

"We have been waiting for you so we can have dinner together this evening," James yelled from his chair in the parlor. "Come join Louis and me while Margaret finishes getting dinner served."

Mary Graybill smiled at him from the sitting room across the hall. Henry sat on the floor beside her, preoccupied with a miniature red, hand-carved horse. "Please tell my darling husband we can talk at the dining table. It appears Margaret is ready for us."

Between mouthfuls of Margaret's Irish shepherd's pie, Louis, James, and Randolph discussed rumors of a Union offensive against the city. Randolph scoffed at the notion and suggested, "We should not add to the reasonable fears and concerns of citizens inside the city."

James laughed at Randolph's expense. "I reckon you slept through most of the louder-than-usual sporadic cannon fire that echoed from downriver."

"I heard some, but I learned about it from Colonel Anderson and General Walker today. Pulaski's supply ship and gunboat escort came under attack from a Union outpost across the river, but we cannot detect any significant movement of men or equipment on the South Carolina side. That's something we are looking into as much as figuring out what they are doing up on Tybee Island."

Lou laughed. "They surely are not slogging around those marsh islands over there and in this weather, that's plain foolish if you ask me."

"Foolhardy or not, they must be up to something even if a ruse to confuse us and get us to take our eyes off their actual movements." Randolph shoved another forkful and nodded at Margaret. "This is mighty fine. A couple nights eating like this, and I will fill my uniform back out again."

A loud rap on the back door followed by voices after Margaret opened it turned all their attention to the kitchen. Margaret said from the back of the kitchen, "Wait here, please. Let me fetch the Colonel for ya."

Hearing his name, Randolph walked around the table and motioned to the others at the table to remain seated. He met Margaret's wide-eyed look. "Who is it?"

"Major Knight, and he brought a sorry-looking black man with him. He asked for you, sir."

Levi met Randolph as he entered the back of the kitchen. "Randolph, I didn't know what else to do. Sentries at Camp Davis caught him snooping around. He told them he came up from South End and needed to find you. It just so happened I am the officer of the day, so they brought him to me. As soon as I recognized him, I dismissed the sentries and took him to my tent straightaway before anyone from the twenty-ninth might see him."

Hector sat with his head hung low, his threadbare clothes, hair, and hoary beard encrusted with mud. He looked up when he heard Randolph call his name. "Hector. How did you get here?"

"Mista Spalding, sir." Hector lifted his bloodshot, tear-filled eyes further than his head. "I be dreadfully sorry, sir."

Randolph placed his hand below Hector's chin and turned his head to one side. He looked closely at the blood-caked gash over his one eyebrow. "Hector, how did this happen?"

"Mista Spalding, sir, two soldier boys stopped me after I walked across a bridge a day's walk from here. They's asked me a bunch'a questions. When I refused to say what they wanted to hear, one of 'em butted me. I hit him and shoved the other before I runs as fast as I could. Mista Spalding, you gots to help me. Your brother comes and gots my wife and girl. I did wrong, Mista Spalding. I knows it. I had to come tell you myself. They gonna kill me, Mista Spalding. Please, help me."

Randolph patted Hector's shoulder. "You will be safe here for now. They know your story." He looked at Margaret standing off in the corner, squeezing the life out of the frilly hem of her apron. "Margaret, can you get me some water and a towel?"

James and Louis stood in the doorway of the dining room. "I take it this is the negro you told us about," James said. "What can we do?"

"Thank you, James. Do you think you can rustle up some clothes that fit Hector? These are wet and muddy." He looked at Levi Knight. "Levi, thank you. I am indebted to you."

"You don't have to thank me. No man, no father, should have faced what they did to his son and daughter and then get hounded like an animal. I figure I would've done the same."

Randolph took the wet towel from Margaret and wiped away some of the crusty blood and mud from Hector's forehead. "Me too, but justice would have been on our side. Not so for Hector. He knew the moment he chased those boys down and exacted his revenge, he would become a hunted man." He looked eye to eye with Hector. "The other boy got what he deserved a month ago. They executed him for running off."

"But that ain't gonna right the wrongs," Hector mumbled. He winced as Randolph wiped the crud from around his wound.

"Randolph, what can I do to help you?" Levi asked.

Randolph stared at Louis for a long moment. "Major Knight, my friend, it may be best that you not get any deeper into helping Hector. I think I know what needs to happen. You best head back to camp before they wonder why the officer of the day is not around."

The two shook hands. Major Levi Knight saluted before he slipped back out the back door and into the night.

"Lou, if you will give me a hand cleaning Hector up and patching his wound, we can talk. I have an idea that requires your help if you're willing."

"Absolutely, Colonel."

CHAPTER TWENTY-SEVEN

19th February, 1862

Hector spent the next two nights on a pallet James prepared in his office on the main floor across from Lou's bedroom, the first restful sleep under a roof since he left Sapelo a month ago. The smell of ham permeated the air the second morning when Randolph came downstairs right after sunrise. Louis sat across from Hector in the kitchen sipping coffee while Margaret fried hoecakes on the stove.

"Good morning, all," Randolph said, pulling up a stool to the table. He stared at Hector and smiled. "You look more like the Hector I remember this morning. I trust you got another good night's sleep?"

Margaret set a mug of coffee in front of Randolph and refilled Lou's mug. Hector hardly touched his coffee. "Gentlemen, give me a few moments, and I'll have your breakfasts ready."

Hector looked at Randolph and nodded. His one eye remained discolored and swollen but appeared far better than when he'd first arrived. Hardly any blood stained his white cloth dressing. "I wants to thank you, Mista Spalding, sir, and Mista Graybill for these clothes." He ran his hand across the osnaburg cotton work shirt James provided along with a pair of trousers, although his shoeless feet remained beneath the table.

"My brother James and Missus Graybill should be down shortly. You can thank them again for your clothes," Louis offered, staring at Hector's feet. "I'm afraid I still need to rustle up some larger brogans to fit you."

Hector glanced at Randolph as if seeking permission. Randolph nodded. "Hector, you will need walking shoes by tonight. Captain Graybill and I will work on that first thing today. Otherwise, you will stay right here."

"Colonel, with your permission, our neighbor is Doctor Read. I would like to ask him to take care of his wound."

Randolph paused, staring at Hector for a moment. "No. We cannot risk it. Word gets out your brother harbored a runaway, a wanted one at that, and he'd get arrested along with us. Our doctoring will have to suffice at least today." He peered at Hector. "Is that all right with you, Hector? You can get proper doctoring after we get you to the other side of the river."

Hector popped his head up, and his eyes opened wide.

"Captain, this is your last chance to back out," Randolph said, glaring at Louis.

"No sir. I'm going with you."

"Good, I'll make the arrangements and get orders from General Walker this afternoon authorizing you to join me on a nighttime reconnaissance mission across the river. You make sure Hector has brogans and a warm coat to wear by tonight."

Once again, Hector swiveled a bewildered, bug-eyed look between Louis and Randolph. "Mista Spalding, sir. Am I gonna go wit'ya? Whats about Alma and my girl?"

"Hector, getting you across the river gives you the best hope to stay alive. Alma and Cecile will be safe at Ashantilly with my brother for now. When this damn war ends, you can catch up to them. I promise. For now, we intend to smuggle you across the river. Trust me."

"Yes, sir. I trusts you. I reckon I gots no choice."

# # #

Late that evening, Randolph and Captain Graybill rode their horses to the supply dock at Fort Jackson. The sentry on duty called out, "Halt! Who goes there?" The ill-humored soldier stepped in front of the two riders. He raised his rifle with the business end of his bayonet pointed between their two horses. He squinted and said, "Sorry, Colonel Spalding. I didn't recognize ya." The crusty, gray-haired corporal from Ochlocknee, the same one who helped Randolph retrieve Jeremiah's dead hog back on Sapelo, lowered his bayoneted rifle and snapped to attention.

Randolph smiled and returned the salute. "Corporal, glad to see you again. How long have you been here at Fort Jackson?"

"This is my second week, I guess."

Randolph leaned forward in his saddle with a friendly, relaxed expression. "Do you miss old Camp Spalding?"

"No sir. The food ain't too bad. At least it's hot, and I got me a real bunk and a roof over my head whenever they let me catch a little shut eye."

Randolph chuckled, glancing at Captain Graybill's quizzical look. He reached into his tunic and pulled out his orders from General Walker, signed that afternoon after several minutes of pleading. His persistence convinced General Walker of the importance of the mission and that he and Captain Graybill knew the river better than most.

"Sir, I don't need to see your orders. The lieutenant told me they received orders to tie up a flat-bottom boat at the supply dock for a late-night reconnaissance mission. I never figured you'd be leading such a wild mission, though. No disrespect, Colonel. You and the captain picked an awfully nasty evening to take a boat on the river."

"Well, neither did I, Corporal. Then again, you recall I was raised on Sapelo Island, and I rowed many a boat up and down the Savannah." He looked at Louis. "Captain Graybill here has done likewise. If we don't get shot by our own trigger-happy patrols, we hope we are lucky enough to avoid any Yankee pickets on the other side."

"Colonel, I'll be here until sunrise. Best of luck to you and the captain. I'll keep an eye on your horses."

"Thank you, Corporal."

They dismounted and tied their horses beneath a sprawling oak near the dock. Randolph stared into the dark underbrush. He whispered, "Hector, get on down to the water's edge. Be ready to climb in the boat when we call you."

A sixteen-foot wooden bateau with two sets of oars and a rudder floated at the end of the dock. The young captain climbed in and positioned a set of oars. Randolph untied the boat and dragged it closer to the end of the dock where Hector waited in the shadows. Storm clouds hid the moon and stars. As soon as the corporal turned his back to them, Randolph waved his hand as he whispered, "Hector, come on. Jump in and lay on the bottom of the boat until I tell you. Hurry!"

Hector clambered onto the wooden dock from the shadows. He stepped clumsily off the dock into the bateau and grabbed onto the opposite gunwale to catch himself. The boat's bowed beam and flat bottom prevented Hector and Louis from an undesirable swim in the cold, dark river before they even got started. Randolph tossed the mooring line, grabbed the rudder, and the boat drifted into the river current just before Louis set his oars in the water and rowed. Randolph steered them downriver into the moonless, pitch-black night. Hector found his seat, grabbed the other set of oars, and stroked in tandem with Captain Graybill.

Leaving Fort Jackson far behind, Randolph navigated the boat across the river's South Channel toward the tip of Elba Island. Once they floated beyond the island, Randolph gave the order to row harder. He held the rudder fast, cutting the bow across the Savannah River's swift current. The current pushed them downriver as they headed for Jones Island's marsh shoreline. The fierce current subsided as they neared the island. High tide flowed in their favor as Randolph maneuvered the boat up to the Mud River. There they rowed upstream until they could find a safe place to beach the boat.

The damp chill in the night air penetrated their clothes. Louis eyeballed Randolph. "Have you been on this part of the river before? I can't see a blasted thing."

"Yes. There's a couple of spots just beyond the mouth of the river. I just hope there's not a Yankee outpost already there."

Hector cried out. *"Shoo, shoo!"* He dropped his oars and swiped wildly at his coat sleeve.

"Damn it all to hell! I hate bats," Louis said in a loud whisper as he swatted at the air over his head.

"Both of you quit making so much noise. Keep rowing." Randolph swatted a bat from the brim of his hat. "Just up ahead there's a patch of high ground even high tide rarely reaches. We can stop there."

The popping of their oarlocks and splash of their oar blades cutting into the murky water made the only sounds as they rowed upstream. Randolph guided their bateau close to the muddy shore. He craned his neck, trying to peer through the darkness. A minute later, he whispered, "Oars in." He cut the rudder, causing the bow to swerve toward the riverbank. Louis leaped from the boat as soon as the bottom touched the mud bank. His boots sank ankle-deep in the dark, cold sludge as he muscled the boat onto the sandy mud of Jones Island. The cordgrass formed a barrier around them. Farther up the river, indecipherable voices along with muffled groans and grunts caught their attention.

"Shh!" Randolph shushed Hector. He motioned with his hands for the eager captain to get low. "Stay put."

Louis whispered, "Colonel, I'll be right back. They sound just around the bend."

"Lou, Louis," Randolph whispered in frustration. He realized Captain Graybill had crept through the waist-high cord grass and headed toward the voices.

Time stood still, measured by the pounding of their hearts. Their rapid breathing was visible in the cold air. Hector leaned toward Randolph. "Mista Spalding, should I go after Mista Graybill?" His eyes grew wider.

Randolph put one hand on Hector's knee and shushed him. "Just sit still."

A few moments later, Captain Graybill ran toward the boat through the thigh-high, brittle marsh grass, struggling to keep his feet. Behind him, they heard one of the Yankee soldiers yelling, "Rebel spy! Rebel spy!"

Another yelled, "Do you see him? I can't see a blasted thing."

"There he is!"

The sound and bright discharge of the bullet from the barrel of the rifle arrived almost simultaneously. A second shot flashed a few yards away from the first. "Don't let him get away, you fools!" Yelling mingled with sloshing sounds of soldiers racing through the soggy cordgrass pursuing Louis.

Randolph pulled a letter from his coat pocket. "Hector, I don't have time to explain, but this declares you are a free man."

Hector stared into Randolph's eyes as he took the envelope.

"I want you to take this, too."

"But Mista Spalding, this is your fancy pocket watch."

"I don't have any money to give you. Keep it tucked away until you can sell it."

"But sir—"

"Hector, hush! We have no time to argue. Now get out of the boat. Remember what I told you. They'll take care of you."

Hector nodded. "Yes, sir. I remember what you told me."

"Now git! Make them believe you were the one they heard in the grass. Scream at the top of your lungs. "No, sir! No, sir. Don't shoot! I am a runaway slave. I am a runaway slave."

Hector nodded at Randolph. "Thank ya, Mister Spalding. Tells Alma and Cecile I'll get word to them as soon as I can." He then released his grip on the seat and leaped out of the boat. He bolted deep into the cordgrass. A moment later, from the darkness, he yelled and waved his arms high in the air. "Please don't shoot. Please don't shoot! I be a runaway!"

Louis crawled out from the cover of the marsh grass, caked in mud.

"Push us off and jump in!"

As soon as he shoved the boat off the mud bank, he jumped in and scrambled for the oars. Randolph switched seats and grabbed an oar. He shoved the boat free from the muddy bottom and into the current just as two shots rang out from the river's edge. "They're getting away!"

Hector yelled all the louder. He galloped toward the Yankee soldiers, his arms flailing high over his head. "Don't shoot! Don't shoot! I be a runaway!"

"Cease fire! You there, keep your hands high in the air." They were the last words Louis and Randolph heard as they slid their oars into the murky waters and glided away into the pitch-black night.

A few minutes later, they found themselves drawn into the Savannah River's powerful current. They rowed with all their might to fight the pull of the river. Randolph struggled to keep up with his much younger cohort as rain fell. He yelled, "The current's too strong," pointing to the faint shoreline of a smaller island. "We need to head to the shallows and then row to that shore over there. That should be Bird Island."

Both men leaned together and rowed their oars harder and faster. Pattering rain swallowed their grunts and groans, rhythmic creaking and cracking of their oarlocks swiveling with each stroke. As soon as the keel dug into the sandy mud along Bird Island's deserted beach, the drenched captain boated his oars and hopped over the gunwale, the bow rope in his grip. Randolph slumped over, beyond exhaustion.

"Colonel, you okay?"

Randolph raised one arm, wheezing and coughing.

"We must find some shelter and rest a bit."

"I need a minute to catch my breath. I'll be fine otherwise."

"I need to get you out of this rain. You don't sound good to me."

Randolph raised his head and glared at Louis until he began hacking.

The captain took off his coat and placed it over Randolph. "I'll be right back."

A few long minutes later, he returned. "We gotta get off this island, fast! There's a Yankee detachment camped not a hundred yards from here."

Their trek from Bird Island landed them farther down the river from Fort Jackson than they had hoped. They beached their boat and walked two miles upriver to Fort Jackson, arriving just before daybreak.

During their pre-dawn walk back to their horses, Louis told Randolph of the miracle the Union engineers had pulled off. Before they'd discovered him snooping on the edge of their fireless camp, he got close enough to see that their engineers had built a stout platform of timbers to support a concealed battery of at least three cannons on Jones Island. Just before they discovered him, he saw two additional guns secured beneath a tarp on a barge along the river's edge.

"Do you think Hector made it all right? What he did saved our lives," Louis said as they retrieved their horses, eager to get back to the house and out of their cold, wet uniforms.

"I sure hope so. Later this morning General Walker needs to know what we found tonight."

"What about Hector?"

"What about Hector?" Randolph said back. He reached into his tunic pocket and pulled out the soggy folded orders from General Walker. "We accomplished our mission. That's all General Walker wants to know about."

CHAPTER TWENTY-EIGHT

25th February, 1862

Randolph struggled to regain his health after he returned from his daring escapade with young Captain Graybill, but he reported to headquarters anyway. Following Randolph's persistent fits of coughing and wheezing, General Walker finally threw his hands up and scolded him privately. After praising him and Captain Graybill in front of the headquarters staff following their report, Walker ordered Randolph to get under a doctor's care or report to the hospital.

The Union floated a barge with artillery to Bird Island, effectively cutting the city off from Fort Pulaski on Cockspur Island. Union gunboats taunted the fort from the South Carolina side of the Savannah River. Concurrently, every dawn revealed new Union batteries added along Tybee's shoreline. Pulaski's artillery crews chased Yankee soldiers off the beach as cannon fire dueled harmlessly. A supply ship attempted to reach Fort Pulaski by navigating the treacherous Lasaletto Creek from Fort McAllister on Wilmington Island. Union artillery on Tybee sank her, and the scuttled hull now blocked the narrow waterway skirting Big Tybee Island.

By the following Tuesday morning, Mary Graybill and Margaret began bringing Colonel Spalding's meals to his room after his symptoms worsened. James Graybill summoned Doctor Read, their congenial neighbor. He prescribed applying a mustard poultice daily along with catnip and horehound herbal remedies to help him sleep.

However, Randolph struggled to remain in bed. Cannon fire echoed downriver, stirring him out from under his sweat-soaked bedding. He found comfort sitting for hours with a blanket wrapped around him, staring out his bedroom window.

A few days later, General Lawton and General Walker stopped by when they learned his conditions had not improved. It would be the last time Colonel Randolph Spalding of McIntosh County would don his uniform. Pale and haggard, he had willed himself to greet them downstairs in the parlor, refusing to see them otherwise.

At the foot of the stairs in the central hallway, Randolph stopped momentarily when he saw his reflection in the narrow, decorative-looking glass in the entry hall. He finger-combed his shiny hair behind his ears and ran his hand across the front of his loose-fitting, double-breasted tunic.

Mary watched from the sitting room with her husband, James, seated across from her. They acknowledged each other with dismal smiles as she stroked her son's curly hair, who sat in her lap preoccupied with his wooden horse.

Warming themselves near the roaring fire in the parlor, Captain Louis Graybill stood beside Generals Lawton and Walker. Randolph coughed as he entered the room. "General Lawton, General Walker, I apologize for keeping you waiting."

"Randolph, my old friend, we wanted to make sure you were on the mend. We need more lionhearted officers like you. You appear to be whipping this lingering illness. We imagine you will be back with us any day now." General Lawton's contrived grin hid the truth.

"I could not agree more," General Walker bellowed. "The North has sheep leading their army, but we have lions like you who inspire our boys to victory. I just notified Captain Graybill that headquarters mustered his volunteer militia unit as A Company, 27th Georgia Infantry, and they will march to Charleston in a few days. But we asked Captain Graybill to remain in Savannah as an aide on my headquarters staff."

Randolph nodded. "Captain Graybill will prove himself as a worthy aide, General Walker." He attempted a congratulatory smile. "Just keep my place on staff empty. I will return in a couple of days."

Walker patted Louis on his shoulder. "We expect you back to mentor the young captain."

General Lawton did not display the same optimism. "Randolph, with your permission, I am going to ask one of our surgeons to call on you. I understand from Captain Graybill that their family doctor has seen you. I would feel better about your swift and complete recovery if one of our better-qualified surgeons examined you."

"Yes, that would be fine with me, General—" A spout of hacking cut him off.

"Colonel, we have taxed you enough with our visit. We will take our leave, so you can get much-needed rest. I want you to mind Missus Graybill and her housekeeper. It sounds as though they are taking excellent care of you. I'll send our best available surgeon to visit you in the next day or two." General Lawton then eyed General Walker and gestured for him to lead the way to the door. "Captain Graybill, we will see you at headquarters."

They saluted Randolph as they exited out the front door.

James stepped beside Louis. "Mister Spalding, you need to return to your bed. Margaret is preparing another mustard poultice for you along with some of the doctor's warm herbal tea to help you sleep."

※ ※ ※

The following afternoon, Randolph watched from his upstairs bedroom window as an army hospital wagon pulled in front of the Graybill townhouse. He sat wrapped in a blanket in the chair beside his bed and heard the footsteps coming up the stairs to his room. Doctor Spalding Kenan entered first, raising a curious look on Randolph's long face. His nephew introduced Major Joseph Habersham, chief surgeon 25th Georgia Infantry and General

Lawton's personal physician.

"Colonel Spalding, General Lawton expressed dire concerns regarding your present condition. He requested I come here and examine you. I guess that means you must be pretty important to him to send me out on a house call like this," Habersham said, gazing at Randolph's droopy, bloodshot eyes.

Randolph forced a feeble grin, casting his eyes at his nephew. "Spalding, how is it you accompanied Major Habersham on this house call?"

"I work under the major at the hospital. When I heard your name mentioned, I told him that we are kin, and I know all too well how you can be a stubborn, quite contrary patient. So, I volunteered to assist him." He watched, arms-crossed, from the door as Major Habersham examined and questioned Randolph.

"Colonel, you need to be under hospital care," Habersham said, looking down at Randolph. "You are exhibiting signs of acute pneumonia." He turned to Spalding Kenan and said, "Would you mind helping Colonel Spalding get dressed and assist him downstairs? I'll speak with Mister Graybill and his wife."

A few minutes later, James Graybill helped Randolph step up into the back of the hospital wagon. Spalding Kenan helped pull his uncle up by hand. James looked up at Randolph as he settled in across from Spalding. "Mary and I will check in on you at the hospital. We'll take care of your belongings and bring you any letters that may arrive for you. Randolph, focus on getting well."

Just as Randolph nodded, Major Habersham climbed up front, and the driver guided the wagon's tandem team of horses around Oglethorpe Park and up Abercorn Avenue toward the hospital.

※ ※ ※

Two weeks later, Randolph slept soundly in his hospital bed thanks to the ample doses of laudanum, though his breathing had become shallow and labored. Standing at the foot of his bed, Captain Spalding Kenan, who had checked on him regularly, gave an update to Captain Thomas Wylly, Captain William Brailsford, and Lieutenant Colonel Charles Spalding. Each stared at Randolph, expecting him to stir at any moment. They laughed as they recalled the last time all four had gathered with Randolph. On that evening, seemingly an eternity ago, each played a memorable part in his drunken tooth extraction.

A nurse shushed them, but she only earned a condescending quip from Brailsford. "Yes, ma'am, we are truly sorry, but we want him to wake up. He's been fast asleep for the past two days."

"William, the nurse is right," Spalding said, glaring at him. "Since he turned for the worse three days ago, Major Habersham told me all we can do now is help him sleep and pray for God's grace. Why don't you three go back to the hotel across the street? I'll join you later."

"Sounds like a good idea to me," Thomas Wylly barked. "I could use a good meal. I'm famished."

Brailsford patted his stomach. "Come to think about it, I feel a bit peckish, and a drink about now will not hurt either." He looked at Spalding. "You'll have someone come get us if there's any change?"

Spalding nodded. "Y'all go on ahead. I'll join you for some dinner shortly."

"Is there any chance he will recover?" Thomas Wylly asked Spalding Kenan.

Spalding's face could not hide the reality of Randolph's fate. "Major Habersham told me he has tried everything, and Uncle Randolph's life is in God's hands now."

"Dammit, Spalding! Do something," William Brailsford railed, turning heads in his direction.

"William, we have seen far too many good men die already because pneumonia beat us. I am afraid, though he has the will to live, his body has lost its ability to fight back. I am sorry, but there is nothing more we can do for him," Spalding Kenan said, placing his hand on William's broad shoulder.

As they walked out of the crowded hospital ward, Charles sighed and said, "I know Mary wants to visit Randolph, but it's far too dangerous. I'm afraid she cannot get a travel pass signed by General Lawton in time to make the trip to Savannah."

"I spoke with James Graybill. He wants to help the family any way he can," Thomas Wylly said.

Charles scoffed. "Let's not bury my brother before he is dead. Let's pray God's mercy will save Mary and their children from having to mourn and grieve."

Two hours later, Spalding walked into the hotel, his frock unbuttoned and hair mussed. He found his uncle and two cousins laughing at a table. Charles stood and put his hand on his nephew's shoulder. "Is he?"

"I am sorry, Uncle Charles. His body gave out a few minutes ago."

Thomas and William raised their glasses. "To Uncle Randolph, the Laird of Sapelo. May God be with Aunt Mary, Sallie, Tom, and Bourke."

※ ※ ※

In the days that followed their visit, the *Savannah Republican* published the following articles.

18th March 1862

FUNERAL INVITATION

The friends and acquaintances of the late Col. RANDOLPH SPALDING and family, and those of James H. Graybill, Esq., are respectfully invited to attend the funeral of the former at the residence of the latter, corner of Oglethorpe Street, fronting Oglethorpe Square, THIS MORNING at 11 o'clock.

Days following, this article circulated in several Georgia newspapers.

> The death of RANDOLPH SPALDING, Esq. will be much regretted by the people of Georgia; for he was a pure patriot and a high-toned, chivalrous gentleman doing good service in the army of the Confederate States. He was formerly a Senator from McIntosh County. His death occurred at Savannah on 18th instant, and his remains were attended to the Laurel Grove Cemetery by a large military escort and a long procession of citizens.

CHAPTER TWENTY-NINE

June, 1868, Sapelo Island

By the Spring of 1868, the ravages of the war remained visible in nearby Darien and on Sapelo Island. A year after Randolph died, the Union army had razed Darien, the once thriving port town, as a dire warning to other coastal towns not to resist. On Sapelo Island, the war left the Spalding family's once grand South End mansion ransacked and uninhabitable.

Charles Spalding and his wife, Evelyn, maintained their residency at Ashantilly, but his plantation holdings he lost or sold off. After President Andrew Johnson allowed Southern landowners with legal claims of ownership to reclaim their confiscated lands, Charles helped Mary Spalding and her family regain their rightful ownership of their properties on Sapelo.

Nearly all of Sapelo's former slaves returned and resettled the land they called home, but now as free men and women. Union General William Tecumseh Sherman's controversial *Field Order No. 15* allowed for the confiscation and paring of plantation lands into small parcels that were doled to the thousands of freed slaves. For three years following the order's execution, opportunistic Northern con men and carpetbaggers swept into McIntosh County like locusts and swindled many of the resettled former slaves. By the time the Spalding family had moved back onto Sapelo Island, they faced the distrust of their former workers, who were already farming plots of land on Sapelo. They felt little reason to welcome the Spaldings, especially after the land they had cultivated for themselves reverted to its former owners.

Undaunted, Randolph Spalding's widow needed money to support the family while they rebuilt South End. Mary Spalding sold Chocolate and Bourbon fields on the north end of the island to a New York investor. In a few more months, Tom Spalding would legally assume ownership of South End as his grandfather had wanted. Until such time, his mother became the de facto Mistress of South End.

As a beacon of hope for all the residents on Sapelo, the lighthouse sprang back to life that spring, once again lighting the night sky from the southernmost point of the island. Alex Hazard moved back into the restored lightkeeper's house along with his new wife and two small children.

On a warm, sunny Sunday afternoon in early June, Mary invited her family for a picnic near the same pristine beach they'd enjoyed before the war. Sea birds of all sorts scampered along the edge of the incoming waves or soared high overhead looking for an afternoon snack in the teeming surf. Squawking gulls and the hypnotic sound of the waves remained unaltered on the island.

Sallie walked along the shoreline with her arm wrapped around her husband, Archibald "A.C." McKinley. She clung tightly to her war-hero husband, still grief-stricken over losing their infant son right after his birth last November. They had named him William after Archibald's father.

Tom and Bourke had grown beyond their years at Beulah after learning of their father's death. They helped their mother salvage what they could after General Sherman's scavenging horde emptied the barns and ransacked their house at Beulah in the final year of the war. They sat atop a dune sharing their grand ideas to begin a new business venture with their new brother-in-law, A.C., and their Uncle Allen. The four had already talked and realized their future on Sapelo needed to include working with the freed workers who wanted to farm their own fields. They pointed out the increase of merchant ships returning to Darien. Rebuilding after the war required lumber and supplies, and they knew South End with Marsh Landing's wharf could sell cut timbers from the island and other naval stores and supplies.

Allen Bass, wearing a sweet grass hat with his trousers rolled up to his knees, sat on a blanket staring at the ships on the horizon and several fishing boats nearer to shore. His son, Charlie, chased after innocent terns on the water's edge with his puppy, aptly named Growler, nipping at his heels.

Standing on the wooden walkway between the lush green grass-covered dunes with clusters of tall, light brown sea oats gently swaying like signal flags, Charles Spalding yelled, "Come and get it! Dinner is served." He waved and repeated the dinner call until everyone diverted their attention and headed to where an end-to-end makeshift ensemble of tables sat in the shade of a grove of cypress and live oak trees. Plain white sheets served as tablecloths and an eclectic assortment of chairs and benches provided adequate seating for the whole family. Charles and Evelyn waited beside Mary at the head of the tables.

"Sorry we are late," Johanna Wylly said in her identifiable English accent as she cradled Marion their newborn, in her arms. Thomas Wylly carried Richard, their giggly three-year-old son, as five-year-old Tom Jr. scampered ahead of his father.

"You're right on time. Come find a seat," Charles said, as the rest of the family found seats around the table.

Allen sat at the far end with Charlie across the table from Bourke and Tom. "Fried chicken! Boys, ya'll go get your own. This bowl is mine," Allen said, laughing as Alma and Cecile examined the three large baskets of chicken, bowls of hot corn on the cob, okra, collards, and cornbread.

"Mista Allen, behave yourself. You hear? Them boys don't need to see you misbehavin'," Alma huffed as she and Cecile sat across from Charles and Evelyn.

Mary stood. She took a moment to inventory the family gathered back together at South End. "Thomas and Johanna, thank you for sharing this day with us. I know Randolph would have been proud to learn how we all not only survived but persevered." Her eyes watered. "I also want us to think about all our family who cannot be with us today. The war took Randolph, Jeremiah, and Hector from our midst, but they remain in our memories of better days. Charles and Evelyn, I have no words that can ever express my sincere gratitude for all you have done and endured. Without you, there would be no Spaldings back on Sapelo."

"Missus Spalding, ma'am. Momma and me want to give you somethin' that belongs to your family." Cecile opened her outstretched hand and peeled back the lace kerchief.

"Oh my goodness. That's Randolph's pocket watch. Where in God's name did you ever get that?" Mary said, bursting into tears.

Alma walked beside Mary and embraced her. "Missus Spalding, you needs to ask your brother-in-law, Mister Spalding. He kept it safe since we got the letter from that newsman from Beaufort." She and Mary leaned on one another, sobbing.

Thomas Wylly asked, "What letter?"

"A parcel addressed to Randolph evidently arrived amidst all the rebuilding that took place in Darien," Charles explained. "The wrapped package got mislaid like a lot of the undeliverable mail in the final year of the war. Captain Web Davis, the new postmaster, showed it to me a few days ago. I reckon not all Yankees are bad fellas."

"They had it all that time?" Allen bellowed from his end of the table.

"Easy, Allen. It's a miracle it survived and didn't get lost altogether," Charles said. "The parcel had no return address. When I opened it, I discovered Randolph's engraved watch with a handwritten note dated December 16, 1864, from John Sears, editor of *The New South* in Beaufort and Randolph's blood-stained letter of manumission to Hector. Mister Sears wrote that Hector had been found shot on the outskirts of Beaufort. He felt obliged to return the pocket watch and the letter they found on Hector to an old friend."

"This proves what we heard from James Graybill," Mary said

as she grabbed her cloth napkin and dabbed her eyes, clutching Randolph's pocket watch.

Tom, Bourke, and Sallie left their places at the table and hugged their mother.

"Well, all these fixings Miss Alma and Cecile made are getting cold. I reckon we need to say grace and then enjoy this feast," Charles declared with a light-hearted chuckle as he returned to his seat.

Souls and Rain-Drops

Light rain-drops fall and wrinkle the sea,
Then vanish, and die utterly.
One would not know that rain-drops fell
If the round sea-wrinkles did not tell.

So souls come down and wrinkle life
And vanish in the flesh-sea strife.
One might not know that souls had place
Were't not for the wrinkles in life's face.

Sydney Lanier, 1842-1881

AUTHOR'S NOTE

After attending a writer's conference on Saint Simon's Island, June 2019, my wife and I traveled to Darien, Georgia, to consider it as a setting for a prospective contemporary Southern novel I contemplated writing. We fell in love with the history of Darien, the second oldest town in Georgia, bowing only to Savannah. After Oglethorpe founded what they had originally named New Inverness, the early Scottish settlers chartered the settlement as Darien in 1736.

We drove through the quaint live oak lined neighborhoods and walked along the docks filled with shrimp boats and pleasure craft of all sizes. After we left, I learned Darien had once been a thriving seaport at the mouth of the Altamaha River, and that the Altamaha split further inland into the Oconee and Ocmulgee Rivers, connecting Darien with Macon and Milledgeville. During Georgia's antebellum period, riverboats hauled bales of cotton and other crops from inland plantations to Darien. They then loaded the valuable cargo onto merchant ships headed to Savannah and Charleston and even across the Atlantic. By the 1850s, the rapidly expanding railway transported much of the cotton directly to Savannah. However, riverboats continued to transport cargo and passengers upriver to cities and towns unreached by the railroad.

August 2020, we returned to further explore Darien and to visit Sapelo Island. We stayed at Open Gates Bed & Breakfast in historic Darien. Our excursion to Sapelo Island changed everything. Our tour guide and host, JR Grovnor, a Geechee descendant, shared how Thomas Spalding had brought his ancestors to Sapelo at the beginning of the 19th-Century. He then told us how following the

Civil War the freed Geechee population returned to the island and bought land. But after Howard Coffin of Hudson Motor Company fame bought the island in 1912, and subsequently sold it to R. J. Reynolds, Jr. during the Depression, the changes they instigated affected the Geechee communities. Of the four hundred Geechee residents on Sapelo at the beginning of the 20th-Century today there are only about three dozen descendants still living on the island. The children no longer attend school on the island but take the ferry to school on the mainland. After the State of Georgia acquired the island from R. J. Reynolds' widow in the 1970s, only parcels of land in the Hoggs Hammock community remain privately owned. Between a lack of jobs and rising taxes, most of the Geechee families at Hoggs Hammock have sold their land to outsiders and moved away.

While in Darien, Zachariah and Carrie Rath, innkeepers of Open Gates Bed & Breakfast, handed me a copy of Buddy Sullivan's book, *Early Days on the Georgia Tidewater, The Story of McIntosh County & Sapelo*. Scouring through Buddy Sullivan's book, I learned more about Thomas Spalding and his family's legacy on Sapelo, in Darien and through out Georgia. I then discovered the overshadowed and mostly overlooked story of Randolph, Thomas Spalding's youngest son. Newspaper accounts recorded Randolph as a revered politician, a successful planter, and a heralded patriot who parlayed his inherited fame and fortune on Sapelo Island in the decade following his father's death in 1851. Further, as a testament to Randolph and his father, following the Civil War, virtually all the displaced Geechee enslaved workers and their families returned to the only home they knew, Sapelo. The question of "why?" led me to writing *The Last Laird of Sapelo*. Though a work of historical fiction, I anchored the novel around actual people and places and events.

While writing the story, in August 2021, my wife and I returned to Darien and also went to Brunswick and Savannah. We likewise visited Ashantilly and chatted with Buddy Sullivan and Harriet Langford, Director of the Ashantilly Center, and then drove over to

Randolph Spalding's house, built in 1857 near the historic homes on The Ridge. Subsequent trips led me to Milledgeville, Columbus, and Russell County, Alabama, where we found the plantation home where Mary Bass Spalding grew up twelve miles from Columbus. When not on the road, I researched and read everything I could about Randolph Spalding and the other characters and events and places in the story. I have downloaded hundreds of photos and files on my computer and filled several three-ring binders that clutter my desk that helped me write the story.

The lone exception in this fictional work, I chose not to depict actual Geechee slaves. Bu Allah (Bilali Mohammed) was the only real Geechee person mentioned—Thomas Spalding's famous black overseer. I contend he had an influence upon young Randolph Spalding as an adolescent growing up on Sapelo Island. All the other slaves depicted in the story are fictional, but representative of those who lived on the island and served the family at Randolph Spalding's mainland farmstead in 1860.

The biggest discovery occurred when I met Miriam Lukken and her husband, Peter. She is a direct descendant of Elizabeth Spalding Wylly, daughter of Thomas Spalding. Her family's collection of journals, paintings, books, artifacts, and photos belonging to the Spalding/Wylly family took my breath away. She and Peter have built a new home on Sapelo Island and support the historical connection of the Geechee community there, as well as preserving the legacy of the Spalding family.

I hope I have written a story that presents the courage to face hard choices and hardships as depicted in *The Last Laird of Sapelo*. Neither did I intend this historical novel to defend any of the wrongs of yesteryear, but to help us navigate the present.

RESOURCES AND FACTS

Annals of Glynn County by Charles Spalding Wylly (1896) annexed to the *Memories and Annals* (1916), were extensively referenced in Caroline Couper Stiles Lovell's, *The Golden Isles of Georgia*, (1932, Little, Brown, New York). Charles Spalding Wylly (1836-1923), brother of Thomas Spalding Wylly (1831-1922), grandsons of Thomas Spalding of Sapelo (1775-1851), wrote other useful books, journals, and articles, including *The Seed That Sown In the Colony of Georgia, The Harvest and Aftermath, 1740-1870* (The Neale Publishing Company, New York, 1910). From these firsthand historical accounts, and others like them, many referenced below, I wrote Randolph Spalding's story, *The Last Laird of Sapelo*.

According to Georgia's founding charter, slavery had been positively interdicted, but Savannah and Ogeechee settlers grew envious of the Carolina planters who watched their slaves work their fields. They became "covetous and restless." Petitions and counter petitions sought the abrogation of the charter's free labor clause, and by 1749 it had been rescinded, stirring a divergence of opinion. Among the counter petitions, the citizens of Frederica and Darien wrote: *"Introduce slaves and we cannot but believe they will one day return to be a scourge and a curse upon our children, or our children's children."* They justified their protest upon humanitarian grounds. Thus, *"nowhere was slavery less objectionable to the humanitarian than on the coasts of Georgia, and to the truth of this fact many visitors have testified...The institution as it there existed, more nearly resembled a patriarchal bondage, than the slavery of the chattel and mortgage type."*

Likewise, Thomas Spalding, at the beginning of developing Sapelo Island, *"looked around from, where to supply the large quantity of crude industrial power. It was at once evident that it could not be obtained from the white population, and must come from elsewhere."* As a descendant of the author of the *New Inverness Protest* against the introduction of slaves into the Colony, he had not forgotten the prophetic closing clause, but rationalized that labor *"was absolutely necessary for the carrying out of his undertakings. His environment and that in which his father had lived, justified and encouraged it; every interest demanded it."* Yet, Thomas Spalding committed, *"They shall be more serfs on the land than slaves; I shall civilize them and better their condition."* But history records that the scourge would fall.

From extensive research, I recognized Randolph Spalding was not only a progeny of his famous father, Thomas Spalding, the Benjamin Franklin of Georgia, but also the original founders of Darien and Frederica. Though his father cleared and planted the fields, and built the plantation known as South End on Sapelo, Randolph parlayed not only his gifted landholdings on the northern half of the island but by 1860 had increased crop production on both ends of Sapelo. I believe Randolph Spalding, the youngest of Thomas Spalding's fifteen children, found himself the laird of Sapelo after his father died in 1851. His father's generous wedding gift in 1843 gave him ownership of the northern half of the island, and in 1851 he became guardian, or proxy-master, of his son's inheritance of South End. His brother in law, Michael Kenan, owned 1500 of the island's 15,000 acres, known as Kenan Fields centrally located on the inland side of the island. Michael Kenan's favorable relationship with Randolph supported Randolph's reputation as the master of Sapelo, until they abandoned the island at the end of 1861.

Below are recommended books, articles, and websites for those wanting to know more.

Sullivan, Buddy. *Early Days on the Georgia Tidewater, The Story of McIntosh County & Sapelo* (McIntosh County Board of Commissioners, 1990)

Sullivan, Buddy. *Early Days on the Georgia Tidewater, The New Revised Edition* (Buddy Sullivan, 2018)

Sullivan, Buddy. *Images of America: Sapelo Island* (Arcadis Publishing, 2000)

Sullivan, Buddy. Images of America: Darien and McIntosh County (Arcadia Publishing, 2000)

McFeely, William S. *Sapelo's People: A Long Walk Into Freedom* (W. W. Norton & Co., 1994)

Cooper, Melissa L. *Making Gullah, A History of Sapelo Islanders, Race, and the American Imagination* (University of North Carolina Press, 2017)

Lovell, Caroline Couper Stiles. *The Golden Isles of Georgia* (Little, Brown, 1932)

Martin, B. G. *Sapelo's Island's Arabic Document: The "Bilali Diary" in Context* (Georgia Historical Quarterly, Fall 1994)

Mulligan, Dylan E., "The Original Progressive Farmer: The Agricultural Legacy of Thomas Spalding of Sapelo" (2015). Georgia Southern University Honors Program Theses. 93

Lawton, Alexander Robert Papers, 1774-1952 (University of North Carolina at Chapel Hill. Library. Southern Historical Collection

Perrine, Rachel Laura DeVan. *Bourbon Field Preliminary Investigations of a Barrier Island Plantation Site, Sapelo Island, Georgia.* University of West Georgia, 2012

Crook, Ray. *A Place Known as Chocolate. A Report on Investigations.* University of West Georgia, Carrollton, Georgia, 2007

Sullivan, Buddy. "Sapelo Island Settlement and Land Ownership: An Historical Overview, 1865-1970," Occasional Papers of the Sapelo Island NERR (2013)

Freeman, Douglas Southall. *R. E. Lee, A Biography* (Scrihner's Sons, 1934)

Witcher, Colette D., *"Our Story, Our Homeland, Our Legacy: Settlement Patterns of The Geechee at Sapelo Island Georgia, From 1860 To 1950"* (2021). USF Tampa Graduate Theses and Dissertations

Berrien Minute Men on Sapelo Island, Ray City History raycityhistory.wordpress.com

Visit tmbrownauthor.com for additional images, articles, and materials used in the story, including profiles of the key charactersy. Another valuable weblink to visit, ClanSpalding.org

ACKNOWLEDGEMENTS

This historical story would not have consumed my life for the past three years had my wife and I not visited Darien in June 2019 following a writer's conference on Saint Simons Island. While we ate lunch overlooking the Darien River, my curiosity intensified with every sight, sound, and smell that filled the air. By the time we drove home on the opposite side of Georgia, we decided we would return to Darien. I knew it would be a splendid setting for a story, but what story? The following summer, we stayed a week at *Open Gates Bed & Breakfast* in the heart of historic Darien. There we met Zach and Carrie Rath, the proprietors, and they became instrumental in pointing me to the history of Darien and Sapelo Island. We had also booked a guided tour of Sapelo Island with J. R. Grovner, a local Geechee descendant. After that long day traipsing up and down the island, Zach and Carrie handed me a copy of Buddy Sullivan's *Early Days On the Georgia Tidewater, The Story of McIntosh County & Sapelo*—nearly 800 pages covering the region's centuries old history. I spent pre-dawn hours in the Open Gates' library poring over page after page. When I read about Thomas Spalding and his family's legacy, I got hooked. Then I stumbled onto Randolph Spalding's tragic story and his role in the Spalding legacy on Sapelo and in McIntosh County.

By the time we left Darien that summer, I knew the story I had to research further and write about: the tragic story of Randolph Spalding and the return of the formerly enslaved Geechee to Sapelo after the Civil War ended. Sadly, history records that Sapelo once touted a thriving community of four hundred Geechee descendants on the island at the turn of the 19th-Century, but they have since dwindled to less than forty in the 21st-Century. The future appears bleak for the remaining Geechee families on the island. I hope this story stirs interest in preserving Sapelo's history, even if it unveils the role Sapelo played as the home of enslaved families. We cannot alter history—but we can learn from it, and aim to create a better future.

In 2021, my wife and I returned to McIntosh County and met personally with Buddy Sullivan and Harriet Langford, Director of the Ashantilly Center. We sat inside the home Thomas Spalding built and his son, Charles Spalding and his wife, eventually lived in until after the Civil War. The original Ashantilly home burned about ninety years ago and, though rebuilt, we saw the original tabby walls when we visited. During our meeting, Buddy made me smile after I shared my research into the story. He said, "You know more about Randolph than I do." By the time we left, I looked forward to revisiting Ashantilly Center after the book got published.

I would be remiss if I failed to acknowledge Kari Lynn Scare, my longtime editor. Beyond her professional editing, her Michigan raised perspective added much to defining the story. She confessed in her assessment that this story reveals much more than the black and white history (literally and metaphorically) she knew, and opened her eyes to the seldom told grayness of history readers should not ignore.

Finally, but certainly not least, I dedicated this book to my mother, who passed away in January 2023. Our conversations while I wrote chapter after chapter over the past two years proved invaluable. She enjoyed reading each book I have written, except for this one. She no longer could read on her own, and looked forward to me reading it to her and Literati Book Club at the Monarch House Assisted Living Residence where she had lived since 2021. Likewise, my wife Connie and I celebrate our 50th anniversary this summer. She has supported me on this journey ever since our lunch in Darien four years ago. Without her unyielding love, encouragement, and patience, I would not have been able to write this story. And thank you to Koehler Books for seeing the potential for this book. John Koehler and his team provided the final touches to help land this book in your hands.

www.ingramcontent.com/pod-product-compliance
Lightning Source LLC
LaVergne TN
LVHW041749060526
838201LV00046B/955